COVER ART

VANESSA WESTERMANN

Cormorant Books

We acknowledge financial support for our publishing activities: the
Government of Canada, through the Canada Book Fund and The Canada
Council for the Arts; the Government of Ontario, through the Ontario Arts Council,
Ontario Creates, and the Ontario Book Publishing Tax Credit. We acknowledge
additional funding provided by the Government of Ontario and the Ontario Arts
Council to address the adverse effects of the novel coronavirus pandemic.

LIBRARY AND ARCHIVES CANADA CATALOGUING IN PUBLICATION

Title: Cover art / Vanessa Westermann.
Names: Westermann, Vanessa, author.
Identifiers: Canadiana (print) 20210363819 | Canadiana (ebook) 20210363886 |
ISBN 9781770866423 (softcover) | ISBN 9781770866430 (HTML)
Classification: LCC PS8645.E7975 C68 2022 | DDC C813/.6—dc23

United States Library of Congress Control Number: 2022932679

Cover art: Nick Craine
Interior text design: Tannice Goddard, tannicegdesigns.ca

Printed and bound in Canada.
Printer: Friesens

CORMORANT BOOKS INC.
260 SPADINA AVENUE, SUITE 502, TORONTO, ON M5T 2E4
www.cormorantbooks.com

In memory of my grandfather,
who found our lake.

COVER ART

ONE

"I DON'T USUALLY DO THIS." Charley Scott stretched on her toes to reach the highest shelf. A long arm snaked past her to snatch the book. As it came down, she caught the faintest whiff of chocolate.

He handed the novel to her with one of those crinkly-eyed, knee-jerking grins only certain men can muster. "Do what?" he asked. "Strike up a conversation with a stranger or rattle off a list of suggested reading?" He leaned against a shelf of books and looked down at her with a mischievous spark in his brown eyes.

He was a good leaner. No, scratch that. A great leaner. He had that casual I'm-so-cool look down pat. It was hard to resist.

"No, I talk to strangers all the time." She glanced at the book in her hands, at the elegant lines of the illustrated couple dancing on the cover. For a murder mystery, the colours were bright and cheerful, deceptively so. Discovering the shelf of books at the back of the convenience store slash coffee bar felt like finding hidden treasure. The selection consisted entirely of crime fiction and appealed to the local cottagers' need for thrills at the dockside. "It's recommending books that isn't the norm for me." Back in town for barely fifteen minutes and she was already slipping into old habits.

"Actually, I found it rather forward. I've always thought that one should at the very least" — he raised a finger to underscore his point, features perfectly serious — "have an intense, mind-blowing

1

physical relationship before sharing the intimacies of one's personal library."

She laughed. "Nice line."

He grinned. "Thank you."

She took a breath of bracing, coffee-scented air. "Can I just remind you that you were the one who started the conversation?"

"Only to point out that you were blocking my way to Raymond Chandler. You don't get between a man and the last copy of *The Big Sleep.*" He shook his head. "I'm sorry, it just isn't done."

"You're lucky it wasn't on my list today." She'd already deviated from her plan. But — she glanced at the mysteries crammed onto those few narrow shelves — wasn't that what this summer was all about? Risk and adventure. "I'm a killer when it comes to books. You wouldn't stand a chance."

"Wait, wait. Hold it!" He waved an impatient hand. "You've read Chandler?"

"Of course. He's a classic in hard-boiled fiction." The 1970s edition had that unsettling and exotic cover image, featuring lush foliage and Venus fly traps. "Dark, smoky settings. Plots filled with deception and pain, not to mention a charismatic, mysterious hero. Glamorous femmes fatales. Brandy drunk 'any way at all' and all the time. Staccato sentences, like the firing of a gun." She stopped, caught herself. "What's not to like?"

He studied her in what could only be described as awe. "Hi, my name is Matt, and will you marry me?"

"I'm Charlotte, Charley for short, and I'll have to think about that." Grinning, she tucked the book under her arm. "Do you always propose this quickly?"

Matt scraped a hand over his chin. "This is pretty much the first time." Casting a glance around the room, he added, "Look, if you don't want to elope right away, at least let me buy you a latte."

He nodded at a cluster of empty tables by the window. "This place isn't called The Coffee Nook for nothing. They're brilliant. Java connoisseurs. Artists of the dark bean. I'd even wrangle some extra cinnamon for you, what do you say?"

Do not be charmed. "Tempting, if only I drank coffee. I prefer tea," she lied. She loved lattes. But she couldn't linger. She headed past the glass case of Chelsea buns and butter tarts, toward the cash.

He followed. "A parting of the minds. And I was beginning to think you were perfect."

"Everyone has their faults." And was that ever true. Watching the girl scan the price into the cash, Charley pulled out her wallet.

"That'll be twenty dollars." The girl behind the counter snapped her gum and looked at them with open curiosity.

Small towns. She'd almost forgotten what they were like.

Oakcrest had the pace of a country village, but the quaint specialty shops and vibrant arts community of a city. In the heart of the Kawartha countryside, the little village nestled on the shores of Blue Heron Lake, at a crossroads between barns and laneways, ploughed fields and sugar bush.

Only a two-hour drive from Toronto, the waterfront cottages, Adirondack chairs, and boats cruising by attracted weekenders to the peaceful getaway. The constant influx of visitors — arriving with the blackflies and staying until the first red leaves fell from the trees — provided locals with fertile ground for gossip.

Placing a hand on her arm, Matt took his own wallet out. "I got it."

"Oh, no." She shook her head. "You can't. Did you hear the price?"

"It's in my best interest." He shot her his crooked smile. "You can repay me by buying me a cup of coffee."

"An ulterior motive, I knew it! Sorry, but I don't believe in debts."

She paid for the book and took the bag the girl handed to her. "Besides, that would have been a rotten deal for you, a cup of coffee in exchange for a hardcover book."

She worked her way around swivel racks and chair legs toward the door and tried not to get distracted by the display of thrillers on the front table.

"That's it?" He trailed after her. "Thanks, but no thanks? I'm sure they have tea, too."

"I'm sure they do, but I'm still going to say no." Charley turned around and smiled. "You seem nice, but that TV show about the psychotic bookstore owner has made me wary of charming men who read. It could be" — she held up the bag and quoted the title of the book she just purchased with a grin — "*An Invitation To Die.*"

A familiar sound came from the other side of the door behind her. A scrape, like nails against wood, and low to the ground. She was running out of time.

Matt glanced at the door. "So, you're new in town?"

An easy guess. Her skin was several shades paler than his mid-summer tan. "You could say that."

"Not a cottager though."

"No." Although, in a way, she was, wasn't she? She had escaped the city to spend her holiday in a cottage. "Well, sort of."

"'Sort of a cottager.' What does that mean?"

"Actually..." Should she? Oh, why not. She had to use every opportunity to advertise now. "I'm opening a pop-up gallery." A warm glow of excitement spread through her.

Pop-up galleries hosted temporary exhibits in unexpected locations, like storefronts or studio spaces. She'd be able to show her work, without having the expense or commitment of a long-term lease. Although success ultimately depended on timing, marketing, and luck.

"Really? Where?" Another scrape, louder this time. And then again. Matt frowned. "What is that?"

"Who is that," she corrected and opened the door with a flourish. She felt like she should be saying, ta da! "Meet Cocoa."

The chocolate Labrador retriever wriggled with barely contained excitement.

"Cocoa?" The glint of amusement in his eyes earned him a demerit point, in her opinion. He asked, "Did she just knock at the door?"

"She thinks she's a person." Charley stepped out onto the porch and into a wall of heat, a contrast to the air-conditioned store, and felt the curls on her head expand with the humidity.

Sunlight glanced off the red brick facades of the old buildings, an unfiltered version of the smog-faded beams she'd left behind in Toronto. Narrowing her eyes against the glare, she glimpsed the wooden siding further down Main Street. The Oakcrest Mews. Her heart thudded against her ribs. Just nerves, that's all.

Cocoa twirled in three tight circles and tried to lick Charley's arm as she bent to untie the leash from the railing, making the whole thing more difficult. "She used to open doors, but I told her that was rude, and so she started knocking at them instead."

"Clever." He squatted down and held out a hand for the dog to sniff. "Well, hello." He rubbed Cocoa's ear and she gave what sounded like a canine sigh of bliss. Shameless hussy.

"Hey!" a man shouted.

Matt straightened. Cocoa tensed and strained against the leash, trying to get down the steps. Charley wound the leash around her hand, held on tight.

Was he yelling at them? Mid-seventies, the man had close-cropped grey hair and a crisp twill shirt rolled neatly to the elbows. He stormed down the sidewalk in their direction, scarred work boots pounding over the pavement. A flick of adrenaline shot along her spine.

But his gaze was fixed upon the man who had just stepped out of the bank. Doing his best to pretend he hadn't heard, he fished his car keys out of the pocket of his dress slacks.

Charley leaned her elbows on the sun-cracked railing to watch. Cocoa sat at her feet, still keyed up and on alert. "Who's that?"

"The angry-looking man is Thomas Kelley," Matt said. "He moved here when he retired."

The name gave her a jolt. Although she'd seen his artwork and spoken to him on the phone, they hadn't met in person yet. His paintings had a restless quality to them, a carefully composed tension. And, right now, the full force of that tension was aimed at the man ahead of him. And there was nothing composed about it.

"The guy trying to make the fast getaway," Matt said, "is Andrew Clarkston, CEO of Clarkston Engineering. He's working on Thomas's house. From what I've heard, things aren't going smoothly."

In his early fifties, Andrew could have been a catalogue ad for business casual. But the slacks and button-down shirt couldn't hide his powerful build.

Thomas caught up to Andrew by the Silverado pickup truck and clapped a solid hand on his shoulder, holding him in place. A tableau at odds with the picturesque storefronts around them. "You've been avoiding me," he growled.

Andrew shrugged him off with a dismissive motion, more annoyed than defensive. "That's absurd."

Face flushed red, Thomas's fingers balled. "I expect you to meet deadlines." The moment simmered, one false move away from violence.

"Should we do something?" she murmured. They were the only witnesses to the scene unfolding on the sidewalk.

Matt looked at her, amused. "Like what?"

"I don't know." She waved an arm. "Get in there and break them up."

He chuckled. "I don't think they're going to get into a fist fight."

"I wouldn't bet on it."

Thomas stepped closer to the other man, his voice carrying clearly. "Let me remind you that you work for me."

"Uh-oh," Matt murmured. "He shouldn't have said that."

He was right.

Andrew bristled, raising his voice in response, "And let me remind you that, while I may be in charge of the project, there are things that are out of my control. Weather conditions. Subcontractors."

"Weather conditions?" Thomas spread his arms. "It's over thirty degrees and sunny and has been for most of the week. I'm tired of your excuses. Get the job done." He punctuated the sentence with a jab at the man's chest.

Andrew slapped his hand away. "Are you threatening me?"

"What if I am?"

She glanced at Matt. "Still so sure it's not going to come to blows?"

"Less sure now," he admitted.

Thomas clenched his fists. "I'd better see your men on site tomorrow, that's all I'm saying." A tense moment passed as the two men stared each other down. Finally, Thomas broke eye contact.

Andrew took a breath as Thomas strode away and glanced at them. "Guess you can't make everyone happy," he joked with a shrug.

In his position, she wouldn't have taken it so lightly.

"Well, that was exciting," she said.

Cocoa shifted, settling into a more comfortable position on the wooden slats of the porch.

Matt watched Andrew climb into his truck with an unreadable expression in his eyes. "Welcome to Oakcrest." He turned to her. "Don't let first impressions fool you. You'll like it here."

"I already do." Oh no, did that sound flirty? "Caffeine and books," she said quickly. "What's not to like?"

"Exactly." He gave Cocoa one last pat on the head. "It was nice meeting you. Both of you." He grinned at the dog investigating his pant leg intently.

"Yes, it was. Come on, Cocoa." The dog looked up at Matt adoringly. Oh God, she'd have to drag her away. "Fine," she told her, "I'll leave you here, then see what you do."

"Don't look at me," he said to Cocoa. "I'd have to feed you steaks and French fries."

The dog's ears perked up.

"You're not helping." Charley had to walk all the way down the steps before Cocoa budged, making her feel like a spoilsport.

A warm breeze fluttered her skirt around her legs. Halfway to her Jeep, she turned back, just for a quick glance. It was fine. He'd be back in the store by now, getting that coffee. He'd never know she looked back.

She gulped. He was still standing there, beneath the yellow-striped awning, and had, in fact, noticed her look back.

Then again, he should be the one looking sheepish. She'd caught him watching them. But he just flashed another boyish grin and waved.

She would not let herself be charmed.

TWO

CAUTION! UNASSUMED ROAD. THE FADED wooden sign at the entrance to Fire Route 22 showed two skulls and crossbones. Hopefully that wasn't an omen of things to come.

Charley made the left turn. The Jeep bounced over the gravel path, bumping over potholes hard enough to jar her teeth. The private road showed signs of wear after the harsh winter. Wide enough for a single car with deep ditches on either side. Deep enough to sink a tire in, and nowhere to swerve to.

"Almost there!" In the rearview mirror, she saw Cocoa sit up and look out the window.

The row of maple trees cast flickering shadows over the ground, playing tricks on her eyes as she followed the winding lane. A glimpse of the lake shot a thrill of excitement through her.

Only fifteen minutes from Main Street, it seemed like a different world here, cocooned and quiet.

Heat radiated off the windshield. The steering wheel was hot, her palms damp, slick. She had the A/C cranked up high, but it wasn't doing much. She put the window down. The breeze tugged at her hair, bringing with it the scent of dry earth, white pines, and lake water.

A flash of movement, off to the right, and something leaped out from between the grey tree trunks onto the road in front of her. Something big.

She slammed her foot on the brake and braced for impact. Cocoa gave a surprised yip from the back.

The deer — a doe — froze an arm's length from the car and looked at her. Direct eye contact. The gaze was eerie, almost human. The animal probably weighed eighty kilograms or more.

The moment stretched. Then broke.

The deer bolted, jumping the ditch, branches snapping. Heart racing, Charley watched the doe disappear into the thicket. A flash of white tail and it was gone.

Shaken, she glanced back at Cocoa. Still safely strapped in by her harness.

"That was close." Too close. Ten years old and rusty, how would the Jeep handle hitting a deer?

The car crept forward. Charley kept her eyes peeled for more wild animals, adrenaline singing through her veins.

Boulders and a fence bordered the narrow road. Another sign, handmade, swung off a post. The engraved figures looked a lot like the gingerbread man and Toto from The Wizard of Oz, '20 KPH' above their heads.

She drove past rental cottages, front yards covered in toys — a plastic tractor, a bicycle, Super Soaker Water Blasters lying like neon rifles in the grass — past a large green building that looked out of place, like some sort of hanger.

That building had caused a lot of speculation — and animosity — at first. Even more so when people found out that it was going to be a workshop. The noise would destroy cottage tranquility, or so they argued. Of course, the tune changed when neighbours realized the convenience of having someone nearby, willing to do cottage renovations at a decent price.

Oh, there it was.

Her heart skipped a beat at the sight of the cabin, nestled in behind the trees. Hit with that same knee-jerk sense of belonging that never changed, even though she'd only spent summers there growing up, and just a few weeks at a time. But all her best memories were here.

Built in the 1950s, the cabin was all one floor. A gabled roof, large windows, and red shutters with sailboat cut-outs. The cherry red colour of the eavestroughs and screen door accented the earth-toned siding. A stone patio wrapped around the house. Shrubs and flowers almost hid the wicker loveseat from view, tucked in an alcove beside French windows. Fieldstone slabs, edged with moss, led up to the front door. Grandma Reilly had kept the garden well-tended, but now it ran wild, with a vibrant mix of orange day lilies, peonies, and fragrant clusters of phlox. The picket fence still looked in good shape and would keep Cocoa in the yard, so long as she didn't try to swim to the neighbours.

The only thing that would make this moment better was if Charley were already sitting on the patio, drinking a gin and tonic.

She pulled into the driveway and the door of the cottage flew open. Foolishly, she half expected to see Grandpa step out with open arms and a wide grin. She shook the thought off and smiled at the sight of her sister. Cocoa gave an excited woof.

"You're here!" Meghan always crackled with energy, but today it seemed to be sparking off her. Even her short-cropped red hair seemed ready to burst into flames.

When had they last seen each other? Christmas, probably. It was the first time she had visited the cottage since Meghan moved in.

Charley got out of the car on stiff legs. "It's so great to — oof!" Hit with a full-force hug, she squeezed back hard, breathing in the familiar scent of rose and magnolia. "See you."

Meghan leaned back and narrowed her eyes. "Are your hands sticky?"

"They might be." A car trip wasn't complete without a bag of Hershey's Kisses.

Meghan rolled her eyes. "What are you, five?"

Charley opened the back door and unsnapped Cocoa's harness, letting the dog out to prance in happy circles around them. "Twenty-nine." She gave Meghan a cheeky grin.

"Almost thirty," Meghan countered, always quick to throw in a jab.

Charley groaned. "Argh, don't remind me."

Meghan laughed, a wicked chuckle. "Hey, I survived it. You will, too. Come on in. Alex is cooking, God help us."

As soon as they stepped inside, screen door still banging shut behind them, the memory of the place hit her, catching at her heart. Cocoa took off, nails skidding over the hardwood floor. Charley winced. "Don't get into trouble!"

"She'll be fine."

She let out a breath. "This place, Meghan —" It was both familiar and different. The past clung to those walls, as real as the faint, slightly smoky scent of stacked wood hanging in the air.

"I know." Meghan did a little spin in the entrance, arms stretched wide. "Aren't you glad you came?"

Cast iron hooks on the exposed wood wall. Most of the interior still unpainted, first-growth pine. Through a door on the left something sizzled and she caught the scent of roasting peppers.

Past the entrance, the space opened up. The living room was as bright and airy as she remembered, the sofa and armchair deep and cushioned. The glass in the wood-stove fireplace blackened after years of use. The bleached spines of Grandpa's private eye novels filled the bookshelves.

But there were little touches throughout that were all Meghan and starting to erase the past. New photographs. A red wool blanket tossed over a chair. The huge widescreen TV that screamed male sports addiction and probably belonged to Alex.

On the far wall, though, Charley's own painting still hung in pride of place. Her portrait of Grandma Reilly, carefully framed. One of her first. Watercolour on paper and nothing like her work now. But it all started here. She'd spent hours over it. Perfecting it, although she hadn't caught all of the mistakes. The colour changes weren't gradual enough, the edges too harsh, but she'd captured that seize-the-moment enthusiasm in the curve of her grandmother's smile.

Charley turned away from the painting, and those eyes, so like Meghan's and full of expectations. "I remember the cottage being bigger."

"The TV takes up a lot of space." Meghan grinned and dropped her keys on the end table. "Just wait until you've had the full tour. You'll see things haven't changed that much. Like the Tardis, the cottage is —"

"Bigger on the inside." She chimed in so that their voices echoed and dissolved into laughter.

"I still can't believe you quit your job. What you're doing is —"

"Insane?" Fear tightened in the pit of her stomach.

"I was going to say 'brave.'"

"You do know that 'brave' means ready to endure danger or pain?"

As if on cue, a yelp and what sounded a lot like, "My eyes!" came from the kitchen.

Cocoa raced around the corner to stand beside Charley, cocking her head. Ready to defend, if she had to.

"That's it!" Meghan yelled. "I'm coming in!" She shoved open the kitchen door, Cocoa right behind her.

Charley's fingers itched to capture Meghan's expression. Determination and amusement. Like a Valkyrie ready to conquer anything in her path, faithful hound at her heels. But she'd have to dig her sketchpad out of her suitcase first.

"Hey!" Alex exclaimed. "Cocoa, out, now. Not on the counter!"

"The kitchen is a mess!" Meghan said. "And what's with your eyes?"

"Nothing."

Charley grinned at the defensive tone. Of course, she could call Cocoa back. But this was so much more fun. And she could listen in.

She glanced at the photograph of her and Meghan on the endtable, faded to sepia now. A cottage snapshot. Aged six and ten, arms slung over each other's shoulders. All bare feet, tangled hair, and wild, carefree laughter. Alex didn't stand a chance.

"Let me see," Meghan said. "Stop turning around. Stand still!"

"Why is Cocoa following me?"

"You smell spicy."

"You're both cornering me," he complained.

Meghan never backed down. As editor of the *Oakcrest Courier*, it was an asset. At home, it was hard to handle. Any second now, he'd crack.

"Fine. Fine!" Charley could just picture Alex throwing his hands in the air. "I rubbed chili powder between my fingers and sprinkled it over the meat like the recipe said. Then I had to cut the onions."

"Oh no." A laugh quivered in Meghan's voice.

"My eyes always water when I cut onions, ok?"

Charley winced in sympathy.

"I hope you don't give up this quickly at work." Meghan's tone was triumphant. "You caved in an instant."

"Knowing when to pick your battles is part of it, Megs. Go back out. I can handle it. And take Cocoa with you."

Time to take charge. "Cocoa, come," Charley called. It took a second, but then a nose nudged the door open and the dog trotted toward her. She rubbed her ears. "Good girl."

"Alex, you can barely see what you're stirring," Meghan tried again. "Let me help you."

"I don't need any help. I can do it." A loud curse followed.

Charley called through the door, "You sound just like Ramsay already!"

"Don't encourage him," Meghan warned.

"Where are you going with that?" His voice rose an octave. "Supper will be ready soon."

"It's for Charley! She's starving." Meghan returned from the kitchen with a bowl of chips in her hand. "Come on, I'll help you unpack." She popped a chip into her mouth and didn't offer the bowl.

"You never did like sharing."

"Nope." Meghan grinned as she led the way through the living room, Cocoa following close behind.

"How are the eyes?"

"He'll live. As a cop, you'd think he'd do better under pressure."

"You can be intimidating."

"True." She lifted her chin, a battle glint in her eyes. Confident of victory. It could make even the strong cower, though Charley doubted she knew it.

Two steps away from entering the next room, Meghan paused. "Ready?"

Heart somersaulting, she braced for change. "Lead the way."

The door swung open and she blinked against the sudden blaze of light. Yellow sheets on the bed. Sun pouring in through French doors. White Adirondack chairs on the stone patio outside. And beyond that, the lake glittered, still and clear. An orange kayak moved along the shore, gliding on the steady stroke of the woman's paddle. The ripples, the reflection, so tempting to paint. A seagull swooped toward the water, skimming low over the weathered wooden dock.

Here, everything was perfect and always had been. And she finally felt like she could breathe again. "Can I steal your identity and live here instead?"

"The cottage is half yours anyway."

On paper. They had both inherited the cottage, but Meghan got the opportunity to make a life here. Doing a real job, as mom would say. One that paid. "There's one minor detail. I have to earn a living."

"You're too short to pass for me," Meghan said. "You'd never get away with it."

"The journalists would notice?"

"They're a perceptive bunch."

"It's a good thing, I'm a city girl at heart." But, oh, it felt like home. When she unpacked her things, she could pretend she was here to stay.

Charley crossed the rug, thinner now, and opened the cupboard doors. And froze. The shelves were full. Linens, board games, winter coats. "Where am I supposed to put my stuff?"

Meghan came to stand beside her and looked at the shelves. "Leave it in your suitcase?"

"You couldn't clear out a bit of space for me?"

"There are fresh sheets." She didn't even look guilty.

"But no space." She tugged one of the board games off the shelf. The corners were worn, the cardboard softer than when they pulled it out on rainy evenings years ago. Clue, The Classic Detective Game. She wiped a hand over the box, felt the dry coat of dust. "No one took the time to clear any of this out?"

"I figured you might want to sort through it, while you're here," Meghan said. "Most of it's yours, anyway."

"And it's so much easier to close the door on the mess."

"That too," she admitted, without any shame whatsoever.

And she'd been worried about facing change? The room was frozen in time. "I've got my work cut out, then."

Even the chest of drawers was full. The nightstand crowded with tattered Agatha Christies, and a few paperback thrillers. The soft-focus photograph of a femme fatale on the cover of one caught her eye. She tugged it free with a waft of musty air and turned it over in her hands.

The Demise of Lady Red. Silver letters, done in a typical pulp fiction typeface with crisp, knife-cut edges. The design moody and striking, but the ex-library copy had seen better days. Rather than cram the book back in the stack, she dropped it on the top of the nightstand. Maybe she'd re-read it.

Meghan snatched the book up. "Can I borrow this?"

That sounded familiar. "It's been in the cottage this whole time, but now you —" She paused. She'd have to clear some shelves out anyway, find a safe space for her art supplies. She sighed. "Sure. Just don't forget —"

"To return it. I know," Meghan said, already skimming the back cover.

Charley sat on the bed cross-legged. So much for unpacking. She'd tackle the storage problem later.

Cocoa rested her chin on the mattress and gazed up at her.

"Not on the bed, you know that." She'd try to hold out longer this time, before she caved and let her up. Cocoa heaved a full-body sigh. Charley avoided making eye contact. "Why is Alex cooking? And what is he making?"

Meghan put the book down on the dresser. "Fajitas," she said with a Mexican accent. She snatched another mouthful of chips. Chewed and swallowed. "I told him, since he's living here now, he should pitch in more."

"Ah."

"I meant replace a lightbulb or vacuum, maybe clean the bathroom. He bought pans."

Alex moved in two months ago. A twinge of guilt hit her at the thought. She'd all but invited herself. "Are you sure you don't mind that I'm here? You're still getting used to each other. I don't want to get in the way."

"You're right," Meghan nodded. "You should leave. Don't bother unpacking."

She whipped a pillow at her.

Meghan caught it in one hand with a laugh. She dropped onto the bed beside her and rolled over onto her stomach. "Let's see. You don't take up a lot of room and you're not messy, so it should be easy for us to pretend you're not here. Fine. You can stay."

"Oh, good." She rolled her eyes. God, she'd missed this. Chatting in person was so much better than over the phone. "I had an interesting conversation in the Coffee Nook today."

"Caffeinating on the way, very wise." Meghan propped her chin on her hand.

"Actually, I got sidetracked by the books."

She chuckled. "What else is new? Which local did you meet?"

"A guy."

"Oh, really?" She scooped the last crumbs from the bowl.

"Good sense of humour, decent taste in books."

Meghan turned her full attention on her. "You're telling me that you've already met a cute guy on your first day in Oakcrest? Your first few hours, actually."

"Did I say he was cute?"

"You didn't have to. It's written all over your face."

Warmth rushed to her cheeks. Going the mature route, she stuck her tongue out at Meghan.

She didn't even blink. "You know how long it took me to find Alex? Who is he?"

"I only caught his first name —" She broke off as Alex appeared in the doorway.

He had a streak of something indefinable along his right cheek, splatters of liquid across his clothes, and a wooden spoon clenched in a death grip. Sauce dripped off the handle in a sticky line down his arm. His eyes looked bloodshot. "It's done. I hope you're hungry."

THE KITCHEN WAS A MESS. Mysterious liquids had splashed here and there, pieces of onion were scattered across the checkerboard linoleum flooring. Used cooking utensils filled the sink. A pair of kitchen shears rested open beside the wooden knife block.

"Hey Alex, this looks a lot like a crime scene," Charley teased. She slid into one of the wooden chairs at the table, the uneven legs wobbling before balancing.

The table had been pushed up against the bay window. Each seat had a view of the lake. A warm breeze drifted through the screen, carrying the sound of waves lapping against the dock and bullfrogs croaking. The paper napkins, pinned beneath the old Jadeite salt and pepper shakers, fluttered at the corners.

The herb pots on the sill were empty. On the pantry door, the chalkboard was wiped clean, just a smudge of white streaking the centre.

A bittersweet ache settled between Charley's ribs. She'd missed so many summers. And for what?

"This looks nice," Meghan said, eyes focused on the table. "Smells good."

"Just wait until you try it." Alex spooned generous portions from the cast iron pan into preheated wraps. With a flourish, he set the plates in front of them.

"Well?" He sat and leaned forward, elbows on the table. "I want to watch your reaction when you take the first bite."

Most of the time, Alex mastered the guy-next-door impression. He played down the crooked nose with a clean-shaven face. Wore Henley shirts and blue jeans. Managing to almost pull off the illusion and blend with the crowd. Until he aimed that laser beam stare.

There was a pause. Charley picked up her wrap. Meghan reached for the sour cream.

She raised her eyebrows. "Wimp."

Meghan pushed the cream aside. "All right."

Silently, Charley counted down. One, two, three. Then took a huge bite.

And choked, mouth on fire. She swallowed and reached for her water glass. Her lips burned.

Meghan wasn't doing much better. Her face had flushed the same shade as her hair.

The flavours were great but, God, the heat. "'S good," she managed. It felt like she'd seared her taste buds off.

"Mmm," Meghan hummed between sips of water.

"You're both terrible liars." Alex planted his hands on the table and stared them down, like suspects in an interrogation room. "What is it? Too spicy?"

She exchanged a glance with Meghan. "You could say that," she admitted.

"Just a little."

"It can't be that bad," he said.

"Why don't you try it?" Meghan asked sweetly and waited.

He bit into his wrap and didn't hold back. "Holy hell!" He coughed, eyes wide. Meghan handed him his water. He chugged it, perspiration beading on his forehead.

"Did you not taste it while you were cooking?" Meghan asked.

"I did, but early on." He looked at his plate. "What do we do now?"

"Sour cream," Charley said.

"More lime juice?" Meghan suggested.

"Both." Already on her feet, she reached for the bowl of lime wedges on the counter. A red bowl. Of course. She held up the Fiestaware dish. "You have a problem."

Alex caught on before Meghan did and nodded. "You do."

"What do you mean?"

She gestured at the evidence. "Red teapot. Red dishes. And don't think I missed the red throw blanket in the living room."

Meghan shrugged. "In some cultures, red is the colour of luck."

"Touché." She placed the bowl on the table, within easy reach. "I could use some luck right now."

Meghan spooned sour cream onto her plate. "I've been telling everyone."

"That I need luck?"

Alex snorted.

Meghan rolled her eyes. "About the gallery. It's haunted, you know."

Charley laughed as she squeezed more lime juice over the vegetables. Then she realized. No one else was laughing. She put the lime wedge down. "What, seriously?"

"Afraid so." Alex stretched across the table for the sour cream.

"Haunted, as in creepy sounds or full-on ghost in a white sheet?"

Meghan grinned. "Guess you'll find out soon enough."

Great. "And you didn't think to tell me this before I signed the lease?"

She shrugged. "I didn't want to deter you. Besides, who believes in ghosts?"

Charley knew there were more things on heaven and earth than people had dreamt of. "You're talking to the wrong person here."

"Just don't go looking for them and you'll be fine."

Reassuring last words.

THREE

THERE WAS A GHOST IN the house. In that room. And Matt had to get his guts up to go in.

He stood in the house his father left him, holding a glass of rye and ginger in his hand. The kitchen bright and inviting behind him, tunes cranked on the stereo. Guitars wailing in the background, way too loud. And he was here, staring at a closed door.

The Viceroy home had seen better days — in the 1980s. The post and beam design originally picked from a catalogue. Most likely because of the window nooks and gallery loft. Sold as a kit, some assembly required. At least the wood frame of British Columbia lumber had withstood enough winters to prove its worth. And now it was his, along with everything in it.

There are no ghosts, Matt told himself. It's an empty room, that's all.

He hadn't been in there since the funeral. Probably not before then either. Why bother? There was no one in there, after all. No reason to go in.

Not until now.

Just another mess to sort out. All part of the process of dying. Just go in. Do it.

He took a swig from his glass, then reached for the door handle.

God only knew what he'd find in there. It could be teeming with ants. And paperwork.

The door swung inward on a creak of hinges that made his hairs stand on end. Like nails on a chalkboard. But nothing a little WD-40 couldn't fix. He made a mental note to add it to his list of chores.

How the hell could his dad still intimidate him?

As soon as Matt stepped over the threshold, the familiar scent hit him full force and almost knocked the breath out of him. Pine sawdust and Old Spice cologne. The musty smell of paper and books.

The thick carpet muffled his footsteps. Even the sound of the music faded, as though turned down a notch. He stood in the centre of the room, feet planted, and took a good look around.

Once meant as a dining room, his dad had repurposed the space long ago, claimed it as his own and left them to eat at a table for two in the kitchen. Probably some nice hardwood flooring hidden beneath that carpet, though you'd never guess it by looking at it.

He could have sworn the office used to be bigger. Didn't help that every square inch of usable space was filled with stuff. At least the window wall behind the desk opened the room up to the deck and yard. No lake view. The house was too close to town for that. If you wanted to see the water, you had to drive there. But, behind the branches of the old oak tree, the sky burned the same glorious red you'd see from the rocky vantage point at the boat launch.

Rustling leaves chased shadows through the room.

"The inner sanctum," he said out loud, because he could. There'd always been something sacred about this room, but now it was like a mausoleum, frozen in time. All those who enter, beware. And wasn't that just typical?

No ants in sight. That was a relief. Nick Thorn had a habit of taking food in with him when he wrote and then letting the plates stack up. Just a bowl on the desk now, some orange crumbs in the bottom. Probably the remains of Cheetos.

Matt set his glass down on the desk, ice cubes clinking. Not on the coaster, but beside it, moisture already beading in the heat.

The floor-to-ceiling maple bookshelves were crammed full, the contents haphazardly stacked, some spines bent. He picked up one of the more worn copies, and felt the dust coat his fingers. Woodworking. Mostly texts on carpentry, which made sense. As a professor of carpentry and renovation techniques at the local college, his dad had collected books on the subject for years. Depending on how out of date they were, he might be able to donate some. Matt flipped to the copyright page, before setting the book aside. He'd have to go through them all. Lots of sci-fi. No surprise there. Some pulp fiction, right down at the bottom. And of course, a copy of *Hamadryads*. The original print run, looked like. Though that didn't mean he'd be saving it.

His dad's armchair caught his eye. Like something straight off a Sherlock Holmes set. He ran his hand over the leather, tempted to keep it. Some cracks, some discolouration, but in pretty good condition. One button missing. Grooves worn into the shoulders of the chair.

Maybe it was that smell, or being in the room, but for one instant, he saw his father sitting there, flipping a book. Glancing up, his eyes taking a second to focus, and that frown that always made Matt feel about ten inches tall.

He blinked, rubbed his eyes. And looked back at an empty chair. Maybe he could just dump it on the curb.

Time to speed this up. Then he could get some food going — a quick crepe, maybe — and settle in to watch the game. The Blue

Jays were playing tonight. Simple rules, and you knew if you won or lost.

The room needed to be vacuumed. Dirt on the floor, trekked through to the desk and back. Some wood shavings too, from the looks of it, like someone walked in straight from a workshop. Which was probably what happened.

When Matt sank into the swivel chair at the desk, he caught himself flicking a guilty glance over his shoulder. Then he laughed and ran a sheepish hand over the back of his neck. There was no reason why he shouldn't be sitting here. Going through his father's things. It was all his now. And yet, an uneasy feeling pricked at him.

"Doesn't feel right yet, that's all." He reached for the padded envelope sitting on top of a stack of papers. Unopened. He turned it over in his hands. Postmarked not long before his father's death. Return address — some company in Toronto. A film service?

Curious, Matt tore it open. A gust of cool air washed over him. Hopefully from the open window and not an angry spirit. "Sorry, Dad." He shook the contents out onto the table.

A CD, a smaller envelope, and an invoice. He picked it up, skimmed it. *Negatives enclosed. Scan to email transfer.* CD *included.* So, his dad had gotten an old film cartridge developed. Maybe a month before things went downhill fast. Looking back to the past right at the end. Full of regret, he hoped.

He flicked on the desk lamp and held one of the negatives up to the light. And caught his breath. A woman, maybe early thirties, grinned at the camera, tossing long blond hair back. A close-up. He recognized her, more so from other photographs than from memory. The film must have been eighteen years old, or more. Just on that turning point, before everyone went digital.

Sorry for your loss, that's what people had said. Like they had 'lost her'. Like the accident was their fault.

Matt held up another negative. Outdoors, view of the lake. He tossed it aside, picked up another. Then paused. This one was different, the start of a series of similar images.

Hard to tell. He'd know for sure when he loaded the CD onto his computer, checked the scans. But if he had to guess, it looked like some sort of construction site. Not unusual in itself. Could have been either his mom or dad on site. Some old project? But why document it on a private camera?

One person would know, but the past was always a touchy subject.

He could let it go. Put the pictures aside, forget about it.

The hell with that. His father had kept too many secrets while alive. Matt wouldn't pass up the chance to expose one of them now. They would all come to light soon anyway. The clock was ticking. Only one week to go.

He swiveled the chair around to look at the room again, tapping the envelope against his palm. His father's study. Fine particles hung in the air, caught by the light.

He was wrong. There was a ghost in the room with him. But, separated by life and death, he finally had his father by the throat. Secrets were trapped inside that house and, one by one, he'd reveal them all.

"'Things crack along the lines of a promise,'" Matt quoted. "Isn't that what you wrote, Dad?" A visionary, the critics had called him. "Let's see how right they were."

FOUR

"NOT THE PRIMROSE!" COCOA FROZE, mouth open, about to bite down on a particularly juicy and well-tended bud. She rolled her eyes up at Charley, who said, sternly, "Leave it be. We don't want to make enemies already." Main Street was still quiet, but it would be just her luck if someone spotted them. Cocoa loved gardening and had gotten her into trouble before.

The dog heaved a sigh and left the flower.

Wandering down the sidewalk, Charley peeked through paneled windows at racks of vintage clothing in the Blast From The Past Boutique, then lingered over the display of handcrafted beeswax candles and bright pottery at Wicks 'N' More.

Just a few years ago, Oakcrest's claim to fame had been a farm supply business and a cheese shop that sold bags of fresh curd and served up giant scoops of Kawartha Dairy ice cream. Now she strolled past a chalkboard sign announcing live music at The Three-Corner Pub on Saturdays.

On the doors of the next building, the peeling red paint looked like a relic of the 1900s, but the old hardware store that once occupied it was long gone. A television costume designer with an eclectic taste in Canadian-made goods had taken over the space and transformed it. Now, you'd have better luck finding Hudson's Bay blankets, small batch bitters, and postal code T-shirts in the

Old General than nails and screws. Proving that the first step to success was a leap of faith.

Watching Cocoa zigzag over the sidewalk, tail wagging, happiness spread through Charley. Quitting her marketing job to spend the summer in Oakcrest was the best decision she'd ever made. She'd enjoy the fresh air and all those little things she hadn't had time for before.

For good or bad, this summer would change everything.

Cocoa was first up the two steps and onto the wooden deck that formed a courtyard in front of the cluster of buildings, complete with gazebo and outdoor fireplace. The Oakcrest Mews. One of those storefronts, the smallest one tucked behind the kitchenware shop, was hers. Temporarily, at least. It was both thrilling and utterly terrifying.

"Who's the pup?"

She whirled around. But, in the glare of the sun, she could only just make out the shape of the woman sitting in the shadows of the gazebo.

Cocoa moved toward the stranger, pulling on the leash. Charley followed.

The air cooled and the light dimmed as they joined the woman. "This is Cocoa," she said.

At the introduction, she plunked herself on the ground and grinned up at the new person.

Dark hair, tinged with grey, escaped from beneath a wide-brimmed hat, placed at a jaunty angle on the woman's head. She wore an over-sized cardigan in a soft shade of moss green. Binoculars hung around her neck. She leaned down and rubbed Cocoa's ears. The dog soaked up the attention. "You're a cute one." She straightened, then frowned in the direction of the sidewalk. "Well, what do you know. He's out walking around, as innocent as can be."

"Who?" Charley turned to look.

Striding down the street was the man she'd seen yesterday. Andrew. Did he have any friends in town?

"The traitor." The verdict was bitter and heartfelt. The stern expression gone in a blink as though the woman realized who she'd spoken to. "Never mind. Just the usual small-town misunderstanding." Sharp eyes peered at Charley from above a defined nose. Despite the strong and weathered features, she must have been beautiful in her youth. "Have a seat and keep an old woman company for a minute." She gestured at the empty space on the bench beside her.

Intrigued by this eccentric woman, Charley took her up on the offer. "You can't be a day past thirty," she teased.

Fine lines — the kind earned from a life well lived — spread around green eyes as she chuckled. "Don't I wish that were true. At seventy-two I'm afraid one is considered — how did little Max Harrows put it? 'Ancient as dirt.'"

She laughed and leaned back. "I wouldn't say that."

The view of the street really was great from here. The intersection within sight provided first-hand information on any new cars turning onto Main Street. She could see the storefronts and customers. The people coming and going from the bank, the grocery store. And in the second-story apartments, above hanging baskets overflowing with bright blooms, the occasional shadow moving behind dormer windows.

Cocoa turned twice and lay down at Charley's feet, pink tongue flashing as she panted. She was probably thirsty after the walk. It was a good thing Charley had tossed the water bottle into her tote bag on the way out. She poured some water into the plastic dish attached to the bottle and offered it to Cocoa, who eagerly lapped it up.

"You, dear," the woman said, "I have pegged as a romantic. No." She held up a hand, before Charley could respond. "That wasn't a question. Hmm?" she murmured, eyes fixed on the Village Grocer across the street. Raising the binoculars, she peered through them and clicked her tongue against the roof of her mouth. "That Stevenson fellow has been after her all week. Look at that! He's practically begging. Silly creature, doesn't he know how to woo a girl? He'll never win her heart like that."

Charley leaned forward to get a better look at the couple inside the grocery store, but she could only make out two silhouettes. "Who does he want to ask out?"

"Jennifer. She's a single mother and won't make that move if she doesn't think he's good enough for her and her little girl. Oh, he's doing it all wrong!" The woman slapped a hand against her knee. She seemed to notice Charley still sat beside her. Reaching into the cloth sack at her feet, she pulled out a plastic bag of sweets. "Chocolate-coated raisin?"

She studied them for a second and breathed in the roasted, earthy scent, that undertone of sweetness. Oh, why not. Already gooey and stuck to the plastic, the chocolate smudged her finger-tips as she chose one. "Thanks." Milky and decadent, the flavours melted on her tongue. It might be the most delicious chocolate she had ever tasted. No way this came from a grocery store.

"Chocoholic."

Aghast, she swallowed. "Excuse me?"

"The local confectionary, it's called Chocoholic's. Here, have some more. Slender as a reed of grass, you could use some meat on your bones."

It didn't sound like a compliment. "They're very good." Incredible, in fact. Sweet but not too sweet, the raisin was plump and fruity, with just the right amount of chocolate coating. "There's a confectionary here in town?" Why hadn't Meghan mentioned it? She'd have some explaining to do when she got home.

"The shop opened six months ago." The woman looked at her, a thoughtful gleam in her eye. Then she gave a decisive nod and said briskly, "If you go down Main Street and turn left onto Union Street, you can't miss it."

"And just when I thought Oakcrest couldn't get any better." Although the place was alive with summer memories, it felt like she was discovering it all over again. Taking another chocolate from the bag, she glanced at the woman's binoculars. "Could I take a look?"

The woman's eyebrows disappeared beneath the brim of her hat. "Certainly not!" Placing a hand over the object in question, she glared at Charley. "They're mine."

"All right. I'm sorry I asked." In silence they watched the figures move behind the glass. "I'm Charley, by the way. Charley Scott."

"Yes, I've been waiting for you."

Goosebumps rose on her arms. She turned to face her. "What?"

"Your sister always has that impish look about her, like she knows something you don't know and she's not going to tell."

"That's her all right." The description was spot-on. "Why were you waiting for me?"

She patted Charley on the knee. "I'm the owner."

This was Sarah Felles? The woman who had sent those clear, precise emails, with an attention to detail that had both impressed her and helped seal the deal at a distance. It wasn't often that someone surprised her. "I thought we were meeting later this afternoon."

Sarah brushed that aside with a cryptic wave of her hand and reached into the pocket of her cardigan. She pulled out a set of keys and shook them, making them jingle enticingly. "You'll need these."

The keys fell into her palm with a chink, the weight heavy with promise. Her fingers closed over them. "I can't wait to take a look around."

"Drat!" Picking up the binoculars again, Sarah trained them on the grocery store's window. "He's leaving. Idiot." Disgusted, she leaned back.

"Do you people-watch often?"

Sarah sat up straight, gaining height and authority in one move. "I am a bird watcher. That is what I do."

"A bird watcher?" She quirked an eyebrow.

Sarah returned her gaze, an enigmatic smile curving her lips. "Shall we go inside?"

Picking up on that hint of adventure in the woman's voice, Cocoa leaped to her feet. Charley didn't need to be asked twice either.

Large front windows threw their reflection back at them. The gabled roof gave the building the feel of a cottage. The wooden siding glowed.

This was it, the moment she'd been waiting for.

The key fit perfectly. With one quick twist, the lock tumbled, and they stepped inside, Cocoa in the lead, like always.

Sarah paused to enter a combination into the keypad by the door. "The code is set to default at the moment, but you can program it however you like. I'll leave instructions with you."

That was one of the plus points. Security, already installed. Along with the open floor plan, wood-paneled walls and whitewashed floors. She'd seen the pictures and fallen hard. Hook, line, and sinker. But it was so much better in person.

Of course, now that she was inside, she could see the imperfections here and there. Some water marks around the window frames, and was that a dip in the floor? But it only added character.

Sarah moved on, to the door in the back. The tour was speedy and efficient, accompanied by a whirlwind of instructions. By the end of it, Charley had seen the bathroom, the earth cellar, the rooms above — meant as living quarters, but they'd need the extra space. She knew where the fuse box was and how to adjust the thermostat, although apparently this was best left untouched.

Back on the ground floor, Sarah said, "Kayla and Thomas are displaying their work, too."

It wasn't a question. "Yes, they are." News travelled fast.

"And contributing to the rent, I assume."

Shrewd woman. "They've offered to help out, but I can pay it on my own, if need be."

Cocoa roamed the room, nose down. Taking time to sniff each corner.

"And what is the theme of your pop-up exhibition?"

Charley shot Sarah a glance. No, the woman didn't miss any details.

Sarah said, "Don't look so surprised, my dear. I know all about these short-term venues, displaying the work of local artists. They're very trendy, these days."

That's what she was counting on. "The theme is Cover Art."

"As in, deception?" Sarah slid her hands into the pockets of her cardigan and looked intrigued.

"Pulp fiction, in my case."

"Thomas does those colourful paintings." For those who damn with faint praise, 'colourful' might have meant 'gaudy' but, the way Sarah said it, the word held no hidden meanings. It was simply an adjective. "Mostly musicians, if I remember," she said. "He has a few pieces on consignment in the café."

"That's right." Thomas's bold and bright pieces replicated the style of vintage jazz album covers. As the only more established artist, they were lucky he'd joined them.

"Jennifer, the woman from the grocery store, is his daughter. There's quite a story there. Have you met him yet?"

"Not in person." Soon, though, they'd be hanging their art on these walls together.

Doubt churned within her. What if her work wasn't good enough? She banished the thought before it could take root.

She said, "I heard there's a ghost in the Mews." The ghost had been on her mind last night, when she couldn't sleep. The haunted gallery — it had great marketing potential. She'd created a blog for the exhibit, intending to post interviews with artists and images of their work. But what better way to draw a crowd than a resident ghost? She only hoped it was just that, a story she could use and not a real spectre.

"Oh, no. Not in the Mews. Right here, above us." Sarah pointed up and the gesture had a shiver running down Charley's spine. "Some claim they've heard mysterious sounds coming from the second floor, but I've never seen or heard her myself."

Her. She tucked that piece of information away.

"But," Sarah continued, "I always say, let the dead rest in peace. The living are so much more interesting. Well, that's that." She clapped her hands and bent to pat Cocoa. "It's yours now, for the time being."

"I'll take good care of it."

"Yes, you will." It sounded only slightly threatening. "Just remember, leave her alone and you'll be fine."

"Leave who alone?"

"Lizzie, our ghost." She placed a hand on her arm, gave it a reassuring squeeze. "Best not to stir up old hurt."

On her own with Cocoa, Charley glanced up uneasily. Marketing potential, she reminded herself. A ghost was a good thing.

And she could always hum to fill the silence.

FIVE

"WHAT CAN I GET YOU, Andrew?" Matt asked, already reaching for one of the small boxes to fill with Belgian chocolates. "Vanilla Cream, Black Forest, or Mocha?"

"They're not for me today." Andrew checked his watch, on edge or just impatient, it was hard to tell. Mouth stretched in a thin line, more grimace than smile. He could be likeable, when he decided it was worth his while to put in the effort. Obviously, this was not one of those times. "Put a box together for my wife. You know what she likes best."

"Sure." Taking time on his lunch break to buy chocolates. Could be an anniversary gift, but if Matt had to put money on it, he'd bet Andrew stopped by Chocoholic's because he had something to make up for. The man never did anything without an ulterior motive. He filled the box with orange apricot white chocolate pralines, dark chocolate, and a few champagne truffles for good measure.

The bell chimed above the door and, for an instant, he thought Charley had tracked him down. But her startled expression when she walked in and spotted him behind the counter put an end to that idea, and fast. Of course, with a dog named Cocoa, he should have expected to see her in the store sooner or later.

She wore loose jeans and a purple T-shirt that, from the looks

36

of it, had been washed to oblivion and back. Those curls, the colour of caramel, were tied back from her face this time. And her sneakers were dusted with — powdered sugar and lime zest? No. Paint. The dark canvas speckled with white and green flecks.

With a jolt, he realized Andrew was talking to him. "Sure, I can wrap the box for you." He was aware of Charley, as she began studying the chocolates. She had the same expression kids got when they browsed the store for the first time. Pure joy. "Can I get you anything else?"

Andrew hesitated. He glanced over at the glass display case. "Yeah, why not? I'll take a bag of the Vanilla Cream too."

He filled the bag with a generous amount, knowing it would probably be empty by the time Andrew got home. If the man had a vice, it was those chocolates. And, for the owner of Chocoholic's, that wasn't a bad thing. He'd expanded his selection of nut-free chocolates because of him.

A ringtone sounded, some tinny musical interlude. Andrew checked his phone screen and frowned. "Sorry, I'm going to have to take this." He moved to the side to answer the call and Matt heard him say, "Actually, I'm just stepping on site now." Sure, he was.

And that's why Matt was in the chocolate business. Less games, less lies.

Finished tying the bow, he headed toward Charley, giving Andrew some space. She gazed at the display of plastic-wrapped bars of specialty chocolate lining the back wall in neat rows.

The antique cupboards at the front of the store — purchased at a yard sale and refinished himself — held milk chocolates shaped like animals, hot chocolate sticks, as well as fudge and jars of honey from local suppliers. The products on those shelves were a hit with the kids, but the bars of chocolate on that back wall were where he could let loose, play with flavours.

Moving closer, Matt snuck a glance over her shoulder to see what she was holding. A bar of Gin and Tonic chocolate.

A flash of colour on the inside of her wrist caught his eye. More paint? No, a tattoo. A dandelion, blowing in the breeze, all delicate lines and pastel yellow and green. Soft as a watercolour painting, the seeds drifted alongside the blue shadowed line, just visible beneath pale skin.

Her left hand kept time to the beat of the song, tapping out the rhythm against her leg. 80s classic rock at noon, just loud enough to be heard. He'd have it cranked higher, if he could get away with it without deterring customers.

"Hi." Not creative, but it got him a smile.

"You own a chocolate shop."

Amused, he said, "Yes, I do." He nodded toward the door where Cocoa sat, looking in at them. Condensation clouded the glass at nose level. "If the water bowl is empty, I can fill it up for her."

She looked surprised that he'd thought of it. "There was still some left, but thanks."

"Let me get you a sample of the Gin and Tonic." He stepped behind the counter and pulled out one of the airtight containers he kept on the shelf. White chocolate, infused with lime zest, juniper essential oil, and coriander.

She took the piece he offered. Her eyes widened as the flavour hit. "It tastes just like the cocktail! It even has that —" She waved her hand, searching for the right word. "— spritz!"

"That's the popping candy." Delighted by her reaction, he leaned a hip against the counter.

Normally, Andrew's full-volume conversation at the front of the store would annoy the hell out of him. But right now, he wouldn't mind if that call lasted another five or even ten minutes.

"I'll take one of those." Charley moved closer to the shelves, skimming over the names of the other flavours. "Do you make all of the chocolate yourself?"

"For The Chocolate Bar, yes."

She looked at the bars on the wall and grinned. "Great name, by the way."

He laughed. "I couldn't resist," he admitted. "Mrs. Callahan helps with the truffles and there are a few ready-made products up at the front, but I make everything else."

She picked up a bar of milk chocolate, filled with strawberry rhubarb mousse. "How did you get into this?"

"Someone my mom worked with taught me how to make chocolate when I was a kid." And let a twelve-year-old boy pound raw cacao beans into a workable mass until he forgot his grief. Until they had more blocks of shiny chocolate than they could eat. "I got hooked. Couldn't stop thinking about it. The process of tempering chocolate, blending ingredients to create something new." Like alchemy. "Trying to balance intensity and bitterness. It's addictive."

"I can imagine." The way she looked around the store, taking in all the details of it, made him think she could.

"Anyway," Matt said. "Enough about me. Would you like anything else?" Spreading his arms, he offered the selection to her. "Truffles? Hazelnut, marzipan, or vanilla cream? Hot chocolate, mochaccino? A date for Saturday night?" Unplanned, the question came out. And he stood there, heart hammering in his chest.

"I think I'll stick with the chocolate for now," she said with a grin.

Fair enough. Shot down for the second time. It had been a while since he'd asked a girl out. Maybe he was doing it wrong. He put the two chocolate bars into a bag for her. Best switch to small talk before he put his foot in it again. "When does the gallery open?"

"So that's who you are." Andrew ended his call and stalked toward them. Deep-set eyes fixed on Charley.

"Excuse me?" She turned to him. And looked up. He towered over her.

"You're the one who convinced my wife to waste her time and money." There was anger there, barely contained. And accusation.

She raised an eyebrow. "I don't know what you're talking about." While Andrew's voice had heated, hers had cooled to an icy tone that froze the blood in Matt's veins.

Andrew didn't seem to feel it. "I will not see my wife get crushed when this goes wrong. You're doing this for fun, for the summer." Disdain and no effort to hide it. "Got yourself nicely covered. No risk, nothing at stake."

He wondered about that. "Got a problem, Andrew?"

"I do, in fact. With her."

Before Matt could respond, she said, "You're Kayla's husband."

Andrew crossed his arms. "That's right."

"Maybe you should let her make her own decisions," she suggested. And if Andrew fell for that sugar-coated tone, he deserved whatever he got.

"So, you can influence her?" Andrew pulled his wallet out of his back pocket, counted bills. "The same way you convinced my wife to use her maiden name for the gallery? I don't think so." He brushed past Charley and dropped cash onto the counter, correct down to the exact change. "You'd better watch yourself, Ms. Scott. I intend to put an end to this exhibit." There was confidence there, and arrogance. The kind that came from years of bulldozing buildings. And people.

That last sentence, it finally got to her, cracking her composure. "We'll see about that!" She shouted, hands on her hips and visibly fuming.

The door slammed behind him.

"That was interesting," Matt said. For a little thing, she could be intimidating.

"It was just talk," she said, more to herself than to him. "What can he do?"

"Probably not much." But Andrew didn't make empty threats.

She took a breath. "Thanks for the Gin and Tonic sample. It was incredible."

A simple compliment and one he'd heard often enough. Still, he felt the grin spread over his face. "You're welcome." Their fingers brushed as he handed her the bag of chocolates, and Matt felt a spike of adrenaline that caught him off guard, had him wishing she hadn't turned him down for that date.

"Sorry about the scene."

He shrugged. "That was nothing. It can get pretty wild in here, especially when there's a good sugar buzz going."

"Fist fights?"

"Only the occasional cocoa-fueled brawl."

Charley laughed. At the door, she paused. "You know" — she broke into a smile that was pure mischief — "your ears go pink when you blush. It's kind of cute." She left before he even had the chance to think of a reply.

Shit. Did they really?

WHAT TIME WAS IT? WARM body beside her, back pressed up right against her side, and it was dark as anything. Then she heard the sound again. A low grunt. The clip-clop of hooves striking stone.

Charley had a vision of a mythical white horse, horn spiraling out of its forehead, walking majestically past her bedroom window.

Obviously, that was insane. She shook off the last remnants of sleep and concentrated. The body beside her was Cocoa, who had climbed onto the bed at some point in the night. Snuffling in her sleep, legs twitching with a dream.

Another low animal grunt from outside, more drawn-out this time, and Charley definitely heard the stomp of hooves.

It could not be a unicorn.

Tossing the covers aside, she slipped out of bed. Wincing at the cool floor beneath her feet, she padded over to the window. She'd left it open a crack. Expecting to look out into the dark, her heart rate kicked up a notch. That tightening of the chest, the shortness of breath. That childhood fear of the dark — of the unseen — could still sneak up on her, even now.

Twitching the curtain aside, heart racing, she peered out. The night air brushed over her bare arms.

But she was wrong about the darkness.

There, on the patio, lit by the pale light of the moon, stood a buck. About seven feet tall with prominent antlers, and much larger than the doe she'd seen on the road. The buck snorted, raising his head with a glitter of eyes. Silvery light caught on the sharp branched tines of antlers, shone white at his throat.

And she'd actually been worried she'd miss the bright lights of the city.

She held her breath as the animal passed, moving around the wrought-iron table and chairs, onto the grass and farther. Like something from a picture book. Hooves sinking into the grass, quieter now. Then it disappeared into the trees beyond.

Goosebumps prickled her skin. Giddy with the scene she'd witnessed, she tiptoed over the chilly floor, back to bed and snuggled down under the covers. In the orange glow of the bedside lamp, she rested her sketch pad against her raised knees, and drew.

And tried not to think about the threat that Andrew had made in Chocoholic's.

So, he was Kayla's husband.

All she'd gotten from Kayla was an email sharing the news of her engagement and a picture of the ring, showcased in its blue Tiffany box. After that, she hadn't heard anything else, even though she'd asked for more details. Like his name.

Hard to believe her husband was so dead set against the exhibit. And Kayla hadn't said anything about it.

Charley's stomach twisted into knots as she glided the pencil over paper. The gallery was her chance to find out if she had the talent to make it as an artist. And she'd hold herself to the promise that, on her thirtieth birthday, she'd make a decision, once and for all. To continue or give up. If the gallery failed, she'd throw away her paints and commit to an office job. At some point, you had to face facts and stop putting time and effort into something that would never pay.

In the meantime, she planned to devote every iota of her being to fulfilling her dream.

With quick, sure movements of pencil over paper, she coaxed the buck into existence until, there he was, standing beside the round-topped table and delicate chairs again, framed by twisting branches. Lake gleaming in the distance.

Nothing — and no one — would stop her.

SIX

"HEY!" CHARLEY SLAPPED AT THE hand reaching over her shoulder, but Meghan was quicker. Always full of energy in the morning, her reflexes were faster. She snatched the square Charley had just broken off the chocolate bar and popped it into her mouth.

"Mmm ..." Meghan moaned and dropped into the chair across the kitchen table from her. "Strawberries and smooth milk chocolate."

She turned her attention away from the mist, rising like smoke over the lake, and scowled at Meghan over the rim of her mug. The coffee still hot enough to singe her tongue. "I was about to eat that." It was the best reply she could come up with. The caffeine hadn't jumpstarted her system yet.

"You snooze, you lose." Meghan slid the chocolate closer to herself, and snapped off another corner, seemingly oblivious to the fact that this could be a risky move. "Last one, I promise."

"It better be." She took the bar back and kept her hand over it this time. Already humid, her bare toes stuck to the wooden floorboards. Somehow, Meghan looked both cool and fresh in her Breton striped T-shirt and white jeans. Pristine and paint-free. "Thanks for telling me about Oakcrest's top tourist attraction, by the way. I stumbled across Chocoholic's on my own."

"And on your second day, too. Not bad sis." Meghan grinned. "I knew you and Cocoa would track it down. It's amazing, isn't it?"

44

"Dangerous, actually." She shifted to prop a knee against the edge of the table. "I could spend a lot of money in that store."

"It is tempting," Meghan agreed. "The owner, too. I'd even go so far as to say scrumptious."

"The chocolate?"

"Matt Thorn." Meghan wriggled her eyebrows.

She snorted a laugh into her cup. "Don't let Alex hear you say that."

Meghan waved a hand. "Looking never hurt anyone." Standing, she headed to the cabinet and took down a ceramic travel mug.

Cocoa nudged her knee. Charley rubbed her ear, the warm weight of the dog's chin heavy on her leg. "From what I've heard," she said casually, "it seems like Matt grew up here, but the chocolate shop is relatively new. What's the story there?"

If anyone knew the details, Meghan would. She'd always been driven by curiosity, always been good at digging up stories.

"Oh, it's newsworthy all right." Meghan reached for the coffee pot and filled the travel mug close to the brim. "It's got all the elements that make a reporter's heart beat faster. Local interest, conflict, scandal, even something a little bizarre, a little eerie. Death." She paused. Spooned sugar in. Returned the half-and-half cream to the fridge. Building the suspense.

Charley waited, knowing that if she showed any interest whatsoever, she would only drag it out longer.

Somewhere along the shore, the whine of an outboard motor started up, cutting through the early morning calm blanketing the lake. On the dock, a blue heron materialized from the haze on a ruffle of feathers. How long had he been standing there, motionless? Lowering its wings, the hunter perched, a grey outline, all but invisible again. The shoreline shrouded and still, the heat trapped between clouds and water.

"Matt grew up here," Meghan finally said, "but he left after high school to go to culinary school in France."

"Ooh la la." She thought of *café au lait*, croissants, and village-square markets. The sun setting over the Eiffel Tower.

Meghan leaned back against the counter. "Exactly. He came back to Oakcrest about a year ago, to take care of his dad. Nick passed away six weeks ago or more now, from cancer. It was pretty rough."

"That's terrible." She'd never have guessed. Was that quick and easy charm a front, to hide his grief?

"Rumour has it," Meghan said, "there was tension between father and son. People are wondering if he'll stay now that his dad is gone or if Matt will sell the house and move on. The ghost of his mother, by the way, is haunting your gallery."

She choked on her coffee. Setting the mug down, she gasped for air. "What?"

"Lizzie." Meghan always did love a plot twist. "She died when Matt was young, just twelve or thirteen years old. An accident on a construction site. I don't know all the details, but she worked as a framing carpenter at the site, where your building now stands."

To say she hadn't seen that one coming was an understatement. Sarah Felles' words came back to her. *Best not to stir up old hurt.*

"That's a lot of history." She felt a twinge of guilt that she had thought about using the ghost to market the gallery.

"I wouldn't blame Matt, if he wanted to leave town. Anyway." Meghan pushed back from the counter. Snapped the lid on her mug. "You promised me a lift this morning. Ready to hit the road?"

THUNK, THUNK.

"I'm sorry, Lizzie." Charley carried the last canvas into the gallery. Her voice echoed back at her in the empty space. "But you're stuck with us, for now. And I don't scare easily." Until Kayla and Thomas arrived, she and Cocoa were on their own. And they'd hold their ground.

In the heat and humidity, her T-shirt already clung to her back. And she still had to bring in the toolbox from the Jeep and the basket of cleaning supplies she'd swiped from the cottage. The bucket, microfibre cloth, and oil wood cleaner soap.

She'd dropped Meghan off at her office on the way, but maybe she should have asked her to help unload the paintings. And seized the opportunity to get more details on the resident ghost. A little intel might have been useful, especially now that the ghost was active and apparently very real.

The next *thunk* had the hairs on the back of Charley's neck rising. Cocoa scratched at the door leading upstairs and growled low in her throat.

Leave her alone and you'll be fine, Sarah said. But they'd have to go upstairs eventually. Charley hoped the spectre was friendly and not out for revenge. Nerves fluttered in her stomach and now she had a ghost to deal with, too.

She knew what she needed. Sugar, butterscotch, and romance. Scrolling through the playlists on her phone, she found the album she wanted. Bubblegum hits. Hopefully the sunny tunes would be loud enough through the portable speakers to drown out the thumping from above.

"Awop-bop-a-loo," Charley sang along as she leaned canvases, safely packed in bubble wrap, against one wall. "Bam-boom!"

As though on cue, thunder cracked in the distance. It hadn't begun to rain yet, but it would soon. And hopefully break this heat wave.

Grabbing the bucket, she carried it into the bathroom. The door-handle banged against the sink. With a twist of the tap, the pipes spluttered to life, running first copper, then clear. The bucket fit under the faucet — jammed at an angle.

Soaking the cloth in lemon-scented oil and water, she wrang it out until just damp to the touch. And tried not to think about the fact that Cocoa hadn't moved from the door.

The first wipe across the floor left a gleaming streak behind. Dipping the cloth into the bucket again, a rivulet of water trickled over the whitewashed boards and ran down to the left.

Sitting on her heels, she swiped the back of a soapy hand at her hair. There was a slope in the floor. And gaps along the baseboard, she saw now. But weren't uneven floors normal in old buildings? Part of the charm. Along with the creaks, groans, and — she glanced up uneasily — bangs. Soon, the place would be glowing, the walls filled with art.

She let herself daydream. And worked until her arms ached and her fingers shriveled.

By the time she had the poster hanging in the window, advertising the opening of the pop-up gallery, she felt better. The building was hers, for now. Ghost be damned.

In the corner of the room, she spread out a fleece throw blanket. Cocoa ignored it and stayed where she was, stretched flat on her belly. Ears on alert.

Outside, the sky had darkened to an ominous shade of slate grey. The air crackled with electricity. Hardly any breeze came through the open window. Charley hit the switch to turn on the overhead lights. The bulbs flickered once, then held.

She jammed her fists on her hips and looked around, trying to get a feel for the space. The size of the walls.

They each had an area to showcase their work, both downstairs and upstairs, all on the theme of Cover Art. Her own canvases and lithographs looked like pulp fiction dust jackets. But instead of coolly smoking private eyes, her paintings featured ordinary women in heroic situations. A woman in a business suit, dropping her children off at the school bus. Even one of Meghan as the reporter, with the sensational title, 'The News Never Sleeps'.

Her bright colours would transition well into Thomas's jazz series. Kayla's art would carry on the storytelling theme.

Of Inuit descent, Kayla had grown up on her grandmother's legends. In a way, so had Charley. She'd seized every chance to be at her cabin in the summer. Now Kayla had transformed those stories from her childhood into delicate line drawings that were both contemporary and rooted in tradition. When they spoke on the phone, she told her that art in Inuktitut is *isumanivi*, which means, "your own thoughts." For those who knew the legends, her illustrations would be at once familiar and foreign, a product of her own imagination and experiences. Together, the three of them could pull off an impressive exhibit.

If things went smoothly.

During a pause between songs, Charley heard it. A light running noise from above, like feet crossing the floor. A chill shot down her spine. This was different. No longer just bumps and creaks, this sounded human. Cocoa leaped up in a flash, her growl turned menacing.

Someone was moving around up there. Not a ghost. Kids.

The alarm though — how did they manage to get past it?

Her heart sank. She hadn't changed the code yet. She'd have to do that ASAP.

Was it just a dare, the thrill of sneaking in without getting caught, or worse? Her first day in the gallery, and she had visions of vandalism and pranks.

She could wait for Kayla and Thomas to arrive. Or catch the hooligans in the act.

Charley strode to the door. She hadn't led an after-school art club for nothing. She could handle a little preteen attitude. And she had Cocoa with her. A happy-go-lucky chocolate lab might not be the most threatening protector, but at least she had company.

The stairs creaked beneath her feet. She kept her hand on Cocoa's collar, holding the dog back. Her heart raced, faster even than the quick beat of the pop song, growing fainter with every step.

On the landing, she paused to listen. The sounds had been coming from directly above them. Which meant that the intruder was in the next room. Beyond the closed door, something scurried.

"Oh boy," she murmured to Cocoa. The handle felt cold to the touch. "Here goes nothing."

The door swung inward on rusted hinges and she tensed, ready for anything. The rain broke, pelleting against the windows.

She stepped into the spacious room. On a sunny day, it would have been bright and inviting. Right now, it looked gloomy and empty.

And without furniture, there was nowhere to hide.

She flicked the light switch. The bulb was dead. The room wasn't dark, not completely. Shadowy and dim, but not pitch-black.

"Hello?" She let Cocoa loose. The dog set off, moving quickly, nose to the ground. Hot on the scent of something.

Had the intruder escaped through the door at the back and taken off down the hall? It was the only logical explanation.

Charley set off across the room. If they got away with it this time, they'd be back, and then the gallery would be filled with art. She couldn't risk it.

Beneath the drumming of the rain, there was only silence. No scrapes, no scurrying. And that silence was so sudden, so complete, it set her nerves on edge. She fought the urge to check over her shoulder.

Lightning flashed, illuminating the room. Except for one corner of the ceiling. That shadow, had it been there before, on her tour with Sarah?

"What is that?" She moved closer.

The shadow looked more like a hole in the drywall, but that couldn't be right.

A furry, black arm reached down from the ceiling, claws extended, like something from a horror movie. A nose popped out, narrow and whiskered, and Charley's heart slammed into her throat.

"Squirrel!" she gasped.

The animal froze, arm stretched out, eyes wide.

Cocoa let loose a volley of barks. Quick as a flash, the furry intruder disappeared back into its hole. Having vanquished the monster, Cocoa pranced back to her. But Charley knew better. It wasn't gone for good.

"Come on, Cocoa." Pulse scrambling, she backed toward the door, keeping her gaze on the ceiling.

A ghost she could handle. Kids, she could handle. A squirrel? That was something different entirely.

They'd need to call pest control. People expected the unexpected in a pop-up gallery, but actual wildlife might be pushing the limits of avant-garde.

SEVEN

TIME FOR SOME ANSWERS.

Driving up the road, Matt caught a glimpse of the lake through the trees, looking like slate beneath storm clouds. So much for taking the boat out this afternoon.

The truck's tires crunched over gravel as he pulled up in front of the large green building.

On Tuesdays, Chocoholic's was closed. His one day off a week, and he'd be using it to interrogate an old friend. To pave the way, he'd brought lunch.

He parked in his usual spot, right out front, and got out of the car. With the height of the roof and the wide garage door, the two-story steel building looked like an airplane hangar. And had been mistaken for one, when Jeffrey first built it, all those years ago. It was actually an agricultural storage building — an economical way to set up a functioning workshop. Simple, sturdy, and filled with memories. Good ones. He'd spent a lot of hours here, growing up.

From the open garage door came the grind of an electric sander, barely overpowered by the sonorous, soul-shaking rhythm of some seventies rock band blasting from the overhead speakers.

Matt grabbed an insulated bag off the passenger seat and headed in.

Sawdust hung in the air, mingling with the smell of wood and metal, oil, and varnish. Seemed like every time he came by these days, he had to find a new path through the maze of lumber, shelving, and extension cords.

"Jeffrey!" he shouted.

No way he'd hear him over the noise of the sander and the music.

Matt crossed the concrete floor, moving around a stack of two-by-fours, past the circle of mismatched chairs, ready for coffee break, and on into the back.

He found him sitting on a stool by the open back door, ear-muffs on, sanding what looked like the side of a bookcase. Oak, judging by the graining — those pinstripes and knots. Through the open door, Matt saw the first raindrops hit the ground. Any second now, it would be pouring cats and dogs.

He moved into Jeffrey's line of vision, caught his eye, and held up the bag. "Lunch?"

Jeffrey switched off the sander and pulled off the hearing protection, resting the padded muffs around his neck. "Pizza?" Edge of humour to his voice. "Or burgers?"

He laughed. "I thought you had better taste than that. I might have to find a new guinea pig."

"You haven't poisoned me — yet."

Out of habit, Matt scanned the notes tacked to the sheet of plywood by the wall phone. Only four in total. That board used to flap with a dozen scraps of paper or more. Probably stored on an app now, but Jeffrey had built his business on those chicken scratches. Orders, types of wood, measurements, paint — a cipher and hardly legible at that. His own cellphone number though was clear as day, scrawled black and permanent, right on the wood.

"Watch for nails over there," Jeffrey warned. "Lonely on your day off, Matt?"

He turned away from the wall. "Nah. I thought I'd take pity on an old man, slaving away out here on his own."

"Old man? Dollars to nothing, I was twice as productive as you today." Jeffrey dabbed sweat off his forehead with a rag. "How are you doing? Must be a lot on your plate right now."

Of course, he'd ask. "It helps to keep busy." And he had more than enough to do.

Jeffrey shot him a glance, looked like he wanted to say more but thought better of it.

Little did he know, this was more than just a social visit.

As Jeffrey turned down the music and cleared the worktable, sweeping away sawdust and shavings, Matt walked around, checking out the latest projects, biding his time. He paused beside one that looked like a large crate, the walls almost five foot high. "What's this?"

Jeffrey glanced over. "A flowerbox."

"This is a flowerbox?" It was huge.

"I had some leftover wood. Thought it would help block the view to the neighbour. Plus" — Jeffrey grinned — "seriously piss him off."

"Don't you think your feud with Andrew has gone on long enough?" They'd been at each other for as long as he could remember. At some point, you had to let it go.

He shrugged. "I'll grow stuff in it. Make it look pretty."

"Skip the peonies. You could plant cedar trees, if you felt like it."

Jeffrey guffawed. "That's not a bad idea." He went over to the small fridge, tucked beneath the stairs. "I'm done with the power tools for today. Want a beer?"

"I'm driving."

"Fair enough." He took one for himself and snagged a water, the kind he still stocked in bulk.

Matt caught the bottle he tossed to him. "No helper today?" For a while, that had been his job. He had worked with Jeffrey on and off all through high school, helping out with residential jobs and some of the woodworking in the shop.

Jeffrey hooked the bottle cap on the edge of the table, gave it a slam with the flat of his hand. Beer fountained over the lip. "I gave the kid the afternoon off."

Matt lowered the water, without drinking. "Getting soft, are you?" July and August were peak months for cottage renovations. "I can't remember getting any weekdays off, not during the summer. At one point, you had me working seven days a week." And he'd never been tempted to complain, not once.

"Times change." Jeffrey straddled a chair backwards and gestured at the bag. "What did you bring me?"

He knew when to push and when to leave well enough alone. He unpacked the bag, setting the plastic storage containers on the table. "Spinach, goat cheese and black olive muffins."

Jeffrey raised his eyebrows and gave a low whistle. He cracked the lid and looked inside.

"A mixed green salad," Matt said. Individual servings, portioned off in Tupperware. He pulled out a jam jar and shook the liquid inside. "French vinaigrette."

He took the jar from him and opened it, took a sniff. "Dijon base?"

"You got it."

"And the chocolate?"

He grinned. "Later." He poured the vinaigrette over the salads and handed one container to Jeffrey, along with a fork. He settled back on the stool, one foot on the rung, and took a swig of water.

Jeffrey eyed the muffin, then broke off a piece. Checking the consistency and texture, looking for an evenly browned crust and rounded top, before tasting it.

He asked, "What do you think?"

As usual, Jeffrey took his time replying, letting the flavours unfold first, before giving a verdict. "Moist and delicate. No paper cups, nice golden finish." He broke off another piece. "Surprisingly fresh taste. Is that dill?"

"Yup."

"Olive oil instead of butter. Clever."

The oil he'd chosen had herbal notes, with a slightly buttery, almost peppery finish. "I thought it would pair well with the bitterness of the olives."

"It does. I like these muffins."

Coming from the man who taught him to cook, the praise carried weight. It was unsettling how much a few words of encouragement from Jeffrey still meant to him. "Good, there's lots." He'd loaded up the container, planning to leave the leftovers with him once they'd finished lunch.

Jeffrey tried a forkful of salad next. "Nice tang to the vinaigrette. Sherry vinegar?"

"What else?"

He chewed, swallowed. "Not enough salt."

And, there it was. Room for improvement, blunt and honest. Jeffrey always had one piece of advice, one point of critique to give. And that was why he still came to him with samples. "You always say that."

"That's because it's always true. Stingy with seasoning, that's what you are." He wiped his mouth on the paper napkin.

"Stingy?"

Outside, the rain began to fall in a hard sheet that drummed on the metal roof.

"Miserly." Jeffrey grinned. "Could be, you've been focusing too much on the sweeter things in life, *chocolatier*. You're out of practice when it comes to savoury dishes." His eyes twinkled.

"Yeah, yeah." He took a bite of a muffin. Maybe it could use another pinch of salt.

"I'd say–" Jeffrey paused, leaned forward, as though about to impart some piece of hard-won wisdom. "Ditch the chocolate-stained apron and make more of these."

He laughed. "My new source of livelihood."

They focused on the food for a while, until Jeffrey said, "Out with it."

Guilt shot through him. "What?"

"Something's on your mind. What is it?"

And that's what happened when you spent too much time with someone. They picked up on all your tells. "Remind me not to play poker with you again," he muttered.

"Your face is an open book, my friend. Always has been."

He shifted his weight on the stool. "Actually, I have some questions for you."

"Questions? Are you sure, you don't have something you want to tell me?" Jeffrey gave him a pointed look, like he should know what he was talking about.

Matt hadn't seen that expression in a very long time. What mistake did he want him to fess up to? "No," he said. "I've got questions."

An emotion flickered across Jeffrey's face, but he shut it down before Matt could decipher it. He nodded. "So, you've finally figured it out."

Matt knew this game and caught on quick. He'd been half expecting a lecture after that buildup, but the tone had changed. And he'd play along. "All your deep dark secrets?"

"The witness protection." Jeffrey kept a straight face. "My past with the mob. The drugs, the women." When it came to tall tales, he could put Mark Twain to shame.

"The money," Matt said, the twists and turns of the story easy to anticipate.

"The price of blood."

He gestured with his water bottle. "Nothing the best chocolate in the world couldn't rival."

"Cocoa beans, worth their weight in gold. And it's all stashed —"

"In the basement. I know."

"Ah," Jeffrey said. "You found it."

"Early on. I've been siphoning it off for years."

"Damn. All right." Jeffrey reached for another muffin, his third. "Ask away."

"No made-up stories this time," he warned. "This is serious."

"Scout's honour." His lips twitched.

"I'd believe that more if you'd been a Scout."

"Details." Jeffrey waved his hand.

"I found an envelope in Dad's office." Keeping his voice level, casual. His dad had been happy enough to let Jeffrey take his teenage son under his wing when he couldn't cope. But those two had always clashed like oil and water, put at odds by different personalities and opinions and that had lasted to the day he died. "He had a film cartridge developed. Some old pictures. Thought you might know where they were taken." And why.

That caught his interest, as Matt knew it would. "How old are we talking?"

"Probably eighteen years."

Jeffrey's eyebrows went up. "My memory's good, but that might be pushing it."

"We can take a shot at it," he said easily. Although it mattered, a lot. "More curiosity than anything."

He pulled his phone from his pocket. Scrolled through until he found the album he'd downloaded off his computer last night. The resolution was good, surprisingly so.

Jeffrey wiped his hand on his jeans and took the phone from him.

"There's about eight pictures there." He wished he could read Jeffrey, like the man could read him.

Jeffrey looked at the first image and shot a glance at him. "A construction site?"

"Looks like. If my guess about the timing is right, and Mom took those pictures, you would have been the general contractor. And these were taken just before the accident."

Those eight pictures, they were all lit by a flash. Taken late in the day. Dusk setting in, throwing shadows. There was something furtive about the photographs. Something that felt off. And, if he was right, that job had been Jeffrey's.

"That's a lot of ifs," Jeffrey said.

"She worked for you, at the time."

If he ran his business the way he did now, he would have kept records, done inspections, been on top of every aspect. Those scribbled notes by the wall phone were just orders, reminders. When a project was underway, Jeffrey was thorough, documenting every last detail himself. Even if it meant putting in an extra half hour at the end of the workday, he never skipped that step or passed it off to anyone else.

Matt said, "Tell me, if you think I'm wrong."

"These are all close-ups. Of supporting structures," Jeffrey said, slowly. He touched the screen, zooming in on the details.

"Do you think Mom took those photographs?" That envelope, those negatives, felt like a portal to the past. Or a message.

Jeffrey flipped back and forth between the images, studying them closely. "Could have been ..." He trailed off.

"What?" He leaned forward. Something on the screen had caught the man's eye. But what?

"No, nothing." Jeffrey put the phone down. "Could you email these to me?"

"You know something." It came out sharper than he'd intended. He had to tamp down on that surge of impatience, that need to know, no matter the cost.

"Let me look into it." Jeffrey must have seen something in his expression, and added, "More guesses won't help you, Matt."

He was this close to pushing for more. He'd seen that flash of recognition before Jeffrey hid it. He was holding out on him.

A gust of wind whipped through the open door, splattering rain on the concrete floor. Bringing in the summer scent of water on scorched earth.

Deception — it seemed like that was his dad's legacy. That and a house full of leaks and creaking floorboards. If he could just get one fact, something that rang true for once, then maybe he could stop wondering, stop dwelling on the what ifs.

Luckily, there was no one in the world he trusted more than Jeffrey. If the man made a promise, he kept it. "Okay," he backed down. "Thanks."

"Now." Jeffrey rubbed his hands together. "Where's that chocolate?"

Matt opened the indigo blue box, revealing the cushioned contents. "Candied orange peel dipped in semi-sweet chocolate. Burnt caramel flecked with *fleur de sel*, enrobed in dark milk chocolate."

Jeffrey shot him a look. "You do want answers."

"Damn straight, I do. Seems like every time I turn around, all I find are more secrets." More lies.

"I'm sure your father had his reasons." His tone was even, but Matt caught a flash of something sharper hidden beneath. "If he'd had more time, I don't think he would have left you with as many loose ends to tie up."

"Loose ends? They're more like knots. Each time I think I've unraveled one, they only get tighter. I can't believe you of all people are defending him." The sting of betrayal caught him off guard.

"All I'm saying is, it's hard to blame a man for dying. I'll help you slice through your Gordian knot. But first" — Jeffrey picked up the candied orange peel — "tell me how you got that crisp, clean break on the coating."

Change of subject. Okay, then. He could talk about chocolate all day long. "Come by Chocoholic's sometime, and I'll show you."

Jeffrey shook his head and wagged a finger at him. "You'll just put me to work."

"Hmm..." He selected one of the caramel chocolates, decided it was time to lighten the mood. "Isn't that what I used to say to you? The tables have turned, haven't they?"

Jeffrey laughed. "Pass me another chocolate, wise guy. Better yet, pass me the box. I'm wary of the day you come to collect your bill."

"Didn't you say, 'Chocolate is worth its weight in gold?' Soon you'll be drowning in debt, old man." But he'd take intel over gold, any day.

"Well then, by now, I must be in over my head. Why struggle?" Jeffrey bit into a chocolate-coated curl of orange peel and closed his eyes on a hum of appreciation. "Death by chocolate?" he asked, his voice muffled by the candy. He swallowed and said, "There are worse ways to go.

EIGHT

CHARLEY WAS ON HER OWN with Thomas in the gallery, and on the defensive. She had last seen him outside the Coffee Nook. He'd been furious with Andrew and close to violence. Was it a personal vendetta or just artistic temperament?

The comments Sarah had made about Thomas's difficult relationship with his daughter and the argument Charley had witnessed didn't paint a pretty picture. Although the man could paint. There was no doubt about that.

His canvases leaned against the wall beside hers. One faced out. Through the protective plastic, the paint glowed, the luminosity barely contained. His portrait, that fragmented profile of a saxophone player, trapped the Bebop beat of snapping fingers in a basement bar, the blue notes of emotions unleashed centre-stage. Even the shroud of plastic couldn't dim the swinging rhythm of those brushstrokes. Colours swirled as though propelled by the pulse of the music. By passion.

Right now, Thomas looked like a kindly grandfather, with a neatly trimmed white beard and twinkling blue eyes. But a rampant squirrel in the gallery might be enough to set him off. And she didn't intend to be on the receiving end of that temper.

Thunder rumbled and Cocoa woofed, as though threatening the gods to stop making all that noise.

Thomas stopped in his pacing, in front of the rain-smeared window that looked onto the courtyard and the street beyond. "When did Kayla say she'd be here?"

She checked her watch again. When Kayla arrived, she'd break the news to both of them. "Five minutes ago."

To some, that might not seem like much, but it wasn't like Kayla. She'd always been the punctual one. But that was in the past, before she got engaged to Andrew. Before they lost touch.

"She's probably just running late." Still, worry nagged at Charley.

Thomas's raised eyebrow conveyed disbelief and more, although he didn't say a word.

Suddenly, a sound came from above them. This time, it wasn't thunder. The scratching echoed down the wall.

His gaze shot up, zeroing in on the fine crack running through the ceiling paint, like he could peer through it and into the room beyond. "What was that?"

"The rain?" It was worth a shot.

"It sounds like someone's up there." He crossed the room, heading toward the door that led upstairs. Each stride dislodging dried dirt onto her freshly cleaned floor.

He reached for the door handle. Cocoa leaped up off her blanket and spun in excited circles, eager for another chance to bark at the squirrel.

"Wait," Charley said. The snap to her voice froze him in his tracks. "You're right. We have a problem."

The glance Thomas shot her was full of patience worn thin. "What kind of a problem?" The resignation in his voice was worse than anger.

Had he been expecting something to go wrong all along? The thought had her back going up.

A bubbly tune cut through the tense silence. Her phone vibrated with the incoming call. She pulled it out of her pocket and checked the caller ID.

Relief washed over her when she saw the name on the screen. "It's Kayla." Finally.

He raised one eyebrow, as though to say it was about time.

Charley answered the phone. "Hi, where are you?"

"I tried to call earlier, but it went straight to voice mail."

She'd had her phone within reach the whole time. But service in Oakcrest could be spotty, at best. "The storm must have interfered with my cell reception. Are you on your way?"

"That's why I'm calling."

That drop in tone. Despite the years, things hadn't changed that much. She could tell right away. Something was wrong.

She moved away, to the door. Rain tracked a path down the glass panels. On top of the gazebo, the weathervane spun to face the storm. She felt Thomas watching and lowered her voice. "You're not coming, are you?"

"No, I'm not."

Not enough panic there for an accident, at least. "Did something happen?"

"I'm going to have to quit the exhibit, Charley."

It took her a full second to form a reply. "What? Why?" Andrew's words came back to her. *I intend to put an end to this exhibit.* Anger flared within her.

Kayla said, "I know this is short notice, but I should never have taken it on. I've got too many other commitments."

Too many commitments? "You approached me, remember?" she said, on a sting of betrayal. "You asked to take part." Out of the blue, after four years of silence. And she'd trusted her. Counted on her.

"I'm really sorry. I know I said I'd contribute to the rent, but —"

"It's fine. Don't worry about it." The rent was the least of her problems.

The bare wall loomed in front of her. White and big. More intimidating than any blank canvas. How would they fill the gallery now?

She'd sort it out. She'd have to.

Thomas shook his head. "Another problem." The words echoed through the space.

"Did someone just say, 'another problem'?" Kayla asked. "What happened?"

Might as well get it over with. "I'm putting you on speaker phone." She gestured for him to step closer and held the cellphone between them.

"Hello Kayla." His clipped tone bordered on annoyance.

"Hi Thomas." Although tinny, the sound carried clearly through the speaker. "What's going on, Charley?"

"Yes," he said dryly. "I'd like to know that, too."

Say it fast. "We're going to have to postpone the opening of the gallery." They'd planned to open that weekend, but maybe the delay was a good thing. With a little more time, she might be able to convince Kayla to change her mind.

"Why?" Thomas demanded.

"There's a squirrel in the gallery. I saw it upstairs." And wished she could erase that image from her mind. "Along with a hole in the drywall."

"A squirrel?" Kayla's voice rose in disbelief.

Thomas shrugged a shoulder. "The building has been empty, for a while. It's no surprise animals got in. There's a reason Sarah put it up for temporary lease. It needs a thorough renovation before some-one will consider buying it." Comforting words from an architect.

But the gallery was a hobby for Thomas, nothing more. He could afford to take it in stride. If the exhibit didn't happen, he might be disappointed, maybe even frustrated about the wasted time and effort, but it wouldn't be earth-shattering. He didn't need this to work. And, apparently, neither did Kayla.

Her heart tightened. So much for being a team and conquering challenges together. "I contacted Sarah Felles. She's been phoning around but, so far, she hasn't had any luck finding someone who can take us on. Apparently, there are too many —"

"Cottage raccoon emergencies?" Thomas shot her an amused glance.

She fought to keep her own temper in check. "Yes, actually. One pest control company offered to put us on a list, but they've already predicted a two month wait."

Kayla asked, "Pest control has a wait list?"

"By the time they get here, the squirrel will have made the gallery it's new home." Shredding insulation and chewing through electrical wiring in the process.

"Let's think this through," Thomas said, suddenly the voice of reason. "The poster in the window doesn't give a specific date. If we have to postpone the opening by a few days, we won't lose out on any of the advertising material we've already paid for."

"A few days," Kayla repeated, as though the words had triggered a thought. "That's it! Why don't you move the opening date to coincide with the Oakcrest Summer Food Truck Festival?" Her voice bubbled with enthusiasm. "I can't believe I didn't think of this earlier. The festival is only a few days later than our original date, and the town will be teeming with tourists."

Street food under the open sky, people strolling down Main Street. Right past the gallery windows.

Thomas scraped a hand over his chin. "That's not a bad idea."

They'd planned for the pop-up gallery to last for four weeks. If they moved the date of the opening, the exhibit would end on her birthday. A shiver stole over her. Well, that was fitting, wasn't it?

"How is it," Charley wondered, "that I'm living with the woman who runs the community paper and I don't know anything about the food truck festival?" So much for having access to all the insider details.

"Trust me," Kayla said. "This is the sort of perfect timing people kill for."

As an event planner, she had gained a reputation for creativity in just a short time and had a track record of success. When she got married, she'd quit her job but, it seemed, she hadn't lost her knack. It just might work.

"So far," Charley said, "we're assuming the squirrel is confined to the second floor. Which means we could set up downstairs." And that was something. "But we'll need a partition wall, to give us more display areas."

Thomas stroked a hand over his beard, thinking. "Some shade cloth, plywood and drywall screws should do it. And L brackets to hang the paintings. I could easily make something."

Finally, things were coming together. "Sounds great. And good thinking about the festival, Kayla."

"It's the least I can do. Don't worry," she said, "This is just a minor setback."

Charley hung up the call. Easy for her to say. She hadn't seen that furry black arm reaching down from the ceiling.

How could they put on a decent exhibit if one third of the art was missing? She'd have to figure that out, too. What was one more problem, in the long run?

They'd need to leave more room between the paintings. Cheat, to fill the space, best they could.

Charley dug her sketchbook out of her bag and scrounged for the 2B pencil. Right at the bottom. "We need to rethink the exhibit's design."

Thomas sighed. "Unfortunately, revisions are all part of the creative process."

Along with the eraser shavings. But that didn't make it any easier. "Let's take another look at our drawings, see what we can save from the original plan."

Freestanding walls would change the focus. But the images still needed to flow through the gallery. To create a coherent route. Tell a story. Anything jarring, or noticeably out of place, would break the illusion. No illusion, no sales.

She refused to wait any longer to fulfil her dream. That had been the entire point of coming to Oakcrest. To finally take action.

Charley flipped open the spiralbound book to the next blank page. She dragged her pencil across the paper, drawing a line for the wall. Then sketched in placeholders. Rectangles and squares. A jigsaw puzzle of hollow frames.

Somehow, she would fix this.

NINE

MATT HAD ENOUGH PRACTICE AT waiting to be an expert.

He could handle the heat and frenzied action of a restaurant kitchen. Had honed his reflexes on boiling stockpots and rapid reductions. But give him the cool, precise pace of the chocolate workshop any day.

He knew when to linger, when something needed that extra time and attention to transform average to perfect. He was careful, thorough.

He rocked the serrated knife over the block of single origin Guittard chocolate, chipping off small chunks from the corners. The bittersweet aroma of tobacco, plums, and black cherries rose around him. Spicy and astringent as a Cabernet wine and just as heady.

Here in his workroom, at the back of Chocoholic's, everything was in its place. Copper pots suspended from the track lighting, exactly where he wanted them. The twenty-pound crate of oranges, ready to be hand sliced and candied, shoved to one side. The air chilled to a brisk eighteen degrees Celsius, kept constant by the PVC strip curtains hanging over the door — thermal insulation and soundproofing, all in one. Which meant he could blast the riff-heavy leads and gravelly vocals of vintage BTO through the overhead speakers as loud as he wanted.

Some days, the crackle of tempered chocolate shrinking and

releasing in the molds as it cooled was all the background noise he needed. But this morning, the quicker the beat, the better.

The blade beneath his hand sliced through solid chocolate to the marble cutting board, riding on the bassline of the song.

Making confections — hell, working in any kitchen — required quick thinking. Fast reactions. A second too slow and risk burning the caramel or the chocolate seizing into hard lumps. But patience was at the heart of it all. And normally, he had it in spades.

Wait for a soufflé to rise? No problem. Take the time to temper chocolate properly? He'd never even been tempted to speed up the cooling process. Now, all he wanted to do was rush. Apply pressure.

Rotating the block, he shaved off splinters.

Turns out, waiting was easy when you could count down the minutes on a timer. Not so much when it came to exposing a lifetime of secrets.

Jeffrey would get back to him. It was only a matter of time. But Matt wanted the phone to ring. Right now. Or the door of the shop to open.

The knife caught on the chocolate, slipped. Razor sharp, the blade nicked his finger. *Damn.* Blood welled to the surface. So much for keeping all five digits high and away from the sharp edge. Even Jeffrey had taught him that.

Turning to the sink, he held his finger under running water to clean the wound. The cut was shallow. Still, the wound throbbed as he applied pressure to it.

Matt opened the right-hand cabinet and grabbed the box of Health Canada–approved supplies. Stocked to treat any kitchen injury you could think of. First-aid kit out already and it was, what — he glanced at the wall clock as he tore the wrapper off a blue food-safe bandage — barely 9 a.m. Great.

Accidents happened when you got distracted. He had the scars to prove it.

Maybe breakfast would help. He could walk to the Coffee Nook, get there and back, and still open on time. Grab a croissant, some caffeine.

Yeah, that sounded just about perfect. Get a change of scenery, forget about those photographs for a while.

And stop dwelling on the fact that he hated waiting.

NOTHING LIKE A LITTLE FRESH air to clear the mind, take the edge off frustration.

Matt walked down Main Street. Sunlight bounced off hot pavement. Not many parked cars yet. A couple of trucks, bumpers rusted from winter road salt. Probably locals, running errands. By noon, they'd be replaced by roadster convertibles, shiny as Matchbox toys. Summer cars. As much a part of the season as pool noodles propped outside the grocery store and splashes of strawberry ice cream on the sidewalk.

He took the weathered steps up to The Coffee Nook two at a time — and stopped short in the shade of the awning.

Kayla stood outside the door, looking in. Or reading the opening hours? He bit back a groan.

The café was normally overrun with customers on the mornings they served their freshly baked croissants. But the way his day had started, he wouldn't be surprised to find the place closed.

"Hey," he greeted Kayla, trying to see around her.

Through the window, he caught a flash of movement. Three, maybe four customers sat at the tables inside. If they were open, why was she still standing out here?

"Hi." She kept her gaze on the door, didn't even glance at him.

Bronzed skin pale against her black hair. She stood there, still as an ornament on a shelf, except for the muscle that jumped in her jaw.

Over her shoulder, he noticed a poster taped to the glass. Bright enough to catch your attention from the street and draw you in. All stark colours and flashy text. The title, done in orange letters, looked like it belonged on a pulp fiction dust jacket. *Pop-Up Exhibition.* Beneath the title, a silhouette of a couple stood in front of a painting, the gilded frame just visible over their shoulders. Through an optical illusion, it looked like strips of the poster had been torn off to reveal the words *Cover Art* beneath. Clever.

But that didn't explain why she was staring at it. And blocking his way inside.

Close enough to catch the roasted caramel sweetness of the Coffee Nook's house Colombian blend, he asked, politely as he could, "Are you heading in?"

Kayla looked at him then, dark eyes flashing with anger. Maybe it was the wrong thing to ask. "Sometimes," she said, more to herself than to him, "I wish he was dead."

The cold fury in her voice startled him more than the words did. "Who?"

She turned, brushed past him, looking close to tears. That show of emotion was like seeing a crack in a porcelain doll that revealed the flesh beneath. The sudden thud of a heartbeat.

On instinct, Matt caught her arm. "Are you all right?"

She took a breath, gave him a shaky smile. "Perfectly."

Could have fooled him.

He shrugged it off and pushed the door open on a blast of butter, pastry, and ground coffee.

The poster for Charley's pop-up gallery had set her off, that much was for sure. And he wondered why.

TEN

FOUR, MAYBE FIVE MORE PAINTINGS. Nerves knotted in the pit of Charley's stomach. Could she do it?

Planks of hardboard slid in the trunk as she touched the gas pedal. The country road unfurled between farmers' fields. Stalks of wheat bristled golden and tawny. On the asphalt ahead of her, the yellow line glared. Cocoa panted on the backseat. The inside of the Jeep was filled with the tang of fresh-cut wood.

The nearest crafts supply store was an hour's drive away, and the price of the canvases would have added up quickly. But Timber-Mart in Brighton was closer, only half the distance, and they'd had the four-by-eight-foot sheet of Masonite hardboard in stock. The service counter even cut it into five panels for her, in varying sizes, free of charge. The wood was dense, impact resistant, and had virtually no grain. Once she'd primed the surface with gesso, she'd be able to build up acrylic paint in smooth, thin layers.

Got yourself nicely covered. Charley's fingers white-knuckled on the wheel. *No risk, nothing at stake.* She wished that was true.

Aim high and take it step by step, that's all she could do. Especially now that Kayla was dodging her calls. She hadn't even had the chance to try to change her mind.

Slowing for the intersection ahead, she moved into the right lane to make the turn back toward Oakcrest.

Gravel widened the shoulder into a makeshift parking lot, shaded by oak trees. Sunbeams sparked off the chrome and tomato-red paint of the seasonal chip truck. Its tires had worn grooves into that gravel every summer for as long as she could remember.

Only three cars parked in the lot. One of them a gleaming Silverado pickup truck with a scrape along the bumper. Recognition hit with a jolt.

She'd seen that truck before, parked on Main Street.

She cranked the wheel, the Jeep's tires grinding over grit and dirt. She pulled into the last free space in the shade. As though scenting the fries on the air, Cocoa sat up, nose held high.

Through the windshield, Charley scanned the people waiting in line. At six-four, Andrew stood a head above the rest, impossible to miss.

Kayla joined the exhibit with her maiden name. She quit after Andrew threatened to put an end to the pop-up gallery.

He held his smartphone in his hand, ignoring everything around him. Picking up lunch, without a care in the world.

An adrenaline-filled whoosh of silence rushed in her ears, the same way it had right before she got on the Tilt-a-Whirl ride at the CNE. This decision had a reckless quality to it, too. Of chaos set in motion. But anger won out over reason.

She opened the windows to let the breeze blow through. "I'll be right back."

Cocoa barked once. A reminder to bring back enough food to share.

Stepping out of the Jeep into hot sunshine, she slammed the car door. Heads turned her way as the sound ricocheted. Only Andrew kept his eyes on his phone. Absorbed in his own world and to hell with everyone else. Wasn't that just typical?

The soles of her sneakers crunched over the ground. She caught the sizzle of hot oil, the salty scent of potatoes frying. The inside of the food truck must feel like an oven.

In front of the serving window now, Andrew glanced up from his phone, long enough to say, "Poutine, with the works."

Everyone — even the cottagers — knew the best, no, the only way to eat Terri's fresh-cut fries was slathered in ketchup, bright with the taste of ripe tomatoes. The fries scalding hot and crispy, not drowned in gravy.

She cut the line, came in from the side.

The burly man she stepped in front of, scowled. "Hey, you can't just —"

"I'm not ordering." Not yet.

Sun flashing in her eyes, Charley glared up at Andrew. "You convinced Kayla to back out of the exhibit." There was more blame there than she'd intended.

He faced her, his expression friendly, almost amused. And why not? He'd gotten what he wanted.

"The gallery, again?" Something dark lurked at the corners of his smile, in the lines around his mouth. "You suggested I let my wife make her own decisions. She did." He reached for the take-out carton, piled high with French fries floating in gravy. Cheese curds melted on top of the soggy mess.

"Somehow, I doubt that."

He shot her an irritated glance. Stabbing the plastic fork into a fry, he said, "Kayla was putting herself under pressure, and for what? A few pretty pictures." They might as well have been count-by-numbers kits or finger-paintings. "Wasted hours."

"They're more than that, to her."

"They're two-dimensional representations of reality." He speared another fry. Gravy dripped onto the side of the carton, staining the cardboard. "You can't build with art, you can't" — he looked at his fork — "eat it. She has better ways to spend her time."

What did Kayla see in the man? Twenty years older and opinionated, he had the tone of someone who ruled the universe. Maybe she'd mistaken arrogance for charisma. And been trapped. "Art feeds the soul."

He chewed, swallowed. Wiped his mouth on the napkin. "It's a hobby." He shrugged. "Just drawings, based on children's stories." Moving around her, Andrew walked past her Jeep, heading for the picnic table in the shade.

For a split second, she stood there, speechless. Then snapped out of it.

She hurried to catch up and stepped in front of him, bringing him up short. "Legends," she corrected. Loud and clear.

Annoyance flickered in his eyes. "Fairytales." The dismissal was casual and vicious.

He stepped forward. Close enough for her to see the outline of a tape measure worn into his shirt pocket. To smell the sour undertone of gravy and cheese on his breath. He towered over her. Fear prickled at the back of her neck. "Now," he said, "I'd like to finish my lunch in peace."

She planted her feet and held her ground. "We're not done yet. Not by a long shot. Art is meant to be shown. Kayla will regret this. And blame you."

He moved forward, his steel-toed boot stomping down beside her sneaker. The impact vibrated through the ground. Dust scudded over the top of her shoe.

She jerked her foot away and stepped back. The hard edge of the wooden bench rammed into the back of her legs, blocking her retreat. Almost knocking her off balance.

Anyone else would have backed off at that point. But not Andrew.

"She might," he said. "If the exhibit is a success." The pleasure of destruction lit his eyes. "From what I've heard, chances of that are slim."

"You're wrong about that." At the serving window, she overheard Terri make her sales pitch to the next customer. Within earshot but out of sight. Blocked by the broad expanse of his shoulders.

"Let me ask you this. Have you seen them?" He loomed, using his size casually and easily in a powerplay meant to threaten. To intimidate.

It wouldn't work on her. "Seen what?"

"The art. All these pieces you keep talking about. Has she shown them to you?"

"Not yet." She had to move. Sidestepping, she put space between them. Forced to retreat and annoyed with herself for giving way.

Andrew picked up his fork again with a satisfied smile. "Me neither. And that's saying something, isn't it? Oh, she sketches, I know that. But how many drawings and paintings has she actually finished? Your guess is as good as mine. She's either hiding them, or they don't exist."

Fury rushed through her, hot and fast. "Interesting. Your first assumption is that she's hiding her art. From you."

The blood drained from his face. She'd hit a nerve.

"What did she just say?" His voice sounded hoarse. He glanced at the chip truck, an intent expression on his face, his attention only half on her.

"Who?" It took her a second to figure out what he meant. The conversation at the serving window. "I wasn't listening."

Was that panic in his eyes? But why?

He pivoted. Before he was even close to the chip truck, he shouted, "Did you say peanut oil?"

About to pass a takeout container to the next customer, Terri froze. "Yes." Cheeks shining and flushed from the steam, she handed the food to the woman. "Fried to buttery perfection. The oil creates that crisp texture and doesn't affect the taste of the —"

"Why the hell isn't it labelled?" Andrew dragged a finger under the collar of his shirt, tugging it away from his throat.

Terri reared back as though slapped. "There's no allergen risk, not without the peanut protein. It's a standard deep-frying oil." Her customers watched the exchange with interest. Her smile became strained. "We've cooked with it all summer. Every single batch. You've eaten your fair share of it already."

Andrew dropped the box, still half full of fries, on her counter, face white as a sheet. His Adam's apple bobbed as he swallowed hard. He muttered what sounded like 'Russian roulette'.

"Are you all right?" Charley asked.

Sunlight caught the gleam of sweat, beading at his hairline. A dark flush spread up his neck.

He shoved past her, bumping into her shoulder. "Fine."

So much for a thanks for asking.

He staggered to his truck, resting a hand on the metal as he yanked the door open. The engine roared to life.

Tinted windows hid him from view. The truck idled. Long enough for her to wonder why. Too long. The minutes stretched and Charley stood and watched and waited. Worry gnawing at her.

Why wasn't he driving away? Maybe Terri was wrong about the peanut oil. Maybe he did have an allergic reaction and he needed help.

Maybe he was just sitting in his truck, making a phone call.

She was about to go investigate when the truck's tires reversed, spewing pebbles and dust. Without a glance in the rearview mirror, Andrew peeled out of the lot.

Nice guy.

She rubbed the back of her right leg, where the bench hit her. That would leave a bruise.

It would take a strong person to withstand that kind of verbal attack day after day and not crumble. If he was right, if Kayla hadn't finished any of her pieces, it was his fault. How much damage had his comments already done?

Doubt was a ticking time bomb that wiped out everything in its blast.

ELEVEN

"ALL IT TAKES IS A little confidence," Alex said.

He leaned against the kitchen counter. The work surface behind him was covered with the evidence of the quick-rice stir-fry they'd tag-teamed for dinner. Broccoli florets, curry powder, and a bowl of cracked eggshells.

Meghan smacked him in the shoulder.

He flinched. "Hey! What was that for?"

"That's the worst thing to say in this situation," she told him. "As if it's that easy." She turned to Charley. "If it helps, we believe in you. Your paintings are brilliant. I love the sketch you started yesterday of the woman kayaking. She looks larger than life itself. You have nothing to worry about."

Meghan had always been on her side, completely supportive and quick to praise, when others held back.

"Thanks," Charley said, "but now that Kayla isn't taking part, there simply isn't enough art on display." She stacked their used plates on the table and carried them to the sink. She had to step around Cocoa, who lay on the floor, nursing a serious case of swimmer's tail after her afternoon dip in the lake. "We estimated our expenses based on potential sales and now those have been cut by a third."

Moving to the stove, Meghan scraped the last of the rice from the pot into a Tupperware container. "Did Kayla say why she had to withdraw?"

"Too many commitments." She could have come up with a better excuse, at least.

Alex tossed the eggshells into the trash. "Do you think she got cold feet?"

"I have a feeling," she said, "her husband had something to do with it." And was that ever an understatement.

"Andrew?" Meghan asked. "What makes you think that?"

"He cornered me in Chocoholic's the other day, to tell me the exhibit was a waste of Kayla's time and money." She took a breath, annoyed all over again. "Then she quit. It's not hard to draw the connection."

Meghan frowned. "You didn't mention that."

She squeezed liquid dish soap into the sink. A cloud of coconut- and jasmine-scented steam rose from the hot water as suds formed. "It didn't seem like a big deal at the time. Although he did threaten to put an end to the pop-up gallery." Bastard.

"Really?" Alex's tone turned sober, his eyes sharp.

Meghan said dryly, "He probably didn't mean sabotage."

He raised an eyebrow. "If Andrew really is behind Kayla's deci- sion to back out, he has sabotaged the success of the gallery."

Charley set the bottle of soap down too hard, and it slammed onto the counter. "No, he hasn't." It was way too early to even con- sider failure. "I saw him at the chip truck and tried to talk some sense into him."

"Uh-oh," Meghan said.

"How did that go?" Alex asked wryly.

She shot him a glance. "Not well."

Meghan opened the fridge door, searching for space to store the leftover rice. "Andrew has always had strong opinions about what Kayla should and shouldn't do with her time."

Alex snuck another piece of broccoli straight from the pan and popped it into his mouth. "Along with every other aspect of her life."

"And it's obvious, art doesn't rank high on his list." She remembered the way he'd loomed over her. Pushing forward until she'd almost stumbled. "He's not —"

"Abusive?" He caught on fast to what she meant. "I wondered, but there's never been any signs."

"Not of physical abuse," Meghan clarified, as she shifted jars and bottles in the fridge. "But he is controlling, and I think it takes a toll on her emotionally."

Sometimes Charley forgot how long it had been since she last spent time with Kayla. "The girl I knew wouldn't give up without a fight."

"But things change," Meghan reminded her. "People learn to adapt, if they want to survive."

Alex shot her a look. "That's a nice view of marriage you've got there, Megs."

She shoved the container into the fridge and rolled her eyes. "Not all marriages. But I do think that Kayla's probably requires some survival tactics."

Self-protection. Was that why she'd quit?

"You've got a point." Alex busied himself scraping the remaining vegetables into a bowl. "So, just charge an entry fee."

She'd already had that idea. And rejected it. "If we have to, we will, but the point of the pop-up gallery is to gain exposure. I don't want to deter people from visiting the exhibit. We'll be fine. All I have to do is fill the gap."

He raised his eyebrows. "Do you really have time to pull off that many new paintings before the gallery opens?"

"I'll just have to make every minute count."

Meghan shot him a glance that would have a lesser man quaking in his boots. "Again, not helping. Isn't there a game on tonight?"

He shrugged. "Not tonight —" Then he met Meghan's eyes. "Ah — I'll just go check. There's bound to be something on," he mumbled and beat a fast retreat.

With her hands full of cutlery, Meghan walked over to the door and nudged it closed with her hip, shutting out Alex and the sound of the television. "Looks like we're on kitchen duty."

Charley tugged on a pair of rubber gloves. "Technically, he's right."

"Of course, he is." Meghan shot her a sly glance. "But he doesn't need to know that."

She grinned as she took the cutlery from her and dumped it into the frothy foam. "Inspiration is for amateurs. I can do it."

"I still think the paintings you have are more than enough." Meghan held up her hands, backing down at the expression on Charley's face. "Hey, you're the expert."

"Two, maybe three more paintings will pull everything together." And, with any luck, she might even be able to do all five. "It'll be a challenge, but it's not impossible." Toeing off her shoes, she scrubbed at the dirty dishes and felt the tension ease. There was something cathartic about cleaning. *Make thick my blood.* As the suds washed over her hands, a line from the Westben Theatre's outdoor performance of *Macbeth* floated through her mind. *Stop up th'access and passage to remorse, that no compunctious visitings of nature, shake my fell purpose.* Of course, she wasn't gathering her courage to commit murder, and she didn't have any malevolent intentions, but still the line echoed through her thoughts. *Thus thou must do.*

"Take it easy." Meghan grabbed a tea towel. "Leave the finish on the dishes, please."

A stray curl brushed her cheek and she pushed it away with her forearm, soap running down the glove. "Sorry, I've been a little stressed lately." Running into Andrew hadn't helped.

"I'm not complaining. If you want to clean anything else while you're here, go for it. Just don't break anything." Meghan grabbed the forks from the rack beside the sink and began drying them with the towel. "I'm looking forward to having dinner out tomorrow."

"My treat, as promised. But are you really sure you want to go to the Blue Heron bed and breakfast for dinner?" She placed the emphasis on *dinner*.

Meghan laughed. "The lounge is a new addition. They only have a small menu, but the food is incredible."

"After all those pictures you sent me, I have to try it. Thanks for those, by the way. They caused some serious food envy."

"It got you here, didn't it?"

Green glass caught the light as she rinsed the soap off the Depression glass tumbler. "Yes, that's why I came to spend the summer with you. Just to try the food at the B&B."

"Your secret's out," Meghan said. "Much as I love Alex, I've missed the girl time."

Touched, Charley felt a smile spread across her face. It had been a while since they'd last done some sisterly bonding. "Me too."

"We've got a lot to make up for. We have to" — ticking items off on her fingers, Meghan listed — "go shopping, get our hair done, paint our toenails."

Placing a pot in the drying rack, she quirked an eyebrow. "Get our hair done?

"It's at the top of the list of things to do with your sister."

"I must have missed that pamphlet when it was handed out."

She grinned. "You know, I don't think we've ever actually done any of those things before."

Meghan frowned. "Are you sure?"

"Absolutely."

There was a pause as they thought about that. "No," Meghan said. "We did once."

"When?"

"I just finished university and you were in your last year of high school." Meghan rested her elbows on the counter. "To celebrate, we decided to give each other new looks."

It seemed unlikely. And, for the life of her, she had no memory of the event. "Are you sure you're not thinking of someone else?"

Meghan snapped the towel in her direction, and she dodged it.

"Cut that out!" She dipped her fingers into the water and splashed Meghan. Water ran over the edge of the counter and onto the floor, a few drops hitting her bare toes. Some things never changed.

"We had aluminum foil in our hair, and looked like aliens," Meghan prompted.

"Wait." She did remember that. "We did those crazy colours! I ended up with hot pink stripes and couldn't leave the house without a hat."

Meghan nodded. "I looked like a skunk —"

"With yellow highlights!" She cracked up. Wiping a tear from her eye, she said, "You're right. Mom flipped. Do you remember her face? Good times, good times," they said in unison, which only made her laugh harder.

"What's going on in there?" Alex shouted from the other room.

"Nothing!" Meghan yelled back, with an impish grin.

"Let's be realistic here," Charley said. "Put burgers on your list." Charcoal grilled and pepper crusted, she'd read rave reviews about the burgers at the Three-Corner Pub. "And shooting some pool."

"Air hockey! And you should plan to come back for the Oakcrest Haunted Carnival in October. You're the only one who can keep cool at the sight of demons and blood."

"Alex can't handle it?"

"Useless. He claims it's an after-effect of work. He doesn't like paying people to jump out at him."

A valid point. "Fair enough." God only knew where she'd be in October. Or what her life would be like. Would she be back in some corporate job in Toronto? Or finally earning some income from her paintings? Spending all her time in a studio, maybe even working on commission. Her heart leaped at the thought.

"Actually, we really do need to go shopping."

"For what?"

"You have a gallery opening coming up, don't you?"

A flutter of excitement danced through her. But — "I have an outfit." She couldn't splurge on anything new.

Meghan waved her hand. "This is big. You can't just grab something you've had hanging in your closet forever. We'll check out the Blast From the Past Boutique, and pull together something amazing. And it won't break the bank. I'm thinking Sunday."

"Has anyone ever told you that you're bossy?"

"Yup." Meghan grinned.

With a loud buzz, Charley's cellphone vibrated on the counter. Kayla's name flashed across the screen. That was odd. Had she changed her mind about the exhibit? She stripped off the rubber gloves and answered the phone. "Kayla, hi."

Meghan raised her brows.

"Charley — Oh God." Kayla sounded ragged, out of breath. Desperate.

"What's wrong?"

"I murdered him. I killed him." Her voice dissolved into sobs.

She gripped the phone, trying to grasp what Kayla just said. "What are you talking about?" At Meghan's questioning glance, she shook her head. "What's going on?"

"Andrew." Her voice broke. "He's dead!" The words echoed through the phone.

That couldn't be right. She spoke to Andrew just hours ago.

"It's all my fault," Kayla said.

Worry hit, an icy wave of it. What did she mean, when she said she'd killed him? "Where are you?"

"At home." Her voice trembled, close to the breaking point.

"Is anyone with you?"

"No. I'm alone. I didn't know who else to call."

"And —" How did she ask this? "Andrew?"

"I found him outside, by the dock. I thought maybe he fell, but —" Kayla broke off on a ragged gasp.

"Did you call anyone else?"

"Not yet."

She covered the phone with her hand and mouthed to Meghan, "Get Alex."

When everything else turned to chaos, Meghan was the eye in the storm, the calm at the centre of it all. She didn't waste time asking questions. Used to emergencies, she grabbed the car keys off the hook on her way into the living room.

Their evening was about to take a turn.

"Stay where you are." Charley hoped she sounded calm and competent. Like she knew what she was doing. "I'm on my way, and I'm bringing Alex. We'll be right there."

TWELVE

IN COP MODE NOW, ALEX steered his Honda down the grey gravel road. Gaze shifting between the speedometer and the road surface, tires biting into chips of stone. "Kayla really said she killed him?

Actually, she said she murdered him. After arguing with him about the gallery. "She was upset, in shock. I'm not sure she knew what she was saying."

In the backseat, Charley gripped the door handle. The headlights picked out the craggy shape of boulders and tree branches, like arms. Reaching. A glitter of eyes, deep in the bush, the height of a dog. So much for 20 kilometers per hour. But Alex maneuvered the narrow lane with confidence.

He flicked a glance back at her in the rearview mirror. "Maybe." But the one raised eyebrow said it all. "Didn't you just tell us they were having problems? A stifling marriage. Being forced to give up a dream. People have killed for less."

"Innocent until proven guilty," Meghan reminded him in a low tone.

There was no way Kayla could have killed anyone.

The tension in the car was thick enough to cut with a knife. Her heart beat too hard, too fast. What would they find when they got there?

Through the windshield, the big green hanger appeared up ahead. Kayla and Andrew's house was just a ways past it, down at the end of the road. Not far from their own cottage.

"Charley, you know her best," Alex said. "How do you think she's going to cope with all this?"

All this. "With Andrew's death? As well as anyone can, I guess. But who knows? It's been a long time since I knew what she thought." And even then, she'd been hard to read. Kayla had always been good at that, hiding what was really going on under the surface. "What happens next?"

"When we get there, you mean?" Alex asked.

Meghan twisted around in her seat and looked back at her. "We keep our eyes and ears open, and don't touch anything."

"Actually, Charley —" He steered around the tight bend. "— I'd like you to talk to Kayla."

"Calm her down?"

That same quick glance up in the rearview mirror, that said more than words. "Sure."

So, that was it. She leaned back, crossed her arms. "You want me to grill her."

"Just talk to her."

The road suddenly opened up, swinging round into a crescent. Two houses sat side by side, the driveways parallel to each other. Andrew's brick house looked like a home snatched from the Oshawa suburbs and dropped here, by the water. Double-wide garage and all. Solid and symmetrical, and completely out of place in cottage country. Only the oak trees provided some privacy between the driveways, between those red bricks and the cedar siding of the house on the right.

Alex pulled up in front, parking on the side of the road rather

than on the driveway. "This is it. The doc should be here next."

They climbed out of the car. A gleaming path of solar lights led up to the door, spilling cool white pools of light over the ground, bright and steady. Not the kind of lights you bought in bulk at the hardware store, hoping they'd last through the summer. This was a decorative border of crackled glass and stainless steel, speared into lush grass and meant to impress.

In comparison, the house next door was dark. Set farther back, there was too much lawn on the roadside, not enough on the waterfront. No lights on. No sparkly, solar lit pathway. The wooden siding looked like tree bark, warped and uneven in spots.

"Who lives there?" Shrouded in darkness, the house had an air of neglect about it. Like it had seen better days.

"Jeffrey," Meghan said. "Doesn't look like he's home. Otherwise, Kayla would have phoned him instead."

"She's lucky to have good neighbours."

Meghan and Alex exchanged a glance that said otherwise.

"I'm not sure that's how Andrew would describe it." Meghan sobered. "Or would have described it."

What did that mean?

Alex pocketed the car keys and started up the path. "Let's see what we've got." Mosquitoes buzzed around the solar lights, flickers of dark against the bright. Swarms of them.

Before they had a chance to knock, the door swung open. Kayla looked out at them, her delicate features drained with shock and grief. "Thanks for coming." She pressed her hand to her mouth. "I didn't know what to do."

"Don't worry about that," Charley said.

Going with gut instinct, she stepped forward and put her arms around Kayla. She stiffened, just for a second, then squeezed back. Charley felt her tremble but, when she moved away, she held her head high and her eyes were dry. People often underestimated her, saw only that doll-like fragility, but Charley knew better. She was tougher than she looked.

Kayla said, "He's outside. I just — left him there."

"That's fine." Another cop might have stripped the emotion from their voice, but Alex's was warm with compassion. If it was empathy or strategy though, she wasn't sure. He asked, "Did you move him at all?"

"Only to check —" Kayla swallowed hard.

"Sounds like you did the right thing," Meghan reassured her.

She moved aside to let them in. Alex was first through the door, gaze sweeping the surroundings in a way that could have been more subtle.

Charley searched Kayla's expression as they entered. For what, she didn't know. Signs of shock? But, deep inside, she knew she was looking for something else.

A sign of guilt.

After all, Kayla had confessed.

The house inside felt cool, almost cold. Instead of making do with a ceiling fan, the space was air-conditioned. During university, Kayla's room in the apartment they shared had been cozy and cluttered, filled with bright colours, stacks of CDs, and antique market finds. This entrance though, it looked like a show room. Sterile and perfect. The spindle leg table was barely big enough to hold a set of keys, let alone a stack of mail.

The living room beyond was more of the same. Country house chic, like something ordered straight from an interior design catalogue, and an expensive one at that. A white upholstered sofa. A wooden coffee table, rustic and aged in all the right places. A slipper chair, a wool blanket draped over the back. Dove grey, folded perfectly and missing cozy by a long shot. Anything personal hidden from view. Either she managed to tidy everything up in the few minutes it took for them to get here, or they actually lived like this.

There was something else missing, too.

Kayla had been raised in homes filled with art. From watercolour butterflies masking-taped to the wall and handstitched quilts to the beaded bracelets her grandmother had worn stacked high on her wrist. But, despite the tell-tale smudge of indigo paint staining Kayla's fingers, there wasn't a single piece of art on these walls. Not hers or anyone else's.

"We can go out the back," Kayla said, her voice hollow. "It's faster that way."

"Was Andrew puttering on the boat again?" Meghan asked in a casual tone.

"What?" Kayla looked startled by the question. "No. He went to sit outside for a bit after dinner."

"On his own?" Alex prompted.

The conversation had shifted ground. Every word now sharp-edged and dangerous, like walking barefoot over broken glass.

"He complained of a headache, said he wanted some peace and quiet." Kayla lowered her eyes, shuttering her expression.

In the living room, two lamps glowed, keeping the dark at bay. Moving past one, Charley heard a frantic *tap, tap, tap* from inside the lamp shade. Moths?

The curtains billowed. The sliding glass door pushed wide open. That explained the insects. The light inside a temptation. She thought of Kayla prying that door open to get to the phone, to call for help. She couldn't imagine how she must feel.

Alex stopped in front of the open door. The breeze ruffled his hair. "What time did you find him?"

Kayla glanced at her wrist. It was bare. Her other hand closed over her wrist, her fingers moving nervously, as she looked around the room for another source.

Charley checked the time on her own watch. "It's nine o'clock now."

"I don't know." Kayla frowned as she thought. "I phoned you right after I found him. Close to eight thirty?"

Alex went through the door first, then Meghan. Charley stepped out onto the stone patio, but behind her she felt the space open up, widen. She glanced back.

Kayla hesitated on the threshold. One frozen beat. Then she seemed to jerk into motion, to force herself forward.

They clustered on the patio, in the line of the wind. The lawn sloped down and away, toward the water. From that elevated position, even in the dusk, the view was stunning. The lake shimmered sunset red. The sky inverted, clouds and spruce and all. The reflection like a lithograph on stone, freshly inked.

Andrew's house looked out onto the bay. The perspective here was different than theirs, the property more secluded. Private. A shield of evergreens blocked the view to the neighbours, the shoreline between the waterfronts thick with cattails and bulrush.

Unless someone was out on the lake, there would be no witnesses. No one to help.

"When did Andrew come outside?" Meghan asked.

"Right after dinner," Kayla said. "We ate late. I'm not sure what time it was."

The tag team questions kept up a steady stream of conversation. A distraction to ease the pain and, in this case, Charley knew, a tool. To gather information.

Alex pulled out his phone. A bright beam of light hit the

ground. He'd switched on the flashlight app. For some reason, that single action sent a shiver down her spine. A loon cried, an eerie, haunting sound that carried across the water.

Meghan turned to Kayla. "You don't need to go through this again. Charley can wait inside with you."

Alex nodded. "We can take it from here."

He caught her eye and she got the message. The offer wasn't an act of kindness. It was a trap.

But Kayla set her jaw, a stubborn tilt to her chin. "I can handle it." As though to prove it, she led the way.

Grass rustled beneath the soles of their shoes. Someone's breath rasped, faster, louder than it should have in that ominous silence as Kayla led them to her husband's body.

In the shadow of the trees, it was darker still. Insects hummed around them, on the hunt for blood.

The beam of light caught the back of a red Adirondack chair. One solitary chair, positioned on its own. Light flooded over the curved yoke, crisscrossed through the wooden planks.

The chair was empty.

The light moved on, sweeping through the air, then down over indistinct shapes, the rocks by the water.

"There." Kayla broke the silence. "Grandmother would say, he's gone to live with the People of the Day." In the sky, where spirits laughed and sang and played. His soul purified by a quick, violent death.

A motionless figure lay on the ground.

When the light hit the man's face, Charley sucked in a breath. The swollen mouth and throat, the welts on the skin —

"His worst nightmare come true," Kayla said in a calm, almost detached voice. "Not being able to breathe and out here alone."

There was little doubt what had caused Andrew's death.

Alex squatted down beside the body. "We can't say for sure until the doc confirms it, but it looks like fatal anaphylaxis. Probably within thirty minutes of exposure, tops."

Exposure to what? A delayed reaction to their dinner? Not from the chip truck earlier. That was hours ago. "He had a history of allergies?" She'd seen the fear on his face.

"He was allergic to peanuts. Severely. Thirty minutes?" Kayla sank into the chair. The back perfectly curved to provide just the right amount of support. And shelter. "No, it would have been faster than that. A reaction wouldn't take long. During an attack, the airways tighten first, making it hard to breathe." Her hollow tone raised the hairs on Charley's arms. "The lips and tongue and throat swell. Skin develops hives. Then blood pressure plummets, and shock sets in."

"Has it happened before?" Meghan asked.

"He nearly died when he was young," Kayla said. "Since then, he's been petrified of it happening again. He had a mild reaction last year and it only increased his anxiety."

No wonder the mention of peanut oil had terrified him. "Didn't he carry an EpiPen?"

"Normally, he always had one on him."

Charley caught the implication, the shift in Kayla's tone. "But not tonight?"

She shook her head. "I couldn't find one."

Alex's hand hovered over Andrew's chest. "How did he carry the injector?"

"An ankle-holster," she answered dully. "Hidden under his pant leg, but within easy reach."

There was a pause as Alex moved. Then a scrape of fabric on skin. He said, "There's no holster."

Far from the house, without the EpiPen, Andrew hadn't stood a chance.

Something gleamed in the grass, just a short distance from where Andrew lay. What was that? It looked like cling wrap or transparent foil.

Charley moved closer, bent down. It was a clear plastic bag. Small. The kind used for storing trail mix or candy. Taking out her cellphone, she shone the light on it. A thin black line crawled over the plastic. She sucked in a breath.

Ants.

The bag lay open where it had fallen. Three round objects inside. The size and shape of Belgian praline chocolates.

One brown orb lay on the ground. The hard chocolate shell cracked, gaping open to reveal the soft centre. Instead of a pillowy cloud of vanilla cream, the filling was dark and dense.

"Did you find something?" Alex straightened from the body, took a step toward her.

"Kayla —" Charley stood and turned to her. Worry twisted inside her. But she had to ask. "What did you mean, when you said you'd killed Andrew?"

The light from her phone reflected off Kayla's eyes, and the expression in them — or lack thereof — was unsettling, like something within her had shut off. Or been closed off. "I bought the chocolates."

The chocolate, grown warm in the heat, gave off a rich, sweet scent that was unmistakable.

A shiver of dread ran through Charley. "Those chocolates are filled with nougat." A nut paste.

Lethal for Andrew.

Had Kayla just confessed to murder?

THIRTEEN

FILLED WITH A LIQUID CENTRE of orange coulis, a citrus infusion, and a hint of mint, the chocolate was decadent and flawless. A carefully orchestrated assault on the senses.

Of the entire batch, Matt chose that square because it was flawless. The edges sharp. The abstract design, in a bright shade of lemon yellow, smudge free. He had silkscreened the design onto the surface of the confection using cocoa butter — a technique he discovered while browsing the website of a Paris-based chocolatier and had actually succeeded in replicating.

The confection was picture-perfect, damn it.

One more try.

He adjusted the lighting and snapped another photograph. He checked the camera's screen and swore violently and creatively.

"I heard that," Mrs. Callahan called from the front of the shop.

Matt winced. Sonar hearing or a sixth sense — either way, she never missed a thing. "Sorry!"

For a Friday afternoon, Chocoholic's was quiet. He'd rather whip up a batch of wafer-thin dark chocolates and practice the silkscreening technique some more, but he still hadn't gotten one decent shot. One photograph, that's all he needed. How hard could it be? Snap the picture, post it and he'd have the shop's social media page up and running.

Something that should be quick and simple had turned out to be time-consuming and frustrating beyond belief.

There was magic on that plate. The chocolate shone, glossy and lustrous. The delicate citrus design popped against the rich tones of the bittersweet couverture. The exterior of the chocolate was smooth as glass. You could tell, just by looking at it, that the coating would break, crisp and clean. That the liquid centre would release a burst of merciless flavor.

Matt glanced at the photograph again. In the image, the rich luster of the chocolate was dull. The yellow had lost its bright hue. The white plate filled the frame, making the chocolate look like an after-thought. And — was that a reflection on the plate?

He knew social media posts were staged, but this was a joke. He had chocolates to make. He was a chocolatier, not a photographer. Sure, a social media page meant more exposure, but he was not going to drive himself insane to get likes and shares. He'd need an artist to make his chocolates look Insta-perfect.

Possibly a very cute artist in a purple T-shirt.

A knock from behind him startled Matt, and for one second he thought it might be —

"Alex?" The sight of the cop propping up his door frame surprised him.

Alex liked Dark Chocolate Mint — could go through a bar fast — and lived with Meghan, but that was all he knew about the guy. They weren't on friendly enough terms for him to pop around back.

"Got a minute?" Without waiting for a reply, Alex moved into the room. His eyes flicked from the stained wooden cutting board to the serrated knife and hammer Matt used to break thick blocks of chocolate into pieces. His gaze took in the melted chocolate sprayed and dripped over the work surface, now hardened. The stained and smeared bowl, the spatula.

When you walked into a man's workshop unannounced, you got what you saw. Matt leaned his hip against the counter and crossed his arms. "What can I do for you?"

"I'm hoping you can give me some answers."

That sounded official. "You're working a case?"

Alex nodded. "Andrew Clarkston's death."

Blindsided, he blinked. "Andrew's dead? Jesus, I saw him the other day." Buying chocolates for his wife. Taking a client call. He'd seemed healthy. Good enough to butt heads with Charley. "What happened?"

A beat passed, as Alex studied him. "He died of anaphylactic shock."

Only one reason why Alex was here, at Chocoholic's. Matt had a sinking feeling. "You're not saying —" He broke off, trying to get his head around it. "— my chocolate killed him?" *Shit.*

The tough cop facade cracked a little. "Chocolate killed him. That's all we know for sure, right now." He pulled out his phone. He scrolled through the files, then turned the screen to Matt. "We found this near the body."

He studied the image, taking in the details. Outside, close-up of grass. Dark and lush and prickly-looking. Sheen of the flash bouncing off plastic. Trail of black spots. Ants, he realized. Crawling over the foil.

"I use the same bags." They were nothing special. Simple and easy to stock. He ordered them in bulk online. But one thing was different. "There's no logo. My bags all have labels on them."

"Charley pointed that out. Kayla confessed —"

Matt's head snapped up.

"To purchasing the chocolates," Alex finished the sentence. He looked amused, like he knew exactly what Matt was thinking. "She says she bought the allergen-safe kind, but..." He trailed off.

"The man is dead."

"Right." Alex flicked to the next image. "Notice anything else?"

Similar to the photograph he had taken, just minutes before, the picture showed a single chocolate against a white background. But this chocolate was far from perfect. It had melted, lost its shape, and cracked to expose the interior. Instead of vanilla cream or the thin layers of berry and chocolate his Black Forest pralines were known for, this filling was brown and more of a paste, the texture thicker than it should have been. "Can you bring me a sample?"

"It's been sent to the lab for analysis. But I can tell you that the chocolates were filled with some kind of nut paste."

"Nougat?" He zoomed in on the image. He used the same mold to make all the allergen-safe chocolates, and this was the right size, the right shape. "At first glance, these look exactly like my Dark Chocolate Vanilla Cream." Andrew's favourite. "By the time Andrew realized what he was eating —"

"It was too late."

Even a trace of the wrong ingredient could be deadly. If anyone wanted to get rid of Andrew, this was the perfect way to do it. Matt levelled his gaze at Alex. "Andrew was murdered."

Stone-faced, the cop looked back at him. Not even a flicker to show if he'd hit the mark. "I'm just gathering facts."

Noncommittal bullshit. He had homicide investigation written all over him.

"Kayla didn't buy these from me." Matt handed the phone back to him. "I haven't made nougat-filled chocolates in months. You can check my inventory."

Alex rotated the phone between his fingers. "But you've made them before."

The insinuation was clear. He tried not to let it get to him. Bracing his hands on the countertop behind him, he fixed Alex with a cold stare. "So has your girlfriend, and six other people in town."

"What?" He looked taken aback.

"I taught a class on making nougat-filled chocolates a couple months ago." He flashed on a memory of chair legs scraping over the red tiled floor, laughter. "Milk chocolate, not dark, but the concept is the same. There were seven participants. Any one of them has the skill to make these."

"I'll need a list of names."

"Done. Anything for the local police." It came out dryer than intended.

The fact that Andrew was murdered didn't surprise him. The man had enemies and plenty of them. But the method, that ticked Matt the hell off.

Who came up with the bright idea of using chocolate as poison? And his recipe, no less.

FOURTEEN

"IT WAS MURDER," ALEX ANNOUNCED. The word pulsed shock waves across the table.

It was the first time one of them said it aloud, though they'd all been thinking it. Charley fought back a shiver.

She sat with Meghan and Alex on the patio of the Blue Heron B&B. They decided to stick to their plan and have dinner out, despite what happened last night. It was that or dig out the two frosted-over boxes of frozen pizza Meghan vaguely remembered buying. Tough choice.

The wrought iron chair was warm from the sun. The air thick with the scent of green herbs and smoke from the charcoal grill.

The restored Victorian farmhouse nestled between maple trees at the top of — well, more of an incline than a hill — just a short drive from Main Street. All around them, flowerpots overflowed with bright blooms. Mason jar lights dangled from wires. The flickering flames danced shadows over the face of the terracotta archer, kneeling between sage and lavender. Past all those green leaves around them, beyond the yellow and red flowering spikes of gladiolus, the lake gleamed, smooth as glass. A white sail flashed. In the distance, a great blue heron rose up from the shore. With slow wingbeats, it flew overhead.

The scene was idyllic. And deceptive. The peaceful lakeside village marred by murder.

"It's official?" Meghan asked. "I'm running a piece on Andrew's death in tomorrow's paper. If you've got a quote for me, now's your chance."

He didn't hesitate. "'The death is being treated as suspicious. The police are currently investigating the incident.'" The chatter from the other tables drowned out anything they said, but he kept his voice pitched low anyway. "Off the record, death occurred within an hour of ingesting the allergen. But the doc's playing it safe with that estimate. It's probably less."

Charley did the math. "At eight p.m.?" She slid her sunglasses on, cutting the glare of the sun ricocheting off the glass-topped table.

He nodded. "Round about then, yeah. Or just before."

"How —" The waitress's shadow fell over their table and she bit her tongue. Her question would have to wait.

The girl smiled, all pink lip gloss and swishy ponytail, and clicked her ballpoint pen into action. "What can I get you?"

"Earl Grey iced teas for everyone," Meghan said, without missing a beat.

Charley shared an amused glance with Alex. "Can we choose our own dinners?"

"Sure." Meghan grinned. "But it's either the daily special or a sandwich."

She put down her menu. "I guess I'll take the special." It sounded delicious anyway. A mesclun salad with fresh black sour cherries and smoked pork tenderloin with a passion fruit balsamic vinaigrette. Followed by a complimentary dessert — a slice of cranberry chocolate coffee cake.

When the waitress left with their orders, Alex leaned back in his chair, kicked his legs out under the table, and stretched like a cat in the sun. "Based upon his medical history and the circumstances, the coroner is confident Andrew died of anaphylactic shock."

"So, Kayla was right." Despite the heat beating down on them, Charley felt chilled to the bone. "It really was Andrew's worst nightmare come true."

Alex's mouth tightened into a hard line. "There's little doubt the chocolates we found caused his death, but an analysis of his stomach contents will confirm it."

"Ah." Meghan sighed and propped her chin on her hand. "Cop talk."

He raised a brow. "Sorry, Megs."

"I should be used to it, by now." The long-suffering expression on her face was half love, half exasperation.

"Only thing is," Alex said, "the doc spotted needle marks on Andrew's thigh."

Needle marks? On his thigh, not his arm. Charley frowned. "Drugs?"

"You could say that." Alex toyed with the stainless steel knife on his place setting. He turned it between his fingers. The vintage-inspired detailing glinted with each rotation. "An EpiPen injection. Two. That same day."

Meghan straightened up, reminding Charley of Cocoa when the Milk Bone box rattled. "We didn't find any injectors near the body."

But just hours earlier, he'd ingested peanut oil. And panicked, even though the oil was refined and allergen safe. What were the symptoms of an anxiety attack? She thought of the last power outage, when the lights cut and she'd spent minutes in total blackness, searching for the candles. Trembling, heart racing, hyperventilation.

Trouble breathing. "When in doubt, they say to use the pen, right?"

Alex nodded. "And to use the second, five minutes after the first, if the medication doesn't take effect. But there's no record of a 911 call."

The truck's engine had idled longer than five minutes. Could it have been seven or eight, maybe even ten, before he drove away? The desperation he must have felt to self-inject, not just once but twice.

Charley said, "I'll bet you anything, you'll find the used injectors in his truck."

Alex put the knife down, with a click of stainless steel. His gaze just as sharp. "What makes you think that?"

She explained about the peanut oil, the chip truck. "You should have seen the expression on his face." Panic. Then terror.

"So that's why Andrew didn't have an EpiPen on him. Luck was on the killer's side." Alex looked thoughtful. "The timing's almost too perfect. According to the doc, using an EpiPen when you don't need it can result in increased blood pressure, lasting a few hours. Along with a racing heartbeat, dizziness, weakness, and a throbbing headache."

She leaned forward, elbows on cool glass. "Which is why he left Kayla after dinner, to sit by the water. She said he wanted some peace and quiet."

The waitress, heading their way with a tray of drinks, cut off the conversation. She set each glass, misty with condensation and full to the brim, carefully down in front of them. Lemon wedges and ice cubes jostled in the amber tea.

Alex waited until the girl was out of earshot again before continuing. "Turnaround time for the lab results of the chocolates can be up to two weeks. So, I went to the source —"

"The source?" Meghan asked.

Charley raised her glass. "Chocoholic's. Am I right?"

He grinned. "And our very own chocoholic gets the prize. I got some interesting intel from Matt." He picked up his drink, tasted the iced tea.

She nearly managed to wait him out. "Which was?"

He set the glass down. "He doesn't sell nougat-filled chocolates. Hasn't for months."

Meghan tilted her head. "So, where did they come from?"

There was only one other explanation. The hairs on Charley's arms rose. "They weren't bought," she said. "They were made."

"Right again," he confirmed. "And someone made them look like Andrew's favourite chocolates."

She flashed on the memory of ants crawling over plastic. "That's why there was no label on the bag."

He nodded. "Matt taught a class on making Belgian chocolates to seven participants."

Meghan tapped her nails lightly against the tabletop as she thought it through. "I took that class. It was well done. Matt's a good teacher. The entry fee covered the cost of supplies. Everyone left with their own chocolate mold and scraper."

To replicate the recipe at home. "In other words," Charley said, "we have a list of suspects." And the scene of the crime, and the weapon. Her pulse quickened.

"We?" Alex looked amused.

No way was he keeping her out of this. To paint a portrait of someone, an artist had to discover their subject's insecurities, their strengths, and, if possible, their secrets. This was no different. "Two heads are better than one," she said.

Catching the reference, Meghan finished the quote with a grin, "'Because they're unlikely to go wrong in the same direction.' CS Lewis."

Alex frowned. "Why do I get the feeling I'm outnumbered?"

"Because you are." Meghan smiled at him over the rim of her glass.

Their food arrived. Fresh black cherries glistened among the bitter greens, a combination of arugula, baby spinach, and radicchio. The pork was tender and rich, glazed with fruity vinaigrette.

Charley lifted her fork and tried the first bite. The cherry tasted like summer. "Who took the class?"

"Meghan." His mouth curved as he caught his girlfriend's eye. "Thomas Kelly, Sarah Felles, Eric Trace —"

"He works at the Blast From The Past Boutique," Meghan explained for her benefit. "And has great taste in clothes."

Alex ticked the names off on his fingers. "Deborah Hamlin."

The librarian had provided Charley with the best cottage reads and, at sixteen, with her first summer job. An unlikely suspect.

"David Nadeau was there, too."

A new name, one she didn't recognize. "Who?"

"A primary school teacher," Meghan said. "Young. The kids love him."

She counted. "That's six." She reached for her glass. "You're missing one."

Alex paused mid-slice, the pork blush pink against the edge of his knife. "Kayla."

The glass jostled in her hand. Ice-cold tea ran over her fingers. She knew exactly what he was getting at. She reached for her napkin. "You think she murdered her husband."

Meghan and Alex shared a glance, the reporter and the cop. The thrill of the hunt in their eyes. You could spot it a mile away.

He shrugged. "She confessed."

"To buying chocolates."

"She's also the only one who could know Andrew used both

his EpiPens. Without them, he didn't stand a chance of saving himself."

"But the EpiPen isn't foolproof, especially when self-administered." She'd googled it, late last night. Life-threatening anaphylactic emergencies could be unpredictable. If injected quickly and accurately, the drug could reduce the chance of mortality. But there were a lot of factors involved and human error was one of them, especially under high stress.

She turned to Meghan. "You've seen more of Kayla than I have in the past few years. Do you really think she plotted her husband's death?" It was insane.

Meghan took her time answering. "I think she was unhappy."

Unhappy enough to kill?

Alex's eyes became bright and intense. "You have to find out how a person lived in order to find out how they died." He leaned forward, with a scrape of wrought iron chair legs over patio stones. "Kayla has an argument with her husband and backs out of the exhibit. Then she plies him with lethal chocolate on the night he's run out of epinephrine. All her problems are solved. And — bonus — she inherits everything. You're the one who put the pieces together, Charley. "

Guilt hooked its claws into her. "No, I didn't. I never said they argued."

He shrugged. "Based on your run-in with Andrew in Chocoholic's and at the chip truck, I'd say it's safe to assume they had a —"

"Marital tiff?" Meghan filled in helpfully.

"The question is, did he unload pent-up anger on you?" He paused. "Or had he already taken it out on his wife?"

It was obvious, Alex had been dying to work a homicide for a long time. "That's a lot of what ifs."

"Kayla had means, motive, and opportunity." He loaded his fork with leafy greens. "It's the best-fit hypothesis."

Charley pointed her knife at him. "Only because you don't have all the facts."

"I don't know," Meghan said. "I think Alex might be right."

He said, "Kayla is the only who took that class and had motive to kill."

"Are you sure about that?" The singed afterbite of meat lingered on her tongue. She set her knife down, metal chiming on the glass tabletop.

"You got any other ideas?"

It wasn't hard to come up with names. "Thomas," she said. "He was furious with Andrew because of the delays on his house. On my first day in Oakcrest, I saw Thomas chase him down the street. Close to violence, he ordered Andrew to get the job done, or else."

"A threat." Alex speared a strip of pork. "That's interesting. But Kayla still has the stronger motive. And the killer had to be able to give the chocolates to him without raising suspicion."

"They could have been a gift." Maybe even an anonymous one.

"That's true," he admitted.

"When I met Sarah outside the gallery, she called Andrew a traitor. She sounded angry." And bitter.

"That doesn't mean much," he said. "She's been after him to do repairs on the building your gallery is in. They haven't been able to agree on terms, which is why she's leasing it. To buy time. If she sounded angry, it's not surprising."

God, he was stubborn. "It means" — she fought to keep her patience — "at least two other people in that class held a grudge against Andrew." She swallowed a sip of her tea, bergamot, icy, and citrus clean.

"And they suddenly decided to off him with deadly chocolates?" He raised a brow.

"It can't hurt to look at the other players," Meghan said. "Sarah moved to Oakcrest after divorcing her husband. Raked him over the coals, from what I heard. She used to be an editor for Hecate Publishing."

That name was familiar. "The romance publisher?"

Meghan nodded. "She owns this B&B now."

"And the gallery." It was an impressive list of accomplishments. And not the only ones. "Thanks to Sarah, a local pest control company is coming by the gallery tomorrow. She didn't back down until they agreed to put us on the schedule."

"Ruthless, that's her all right. And" — Meghan clinked her glass to hers — "hurray for some good news."

For a change. "We need it."

At the table nearby, laughter broke out on the punchline of a joke.

"Fine," Alex said, "if you want to look into every single person who took that class, be my guest. But I have two people in my sights."

Two? "Kayla and..."

He waited a beat. "Matt."

Her stomach twisted. "Sure, he had the means. But what's his motive?"

Alex broke off a crusty piece of bread, used it to mop up the remains of the balsamic vinaigrette on his plate. "His mother worked for Clarkston Engineering as a framing carpenter. She died on one of Andrew's sites."

"The gallery. But it was an accident."

"Matt's father blamed Andrew for his wife's death, and he didn't try to hide it." He shrugged. "Maybe the apple doesn't fall far from the tree."

"Why wait? Why take revenge now?" It didn't make any sense.

"His father died."

As though that explained everything. "And you think he waited for his dad to die before carrying out some twisted plot for revenge?"

Meghan told Alex, "She has a thing for the chocolatier."

He gave a wry smile. "You might not want to act on that right now."

On a surge of annoyance, Charley gritted her teeth. "You mean, wait until we know he's not a murderer?"

"I'd recommend it, yeah." As if hit by a thought, he added, "Don't mention the chocolates in the article, Megs. Let's keep that under wraps, for now."

But rumours spread quickly in Oakcrest. "Kayla isn't capable of murder." And neither was Matt. She was sure of it.

"You want to play detective, that's fine," Alex said. "In the meantime, I'm going to do my job."

Playing detective. She wasn't about to sit by and let him arrest the wrong person. There was another explanation. She just had to find it.

FIFTEEN

MATT SHOULD HAVE BEEN DRIVING through predawn streets. Instead, the sun slanted white-hot through the windshield as he turned off Pine Ridge Road onto Main Street. At a time when he should have been a good couple hours into cutting slabs of ganache.

He couldn't shake the feeling that he'd handed the killer the murder weapon.

He'd spent most of the night staring up at the dark ceiling, circling around the same two questions. Who? Why? Wracking his brain to figure out the answers. If anyone could do it, it should be him. He'd been there. He'd taught the damn class.

But, after all that tossing and turning, he still had no idea.

He woke up bleary eyed and beat. Hit the snooze button one too many times. Luckily, if he chose to linger, eat a waffle straight from the toaster, smeared with hazelnut-chocolate spread, while zoning out to SportsCentre, he could. He wasn't about to fire himself.

Matt grinned at the thought and reached for his Thermos. He took a swig of coffee. The liquid seared his tongue. He sucked in air through his teeth. Hot. And sweet as syrup. He'd been heavy-handed with the sugar, though that was probably a good thing. He needed the kick. Preferably straight to the blood stream.

A few open signs already out on the sidewalk. Shit. But Main Street was so postcard perfect, it took tourists a while before they even realized there was more to see one street over. And if any-one came by, saw the CLOSED sign still dangling in his window, cottagers were patient enough to grab a coffee at the café and wait for Chocoholic's to open.

The street was cloudless and sun soaked. But on the best of days, Oakcrest was pleasure and pain, mixed into one. Like biting your tongue and tasting blood and chocolate at the same time. All that quaint charm, along with the memories he'd rather forget.

When he was tired or run down like today, the past had a raw edge to it, making it harder to ignore.

Maybe that's why he glanced in the direction of the Mews as he flicked the turn signal on. Gut instinct, and not enough caffeine yet for self-preservation to kick in. Either way, the vehicles parked in front — that flash of red — caught his eye.

He touched the brake, took a longer look. Hold up. Was that a pest control truck, parked outside the Mews? Beside a red Jeep. Charley's? Before he could think it through, he'd switched off the signal and was driving straight ahead.

He was already late. A few more minutes wouldn't make a difference.

Cranking the wheel, Matt did a three-point turn and pulled his pickup in behind them, taking the last free space. He parked, yanked the keys out of the ignition.

What the hell was he doing?

Worrying at the wound, that's what.

Matt got out of the truck. Might as well take a closer look, since he was here.

The wooden boards of the deck creaked beneath his shoes. He walked past The Oakcrest Pantry — kitchen gadgets gleaming in the window — toward the building at the back.

He had a flash of what the place must have looked like while it was being built. Bare bones framework exposed. The sawdust, hot iron smell of construction heavy in the air.

Cinnamon. Mom always had cinnamon gum in her pocket. Christ, he'd almost forgotten that. Not a whole pack, just a few sticks in papery wrappers that left a spicy scent on her sweaters, her coat.

Matt shook off the thought before it could take root and opened the door. Stepping inside on equal parts curiosity and guilt. Like he was about to get caught breaking and entering.

It wasn't much cooler in than out. The room worked well as a gallery. Good, natural light. White walls, nothing to distract from the art. Though he'd expected to see more pieces on display. Then again, they hadn't officially opened yet.

The space inside was smaller than he'd imagined. Friendlier. Not at all the way he'd built it up in his mind.

With a scramble of nails over wood, Cocoa came racing toward him.

"Hey." He stopped to pat the dog, who vibrated with excitement, and looked around. Besides Cocoa, there was no one else in sight.

Matt crouched, hand on warm fur, and looked at the book covers on the walls.

No, not book covers. Paintings, like pulp jackets.

Showing the battlefields of everyday life and the heroine at the heart of each. Bold, vivid, and unexpected. Little tricks — shading, creases — turned the canvases three-dimensional. The portraits rich with details that added gritty realism, despite the vibrant colours. The newsprint stain on a fingertip. The hairline crack in the handle of a porcelain teacup. The splash of dirty water caught in headlights. The weary determination somehow different in each face, but always there.

It took a certain kind of personality to look for, and capture, the good in other people. To recognize those small acts of kindness and courage and put them on display. Preserving them in paint and ink. It made him all the more curious about the artist.

He rubbed the dog's ear one more time and straightened.

From above, footsteps crossed the floor, echoing through the empty space.

Standing here now, he knew why the rumours had started. Oh, he'd heard them all right. The ghost in the Mews. Sure, people clammed up fast, switched to a whisper when he came close, but he'd caught enough. The hair-raising thrill in their voices when they tossed around ideas about what held her soul down, trapped on earth.

An unnatural, untimely death. Anger. Pain.

Not exactly the way he wanted to envision his mom's afterlife.

The story had ticked him off at first, but there wasn't much he could do about it. A fatal accident. An empty building. It was easy to see the temptation to embellish. But that's exactly what it was. A story. Nothing more.

If he was a little jumpy — catching shadows darting out of the corners of his eyes, the faces on the walls — it was just the caffeine, the sugar high, hitting him harder because he was missing sleep.

Matt looked at the dog. "Are you going to bark at me, if I head up?"

Cocoa sat and panted at him. He'd take that as the go-ahead.

He crossed the room, closing the door behind him. There was probably a reason why Cocoa wasn't allowed upstairs.

The wooden stairs groaned beneath his feet as he made his way up. Trying not to count how high, how far off the ground.

The scream stopped him dead in his tracks. Slammed the image into his head. Of a woman falling. The sickening thud of impact.

He hadn't heard that sound echoing through his mind in years.

Heart hammering on a surge of adrenaline, Matt jumped the last two steps and charged through the door.

Blinking against the sunlight pouring through the windows — blue sky filling his vision — he registered Charley spin toward him.

Yellow T-shirt. No blood, no injuries.

It took him a second longer to realize that the screams — short and high-pitched — came from a wiry man standing at the far end of the room. He was looking up at the ceiling, making animal sounds. His tangled beard was timber wolf grey and as feral as the growls coming from his throat. An open bag of tortilla chips clamped in one hand. Barbeque-flavoured Doritos.

"Matt? What are you doing here?" The surprise on her face bordered on shock. He figured it about matched his own expression.

He had just made one hell of an entrance. All he could do now was play it cool. "I was on my way past, saw the truck outside." He dug his hands in his pockets, trying not to shift his feet. "What's he doing?"

"Squirrel mating sounds."

As though that explained everything. "And the chips?"

She shrugged. "Breakfast, apparently."

A brown-and-white spaniel zipped from one end of the room to the other, doing sweeps, nose to the floor.

The man spoke in a gravelly rasp, at odds with those earlier shrieks. "Yup, you've got yourself a squirrel problem."

Charley said, "That's why you're here." She sounded close to losing her patience.

The man tossed back a fistful of chips. Red crumbs dusted the front of his canvas work shirt. He squinted up. "Trouble is —" He chewed, swallowed. "— the dog can't get up there."

She looked at the spaniel. "Why would —"

"If there's a squirrel here," the man said with satisfaction, "you better believe that dog there will find it."

"And then?" Matt asked. He had a bad feeling about the answer.

The man grinned, flashing yellow canines. "There's nothin' that dog likes better than squirrel. Dontcha boy?"

Holy shit. Matt looked at the dog's lolling tongue, the bright eyes and wagging tail. Hard to imagine something that cute could turn vicious.

Charley shook her head. "Hold on. Your website says you offer humane pest-control solutions."

"Those cost extra."

She blanched. "Excuse me?"

"You wanted a fast fix." His hand disappeared in the bag again with a crackle of laminated foil. "The squirrel doesn't seem to be in the building right now, but we'll wait it out. They're busy critters during the day — looking for nuts, scampering up and down trees. Around your attic." Creases spread around his eyes, though the beard hid most of his grin. "Got my gun in the truck, too, if need be. We'll get you sorted in no time, just you wait and see."

An angry flush coloured her cheeks. "Right. That's it."

Torn between fascination and pity for the man, Matt leaned a shoulder against the wall. This should be good.

He watched as Charley strode to the door and held it wide open. "Thank you for your time."

Both the man and the dog looked up at the ceiling with longing. "You sure?"

"Absolutely."

"You won't find anyone else this time of year," he warned.

A fierce set to her chin, she said, "I'll figure it out."

Matt would have said the same thing.

"That's your choice, then." The man slapped chip dust off his hands. "Better get to it fast though, before the critter puts another hole in your ceiling." He reached into his pocket and pulled out a Bic ballpoint. Uncapped it. "There's still the service charge."

Ten minutes later and fifty dollars shorter, Charley slammed the door behind the man and his dog. Matt made a mental note to stay on her good side.

"Did you see what he wrote on the invoice?" She waved the paper in the air. "'Good luck.' Well, I say, good riddance!"

He bit back a smile, more comfortable now that they were back on the ground floor. Harder to dwell on ghosts here, with all that hardboiled courage on the walls and a blissed-out trumpet player improvising a silent solo on his right. "You don't need luck. You need steel wool and spray foam."

That stopped her. "What?"

"If you're going to take care of it yourself, you'll need to get some."

Charley narrowed her eyes and stepped closer. "Tell me everything you know."

He laughed. "You'll have to find the entry point in the attic. It's probably no more than a crack. Fill the hole with steel wool and seal it with spray foam, and you just might solve your problem. You can get both at the hardware store. Although —" God, she was cute mad. "I know a guy who has everything we need, including a live trap. We could pay him a visit."

"Now? Doesn't Chocoholic's open at ten?"

And he should have been there long before now. "The gallery can't open if you don't get rid of that squirrel, right?"

She nodded. "Yeah, but I've got this. We'll be fine."

Cocoa wagged her tail, a full body wriggle.

"I like you a lot better than that other dog," he told her.

He checked his watch. Odds were good that Jeffrey would be in his workshop. And that's exactly where Matt should be. In his own workshop. Working. But this would only take half an hour, there and back. He could leave her with the supplies.

He said, "We're opening late today. Come on." He held the door open for her.

"I'll owe you one."

"Don't worry about it." He looked down at Charley as she passed him in the doorway and couldn't resist stealing an old line from the best. "Anything for you, doll."

She paused, edged in close against him, and gave him a cool, long look that almost stopped his heart. With a husky voice, she said, "You like to play games, don't you?"

The air thickened, crackling with tension. With anticipation. Should he —

She cracked up. "God, you should see your face. Bacall trumps Bogart any day." She went out chuckling. "That was a pretty decent imitation, I'll give you that." She added over her shoulder, "But don't call me 'doll.'"

He should have known better than to quote Bogart to a woman who painted pulp fiction covers.

"Tough crowd." He rubbed the heel of his hand over his heart, hoping to kick-start it again, and followed her out.

"So —" He waited for Charley to lock the gallery door. "— who's riding shotgun? You or Cocoa?"

He just managed to sidestep the quick elbow to the gut.

SIXTEEN

SPARKS. SHE'D HAVE TO BE blind, deaf, and dumb not to notice them. And she'd practically set them off. Charley's nerves hummed, running as steady as the truck's engine.

Matt seemed edgy when he first got to the gallery, but he looked relaxed now, arm hanging out of the driver's side window. The breeze ruffled his hair. His fingers kept time on the steering wheel, to the rhythm set by the Boss. Eyes hidden behind Ray-Bans.

He smelled like lemon shower gel with a hint of dark chocolate. Maybe she should just not breathe.

"You okay?" He glanced over at her.

Caught out, she nearly flushed. "Yeah, fine." She looked out the windshield. Along the shoulder, bleached ditch grass danced in the wind.

A stainless steel Thermos mug rattled in the cupholder between them, sloshing and probably more than half-full, from the sound of it. He hadn't even finished his coffee before offering to help her.

Matt flicked on the turn signal, and she sat up straight. That was their lane up ahead. The one that led to their cottage, and to Kayla's. "Where are we going?"

He made the turn. On the backseat, Cocoa shifted, sensing their trip was about to end.

"Jeffrey's workshop," he said.

Of course. Everyone went there when they had a problem that needed fixing.

She cast a glance at him out of the side of her eye. Should she bring it up? They were alone in the car. The timing couldn't be better. "Alex said he went to see you yesterday."

His grip tensed on the steering wheel, knuckles shining white. "Yeah? You know about —"

"Kayla called us when she found the body." *And I found the chocolates*. But she wasn't about to say that out loud.

"How is she?"

In shock? Heartbroken? None of those descriptions seemed quite right. "She's ... dealing with it."

"Good for her."

"She's tougher than she looks." Or she hid her emotions well.

"Who knew I was teaching a class on murder?" Matt murmured under his breath.

And that would be hard to live with. "The fact that you did teach that class narrows down the suspect list." Cold comfort, she knew.

"I guess there's always a silver lining." His mouth twisted in a smile. "Alex seems to have a lot of theories."

Bitterness there. Did he know Alex had him on his list of suspects? "What's yours?"

"About Andrew's death?" He took his eyes off the road, and looked at her, one long second, reflections shifting in his sunglasses. "I think it was a damned convenient way to kill him."

A chill stole over her. "I'm with you on that one."

The green building appeared up ahead, a beat-up flatbed truck parked out front. Matt pulled up beside it. He lowered the back windows a crack for Cocoa before turning the engine off.

He looked at Charley over the rims of his shades. "In case

you're wondering, I didn't do it." He got out of the car. "But I'd love to get my hands on the person who did." He slammed the door. The sound echoed like a gunshot, sharp and final.

She had no doubt he meant every word.

Charley unbuckled her seat belt and stepped out onto sun-dappled gravel. Standing here now, she noticed a narrow ATV trail cutting a path through the thicket of oak and papery birch trees, back out toward the main road.

"Watch where you walk," Matt told her. "There could be nails."

End of conversation. Her questions would have to wait. For now. But she had more, a lot more.

An octagonal shimmer of coloured light above the open door caught her eye. Carefully cut and soldered prisms of stained glass, but not just a single panel. The design filled the entire window frame. A hawk in flight. "I've been dying to get a glimpse inside this place for years," she said.

"Really? Why?"

"Are you kidding?"

Behind the big white truck, the garage door stood open, revealing a glimpse of tools, and a floor coated in a layer of sawdust. Music blasted out, heavy on the drums. Whiskey-fueled vocals sang about darkened streets and reckless feelings.

She said, "There's a stained-glass hawk in that window. The building is large enough to house an airplane. Sometimes, you can hear the sound of a chainsaw all the way up the street."

"It does catch your imagination, doesn't it? But it's a lot less exciting than you think." Matt led the way inside.

The relentless drumbeat pounded from the speakers, shifting to a joyful and frenzied piano part that kicked up the rhythm of her heart. Those driving notes echoed into the rafters, the ceiling high enough to allow for scaffolding. Beneath the sharper bite of sealant, she caught an undertone of beeswax and the deep, fresh-cut scent of maple and walnut.

"Hello," he shouted.

No reply.

Matt said to her, "We'll check the back. He's probably there."

She followed close behind him as he moved through the space, leading the way around tables, ladders, and planks of wood. She had a feeling he could find his way through that workshop blindfolded.

He reached for her hand with a quick grin, his fingers lacing through hers, and she let him. Even though it meant she couldn't stop to take a closer look at the jars of nuts and bolts on the shelf. A still life waiting to be drawn, light caught in the cloudy glass, fracturing through the red plastic handle of the screwdriver, to cast reflections on the metal file.

"There he is," Matt said.

In the shadows, a man lifted the last shelf out of a beautiful wooden bookcase. She fought the urge to run her palm over the honey-toned surface. Lustrous and sanded to perfection. The tang of varnish still fresh in the air.

"Need help with that?" Matt raised his voice to be heard.

A flash of pleasure lit the man's face. Followed by curiosity when he spotted Charley. He had the lean, tough build, the broad and calloused hands, of a man used to physical labour. Thick brown hair just starting to streak silver, shot through like wood grain.

He reached for a control resting on the stool nearby and lowered the volume, taking the edge off the music. "Back so soon?" Stance easy and hipshot, he turned to her. "I can't seem to get rid of him."

"And you tried your best. Gave me all the worst jobs when I was a teenager. Crawlspaces." Matt shuddered. "I still have nightmares."

"Had to test your mettle, didn't I?" He winked.

"Did he pass?" she asked.

"With flying colours." Warmth and a great deal of pride filled his voice. "Jeffrey Haste. I'd shake your hand, but, well." He looked ruefully at his varnish-stained fingers.

"I'll take a rain check. I'm Charley Scott."

"Meghan's little sister?"

Amused, she said, "That's right."

"The one with the gallery." He raised his eyebrows at Matt in a silent male exchange she pretended not to see. "I knew your grandfather." He bent to align the shelves, stacking one on the other. "Good man. Loved fishing, if I remember right. And telling jokes."

"He did." All the time. She decided at that moment that she liked this gruff man.

"Maybe we met before," Matt said. "Passed each other by one summer without even realizing it."

It was Oakcrest. They probably had. But she was sure she would have remembered.

"Fate?" Jeffrey teased.

"A grand design?" Charley grinned.

"Could be." Matt put his hand on the bookshelf. "Are you loading this up?"

"If you take one end, that'd be great." A beat went by. "Unless you're trying to impress the lady and want to carry it on your own." The grin was quick, the tone tongue-in-cheek.

Matt shot him a glance and got a grip on the top of the bookcase. "The lady's already impressed."

"Is she?" she asked dryly.

They tilted, lifted the shelf. "Has he cooked for you yet?" Jeffrey asked.

"No, he hasn't." She picked up two of the shelves. Even tough guys wouldn't turn down a little help.

"His cooking, I have to admit, is impressive," Jeffrey said. "He had an excellent teacher." Humour there.

"And a modest one at that." Matt backed his way through the space, feeling his way heel first. Well-coordinated, they moved in step, with just a nod or a glance needed to shift, adjust. A practice honed over time.

A wool blanket was already laid out in the bed of the truck. She waited for them to hoist the bookcase in, then slid the shelves in beside it.

Matt stepped back. "Where's this going?"

The pause was too long. Jeffrey scratched his throat, eyes on him. "The Coffee Nook."

"Yeah? New display?"

"For a local author." Again, that same expression in his eye, at once sharp and watchful. "Book's being released on Monday."

Matt's head snapped up, attention all on Jeffrey. "That so?"

She wished she could read the subtext. Because the air was thick with it. "What's the title?"

"*Hamadryads.*" The title was wielded like a weapon, and she wondered why. Then Jeffrey turned to face her. "By Nick Thorn."

Matt Thorn. Nick Thorn. Oh, there was history there. Painful, by the looks of it. "Your dad wrote *Hamadryads*?" She hadn't read it, but she'd heard of it. Of course, she had. It was a sci-fi cult hit. One browse through a bookshop and you'd come across a copy. Anywhere in the world.

Matt shrugged, wary eyes still on Jeffrey. "He did."

"Originally published under the name Sam West." Jeffrey hooked his thumbs in his pockets, stretched his back. "But all secrets come out at some point, don't they?"

"Yeah." Matt shifted his weight. "Listen, we actually came to borrow a live trap."

The flicker of disappointment in Jeffrey's eyes was shut down quick, but not before she'd spotted it. She saw the shift, as they moved back onto safe ground. Neutral territory.

"Rodent problem?" Jeffrey asked.

"Squirrel," she replied.

"At the gallery?"

"Sadly, yes."

"Nasty buggers. Might as well take some steel wool and spray foam too."

Matt smiled, though it fell short of his eyes. "I was hoping you'd say that."

"Paying off my debts, remember?"

That comment brought back his grin, full wattage. "That'll take years." Their banter had a well-worn rhythm to it.

"I plan to lead a long and healthy life." Jeffrey rocked back on his heels. "Help yourself. You know where everything is."

Matt was already heading back inside. As he passed, Cocoa gave a joyful bark from the back seat of the truck.

Jeffrey squinted up at the sizzling sky. "So, you're opening the gallery."

"Yes, I am."

"Why cover art?"

The question took her aback. "Excuse me?"

"'Cover Art'. I've seen the poster. Where's that come from?"

"Oh." She relaxed, focusing on the light breeze, the warmth on her face. When would she stop assuming a comment or question about her art was a set-up for criticism? Probably long after the exhibit ended.

She said, "I got my first summer job at the library here in Oakcrest. And discovered that the gateway to that magical world, filled with stories, was art." Yellowed paperbacks and pulp fiction covers. "I got hooked. Completely. The best designs have this quality about them that goes beyond words, that speaks directly to you. Book covers charm and they make a promise."

"About?"

"Thrills. Happily ever afters." She didn't have to think about the answer, it was right there, waiting. "Dell paperback mysteries had a 'mapback' cover that showed the location of the murder so that the reader could visualize the setting. You knew right away what you were getting when you picked one of them up. And, of course, some covers become iconic. And valuable. Especially in a small print run. Some are worth thousands." Rare and ephemeral, dust jackets were icons of graphic art and could increase a first edition's value. "A rejected Tintin cover illustrated by Hergé sold at auction for €3.2 million."

"All thanks to a pretty picture on the cover?"

"That makes a promise." She smiled.

"Heads up." Charley just managed to catch the cardboard box sailing toward her. She looked at the bulldog on the front. Steel wool. Matt walked toward them, carrying a rectangular metal cage, two cans of spray foam clamped under his arm. "We're good to go." He dropped the cage into the back of the truck.

Jeffrey walked around the side of the vehicle. "Best give the critter a bath after." He nodded his head at the cage.

Drown it? Her stomach twisted. It was a gruesome thought. "Oh no," she said. "That's not happening. Not on my watch."

Matt shook his head. "If Charley catches anything, we'll release it somewhere far away."

Jeffrey raised an eyebrow. "Find it a happy new home? Sometimes kindness can be a weakness." He looked in the backseat of the truck. "Who's this?"

"Cocoa." She made the introductions as Cocoa stretched her head out of the window as far as possible, angling for an ear rub.

Jeffrey shot Matt an amused glance. "Seventy percent?"

"Nah." He climbed in the driver's seat. "Sweeter than that."

The tone was casual.

And dangerous. Because, if she wasn't careful, that kind of line could melt her heart.

BACK AT THE GALLERY, CHARLEY was ready to roll up her sleeves and get to work.

With a clank of metal, she unlocked the stepladder she used to hang paintings. And banged her elbow on the wall. Pain shot up her arm, straight to her shoulder. She rubbed a hand over the ache and grimaced.

The trap door leading to the attic was in a closet off what was meant to be the living room in the upstairs apartment. A very small closet.

Fighting the urge to swear, because that wouldn't help anything, she positioned the ladder under the door. The base wobbled on uneven floorboards before settling.

From the other room, she heard Matt say, "Some apple slices should do the trick."

"An apple as temptation." She climbed the stepladder and reached over her head, pressing her fingertips to the fitted square cover. "Works every time, I guess."

"Need any help?"

She looked down at him. Not too far down. He was taller than she thought. And close.

Matt crossed his arms and settled a shoulder against the door-jamb. "I thought you might want someone to scout out the terrain. Give the all-clear, before you go up."

"Check for monsters?" She stood on her toes, the soles of her Keds flexing, as she applied more pressure. She felt the shift, the give as the square cover lifted off the frame. "Do I look like a wuss?" She angled the panel and gave it a shove, to slide it out of the way. Hot musty air washed over her. The opening gaped into darkness.

"Okay, so I'm off then."

With a knee-jerk reaction, she glanced back.

Matt grinned. He hadn't budged. "I'll follow you up," he said.

"Thanks," she muttered. She got one knee up on the top of the ladder and a good grip on the frame of the attic access hatch. Her palms on solid ground, she levered herself up.

And felt a helping hand on her hip.

She froze. Through gritted teeth, she said, "Unnecessary."

The hand disappeared.

When she was through and up, she looked back down and frowned.

"Sorry." He didn't look sorry at all. Matt handed up the box of steel wool and spray foam. "Move over. I'm coming up."

Charley stood. The attic was dark and unfinished. Too many shadows clung to the walls. One bare, burned-out, useless bulb hung from a roof joist down at the far end. A few slats of light filtered through the intake vents under the eaves, but not enough to slow the pulse throbbing in her throat.

The heat was stifling beneath the low rafters. "Watch your —"

Thunk. He swore ripely.

"Head," she finished.

"Yeah, got that." Matt rubbed the back of his head, where he'd whacked it on the wooden beam. He seemed to take up all the space in the attic, filling it with long legs and broad shoulders.

Ducking beneath the sloped ceiling, she stepped carefully along the floor joists, spreading her weight evenly. It was too much to hope there might be floorboards. One wrong step and she'd crack the drywall ceiling of the room below or fall right through. The landing wouldn't be pretty.

Sticky threads hit her cheek. Cobwebs, ugh. Thick and old. She brushed the silvery strands away and wondered where the spider was hiding. Hopefully somewhere far away.

There were scratches in the grime coating the wooden joists. Animal tracks? And dead moths.

A pile of debris in the corner caught her eye. Squatting down for a closer look, she smelled the faint but unmistakable odour of rot. Brittle pinecones and dry leaves, crumbling to dust. Nuts, too.

"Looks like prime storage space." She picked up a pinecone and tossed it to Matt.

It was a good throw. Nice and easy.

The pinecone bounced off his shoulder and fell to the floor.

Matt just stood there, staring. His eyes following the line of the floor. The expression on his face — it looked like he'd seen a ghost.

The thought had the hairs on her arms rising. She swallowed hard and fought the urge to check over her shoulder. A cramped, dimly lit attic. The prodigal son. What better time for Lizzie to make her appearance than right at that very moment? "Matt?"

He jolted. "Yeah. Sorry." He seemed to shake it off, refocus on her. "I thought I saw something."

A shiver ran through her, but she smiled. False bravado never hurt. "Probably stars, after that bump on the head."

"Could be." He moved toward her, balancing along the joists like a gymnast, ducking carefully to avoid the beams. "There's light coming through there." He pointed behind her, to the sliver of daylight seeping through the wall. Just above her head, but not out of reach. "Looks bigger than an airflow vent. You might want to start there."

She'd already spotted it, but she'd let him have that one. He'd hit his head, after all. "Got it."

She had her back to the wall. In that small dimly lit space, he stood close to her. Almost hemming her in. If she angled her chin the right way, their lips would brush.

Their eyes locked and her stomach did a slow roller-coaster dive.

"Chocolate." His voice sounded husky. "I should be making chocolate."

"And selling it." Her own voice was suddenly thick.

He braced his hands on the wall on either side of her, caging her in. Or steadying himself. Seemed like she wasn't the only one off-balance.

His eyes moved to her mouth. Danger-zone close. "I should go."

"You're already late," she murmured.

The corner of his mouth twitched. "That detour to the workshop did it." He moved in, a little closer. Their legs brushed, denim to denim.

His eyes were like molten chocolate. The air in the attic suddenly seemed several degrees hotter than before.

Something clattered downstairs.

"Charley?" A voice called. "Are you up there?"

They leaped apart, putting space between each other. Lots of it.

Her heart thundered. "Is that Kayla?"

"Sounds like." Matt rubbed a hand over the back of his neck. "Guess that's my cue to leave."

"Thanks for your help." Just a second longer... But it was probably better this way. She couldn't handle any more complications. She had more than enough as it was.

"Call me if you need me." He shot her a wicked grin over his shoulder, before disappearing down through the trap door.

Whew. Alone in the attic, Charley blew out a breath. Next time she saw Matt Thorn, she'd be keeping her distance.

Two feet apart or more, from now on.

SEVENTEEN

"I CAN'T BELIEVE MATT WAS here," Kayla fumed.

Charley eyed the two take-away cups she held. Coffee scented the room. "Is one of those for me?"

"What?" She blinked. "Oh, yeah. Lattes from The Coffee Nook." She passed one of the cups over, then started pacing again.

"Hallelujah." To handle this conversation, she needed caffeine in her system. Her hands felt grimy from the attic, but she wrapped them around the paper cup and breathed in the fragrant steam.

She settled on the floor, back to the wall. They'd have to get some chairs in the gallery soon.

Propping the cup on her raised knees, she watched Kayla circle, past the cage and back. The steel rod door of the trap was raised, fastened and set to capture. Hopefully, they wouldn't need it. From where she sat — with a little imagination — the hole in the drywall looked like a dark stain in the ceiling, nothing more.

"You're not blaming Matt for what happened to Andrew, are you?" Charley asked cautiously. Because he already blamed himself.

"Why shouldn't I?" Kayla dragged a hand through her hair. The blunt cut fell back into place in a black curtain, glossy and perfectly styled. But her normally golden skin looked lifeless. Sleepless nights shadowed her eyes. "Alex is investigating Andrew's death." She whirled on Charley. "Your sister printed that in the paper.

Everyone's talking about it. That his death is 'suspicious.'" She framed the word with air quotes. "Murder, God. He died because he ate those chocolates. It doesn't take a genius to figure out whose fault that was. I should sue, take Matt for all he's worth."

Kayla dropped to the floor beside her and tipped her head back. Gaze fixed on a distant point, like she was staring into an abyss. "This isn't my life," she murmured. "I feel like I'll wake up tomorrow and realize it was just a dream."

A dream. Not a nightmare? "There are a few reasons why Alex thinks —" How could she say this? "— that his death was more than an accident."

Kayla's fingers tightened on her cup. A delicate silver bracelet winked at her wrist. "Alex is an idiot if he thinks I killed my husband."

Charley choked on her coffee, spluttered. And she thought she'd have to dodge around the topic. "Did you?"

"Jesus." Kayla leaped up like a coiled spring. "No." She moved to the window.

At a better angle, Charley might have caught a glimpse of her reflection. Somewhere beneath that chic exterior was the girl who scribbled caricatures on cocktail napkins and went on candy runs with a bad case of bedhead, nowhere near artfully messy. But the noon sun burned the glass white, a blank slate.

"I didn't kill him," Kayla said. "Alex doesn't know me. People make assumptions. They always do. I need someone on my side." She faced away, her back ramrod straight.

Charley wished she could see her eyes. "I am on your side." And that would never change.

Kayla turned back to her. Hope dawned on her face. "So, you'll help me?"

A memory flashed through her mind. The sting of scraped

knees at the end of a long summer day. A handshake and a promise, binding as a blood oath. "Get answers? Of course, I'll help." And they'd prove her innocence.

Kayla shook her head, stepping closer. "I need you to convince him to drop this." No hesitation, not a trace of a smile. She was serious.

It took Charley a full second to process it. "What?" Why? Because an investigation would open old wounds? Or unearth a truth best left buried. The thought brought with it an uneasy trickle of doubt. "I can't do that."

A cat slant tilt to her lids turned Kayla's expression fierce. Then that ruthless stare was gone, drowned out by sorrow, and she wondered if she'd imagined it. "Alex is wasting his time," she said. "It was an accident, you'll see. Probably some mix-up at Chocoholic's."

Stage one of grief. Denial. "Maybe."

Kayla took a last sip of her coffee, draining the cup. "I've changed my mind about the exhibit. I want back in."

"You what?" Talk about a change of topic.

"I want to rejoin the exhibit."

She got to her feet, trying to wrap her head around it. "Now, with everything else going on?"

"The funeral arrangements, you mean?" Her voice bled ice. "I've had a lot of practice preparing tasteful events for Andrew. This isn't any different."

And now that Andrew had died, Kayla could pursue her dreams again. To some, it might seem callous. But in her position, wouldn't she do the same thing? Seize the opportunity to forget about everything else but art. "If you're a part of the exhibit, we'll be counting on you."

"I'll go up into the attic with you," she promised. "I can hang paintings and help with the opening. Walk Cocoa."

"Who's spent the last hour napping in a patch of sunshine downstairs."

"I can watch the gallery, when you need a break."

It was tempting to give in, say yes. Still, Charley hesitated. "You can't back out again."

"I knew you'd say that, so I brought a sign of good faith. Three of my illustrations."

"Collateral?" she asked dryly.

"You could call it that."

So, Andrew was wrong. Kayla had finished her drawings. To think, he'd almost convinced her. "Let's see them then." And prove they'd existed, all along.

IF SHOWING YOUR ART TO someone took a leap of faith, committing to an exhibit took an act of bravery.

Charley looked at the frames wrapped in scuffed brown paper. Tightly sealed and taped at every corner. "Has anyone else seen these?" They stood in the main room of the gallery.

Kayla moved a few steps closer to her art and braced, as though ready to defend against an attack. She shook her head. "Only Sarah, months ago. She stopped by the house one day, caught me by surprise. She's convinced I need to show my work. It's one of the reasons why I'm here." She glanced over her shoulder at Charley. "Ready?"

Curiosity thrilled through her. "Do you have to ask?"

Cocoa stood and wagged her tail.

Kayla hesitated, just once, then grabbed a corner of tape and pulled. Packing paper ripped, tearing through the red tissue beneath, revealing burnished, wax smooth layers. Crosshatched pencil lines. An eye, the curve of a cheek. Soon the floor was littered with pieces of wrapping, sticky curls of cellophane, and tissue paper. Cocoa pounced on a red scrap, playfully shredding it with her teeth.

If Thomas's work was a shout, Kayla's was a whisper.

Charley felt a tiny stab of doubt. Would anyone even notice hers?

Thomas's paintings captured the very motion and colour of music in oil and canvas. Kayla's told a story composed of delicate lines. Her illustrations had a magnetic draw that pulled the viewer in, until they stood, absorbed. Transfixed.

Tattered strips of paper and plastic wafted over the floor as Charley moved closer.

In the illustration, a woman floated in a starry sky, darkness swirling around her. The gossamer hood of her parka lit from within. She held a bone to her face, the socket of the shoulder blade shining clean and white. Peering through the hole in the bone, the woman looked down on a man standing in a busy city street below. He seemed separate from the activity going on around him, a sneering twist to his mouth. His clothes were tattered, his features gaunt and worn. His skin tinged a pale shade of blue. Frost clung to his clothes.

The woman in the sky smiled, radiating satisfaction.

The man's face — Charley fought to hide her knee-jerk jolt of recognition. To keep her eyes from flicking to Kayla.

The cold and ragged man was Andrew.

"So, what do you think?" Kayla asked.

It might be a coincidence, a form of catharsis. Maybe she hadn't even noticed the similarity. "They're good," she murmured. And they were. Still, there was something disconcerting about them. The pain inflicted, the features too true to life.

Unsettled, she moved on to the next drawing.

The girls were playing near the beach. The first line of the story swept through her mind. An old woman's voice, the crackle of a bonfire.

The story of the three girls — Kayla's grandmother had told it to them, so many summers ago. How did it go?

The first girl married a whale, who sacrificed his bones to build her a house in the water. But she missed her family and her life on land. When she returned to the island, to visit her father and brother, the whale became angry. He tore down the house he'd made for her and took back all the bones, except his breast and hip bone, which he forgot in his fury. The whale hauled the girl back, but her father and brother rescued her in their boat. They pulled the boat over a reef and the whale became stranded. When the tide went out, the people killed the whale and set the girl free.

The second girl chose an eagle for her husband. He carried her away to his nest on a cliff. But she could not be happy, living there. Every time the eagle went hunting, she braided caribou leg sinews to make a rope. When she saw her father and brothers coming to rescue her, she distracted the eagle by telling him about a place far away, where he could hunt caribou. He believed the lie and flew away. She finished the rope and climbed down to her father's boat. Furious at the betrayal, the eagle flew to the village to bring her back. He broke the window of her father's house with his wings, but her father shot him with an arrow and killed him.

But Kayla's drawing showed only one of the girls — the third girl. She stood in a vast Arctic tundra. The stark landscape of frozen soil, ice, and barren rolling hills spanned the width of the paper, stretching from horizon to horizon. The natural habitat of polar bears and caribou. The girl's bare hands rested on a boulder, but she strained away. Her fingers looked fossilized, fine shading turning skin into exposed rock surface. People in caribou parkas and mittens brought baskets of food to lay at her feet. For survival, not rescue.

The third girl took a boulder for her husband and gradually turned to stone. The only one of the three who couldn't escape. And Kayla had drawn her story.

"Be careful what you wish for," she said aloud. And regretted it when Kayla's smile turned bitter.

"Because," she said, "you might regret the consequences."

No need to ask what Kayla meant. It was all there, in those drawings.

In the last illustration, Sedna, the mother of the sea mammals, sank down to her house beneath the water. A house built of stone and whale ribs. Seals, whales, swordfish bled from her severed fingers. According to legend, she didn't want to take a husband but was forced to marry a man who deceived her. She fled and suffered for it. So, she became Sedna, the bitter woman below the ocean, who punished those who break taboos, showing no mercy, as none was shown to her.

Those strokes of coloured pencil on paper spoke of anger and anguish. Of violence.

"You remember Grandmother's stories." Kayla stood beside her.

The smell of wood smoke, the taste of sweet tea. The thrill of monsters and strange creatures brought to life by words alone, spoken aloud on a hot summer night. "There was always a lesson." But the listener had to interpret the characters' actions, to decide whether or not to accept them. "Kayla, people might think —" Charley cut herself off. Might think what? That she killed her husband?

"That we put on a hell of an exhibit?" She smiled.

"Only if we solve the squirrel problem and actually hang the art on the walls." A cold and wet nose nudged her hand. Cocoa wagged her tail, holding a strip of paper clamped between her teeth.

"Then let's get started."

Kayla had told her the word for art meant 'your own thoughts'. Had she purged them on paper?

Or put her motive for murder on display?

EIGHTEEN

HE LIED. THAT WAS THE only thing going through Matt's mind as he pounded his fist on the wooden storm door, hard enough to rattle it in the frame.

For the first time ever, he had caught Jeffrey out in a lie.

Rough and aging wood bit his hand as he banged on the door again.

All signs said Jeffrey was home. Wide open windows, his truck parked in the drive. From the back of the house came a fiery guitar lick, blurred by the low-level buzz and rumble of an outdated subwoofer. Classic rock, hard and fast and loud.

"Open up, Jeffrey! We need to talk." He could hear the anger in his own voice.

He should wait to cool off. But he'd already put in a full day at Chocoholic's, and those extra hours hadn't helped. Time had acted as a pressure cooker.

Patience wearing thin, he yanked the storm door open and tried the handle inside. Locked. That wasn't unusual. After one too many uninvited guests, Jeffrey had a rep for throwing the deadbolt.

Matt skirted the side of the house, following the path around to the waterfront. No fancy flagstones here, just grass worn down to solid earth beneath. Jeffrey had talked about laying a walkway, but it hadn't happened yet.

That burnt charcoal taste to the air — Jeffrey had the grill going. Round the house, the wind picked up, gusting fresh and sweet off the lake. The property, like so many on that road, sloped down, giving a clear view of the water. In the distance, waves crashed toward shore, frothing white at the crests.

Music blasted out through the screened-in porch. The radio tuned to central Ontario's favourite cottage rock station. Request a song on a Saturday night and you'd better be prepared to howl like a wolf before it got played.

Matt stepped onto the deck. The wood had faded to grey and mildew was starting to set in. It could use a little TLC. Nothing a good cleaning and stain couldn't fix. But most times you didn't even notice, not with the sunset turning everything to sheet gold.

Jeffrey sat in one of the Adirondack chairs, looking out at the lake. He wore cut-off shorts, bare feet kicked up on the low table. On a wooden board rested a red slab of marbled sirloin steak, shiny with marinade and studded with herbs. A bottle of whiskey nearby, and a glass, cloudy with condensation, within easy reach. A copy of the *Oakcrest Courier* lay on the table, pages fluttering. Today's edition?

The breeze caught at Jeffrey's hair. His gaze, sober and distant, was fixed on the horizon.

"The photographs." Matt pitched his voice above the Stones belting *it's all right.* "You know why dad got them developed."

"This again?" Eyes on the water, Jeffrey said, "Get yourself a glass."

Since that seemed like a good idea, he did what he was told.

The screen door slammed shut behind him, as he stepped into the galley-style kitchen. Two parallel runs of units optimized the compact space. The peninsula, with a couple stools shoved beneath, perfect for rolling out pastry. The pro-style range, about ten years old now, was restaurant quality, without the eyewatering price ticket. And close enough to the one he'd earmarked for himself, if he ever felt ready to admit he wasn't leaving Oakcrest anytime soon. Four cast iron grates, high-BTU burners and a griddle. Convection oven. Yeah, he wanted one.

The baked potatoes sat on the counter, prepped and ready to go. An aluminum dish of mushrooms, tossed in oil and parsley. All the work surfaces wiped down clean, the old butcher block cutting board scrubbed with lemon and coarse salt. Same way he kept his.

He was pretty sure he could find anything in here just by going on gut instinct.

Matt grabbed a glass off the shelf — Captain Morgan's grin dishwasher faded — then twisted the knob on the old stereo, taking the volume down a notch. He wasn't about to be drowned out by Jagger.

He carried the vegetables out with him.

Jeffrey levered himself to his feet. "Gotta get the steak on. There's enough for two, if you're hungry. I liked the girl you brought by this morning — Charley." He picked up the board. Those careful movements gave him away. That gentle sway. Almost steady on his feet, but not quite.

Matt sank into the other chair and picked up the bottle, tipped it. More than half empty.

Jeffrey was well on his way to being stinking drunk.

The meat hit the grill with a hiss. "Something on your mind, Matt?" Slight slur to the words.

"You could say that." He filled his own glass. The label was nothing fancy. The kind you drank with an end result in mind. He didn't know why Jeffrey was drinking, but he hoped the liquor would loosen his tongue. A truth serum would be perfect, right about now. "You knew where those photographs were taken." Admit it.

"It was a hunch."

"It was more than that. You knew the moment I showed them to you." He'd seen that flicker of recognition. Betrayal twisted inside him, black and bitter. He chased it down with the oak and vanilla finish of the whiskey, but still it burned in the back of his throat.

"It was a long time ago. I had an idea, but I wasn't sure." Leaving the grill, Jeffrey returned to his seat, dropped heavily into it.

Charred meat and roasted mushrooms began to scent the air. A deerfly buzzed around Matt's head, ready to take a bite out of him the second he let his guard down.

He slapped it away. "Any half-blind idiot can see those photographs were taken in the Mews." Once he'd been there, he'd spotted it. The bay window. The layout of the room itself. It was all there, plain as day.

"And I was supposed to tell you that the photographs were taken in the building where your mother died?" Anger had started to heat Jeffrey's voice now, too.

"Yes."

"Fine. Your mother took those photographs."

Finally, he was getting somewhere. But he wanted more. "At the Mews, while it was being built. Why?"

Starting to rise, Jeffrey said, "I should check the meat again."

His hand shot out, clamped down on Jeffrey's arm, holding him in place. He felt the muscles tense beneath his fingers. "I asked you if you knew where those photographs were taken. You lied. Now I want the truth. All of it." So he could shine a beacon on all those shadowy unknowns still lurking in the corners. A blinding white, high exposure beam, powerful enough to burn away the darkness.

"No" — Jeffrey broke his grip and stood — "you don't."

He blinked. "What the hell is that supposed to mean?"

"Leave it be, Matt."

Shock or anger, or a bit of both, had him up on his feet and following. He knew he was on the edge. But there had been too many years of silence and closed doors, of secrets stored away. And all along, Jeffrey had been keeping his own. "You said you were going to help me."

The grill radiated heat waves, smoke curling off the embers. The deerfly was back, buzzing around his ear again.

"Trust me," Jeffrey said, "I am."

"The hell you are."

The grill tongs slammed down on the Weber's side table and Matt felt a flash of satisfaction.

Jeffrey stepped forward, hands clenched, muscles rigid. "Don't lash out at me," he snarled with a jab of his finger, "because the man you're angry with is dead."

That hit like a fist to the solar plexus. "I came here because you've been holding out on me."

Jeffrey laughed. It had a bitter edge to it. "That's rich, coming from you."

The accusation settled somewhere in his chest. "What's that supposed to mean?" Matt was starting to lose control of the conversation.

"*Hamadryads.* You could have mentioned it."

"It wasn't my secret to tell."

"Neither is this."

He had to argue that one. "My mother took those photographs late at night, in the building she died in. You can't tell me that isn't my business."

Jeffrey blew out a breath, rubbed a hand over his eyes. Then he levelled him with an assessing gaze. "Those photographs. What else did you notice about them?"

He thought back to those close-up images. Supporting structures, beams, and wall studs. Hard to tell what type of lumber in the dark, maybe pine. Some electrical lines laid out, the project just passed framing and heading into the rough-in stage. But the camera lens always carefully zoomed in on — "The floor joists." That was it, every time.

"Yeah?" Jeffrey said. Waiting for him to hit on the answer.

There must have been something about those joists worth documenting. As a rough carpenter, she would have been in during the early phases of construction, assessing the framework of the building. But she'd taken the photographs on her personal camera, recorded evidence. It could only mean one thing. "There was something wrong with the structural integrity of the building."

"And then she died."

It fell into place with a neat chink, all the edges matching up in his mind. One piece of the puzzle. Jesus. "Did she come to you with this?"

"Leaving the problem as is could have called into question the integrity of her work on other sites. But she didn't come to me with it."

Then who? Someone who could fix the error, take responsibility. The engineer.

Suddenly he knew what Jeffrey was hinting at.

"Andrew." Fury rushed through him. "You think the son of a bitch killed her." His thoughts reeled. "Because she, what, wanted him to fix an error?"

"An expensive error."

Matt glanced to the left, toward the tangle of black-eyed Susans, the thicket of evergreens. Cattails and bulrush and water sparked in the lowering sun. Just past that, only a stone's throw away, Andrew had laughed and slept and lived his life. No wonder Jeffrey had planted that shield of trees.

He had been Andrew's go-to contractor, up until — the realization knocked the breath right out of him. "You stopped working with him after Mom died."

Jeffrey turned back to the barbecue. "There were other reasons for that."

Bullshit. He paced the deck, adrenaline surging through him. Jeffrey knew. Or had at least suspected enough. "Did you confront him?"

"We were friends. He donated a grant to the college in your mother's name."

As though that somehow made it better. "Blood money, it seems." He thrust his hands in his pockets, nails digging into his palms.

The deerfly zoomed in on the skin at the base of his throat, bit with a razor-sharp sting he ignored.

Jeffrey had all but told him Andrew committed murder and yet here he was, defending him. Making excuses for an old friend, never mind how long ago that might have been.

Was that why Jeffrey had the whiskey out? To toast their friendship now that the man was dead? "Andrew screwed you over. Dropped you on projects. You said so yourself."

"It's never a good idea to speak ill of the dead." Jeffrey slid the steak onto a plate, juices running red. "Andrew's death was in the paper. The cops are investigating. My advice? Keep your suspicions to yourself."

"Why? So that Oakcrest can keep mourning the great philanthropist?"

"Because people make assumptions. And it's a well-known fact

147

that revenge," Jeffrey said, handing him the plate, "is a dish best served cold."

NINETEEN

NO WONDER THOMAS WAS MAD. Despite the solid foundation, his house was still just a skeleton.

His argument with Andrew put him at the top of Charley's suspect list. And the interview for the gallery's blog gave her the perfect excuse to ask questions.

She slammed the door of the Jeep, inhaling the scents of timber and lake water and torn-up earth. Although it was early yet, the sun on her shoulders promised another blistering day ahead.

In comparison to their own busy cottage road, this part of the lake seemed untouched. The land on either side of his property untamed and wild. In the distance, the soil, swampy and studded with cattails, transitioned into open water. Iridescent green heads bobbed between lily pads — a brood of mallard ducks paddling, one after the other.

There were no neighbours, no reason for anyone else to venture down that road at all. Just a finished shed, a bare-bones house, and a camper trailer. Had Thomas chosen isolation on purpose?

Thomas sat at the picnic table, the lake behind him. Instead of facing the water, he had his back to the view. His gaze aimed her way, or maybe toward the house, as he nursed a cup of coffee. Waiting for her. Despite the shabby shirt, his carefully combed grey hair emphasized that sense of urban polish that even hours of work outdoors couldn't dull.

He raised a hand in greeting.

A surge of adrenaline shot through her. Show time.

Charley waved back but didn't head over, not right away. She wanted to take a look at the place first. Get a sense for the cause of so much anger.

The roof was covered, with enclosed eave overhangs, but they hadn't started on the siding yet. Sunbeams cut angles through the framework. Some sections had been covered with plywood, but others were exposed to the elements.

She pushed her sunglasses on the top of her head.

Oh, there was work to be done. Even she saw that, and she had no idea how a house was built. There'd been some progress, but not much.

Still, there was promise. She might not know much about construction, but she knew art. And this house, when finished, would be a work of art. The careful composition worked with the landscape, not against it, following the path already created by rocks and spruce. The two-story house had character, atmosphere, and a view of the water from almost every room.

But it was the wooden shed that stood out, caught her eye. Someone had taken their time over the details. Stained the siding ochre, installed barn sash windows to let the light in. The slanted roof hinted at loft space, and the overhang shielded the door from rain and snow. Maybe a glorified toolshed or a bunkie — a single mattress might fit but barely. Everything finished down to the solid door and deadbolt. High security for a shed in an isolated place like this.

Making her way toward Thomas, she was glad she'd swiped

Meghan's boots for the visit. Tires had carved thick ruts into the ground, the churned-up earth baked solid in the heat.

"What do you think?" He raised his enamel mug at the house.

She sat on the bench across from him. "It's got potential."

He choked on his coffee and she grinned. "Potential," he spluttered. "It's damned brilliant." He set the mug down and gestured, illustrating his point. "Clean lines. A rustic simplicity I pilfered from the Arts and Crafts movement. Vaulted windows. Open-plan spaces, exposed beams, and a semi-floating staircase leading up to the loft. See that?" He stabbed a finger at the house. "That is an architectural haven."

"It does look inviting." Or it would, once it had walls.

He leaned forward, eyes bright and intense. "Landscape architect Andrew Downing once said that a cottage without a porch is like a book without a title page. Strangers plunge *in medias res* into the house without a single word in preparation. My house will have a porch."

"Cover art," she murmured. She would have to work that into the blog post.

"Right." He smiled. "An ornamental transition from outside to inside, from garden to home." Gaze on the house, his voice softer, he added, "And that is going to be a fine home."

And a great quote for her. "Will there be a delay before Clarkston Engineering can finish the project, now that Andrew has passed away?"

She glanced at the cramped RV parked by the water. Weeds bristled, tall as the tires.

"'Finish the project?'" He roared with laughter. "That's a good one. No." He chuckled. "I'm happy to say I've seen the last of that team, and good riddance to them. I figured I'd be waiting on

Clarkston Engineering to finish the job until the end of my days, but Andrew's death — may he rest in peace — finally gave me the out I needed."

Keep it casual. Don't react. Her heart raced. Thomas had motive. Relief rushed through her. Better him than Kayla. All she needed was the evidence. "You couldn't terminate the contract before?"

A frown knit his brows. "Tried my best to, but everyone's covering their asses these days — pardon my language." As though she hadn't heard it all before and more. "In order to terminate a construction contract, there has to be legal grounds for it. Failure to perform according to schedule seemed like a good enough reason to me, but hey, what do I know?" Anger there, still. "Andrew always did just the right amount to scrape by." No attempt to hide the grudge, the bitterness.

"What are you going to do now?"

He took a swig of his coffee, grimaced, and upended the mug over the ground, pouring the rest onto the dandelions. "I asked Jeffrey to step in. I wasn't sure if he'd have the time or the manpower to take the project on, but he seems confident he can do it."

"That sounds perfect." Too perfect.

He stood. "You didn't come here for a lecture on architecture, and I've already prattled your ear off. Come on. I'll show you the studio." Humour caught on that last word.

He led the way to the shed. She wished he'd just gotten a portfolio from the RV and brought it to her.

The padlock glinted in his hand as he fit the key in the lock. The pins aligned with a sharp metallic click.

He pushed the door open and something rustled within. A dry scrabble of sound. Like something alive.

Pausing on the threshold, he said, "I built this myself, and faster than anything Andrew's people got done." Pride filled his voice. "Watertight, sturdy, and ideal for the job." He rapped a knuckle against the wall so the wood echoed.

She followed him inside. Instead of stepping onto solid ground, something slid beneath the sole of her shoe and she caught her hand on the wall to keep her balance. She glanced down.

A sheet of paper? Awash with colour and fluid lines.

A watercolour sketch, one she recognized as a rough version of a painting hanging in the gallery.

There was something living and breathing in that shed, after all. Art.

Paper was everywhere. Spread over the table, tacked to the walls, lying on the floor, set adrift by the open door. Softly rustling. Whispering.

Charley bent to pick up the watercolour as she looked around. A ladder led up to a narrow loft filled with canvasses. Light cascaded through paneled windows, falling over an easel and the worktable lining the back wall. And the sketches. All those sketches.

Endless variations of one subject. The house.

"Well, this is it," he said. "Organized chaos, if you can believe it. Browse. Make yourself at home."

She reached into her bag, pulled out her phone. "Mind if I take some photos?"

He shrugged. "So long as I give the final okay on the ones you use in the post."

"Deal." If only she knew where to start.

"I'm going to head to the trailer, put another pot of coffee on," he said. "Want a cup?"

Yes. But from a potential poisoner? Not a chance. "I'm fine, thanks."

"Suit yourself. I'll be right back." The door slammed shut.

She listened for the chink of the padlock, heard only the blood pounding in her ears.

She was on her own. Alone in a space that unsettled her. But why?

Blueprints shared wall space with charcoal illustrations. Half-squeezed and mangled tubes of oil paint lay on a stack of sketch-books. The rough outlines of Thomas's jazz series were few and far between. The focus was on the house.

The finished house.

She walked along the wall, studying the drawings. The house in darkness, lights glowing within frosted windows. Snow-swept, footprints leading up to the front door. That bright hot glow of summer in another. Then a heap of autumn leaves on the lawn, swirling to form a border, as though caught by a fall wind.

She ran a finger over the rent pencil had made in paper and shivered.

Obsession. The proof was here.

Raising her phone, she zoomed in on the sketches, snapping pictures of the easel, of a jar of old brushes that caught her eye.

Turning to the table, Charley flipped the first sketchbook open, thumbed through designs that showed the blend of architect and artist. A paper was tucked inside the book. A recipe.

She froze. The world centred, crystal sharp.

Don't touch anything. Tell Alex.

She hesitated. The weight of the moment pressed in on her. Leave the evidence here and she'd risk it disappearing. They'd never make it back in time. Or something might tip him off, along the way.

She had to act, now.

Outside, boot steps crunched closer over hard-packed earth. She shot a glance over her shoulder. Any second, he'd walk through that door. What should she do?

The only thing she could think of. She shoved the loose-leaf sheet of paper into her purse and spun around to greet Thomas with a smile, heart hammering in her chest a mile a minute.

He stood there, a backlit silhouette, steam curling from the mug in his hand. He nudged the door closed behind him. The heavy wood slipped into the latch, sealing shut. "You've probably figured it out by now."

Trapped, with no way out. Heart in her throat, she held her ground. "Figured what out?"

"My secret." He nodded at the walls. "One hobby bleeding into the other."

What did he mean? "I don't —"

"You caught me at the right time when you asked if I'd join the Cover Art exhibit." He stepped forward into a patch of light that stripped the years off his face, turning it younger and leaner. Skin on bones. "I'd just finished the jazz paintings. Now, I'm onto houses. No mystery, why." He waved his mug at the worktable. "I'm working on some new ideas." His hand hovered over the sketchbook. The one she'd stolen from.

She had to distract him. But how?

"The piece you're working on," she said, "I'd love to find out more about it." Drawing his attention to the half-started painting on the easel, far away from the table and the sketchbook.

The canvas glared white, but the structural points had been mapped out, the details started. She focused on the horizon line that split the sky and ground in two.

His eyes lit up and she breathed a sigh of relief. Give an artist the chance to talk about their latest piece...

"A house is a symbol of permanence." Launching into a description of his creative process, he took her through the stages from inspiration to finished piece, pointing out the delicate dimensions of the building, and how he would layer the paint.

Still just a ghost of graphite pencil, the porch wound around the house like a vine, like something organic.

But a vine strangled the tree it covered, trapping disease and decay in the roots. Was there disease and decay here?

Charley thought of the paper tucked away in her purse. A typed-out recipe for nougat-filled Belgian chocolates, with hand-written annotations done in soft graphite pencil.

"YOU STOLE IT?" ON THE phone, Alex's voice rose, cracked in disbelief.

Not the reaction she'd hoped for.

Charley frowned, concentrating on the road. She was on her way back to the cottage to take Cocoa for a walk before meeting Meghan at the Blast From the Past Boutique. The Jeep juddered over loose gravel and potholes, haphazardly filled.

She said, "I was holding it when Thomas came back. What was I supposed to do?"

"You should have left it where it was, then told me about it. If this turns out to be evidence, we won't be able to use it."

"You'd need more to convict anyway."

"Oh, so you're the expert now?" he asked.

"Thomas took the class, and he made notes. The recipe isn't exactly a smoking gun." Still, the thrill of the find sang through her veins.

She slowed for the single lane bridge ahead, keeping a careful eye on the kids, dripping and jostling to cannonball next into the water below. A boy balanced on top of the guardrail, wet hair gleaming, coiled to jump. Knees bent, he launched himself into the air, one arm outstretched to the sun, fingers splayed and reaching. Frozen mid-air, legs kicked out in a parkour leap, he hung suspended. She framed the image in her mind, held onto it. He broke the tranquil water with a splash that rippled toward shore.

The Jeep's tires rumbled over the wooden boards, then bumped back onto gravel on the other side.

"But" — she followed the winding lane — "Andrew's death allowed Thomas to get out of his contract with Clarkston Engineering."

"Maybe he wasn't hiding the recipe. Maybe he just tucked it into the sketchbook and forgot about it."

Possible, but unlikely. She gritted her teeth. "He's hired Jeffrey to finish the house. A house he happens to be obsessed with. I'll show you the photographs I took of his sketches." If that didn't convince Alex, she didn't know what would.

"Yes, he has motive. And I'll look into it. But we still have a problem. You were in that shed. You stole the recipe. What if he notices it's missing?"

Hindsight was always 20/20. "I wish I'd just asked him what it meant," she muttered. She might have caught him in a lie, had more to go on than a guess.

"I'm glad you didn't," he said, his tone grim. "You and Meghan both ask too many questions."

He was right. Odds were good Meghan had more intel than he did. And she knew just how to get her to spill. "Don't tell me curiosity killed the cat."

Sun-dappled light poured through the leaves above. Everything stippled deep green and blue, a medley of broken colours and hanging branches. It felt like driving down Renoir's wooded forest path.

"What if this was a recipe to murder?" he asked, exasperated now. "How do you think Thomas would have reacted, if you'd asked him about it?"

"That's why I didn't."

Alex groaned. "My life used to be stress-free."

"You're a cop," she pointed out. "How stress-free could it have been?"

"More than now."

Charley grinned. "That's because you're emotionally attached. It ups the pressure."

"You're telling me."

TWENTY

THE BLAST FROM THE PAST Boutique was a maze of small rooms and slanted ceilings, a treasure trove of vintage finds. Cashmere and old leather. Elbow-length gloves, collared shirts, and backless gowns. To Charley's left, a trench coat slouched on a hanger, the pockets deep enough to hide a gun in. In an open jewelry box, Double Indemnity cocktail rings sparkled. Princess cut, heirloom worthy, and cubic zirconia through and through.

"It was nice of Matt to stop by the gallery yesterday." Meghan disappeared behind a rack of dresses with a rustle of taffeta.

Cocoa lay beside a row of stiletto heels, patiently waiting as they browsed.

"You heard about that?" The brooch Charley picked up was a blaze of art deco rhinestones.

Meghan's voice echoed from behind reams of draped fabric, "It's kind of what I do."

She set the brooch down. Meghan probably had sources all over town. "Intel from the local CI?"

"Nailed it. Jennifer was working the register at the window of the grocery store and saw him enter the gallery at 9:30. You both left together in his truck." She reappeared to wriggle her eyebrows, before ducking out of sight again. Wire hangers rattled. "In about half an hour, you were back. Matt had a cage. That sounded odd, but she explained it. How great is it, that he helped you, by the way?"

Charley flashed back to that moment in the attic, the feel of his breath warm on her cheek. Butterflies danced through her stomach. "I was handling it."

"Natch, but it was still nice. Especially since he opened Chocoholic's an hour late. Matt never opens late."

She caught the hint. A flush spread under her skin, hot and fast. Time to move the topic to less dangerous ground. From romance to murder. "Speaking of Chocoholic's, I've been thinking about that class Matt taught. You were there. Who was the best student? There's always someone who stands out, who has the most talent." And the skills to replicate the chocolates on their own. To adapt the recipe with penciled annotations. The way Thomas had.

"You mean, besides Matt?" Meghan pulled a gold sequined dress off the rack, fringe swinging, and held it up.

She wrinkled her nose at the gown. Definitely not. "The students, Meg."

"I was good." She grinned. "Okay, okay. Not the best. But by the end of the lesson, everyone could make chocolates on their own, and do it well. Matt's a patient teacher. If I had to pick one person with the most talent, I'd have to say Sarah. Her chocolates were amazing. But Charley" — her expression sobered — "you can't ignore it, if you find proof that Kayla killed him. She rejoined the exhibit. That's quick. Maybe even heartless?"

At least she'd said if. "I know that's what Alex thinks." He was determined to trap Kayla in a lie. "But if she made those chocolates wouldn't Andrew have noticed?"

"He often worked late. She'd have loads of time on her own. Besides, Kayla refused to allow the police to search her house."

As though that proved anything. If Charley knew her at all, she had done it on principal. To keep some kind of control. "She was within her rights to do so. They didn't have a warrant."

"Yet."

As if it was only a matter of time.

Outrage on Kayla's behalf flared, sharp and swift. "Would you let a stranger search your home?"

Meghan shrugged. "Hey, I'm just playing devil's advocate. She did confirm the used injectors were in Andrew's truck. But she disposed of them, instead of handing them over to the police." She left a beat, let that comment sink in. "You want to find proof of her innocence. But maybe you're searching for something that isn't there."

No way. She leaned a hip against the table, crossed her arms. Beside her, a collection of vintage compacts glinted inside the glass case. "Kayla wouldn't kill a spider." She'd trap it and carry it carefully outside. Not to set it free on pavement, or on stone. But in safety, on the bough of a tree.

"That was then, this is now. And sometimes people get pushed to the extreme."

No one changed that much. "There were others in that class with motive to kill."

"Just because Thomas cracked and yelled at —"

"Threatened," she corrected.

"Fine, threatened Andrew, doesn't make him a killer."

No, but the recipe might. "You didn't see him on the street that day. Thomas looked ready to kill." He'd been livid. All but shaking with fury.

Meghan pressed her lips together. "If Andrew's death had been quick and violent, I'd be with you. But making lethal chocolates takes planning and foresight. It's cold, calculated."

True. "So, this wasn't a crime of passion," she admitted. "But aren't architects known for their problem-solving skills?" Maybe Andrew had just been one more problem to solve.

"This could end up leading straight back to Kayla." Meghan draped the thin strap of a beaded evening bag over her shoulder and struck a pose in the mirror.

"Or to someone else." The real killer.

She hung the purse back on the metal hook. "If that happens, I'll be the first to set it in ink and double the print run."

Snagging a tweed newsboy cap from the shelf, she dropped it on Meghan's head. "Triple it." And she'd hold her to it.

Tipping the brim at a jaunty angle, Meghan smoldered. "How do I look?"

She walked around her, checking the angles. Pressed her lips together and gave it some careful consideration. Then she grinned. "You found yourself a crook cap."

Meghan laughed and turned to the mirror. "Speaking of murder..." Eyes on her reflection, she hooked her thumbs in the pockets of her jeans and rocked back on her heels, in full vintage reporter mode.

"Fantastic," a male voice drawled behind them.

Charley whirled around.

Electric-blue eyes. A lean frame clad entirely in black, from T-shirt to jeans. His crossed arms showed off the word *VOGUE* tattooed on one toned forearm. This was Eric Trace.

Cocoa stood, tail thumping against skirts.

He said, "And here I thought, Meghan, your cheekbones were one of a kind. You must be Charley." He strode into the room, moving over creaking floorboards like the runway of an *haute couture* show. "I caught the word 'murder'. So, I can't help but wonder if you're discussing dark family histories and bodies decomposing in the attic? Or if the topic of conversation is, in fact, dressing to kill and slaying hearts?"

"Some of all of the above," Meghan replied, moving to give him a quick hug in greeting.

Eric gave her an affectionate squeeze. "I read about a 'suspicious death' in the paper. Now I come upon the local journalist in my very own boutique, discussing murder with her sister. But is it a coincidence?"

In that maze of rooms, they'd made a mistake. The sloped ceilings, the wooden floors had perfect acoustics. Their voices carried through the space.

"How much did you hear?" Charley asked. Rumours, half-based on facts, could tear through Oakcrest like shrapnel.

Eric straightened a stack of sweaters on the table, lining up the corners. "Enough to make me wonder how Andrew Clarkston died." He held up a hand. "I know, I know. Alex would be furious, if you so much as breathe a word about an ongoing investigation." A quick-fire, canny gleam lit his expression. "But I am very good at keeping secrets. And Andrew was positively odious."

Had anyone liked the man? "Odious?" she prompted.

He shuddered. "He once made Kayla return a dress she bought from me because he didn't like it. It was stunning, made for her." He smoothed the neckline of a sweater. Raised a brow. "Maybe that was the problem. Or it was a petty reaction to the sparks flying between Kayla and that teacher."

A harmless flirtation? Or something more.

She caught Meghan's eye, and read her mind. Another clue pointing toward Kayla. But they had a teacher on their list of suspects. And, if it was the same one, well that changed things. "David Nadeau?"

"Too handsome for school, is what I say." He winked. "Meghan, you took the class, too. Those two were as conductive as a silk slip dress in winter."

During Matt's class? It might just be gossip. Eric seemed to relish it. Or Kayla really did have another reason to escape her marriage. But love — or lust — was a strong motivator, and one that had her bumping David higher up on her list of suspects. "They were flirting?"

Meghan shook her head. "I didn't notice anything."

He rolled his eyes. "Darling, you were intent on tempering chocolate. Those less absorbed with melting cocoa nibs watched the heat level rise between those two. It was steamy." He fanned himself.

"Ooh!" Meghan's exclamation startled her, had her turning. "Charley, you've got to try this on." She pulled a dress off the rack. The fabric rustled. 1950s blue and white gingham. Off the shoulder, cinched waist and a full circle skirt. "It's perfect for the gallery opening."

"No." She backed up, but the shelf behind her blocked her retreat. Back to the wall, she said, "Absolutely not."

Eric studied the dress. "The blue would make your eyes pop."

"And it swishes." Meghan held the dress up to herself and twirled. The skirt flared out.

Cocoa leaped to her feet to sniff the hem and ended up with blue gingham draped over her head. They looked at her.

"I'm not wearing that."

"Add some drop earrings —"

"Meghan, darling," Eric interrupted. "We all have our area of expertise and fashion is mine. Leave it to me."

Moving past them, he pulled an item off a hanger here and one there. Rejected the latter, then turned back to them, and held up a pair of pants. But not just any pants. Masculine, wide-legged and high-waisted, with crisp pleats.

She fingered the grey cotton twill. They looked classy and comfortable, and she would need to be comfortable. She'd be on her feet for hours.

"Oh." Meghan draped the dress over her arm and studied the pants with a critical eye. "With a blouse?"

"A shirt," she said. A thrill of excitement shot through her. "I saw one downstairs that would be perfect." Tailored teal, but affordable. Maybe, just maybe the outfit would bring her luck.

Eric shot her a glance of approval. "Good eye."

Meghan nodded thoughtfully. "With your killer red lipstick."

"Like Hepburn in *The Philadelphia Story*," he said. "You'll make an entrance. Watch out art world, Charley Scott is on the scene." The clipped syllables, like an old Hollywood voiceover narration, echoed to the rafters.

"You had me at Hepburn." She took the pants from Eric with a grin. "You can put that dress back where you found it, Meg."

"Oh, all right."

Ouch. Charley hissed as pain pricked her fingertip. The price tag fluttered to the floor. She lifted her hand and saw a drop of blood, beading the skin.

Almost buried in a pleat of grey fabric, metal gleamed. The point of an open safety pin jutting upward, needle-sharp.

Swift as a flash, Eric grabbed her wrist. Tensing, she jerked away but his grip was strong, and he held tight.

"Don't bleed on the fabric," he warned. Removing a cloth handkerchief from the pocket of his jeans, he dabbed at the wound.

"It's fine, thanks. Though I really hope it isn't a bad sign."

"The shop may be run by a queen" — he grinned — "but there are no wicked witches here." He turned to the laden shelves and chose a velvet ribbon in a rich shade of emerald. Bending, he tied it to Cocoa's collar. She gave his arm an excited lick, right across the VOGUE tattoo. "A gift for the little lady. Because everyone should leave the boutique with something, even those with four legs."

And he just scored himself some return customers.

They paid for their things and thanked Eric for his help. Loaded up with bags, they left the shop, Cocoa pulling ahead.

Outside, the heat was cloying and sticky. Meghan still wore her newsboy cap and looked like an extra from the set of *Peaky Blinders*.

Charley thought longingly of sitting on the dock and dipping her feet in cool lake water. But she had one more item on her list to get. "Before we leave, I want to stop by The Coffee Nook."

"Caffeine?" Meghan perked up. "Yes, please."

"And books. I'm going to buy a copy of *Hamadryads*."

Meghan cast a curious glance at her. "Sci-fi? It's not really your thing, is it?"

No, but it seemed like it might harbor as many inner demons as a hardboiled PI novel.

When she explained why she wanted a copy, Meghan stopped short, dead centre on the sidewalk. "Matt's dad wrote *Hamadryads*?" Her gaze turned ruthless. "Now that's a story I have to have." She drew a breath, her eyes flashing. "A killer outfit for you. Deadly chocolates, and a *nom de plume* exposed. Charley," she said, "life is good."

12:04. THE NEON GREEN FIGURES glowed eerily in the dark.

Charley lay on her side and stared at the alarm clock. A thousand and one thoughts raced through her mind. Death. Fragments of the past. Molten chocolate. A darkened attic, and that slow build of anticipation. Nerves and excitement about the opening of the gallery.

She shifted and rolled onto her back. She bumped against Cocoa, snoring beside her.

Scrubbing a hand over her face, Charley cast another glance at the clock. Ugh. 12:05. It was hopeless.

She had to do something. Hot milk? No thanks. Counting sheep? She tried that an hour ago. Tea, bubble baths.

Actually, the last one wasn't such a bad idea. A bath might be just the thing she needed. Sure, it was the middle of the night but why should that stop her?

Pushing aside the sheets, she slipped out of bed. Tiptoeing across the room, she rummaged in her bag until she found the soothing bath oil she'd brought with her. This was the best idea she'd had in a long time. Grabbing the brand-new copy of *Hamadryads*, she snuck out of the room and down the dark hall.

She shut the bathroom door quietly behind her and flipped on the light. Squinting in the sudden glare, she dimmed it to a dusky glow. Much better. She sighed with pleasure as she looked at the deep curve of the claw foot tub. Oh yes, this was perfect.

Turning the knob, she poured a healthy dose of oil into the running water. The room began to fill with warmth and herbal scents. As the water burbled into the tub, she opened the window wide. Leaning on the sill, she breathed in the night air and looked up at the stars. Too many to count.

The witching hour. That moment when anything could happen, where the mind hovered between sanity and the fantastic. And she was the only one awake to witness it.

The air turned thick and humid as the bathroom filled with steam. She slipped out of her boxers and loose T-shirt. With a twist of the knob and one last slosh, the stream gurgled to a stop.

Tying her hair up and out of the way, she slid into the water. Stillness filled the room. Lavender, sweet orange, and geranium scented the air. She reached for the book on the floor beside her.

A hardback reprint, the cover showed a sepia-hued photograph of a woman turned away. Her arms stretched high above her head, as though prepared to dive. The lettering of the title, like foliage itself, swept in an arc above her clasped hands. A pattern of twisting leaves and branches overlaid her bare back. Her hair was short, cropped at the neck. The rest of the image was a blur of muted tones, a subtle wash of green and gold. The woman stood on the edge, about to jump.

Cracking the spine on the book — God, how she loved that sound — Charley skimmed over the foreword. An erudite introduction by a fellow writer praised the work. The first edition's limited print-run had sold out in months, thanks in part to the original cover — she'd have to look that one up. She skipped on.

Page one. She waited a beat, then dove into the story.

The characters and their actions came to life before her eyes.

In a post-apocalyptic world, the damage to the planet was irreversible. Plagued by epidemics and harsh weather conditions, companies were building elaborate bunkers that only the rich, the elite, could afford. Until a young female engineer started to doubt the integrity of the company she worked for. Like the Hamadryads of Greek mythology, humanity would come to an end with the rainforest. But some people, consumed by greed, saw the opportunity to profit from destruction. Wreak havoc on the world and they could provide the solution, at a price. A controlled ecosystem below ground only the rich could afford. Survival was a privilege, and a costly one at that.

Charley's skin crawled as Liselle crept into the building late at night. Her heart raced as the suspense built. Subtle, but effective. The world between the pages of the book as three-dimensional as though it had been built with bricks and not words. The author's voice, the rhythm of the prose, familiar as an old friend's and irresistible.

It probably wasn't the best story to read before trying to get back to sleep. But she knew Liselle would save the day in the end, and seriously kick ass doing it. Tough, educated, and creative, so far she had overcome every obstacle thrown in her path. And that was the magic of fiction. Anything was possible.

"Borrowed time, nestled in the palm of my hand," she murmured aloud as she read. "Egg-white shell of memories." She leaned her head back against the tub. The water was lukewarm now and cooling fast. With a sigh, she reached for the bookmark to hold her page.

Liquid coursed off her body as she stood. Shivering, she snagged one of the thick towels stacked at the side of the tub. Still half caught up in the story, she pulled the plug and watched the water drain away.

Nick Thorn had a way with words. And wasn't it wonderful that everyone now knew those lines were his?

TWENTY-ONE

IF ONE MORE PERSON CAME into Chocoholic's to talk about *Hamadryads*, Matt would lose it.

He'd been tempted to hide out in the kitchen but, on Mrs. Callahan's day off, that wasn't an option. And with that clear blue sky, the weather forecast not high or humid enough to anchor cottagers to the water, the shop had been busy all morning.

He unpacked the shipment of Molinillo hot chocolate whisks and fought to keep his temper in check. So far, he hadn't snapped at anyone. But if he had to field one more question about that book — Matt slit the tape on the box with a satisfying jerk of the knife.

He reached for the blue stoneware pottery mug on the counter and pulled it closer. On loan from the local potter in exchange for some free promotion, the mug would make for a nice display. One-of-a-kind and durable, that rustic appeal cottagers couldn't get enough of, would help sell the whisks. But all that was just an excuse to keep his hands busy, because they were itching to do some damage.

Ever since his conversation with Jeffrey, it felt like the world had tilted beneath his feet.

He had never craved violence before, but all he could think about now was breaking bone. Drawing blood. Inflicting pain until he'd forced out the truth and his victim begged for mercy.

But Andrew was dead.

The killer had robbed Matt of that chance and tainted the one thing in the world that was perfect. Chocolate.

He tore the plastic off the next whisk.

The bell chimed and a little girl entered the store, clutching a handful of coins. A smattering of freckles beneath the sunburn, cut-off shorts, and a fraying friendship bracelet screamed carefree summer holidays. Focused on the milk chocolate seashells, she headed toward the shelf, flip-flops slapping against the floor. Rattling the coins thoughtfully in her hand, she studied the selection with a frown. The kind of make-or-break concentration devoted to the biggest decisions.

Matt dropped the first whisk into the mug, wood ricocheting off stone. The girl jumped a foot, shot a glance at him over her shoulder. Wide-eyed, she took one look at him and gave a squeak of terror.

Before he could wipe the scowl off his face, or work up a smile, she turned and fled. Hightailing it out of there, fast as possible.

The door clattered shut behind her.

"Great." He sighed and scrubbed a hand over his face. Now he was scaring kids.

A fatal fall on a construction site. That's what the cops had said when they broke the news. An accident. Only that wasn't true. His mom had died — been murdered — because she tried to do the right thing. And Jeffrey kept that information to himself until it was too late.

Forgive and forget? Maybe Jeffrey could, but hell if he would. Anger clamped in his chest, tight as a vice. Not a chance.

The bell chimed as the door opened again, and he scowled. What now?

Meghan stepped into the store like a woman on a mission.

Something told him she wasn't here for the chocolate seashells. Not with that gleam in her eye.

She smiled as she approached the counter, but he knew enough not to trust it.

"Meghan." He nodded, as he set the mug, full of whisks now, beside the cash register.

"Pretty," she commented. She looked around, gaze sliding over prepackaged bags of chocolates, the gleaming display case. "There's probably always lots to do here."

In the shop? He relaxed a bit. "It keeps me busy, yeah."

"I believe it. Which is why I won't hold it against you."

What was that supposed to mean? Wary, he asked, "Hold what against me?"

"We've known each other a while."

"Yeah, we have," he agreed cautiously.

"I'd say we're friends, wouldn't you?"

And there it was. The conversational equivalent of a bear trap, and no way around it. Say no, and you're a jerk. Say yes and you're committing to anything. "Sure," he said finally.

"I gave Chocoholic's some nice promotion, when you opened, ran a feature on the shop in the paper. And it didn't cost you a thing."

She had him there. Snapped the jaws of the trap shut in one neat move. Though why she came here to bring it up now, he had no idea. "You did." To be safe, he added, "And I appreciated it."

She nodded, fingered one of the whisks. "Imagine my surprise when I saw the display in The Coffee Nook."

So that's what this was about. He'd been expecting it, but not this soon. Not today, not with everything else. "Listen Meghan —"

She held up a hand, cut him off. "Your dad wrote a book. An

important book. And it's just been revealed that he was the author. Don't you think it might have been nice to give me a heads-up? As the editor of the *Oakcrest Courier*."

He hadn't even thought of it. Probably should have. "It really wasn't —"

"I only found out about it when Charley bought a copy."

"She bought a copy?" Panic simmered.

"This is big news, Matt," she continued, relentless. "Huge. The kind of news that could put this town on the map."

"Oakcrest is already on the map," he said dryly. "That's how the tourists find us."

Meghan stalked around the counter, and he backed up in defense. She drilled a finger into his chest. "A tip, that's all. Is that too much to ask?" She punctuated it with another jab.

"Hey!" It felt like she'd bored a hole straight through his ribs. He rubbed the spot. "I think you hit an organ."

"The heart, I hope." Her eyes flashed fire, reminding him of Charley. Seemed both sisters had a hell of a temper. "One measly text message and I could have run with it. Your dad lived here most of his life, and the local paper had nothing. Not a single word. How do you think that makes the *Oakcrest Courier* look?"

No right way to answer that one either.

She stood all but toe to toe with him. He looked down at the top of her red hair. Although she was taller than Charley, it still felt like being told off by a tough pixie. With a blood-stained dagger tucked up her sleeve. "Um —"

"An interview."

"What?" He tried to keep up. Any other day he could have handled this confrontation better. Maybe even saved his ass. But today, the quick-fire exchange was messing with his head.

"I want an interview." She hoisted her bag higher on her shoulder. The tote looked heavy. It wouldn't surprise him if it turned out to be filled with all the town's secrets.

"I'd love to help you with that, Meghan." He fought to keep his patience. "But there's one minor detail. The man you want to talk to is dead." She'd run the obit herself.

She eyed him, sizing him up. "From what I can see, you're alive and kicking. And full of information."

Jesus. She made him sound like a human vending machine. He put the counter between them. "No."

"You owe me." She stalked after him.

"Free chocolates, sure. You like the dark chocolate orange slices, right?" He took a box off the shelf — the closest thing he had to a peace offering — and set it on the counter, slid it toward her. "Take them. But I'm not doing an interview." Place some tape recorder in front of him and grill him about his childhood, about his dad? No way.

She ignored the chocolate. "It'll only take half an hour — maybe forty-five minutes, tops."

He'd always figured selling his soul would take a little longer than the average Netflix episode. His mistake, apparently. "Hounded by the press," he muttered beneath his breath.

"Just one determined journalist," she shot back.

Pain in the backside, was what she was. He shook his head. "It's not happening. You're wasting your time."

She shrugged, like she knew that's what he'd say. Expected it, even. "Your dad was a dark horse, and the word is out." Not cruel. Just honest. "I'm not the only one who's going to ask questions."

It didn't help that she was right.

At wits' end, he gritted his teeth. "And everyone will get the same answer."

"Until you crack."

His vision turned red at the edges. "What's that supposed to mean?"

"Just a warning. You will crack. Everyone does. And I'll be there when you do. I always get my story." The smile she gave him was sweet as caramelized sugar. She picked up the box of chocolate orange slices. "I think I will take these, thank you."

"Help yourself." Anything to have his peace and quiet again. Knowing he sounded sulky and annoyed with himself about it, he crossed his arms.

"By the way —" Meghan paused on her way to the door. "— what's with the box of books outside the shop?"

"Belated spring cleaning." How many were left? Putting them on the sidewalk was the fastest way he could think of to get rid of the books in his dad's office. He'd dumped some in an old box, scrawled *FREE* on the cardboard with a fat black marker and left them there. His dad would hate it. Hopefully, those books would be gone by the end of the day. He didn't intend to cart that box home with him again. "Take whatever you want. There are text-books, novels. Actually, there's some that Charley might like." He should have thought of that sooner, set aside some for her, and kicked himself for missing that chance.

"Good idea. I'll take a look." She gave him a cheery wave as she went out, leaving him feeling like he'd played right into her hand. The glass rattled in the door.

Matt scowled at the chocolates. He was surprised they didn't melt before his eyes.

He had two options. Let the anger, the bitterness, destroy him from the inside out. Or focus on the good.

Bracing his hands on the counter, he took a steadying breath, filling his lungs with the scent of cocoa butter, spices, and fruit.

The past had shifted ground on him, but the present was rock solid. And that was all that mattered.

TWENTY-TWO

CHARLEY NEEDED TO KNOW MORE about Andrew. What had Alex said? Find out how a person lived, and you'll find out how they died.

Lost in thought, she strolled toward the Oakcrest Mews. Leash slack, Cocoa wandered ahead, crossing from one side to the other — although Charley made wide circles around any flower beds.

Soon racks of clothing would be wheeled out onto the sidewalk in front of The Blast From The Past Boutique, and Wicks 'N' More would set up their chalkboard sign. But for now, most of the storefronts were still shuttered. In the window of the Oakcrest Pantry, early morning sunlight shone off a colourful display of London Pottery teapots.

Nose down, Cocoa roamed over the wooden deck as they walked toward the gallery.

Thomas's motive was connected to Clarkston Engineering. But David's motive was personal. Had he fallen in love with Kayla? If Eric was right about the chemistry between them, maybe David murdered Andrew to protect her. Or eliminate the competition.

Out of the corner of her eye, Charley caught something dark streaking toward her, arcing through the air. Straight at her head.

She sidestepped and the breeze brushed her cheek as the object hurtled past. Cocoa bolted, straining on the leash.

Thwack! Something landed on the deck in front of them.

"Hey!" Furious, she whirled around.

There was no one in sight.

A book lay on the ground. Gilded edges sparking in the sunlight.

Cocoa pulled toward the hardcover book and sniffed at the corners. On the cover, pastel blossoms contrasted with a black background.

Charley bent to pick the book up. Twisting branches, delicate as lace, pressed against her fingertips. The design was raised, embossed onto the cover. The pages creamy, the binding stitched.

Wuthering Heights. She turned it over in her hand and felt a dent where the spine hit the ground.

Cocoa looked up at her, as though asking, what next? Good question.

Straightening, she scanned the area.

The book had come — no, been hurled — from her right. From the gazebo. The sun reached fingers beneath the roof but hadn't gotten hold of the bench yet. And the planter of day lilies blocked most of her view.

"Come on." She'd like to meet the person who threw books at people. By one of the Brontë sisters, no less. She strode toward the shadows, Cocoa prancing at her heels.

"Fixating on the past."

The words, filled with disgust, had her step faltering. But Cocoa strained forward, tail wagging. It took a second longer for Charley to see the figure on the bench.

She should have guessed.

She let Cocoa take the lead, the dog's tail whipping in recognition.

The woman raised her head as they entered the gazebo. The

straw brim of her fedora cast crosshatched shadows over sharp cheekbones, the curve of a smile. Her binoculars lay beside her, along with a small plastic bag of chocolates. Cocoa nosed forward to be petted.

"You found my book." Sarah held out one hand, fine-boned but far from delicate, palm up.

"It found us," she replied dryly, as she passed it over.

Sarah looked startled, then laughed. "Oh no. Before stores open, the Mews are normally deserted. And it's quite safe for me to throw books." She winked, a green glint of conspiracy.

"Next time, I'll be more prepared." She'd know to duck, anyway.

"It's best to expect the unexpected." Sarah scratched Cocoa behind the ear one more time, then leaned back. "Have you never been tempted to throw a book?"

She sat down on the bench beside her. Cocoa sprawled at their feet and rolled onto her back, in case anyone felt like rubbing her belly. "Not one that looked like that."

"The flowers of a briar bush." Sarah stroked her palm over the design. "But it's the content that matters. Though, I suppose, you'd disagree." She nodded at the gallery.

"Cover design, that's a separate form of art."

"To writing, you mean? And yet, the cover wouldn't exist without the story." Sarah let the book fall open. The pages riffled, the text a blur of black on white. "Emily's words are branded on my memory, the way Catherine's were on Heathcliff's."

Maybe that explained why no bookmark had fallen out, why there was no slip of paper marking her place. "How many times have you read it?" Her own paperback of *Wuthering Heights* was tattered and well-loved. And stored on her bookshelf in Toronto.

"Too many to count." She leaned closer and lowered her voice. "But I haven't managed to unlock it's secrets yet."

Charley thought of *Hamadryads*. "I suppose every story holds secrets."

Sarah raised a brow. "This one" — she tapped the cover — "raises more questions than answers. Is Heathcliff a romantic character or evil? Villains go unpunished. There are unresolved puzzles, unexplained dreams and unquiet ghosts. Love is corrupted by a lust for revenge, and revenge leads to downfall. There is no happy ever after, but still the story withstands the test of time. Why?" she demanded.

"Passion." She didn't need to think about that one.

Sarah laughed. "Oh, there is that." She shot a keen glance at her. "Did you visit Chocoholic's?"

Amused at the transition, she replied, "I did."

"And?" It was imperious.

She smiled. "The chocolate is wonderful."

"Hmm." Impatience radiated off of her.

How many matchmaking schemes did Sarah have in the works? She watched and assessed. Manipulated, if need be. "Can I ask you something?" The question burned on the tip of her tongue.

"You can." She folded her hands on the cover of the book. Her skin was paper thin, but those laced fingers were strong and capable and unadorned by rings. "I might even answer it."

The question had to be worthy. Get it wrong, and she might not get the chance to ask another. And Sarah knew things, that much she could tell. Best to acknowledge that and play on it. "What did you think of Andrew?"

"Ah." She glanced down at the book on her lap. "Another love story built on loss and secrets." A moment passed and Charley thought she wouldn't continue, that she'd somehow gotten it wrong, after all. But then Sarah drew a breath and said, "I doubt that Kayla believes her soul is buried in Andrew's grave."

A shiver ran down her spine. "Why do you say that?"

Picking up on the change in her tone, Cocoa rolled over and shook, tags jangling on her collar.

Sarah sighed. "Do you know what mistake Catherine made?"

The moment of revelation. Her heart raced. "Tell me."

"She pictured Edgar as a hero of romance, and then was disillusioned." Sarah's eyes met hers, her glance quick and sharp.

"Are you saying the same thing happened to Kayla?" She thought of the last email she'd gotten, before those years of silence. *Let's just say, I'm starting the next twenty-six years of my life with a bang! I've never met anyone so hardworking, caring, and generous.*

Sarah looked at the picturesque street spread before them. But instead of enjoying the yellow awnings and the promise that life was better on the lake, it seemed like she saw and counted the flaws that needed fixing. "Catherine resorted to self-destruction, breaking their hearts by breaking her own. I think Kayla's heart was broken, too."

"By Andrew?"

"On many occasions."

Pieced together at the fault line. At what point did self-destruction become a way out? "And you think she broke someone else's heart?" Did she mean David's?

Instead of answering, Sarah picked up the bag of chocolates. Charley spotted the by now familiar label. Chocoholic's. The plastic rustled and Cocoa stood, attention all on her.

Sarah took her time, choosing one. She finally plucked out a round chocolate, milky brown and shiny. She held it up, trapped between thumb and finger, and smiled. "It's a vice. But what would life be, without our wrongdoings to guide us?" The chocolate disappeared with a lick of her fingers.

Charley grinned. "Not half as much fun, I guess."

"Although there is something to be said for the suspense created by anticipation." The bag of chocolate rested on the gold-lettered title. "I do wish that Catherine and Heathcliff's story didn't depend on separation. That's why I threw the book," she confided. "Of course, it's economically inevitable that Catherine marries Edgar, not Heathcliff." A darker inflection crept into her voice.

"He had nothing to offer her." Was she implying Kayla married Andrew for his money?

"Only a love that defies death. Sadly, Heathcliff's fixation on the past, his determination for revenge, is his downfall."

And revenge could be a powerful motive. So could betrayal. "When we first met, you called Andrew a traitor."

"Did I?" she asked, her tone noncommittal.

"What did you mean by that?" She looked at the woman's profile, Merciless and intelligent.

"Well, now. If there's one thing we can learn from Emily, it's that it's up to the observer to provide the narrative framework." She let that linger. "To make sense of it all."

The challenge was clear. "To uncover the secrets?" She planned to.

"Exactly." Sarah leaned back. "I've always enjoyed fixing a story. Often, it's simply a matter of removing elements that don't serve the greater good. All it takes is courage, really." She tilted the bag of chocolates, shaking one the colour of caramel to the surface. "The courage to kill your darlings." The words echoed in the gazebo, ominous and ruthless and heavy with meaning.

Was that what Sarah had done? Taken the plot into her own hands and removed the element that didn't serve the greater good? "Without Andrew, Kayla's story has the hope of a happy ending." And maybe she had helped it along.

"I'm looking forward to the opening of the gallery," Sarah said. "I'm so glad you and Kayla are pursuing your dreams."

LATE AFTERNOON SUNLIGHT STREAMED THROUGH the bay window on the second floor of the gallery. Without music playing, without the thud of a hammer driving a nail into drywall, and empty of other people, the space was quiet. Hushed.

No ghosts. No squirrels. Fingers crossed they'd actually managed to seal all the entry points in the attic.

Charley cast a glance at Cocoa, who stood beside her, tail wagging. Soon people would walk through those rooms, looking at their art. At her paintings.

Not much to do now. Together, they'd pulled through a lot of the work. They'd have to check through once more before the opening, to make sure they hadn't missed anything. Add the title cards, discreet beneath each piece. But, for today, they were finished. Kayla had left already, and so had Thomas. She'd lingered, to have this moment to herself.

On a heart-skip, she breathed in the faint Linseed Oil–scent of paint and fixative and turned in a slow circle. Taking in the colours, the vibrance, brighter even than the light pouring in through the window. The abstract, painted instruments. A saxophone. A trumpet. Stark, frigid landscapes. The soles of her sneakers squeaked on the hardwood floor as she turned. Water-washed rocks and oval faces. A chin raised with courage and defiance. Each brushstroke of that woman's determined expression a memory she still felt in her fingers.

The room glowed. It looked like a real gallery. Charley let that thought soak in.

God, it felt good.

Except, she was starving. The slapdash ham and cheese sandwich she'd had for lunch — eaten between hanging paintings — was a long time ago.

"Okay, Cocoa, time to head —" She caught herself. She'd almost said home. "— to the cottage."

She went down the creaking steps. Clipped the dog's leash on and grabbed her tote bag off the bench. Checked for her keys. Right at the bottom of the bag.

But a shadow on the floor had her fingers tightening on the keyring. A rectangle, charcoal-dark on whitewashed wood and wrong.

Maybe she was trying too hard to make everything perfect, was too in tune to the tiniest details, that even a shadow jarred. But what cast it?

She glanced up and spotted it.

The door. Dark against the sun, something covered the centre of one panel, where there should have been nothing but glass.

Cocoa trotted beside her as she walked closer. The glare out of her eyes, Charley saw the white cardstock.

The back of a postcard. Taped to the glass.

Letters pasted on in a diagonal line, spaced wide — black and white newsprint, carefully cut out, the edges neat. All capital letters, probably taken from headlines. M-Y-O-B. Like an acrostic poem, only at an angle. Printed at the bottom of the card was the name of an artist. Peter Claesz.

An art print?

The picture on the postcard faced out and could be seen from the street. Had Kayla or Thomas put it there?

She pushed the door open and stepped outside for a better look, Cocoa right behind her.

There on the glass, at eye level, was a skull. Bone white against a black background.

The keys slipped from her fingers, hit the pavement.

It was a postcard replica of a painting. A Dutch *vanitas* still life.

The skull rested on a book with yellowed pages. An overturned wine glass glinted, struck by light from an unseen window. In the foreground, an ink-stained quill pen lay forgotten. In the background, smoke rose from a burned-out match, tip still glowing red.

A collection of objects symbolizing the inevitability of death.

And it was — she brushed her fingers over a corner of the image, over cold, smooth glass — taped to the inside of the door.

Someone had been in the gallery. After Kayla left, otherwise she would have noticed the postcard and said something. Whoever put it there had waited just long enough. They wanted her to see it. To react to it.

Her hand tightened on the leash. Cocoa's body leaned warm against her leg. Focus on that. She took a deep breath. Think.

The postcard was a threat. That much was obvious. But why? Cocoa bumped her knee with her shoulder.

A reflection shifted in the glass door panel. Growing larger, it took on human shape.

"Still Life with a Skull and a Writing Quill," a male voice said behind her.

Charley whirled, heart hammering against her ribs.

The man smiled. "From the Dutch Golden Age. It's a wonderful work of art." He studied the postcard with the intensity of someone who viewed the world with equal parts wide-eyed curiosity and boyish enthusiasm.

"Yes, it is."

Maybe a few years older than her, he had the lanky build of a swimmer and a tan that implied he did most of his swimming in the lake. Probably at first dawn in frigid waters. He was hand-some in a wholesome sort of way. But she knew enough not to let appearances fool her.

He recognized the painting. Knew the title, the artist. Not many would.

With a tug on the leash, Cocoa shot forward and investigated the hem of his jeans. He bent down, holding out his hand for her to sniff.

"Hey, Mr. Nadeau!"

At the bright shout, he turned and waved to the three boys, leaving the kitchen shop with ice cream cones in their hands. The kid who'd shouted the greeting got jostled by the others. Although he almost fumbled his ice cream, he shrugged it off with a laugh and kept his cool.

So, this was David Nadeau. Speak of the devil. Had his clean-cut, casual intelligence caught Kayla's eye?

"I thought you might be gone already." His expression alive with mischief, he said, "I have to admit, I was hoping to catch a peek through the window."

A few people had tried that already, but the angles weren't right. They might see the corners of canvases, the side of the partition wall, but not much else. "We open on Friday. Come back then and you'll be able to explore the entire gallery."

"I'm planning on it." He hesitated.

Charley bent to pick up her keys. "Kayla left earlier, if you're looking for her." If she hadn't been watching for it, she might have missed that flicker of surprise, that shift of awareness.

"Actually, I was —" He rubbed a hand over the back of his neck, looking uncomfortable. "Look, you might not know this about teachers, but we love to give advice. A hazard of the job."

Would she want to hear it? "If you managed to catch a glimpse through the window, I can tell you right now, I'm not rearranging those paintings."

"I guess you could call it more of a warning, actually."

About the gallery? "That sounds ominous."

"Be careful around Thomas."

Whatever she'd expected, it wasn't that. "Why?" She thought of the recipe she'd handed over to Alex. The air crackled with tension.

Cocoa sat on her feet and stared at David.

"Years of playground duty." He made it sound like a war zone.

"Excuse me?"

"Experience. Teachers develop a sixth sense for this sort of thing."

"Murder?" she asked wryly. Though her heart was pounding.

He smiled. "For preventing it. It's none of my business, really, except Thomas's granddaughter is in my class. His arrival in town has caused stress at home."

The leather leash dug into the palm of her hand, and she loosened her grip a little. "In what way?"

He shrugged. "Let's just say, when Thomas moved to Oakcrest, his family didn't welcome him back with open arms."

Sarah had implied there was tension between father and daughter. A history of it. "What does that have to do with Andrew?"

"Finishing his house has become all-consuming for Thomas. Andrew made achieving that goal ... difficult."

She'd figured that out already. "You think Thomas killed him?"

He shrugged. Feet apart, hands in his pockets. A crossbeam of sun bleached his blue-gray eyes to steel. "Sometimes feeling unimportant, feeling left out, can lead to defensive, threatening behavior. And anxiety can turn into violence."

"You think he's dangerous." Cryptic threats and poison. Whoever was behind it all preferred solving problems from a distance. No clues pointed to violence.

"Best to avoid confrontation, if you can. That's what I always tell the kids." David nodded at the door behind her. "Course, I'm sure Alex is looking into it and the case will be solved soon. Until then" — he squinted up at the angles of the roof — "I'd concentrate on the gallery."

And leave the questions to Alex? Yeah, right. "Thanks for the advice." And the thinly veiled threat.

He smiled. "Anytime. Say hi to Alex for me." Whistling a bright tune, he strolled away, the clear notes echoing off the wooden deck.

Cocoa watched him leave.

Had David put the postcard there, then followed it up with a warning? But why? Had he wanted to witness her reaction? The thought chilled her.

Yanking the gallery door open, she peeled the tape off the glass. The four strips, one on each corner, left a sticky residue behind. Looking at the marks on the glass, a fresh surge of anger rose within her.

The postcard was sneaky, creative. Subtle. And a mistake.

Using a *vanitas* painting to reference death and mortality showed a knowledge of art history. David had it, that much was obvious, but so did Thomas.

Holding the postcard by one corner, she slipped it into her purse. She locked the door and double-checked that the latch caught.

Most people wouldn't risk planting the postcard here in broad daylight. But no one would question Thomas.

The postcard showed fear. Desperation. Something she'd done or said had triggered it. Which meant that, whatever Alex might think, she was on the right track.

But whoever left the postcard here had underestimated her.

It would take more than a replica of a still life painting to scare her.

TWENTY-THREE

FOCUS ON THE GOOD, THAT'S what Matt planned to do. And he'd go after it.

Soon as he worked up the courage.

He rinsed his plate and set it in the dish rack to dry. Then took one last look around the spotless kitchen. Not that the quick dinner of thick-sliced white bread and melted Gruyère cheese had made much of a mess in the first place.

Function hadn't been at the top of his dad's mind when he'd done the kitchen's layout. It was easier to nuke a meal than to cook in it. The kitchen needed more open shelving, preferably in sturdy, rough-cut wood. All those closed cabinet doors were just another obstacle to slow the chef down.

For his own sanity, Matt had cut down on the clutter, added labels, and lidded storage containers. Drawer dividers for the cutlery, pull-outs for spices. There wasn't much he could do about the microwave-centred design or the shaker cabinets besides a full reno, but he could make sure things were in the exact same place every time he reached for them.

The cut-out in the wall over the sink though, that was the one thing his dad got right. The view onto the living room and the widescreen TV meant he could wash the dishes without missing a grand slam.

Time to go. It was now or never. Never mind that his heart was pounding, and his hands felt clammy.

Get a grip. Charley had been staying late at the gallery. She might not even be home yet. This could all be wasted effort.

Dropping by unannounced was a risk. But a man bearing chocolate was hard to turn away — at least, that's what he was counting on. The bar of strawberry and saffron white chocolate would be his ticket over the threshold.

A grin spread over his face as he grabbed the chocolate from the counter and headed to the entrance. Shoes. He'd need shoes. And car keys.

Just a smile from her would make the trip worthwhile.

Holy hell. He paused in the process of yanking on his sneaker and froze. What did it mean when a smile from one woman could make your day? He took a breath, sucked it in through his teeth. Nothing good, that's what.

"You like her, that's all," he muttered, tugging the shoe on. This was no big deal. He tied the laces with a sharp tug. "It's physical attraction." That moment in the attic had sparked a hunger. And a healthy craving was meant to be indulged. So what if he also wanted to impress her, maybe even sweep her off her feet? It was normal. "Happens to everyone," he said out loud as he straightened.

She'd gotten into his head. Just because he thought about Charley — a lot — didn't make this any different. Eventually, the heat between them would fade to a slow simmer, then cool off entirely. The way these things always did.

He jiggled the keys in his hand as he yanked the front door open. And came face to face with Jeffrey.

Surprised, Matt fell back a step. "Hey."

"On your way out?" Jeffrey had his hands shoved in the pockets of his Levis. He wore an old and faded sweatshirt, a sign he'd come straight from the workshop.

"Yeah." He took in the grey stubble of beard, the tired eyes and held the door open. "But I can change my plans."

Seeing Charley had been a spontaneous idea anyway. And it was probably better if he didn't follow through with it.

"You sure about that?"

When Jeffrey stopped by, he normally had a good reason, and Matt wasn't about to turn him away. "I wouldn't say it if I wasn't. Want a coffee?"

"Just a pop, thanks."

Matt led the way to the kitchen. He set the bar of chocolate on the counter, to the side but not out of sight.

Jeffrey flicked a curious glance at it but didn't say anything.

Cracking the tab on a can of ginger ale, Matt wondered briefly if there should be whiskey in it. He poured the drink in glasses with a snap of ice cubes but held off on the shot of Jameson's, for now. "Been busy today?"

Jeffrey took a seat at the green Formica table. "You could say that. I've been wrapping my head around a new project. Thomas's house."

"Really?" The project was big. Bigger than most of the contracts Jeffrey had taken on in the past few years. "That's good."

He folded his hands, spent a second frowning at his thumbs. "I wanted to apologize to you."

About the photographs? Matt slid the glass over the table to him. "For what?"

"The way I broke the news to you."

So that's what this was about. He took the chair across from Jeffrey, the chrome frame cool against his back, and shrugged. "I get it."

Jeffrey swirled his glass, so the ice rattled, then set it down. Levelled his gaze at him. "You didn't see me at my best the other night, and I'm sorry for that."

"You're not allowed weakness?"

"Don't get smart with me." The grin almost reached his eyes. "I have no weaknesses."

Bulletproof and invincible? He'd believed that at one point. "Even Superman had kryptonite," he pointed out.

"God, that takes me back." Jeffrey blinked and shook his head. "Andrew used to call his allergy that, when we worked together. Kryptonite."

And cast himself in the role of hero. Anger twisted, low in his gut. "I keep forgetting you were friends." It was hard to imagine.

"That's ancient history now. I came to talk about the past, but not my own." Jeffrey shifted, pulled something out of his back pocket. He laid it on the table. A square of folded paper, heavy, the finish glossy. A photograph? He smoothed it flat, turned it to face Matt. "I found this the other day, thought you might like to have it."

Curious, he reached for it. It only took one glance for recognition to hit, a jolt straight to the heart. A birthday, long ago. How old had he been there? Just a kid.

Chocolate cake in front of him, heavy on the icing, an elephant design and blazing candles. At their old dining room table with the rustic, oak planked top and enough chairs to seat six. A face-splitting grin showed the gaps in his teeth. His mom leaned over him from behind, arms wrapped around his shoulders. Her smile just as wide as his. The scent of cinnamon hovered at the back of his mind, along with the sweeter, burnt sugar undertone of cedar resin.

Jeffrey leaned back in his chair. "Biggest birthday bash for a seven-year-old I've ever seen. Your mom went all out."

"Looks like." He cleared a throat that suddenly felt tight. "That's some cake."

"She came up with the design, got me to bake it by calling in a favour. I had strict instructions, too. She knew exactly what she wanted."

"An elephant?" He raised a brow.

"Elephants" — Jeffrey tapped a finger on the edge of the photo — "don't forget. Your mom was big on making memories last."

"That she was." And she'd had less than four decades to enjoy them.

"You were barely seven and already a hassle and a half," he said it with a wry grin. "Asking questions all the time. Grilling me about how I made the icing, the elephant. Made from marzipan. I told your mom you wouldn't like it, but she was set on it."

"And you were wrong." His chocolate marzipan truffles were as close as he could get to reliving that first taste of almond paste, honey, and sugar. And it was never quite the same as that first bite.

"Yup." Jeffrey chuckled. "You went through three slices of cake that night."

"I remember the sugar high." Buzzing through his veins, sending his heart racing so he couldn't sit still.

"It left an impression on all of us." Jeffrey raised his glass, gaze fixed on him. "Who do you think killed Andrew?"

From cake to murder. It took him a whole second to catch up. "The obvious answer is Kayla, isn't it?"

"I knew there were problems. I wish she'd gone to someone with them. Matt —" Jeffrey broke off, took a sip. The liquid trembled in the glass, as he set the drink back down, his hand not quite steady. "There's another reason why I'm here."

He'd already figured that one out. "Yeah?"

"If I had another option, I wouldn't come to you with this."

An uneasy feeling washed over him. "Okay." Jeffrey didn't normally beat around the bush like this.

He gave a short laugh and scraped a hand over his jaw. "This is harder than I thought."

Asking for a favour? That had never come easy for him. For either of them. "Better get it over with fast then."

"Right." He frowned at his glass. Silence fell.

On edge, Matt broke it first. "Thanks for this." He nodded at the photo. Hard to believe Jeffrey managed to dig it up. "Dad never talked about the past much, not after. Never talked much at all, actually. He saved all his words for the page."

More at ease, Jeffrey smiled. "As it turns out, with great success."

The shard of bitterness buried beneath his skin ached, a dull pain he'd grown used to. But that didn't mean he was ready to rave about his father's hidden talent. "I've been clearing out Dad's office. You should have a look at his books while you're here, take the ones you want."

Jeffrey seemed to consider it. "He still have that book on residential framing?"

"That and more. I've only managed to get rid of a few so far. There are some boxes in the room. You can load one up." Or two.

"Might as well take a look at them now then." Chair legs scraped over the floor as he stood.

Matt narrowed his eyes at him. "Dodging the topic?"

"I'm getting to it," he growled. "Patience is a virtue."

"So is openness."

"And, right now, I could use some understanding. Come on. Show me those books." Jeffrey clapped him on the shoulder. Solid enough for Matt to figure it was a good thing he hadn't just taken another sip. He'd be choking on his ginger ale.

Matt led the way. This time, the door didn't creak and the office smelled of citrus cleanser. "Some books are already in the boxes; the rest are on the shelves. You'll have to do some digging. Or leave it up to fate and take the lot." Might as well plant the seed.

Jeffrey moved into the room slowly. He rested his hand on the back of the armchair, same way Matt had. "Jesus, it's like time stood still in here."

And he was setting it back in motion, one cog at a time. "It's cleaner." He leaned back against the desk.

Jeffrey stopped in front of the bookcase, scanned the titles. Books tilted in the shelves, no longer packed in tightly as the numbers dwindled.

All he had to do was wait for Jeffrey to bring up the topic again. And, if he didn't, he'd pry.

From the other room, the phone rang.

Jeffrey shot him a glance over his shoulder. "You gonna get that?"

"Wasn't planning to."

"You don't answer your phone anymore?" He might as well be saying, *you gonna operate that saw without eye protection?* The tone was the same.

"They can leave a message." At the look Jeffrey gave him, Matt swore under his breath, pushed off the desk. "I'll be right back." Shaking his head, he went to track down the phone.

Where the hell had he left it? Kitchen table? No. Living room. The couch.

He leaned over the back and there it was, on the seat cushion. He grabbed the phone.

Meghan. He answered on the last ring. "Yeah?" Couldn't keep the irritation out of his voice.

"Nice way to answer the phone, Matt. I have a proposition for you."

He dropped onto the couch, a headache building behind his

eyes. He pinched the bridge of his nose. "The answer is still no."

"Hear me out. How about an interview via email? You veto the questions, answer the ones you like."

"No."

The sigh crackled in his ear. "You're being stubborn," she said.

He tipped his head back against the upholstery, looked up at the ceiling. "Meghan, I like you. I really like your sister. But you're starting to become very annoying."

"Let's call it pesky. It sounds nicer."

It might as well have been a compliment. "The pesky reporter?"

She laughed. "Plosives, always a hit."

He remembered enough from English class to know she was talking about consonants, not dynamite. Though either one would work in this scenario. "I'm ending the call now, Meghan."

"I'll get back to you with another idea," she said cheerfully.

He shook his head, torn between frustration and amusement. "Bye." He pressed the end call button.

It's no wonder the *Oakcrest Courier* was known for its content. Meghan simply didn't back down until people bared their souls and agreed to publication.

But not him.

He returned to the office to find Jeffrey had filled a box. The remaining books narrowed down to three shelves.

"You sure you want to get rid of all these?" Jeffrey looked at him like the books should hold some kind of meaning. Some sentimental value. Maybe they should.

He shrugged. "I don't need them." Or want them.

"Then I'll make sure to put them to good use." Jeffrey folded the flaps down with a scrape of cardboard, sealing the box shut.

One less problem for him to worry about. "So." He sat on the edge of the desk, waited until Jeffrey turned, made eye contact. Held it. "Out with it. What were you trying to say before?"

"Ask." Jeffrey dragged a hand through his hair and shrugged with a sheepish grin. "The muffin recipe. I've tried to replicate it, but it's not the same."

"You want a recipe?" He blinked. All that lead up, for this? He'd been thinking the favour was along the lines of a kidney donation or unpaid labour.

"It's never easy admitting defeat, but this one's got me stumped."

Maybe. More likely, he'd decided to keep whatever was on his mind to himself, for now. "Sure. I can give it to you." He looked at Jeffrey, but he couldn't see past the open grin.

TWENTY-FOUR

"M-Y-O-B?" ALEX LOOKED AT THE postcard, now sealed inside a zip-lock bag. Preserved for prints. "What's that supposed to mean?"

"I'm guessing Mind Your Own Business," Charley said.

Perched on the edge of the couch, Alex studied the postcard on the coffee table like he was ready to jump at the first sign of a fresh lead.

The sliding door in the living room stood wide open to catch the breeze off the lake, tinged with a hint of burnt sugar and wood smoke from some distant bonfire. The water mirrored the thick brushstrokes of colour that deepened the evening sky to shades of violet and red.

Curled up in the armchair, sketchbook on her lap, Charley moved her pencil over the paper, but somewhere along the line her motif had changed. From the pines silhouetted against the sunset to a clear plastic bag and cracked chocolate. The soft texture of the filling. The image she couldn't get out of her head, no matter how many lines she drew on the page or how photorealistic the sketch became.

She said, "A couple of kids were hanging out on the street, but they didn't see anyone come or go from the gallery except me and David."

On the TV, the talk show host wrapped up his monologue to

canned laughter, but Alex's attention was fixed on the clue in front of him. "Kayla could have put it there, when she left."

The tip of her pencil hovered over the brittle shard of broken chocolate. Of course, that would be his first thought. "Or Thomas, while I was working upstairs."

"I can do an iodine test for fingerprints at the station tomorrow, but I doubt there'll be any." His focus was trained on the title, the details typed discretely on the bottom left corner. "Doesn't look like it came from a museum shop or an art gallery. They normally include their information on the back, don't they?"

"And the dates of the exhibit." But the few lines of text only revealed the name of the artist, the dimensions of the painting, and the medium. Oil on wood. "My guess is it's from an art-themed postcard set. You can order them online, and the selection is huge."

He flipped the postcard over, to the side with the painting. The arranged objects, reflections, and shadows rendered in monochromatic tones of brown and black and grey. "The skull is resting on a book. The *cover* of a book."

"I noticed that." Was it a threat to the gallery? Her stomach seized into knots at the thought.

"Art and books. Symbols of death." He rubbed a hand over his eyes. "Jesus, Charley."

At the worry in his voice, Cocoa raised her head and eyed them from where she lay on the threadbare rug.

But there was one good thing about all of this. "At least the postcard proves that Kayla didn't kill Andrew."

"How do you figure that?" Alex asked.

Did she really have to spell it out for him? She put her pencil down, trying hard to keep her patience. "If she killed him, she'd be threatening you, not me."

"Definitely not by way of a Dutch still life. There's a problem with your logic." He leaned forward, elbows resting on his knees, and levelled his gaze at her. "Misdirection. Criminals lie, throw suspicion on others. This postcard" — he held it up — "is probably a decoy. To get us to look at someone else."

"Which is exactly what you should do." Annoyed, she closed her sketchbook with a snap. "There's a reason why David felt the need to warn me about —"

"Putting yourself in danger." He leaned back. "That's all this" — he gestured at the postcard — "proves. It's a threat, to you or the gallery."

Because sitting in the armchair made her feel like a kid getting a lecture, she stood. Cocoa raised her head, then settled back down when she decided Charley wasn't going anywhere.

She said, "Which means we're getting close to the truth."

He didn't call her naïve. He didn't have to. It was written all over his face, in the clenched jaw and the muscle twitching in his cheek. "I can tell you one thing. This will escalate. You piss someone off enough to threaten you, you can bet they won't stop at hanging a pretty picture on your door."

She should — what? Let it go? No way. The force of Grandma Reilly's gaze, those watercolour green irises, prickled between her shoulder blades. She didn't need to search her memory for the voice already ghosting through her mind. *Never back down, kiddo. Life's too short to waste on what ifs.*

Charley stood by the open door and took a breath of lake-fresh air. "So, we catch them first."

"There is no 'we.'" This time, he didn't try to hide his exasperation. "I've got a search warrant for Kayla's house in the works. Her lawyers had us jumping through bureaucratic hoops, but I'm betting that we'll find evidence there that will help us crack this case. Until then, stay out of my investigation."

"But —"

Meghan strolled into the living room, a bowl of ice cream — three scoops full — in one hand and a cellphone in the other.

Scenting food, Cocoa whipped her head around to eye the dish.

Meghan headed toward the other end of the couch, then paused as she looked at them more closely. She narrowed her eyes at Alex. "You look frustrated. And you" — she turned to Charley — "look stubborn. What's going on?"

Charley dropped back into the armchair, settling into the familiar dip worn into the seat cushion. "Alex is hogging the TV remote." She shot him a warning glance.

The postcard in the gallery window was exactly the type of story to catch Meghan's interest. And her investigative techniques weren't always subtle.

He raised his brows but got the hint. He slid the postcard under the latest *Food & Drink* magazine, out of sight. "Not everyone wants to spend their evening watching some black-and-white flick."

"Classics." She reached for her sketchbook and watched Meghan swirl her spoon through an already melting scoop. "There's ice cream?"

"There was," she said.

The flavor looked like Kawartha Dairy's Pralines and Cream. A summer staple and she hadn't even had any yet. "You're just going to eat it in front of us?"

"Yes, I am."

Alex stretched, arms over his head, circling his wrists. "That's love for you."

Cocoa rested her chin on Meghan's knee and stared up at the bowl, as if trying to burn a hole through the bottom. Reaching around her, Meghan put the phone on the coffee table. Charley caught a glimpse of the plastic case. Of honey and gold, and swirling patterns. Alphonse Mucha's *Chocolat Masson*, the spring poster.

She sat up straight. "That's my phone!"

Around a mouthful of ice cream, Meghan said, "Yup."

Not a trace of guilt. "Did you take it from my purse?"

Meghan carefully loaded her spoon with more ice cream, Cocoa watching her every move. "Yes, I did."

Alex groaned. "Great. Theft runs in the family. First a stolen recipe, now a phone."

Grinning at that, Meghan caught her eye. "Shame on you."

A smile curved her own lips. "Back atcha."

Meghan pointed her spoon at her, heaped high with caramel-swirled ice cream. "I read your blog post about Thomas. It was good." She licked the spoon, before it dripped. "It gave me an idea."

She didn't like the way Meghan was looking at her. "Whatever it is, I'm not doing it. So, give me back my phone."

Alex snorted a laugh. "I've tried that tactic. It doesn't work."

Meghan grinned. "He's right. You might as well just give in now."

As if. "I've had more practice saying no to you than he has," she pointed out. A lifetime of it.

"It's just a phone call."

It was never that simple. She tapped her fingers on the cover of the sketchbook. "Why can't you make it yourself?"

"Good question," Alex said, too innocently. "Why can't you call, Megs?"

She cut her eyes at him. "You know why." There was subtext there.

Why would Meghan need someone else to make the call for her? It hit her. "Caller ID." At the flash of guilt that crossed her face, Charley knew she'd gotten it first try. "Someone's blocked your number and you want to get around it by using mine."

"That makes it sound so" — Meghan waved her hand — "sordid."

"It is," Alex said.

"Then I'm staying out of it." She flipped her sketchbook open to the next blank page.

Meghan glanced down at the nearly empty bowl she held. "What if I bought you a fresh pint? Any flavour. Your choice."

She propped her feet on the footstool and picked up her pencil. "No deal." Not even for black raspberry and white chocolate. "Find someone else to do your dirty work for you." In fact... "Get Alex to call."

He held up his hands, palms out. "Leave me out of this."

"It has to be you," Meghan said. Too fast.

Cocoa straightened and licked her chops, ready to dart for the ice cream first chance she got.

"Why?"

"Because —" Meghan paused just long enough to make her suspicious. "— I'm your sister and you love me."

"Emotional blackmail?" she asked. "You must be desperate."

"I am."

Curiosity tugged at her. "Fine," she said. "Who am I supposed to call?"

Meghan hopped to her feet with a triumphant grin. She held the phone out to her. "Matt."

Mid-reach, she froze. "What?" Charley crossed her arms. "Oh no. The only reason you'd need me to call is if he already turned you down for an interview."

"He did," Alex said. "Course, that means she wants the story even more."

Meghan ignored that. "Matt likes me. But he really likes you."

The comment had a tingle spreading through her, which she tried hard to ignore. "Did he tell you that?" she asked casually.

But not casually enough. Always skilled at sensing weakness,

Meghan pounced. "Yeah, he did. He'll answer, if you call. All you have to do is dial the number, then pass the phone to me."

And Matt would be trapped because, once Meghan had her chance, she normally got what she wanted. "Not everyone wants their secrets printed in the newspaper."

"What secrets? I just want a few comments about his dad's writing process and his inspiration. It'll be painless." She shrugged. "If he says no again, I'll leave him alone."

She caught the lie in Meghan's voice, but let it go. He would have to handle that himself. "All right." She took the phone. "What's his number?"

Meghan rattled it off.

The dial tone rang in Charley's ear. Her heart thundered. The last time she'd seen him was in the gallery when they'd been this close to — Taking a breath, she steadied her nerves. He might not even answer. It was still ringing. It might go straight to voicemail.

"Hello?"

No such luck. "Hi." Her heart felt like it was going to leap right out of her chest. "It's Charley."

"Hey." Warmth filled his tone. "Don't tell me, you changed your mind about that date."

Two feet or more. "Not yet."

"'Not yet.'" She heard the smile in his voice. "That's better than the answer I got before."

"Don't get your hopes up."

"Too late," Matt said cheerfully. "Is everything okay at the gallery?"

"Yeah, thanks." He'd thought to ask. She stood, paced again. She felt Meghan and Alex watching her and tried to block them out. "I think we solved the squirrel problem."

Meghan rolled her eyes and circled a finger in the air, as though to say, *wrap it up*.

Charley turned her back on her and faced the door. Moths fluttered against the screen.

Matt asked, "Did you run out of chocolate?"

She grinned. "I still have some."

"Then there's only one explanation. Did she bribe or blackmail you?"

She choked on a laugh. "A bit of both. I tried to save you."

"You still can." He had a nice phone voice, low and rich. "Tell her the answer's no."

"It won't work," she warned him, but she held the phone away from her ear anyway. "He says no."

Meghan sighed. "Give me the phone."

She told him, "She wants to talk to you yourself."

"I figured as much." He sounded resigned. "It was worth a shot."

"Brace yourself." She passed the phone to Meghan. "Be nice."

"I always am." She put the phone to her ear. "Counter-offer. What if Charley does the interview?"

She spun toward Meghan. "Wait, what?"

Alex chuckled. "I hate to say it, but I told you so."

"Not helping."

Meghan ignored them. "Charley's read the book, and I haven't."

"Not all of it." She was barely two-thirds through.

"She did a great interview with Thomas the other day," Meghan said. Charley made a grab for the phone, but she danced out of reach. "You can check it out on her blog. She could link the cover of *Hamadryads* to the theme of the exhibit in the article, and promote the gallery, too." She smiled. "It's a win-win."

Fuming, she tried again, but Meghan dodged away. "I don't have time for anything else."

Meghan grinned at something Matt said to her. "He says he heard that." She listened for a second. "He says he's busy too, but he'd make time for you."

Alex lifted a brow. "He's got you there."

She knew when she was beaten. She huffed out a breath. "Oh, for God's sake."

Meghan listened again. "Right." A pause. "Sure. I told you, I'd get back to you with another idea."

She put her hands on her hips and glared at Meghan. Cocoa snuck a lick from the bowl, now sitting unguarded on the coffee table, and she didn't even try to stop her.

"Perfect." She hung up the phone. "He's cooking dinner for you tomorrow night."

"Meg —"

"Be there at six. And he said to bring Cocoa."

At the sound of her name, she glanced up, whiskers smudged with ice cream, tail wagging hard.

"You are so —" Charley searched for the right word. Devious, sneaky, underhanded? She went with the most fitting one. "— annoying."

"And you" — Meghan grinned — "have a date."

She sucked in a breath. "It's not a date." It wasn't. How could it be? "It's coercion."

Alex reached for the TV remote. "He's cooking dinner for you, and you're going to ask him questions about his personal life." He switched the channel, turned the volume up on the squealing tires of a car chase. "Sounds like a date to me."

She sank into the chair. "It's a date?"

Meghan nodded. "And you're going to get my story for me. I'm a genius. You can thank me later."

"Or kill you," she muttered beneath her breath.

"Just keep your phone with you," Alex said, focused on the get-away car barreling down the highway. "He's still on the suspect list."

"I thought you had your sights set on Kayla."

He shrugged. "Better safe than sorry."

TWENTY-FIVE

DINNER, MATT COULD HANDLE.

He'd buttered the ramekins for the *gateaux au chocolat*. From the sounds of it, the pot of salted water was close to a boil. The sauce for the pasta simmered, filling the kitchen with the aroma of late-summer Ontario tomatoes, hot chili, white wine, and basil.

No, it was the questions that worried him.

If only he had the book. The first edition would have distracted Charley, taken the heat off himself. But he'd spent the past few days giving books away, emptying the shelves. Carelessly, as it turned out. *Hamadryads* was gone.

He shot a glance at the digital clock on the oven. Just enough time to finish prepping the cakes. He reached for the sieve. A dusting of cocoa powder would stop the batter from sticking in the molds.

The doorbell rang, and he jolted. A cloud of cocoa powder rose into the air. Grabbing the cloth draped over the edge of the sink, he wiped up the worst of the mess.

Despite the rain that had picked up just half an hour ago, she was right on time.

Matt ran quick fingers through his hair on the way to the entrance. His pulse scrambled and it wasn't just the interview that had his heart racing.

He swung the door open, a clever line all ready, but his tongue tangled.

Charley wore jeans, and a T-shirt the colour of cornflowers. Twists of silver dangled at her ears and she had her hair caught back in a clip. She'd done something with her eyes too, something dangerous that could have a man drowning in them, if he wasn't careful. It took a second before he even noticed Cocoa. "Hi." Smooth.

Charley grinned. "Hi."

Behind her, water splashed off the porch gutter. Drops of moisture glistened in her hair and on Cocoa's fur from their run from the car. She'd had to park her Jeep on the curb, then make a dash for the door because he'd forgotten to move his boat and trailer off the driveway. Mentally kicking himself, he moved aside. "Come on in."

Cocoa nudged in ahead, tail wagging, and Matt grabbed for the leash before she tangled his feet.

The scent of the rain on Charley's hair as she brushed past him, a subtle undertone of cassis and honey, had his brain stuttering again.

She glanced at the wooden storage bench and the loon carved in the lid — the result of his dad's test run with the college CNC machine. He just hoped she didn't also notice the scuff marks in the oak finish or the flaking paint on the folding closet door. Which he had no intention of opening while she was here. His dad's out of sight, out of mind attitude toward cleaning, hiding the mess behind cupboard doors, had come in useful today.

"Sorry about my sister." She bent to unhook Cocoa's leash.

The dog sniffed the sneakers that he'd ditched by the door — probably should have moved those — then ran at him. But fending off her enthusiastic greeting gave him something to do with his hands. "Don't be. I'm thinking she did me a favour." He rubbed Cocoa's ears, then glanced back at Charley. "You look pretty."

"Thanks." Her cheeks flushed pink. "Just to be clear" — she dug in her purse, pulled out a notebook and ballpoint pen — "this isn't a date."

His lips twitched. "It's almost a date."

"I'm here for the interview, and —"

"My boyish good looks?" He tried for a winning grin.

She laughed. "I was going to say 'chocolate.'"

"Good thing, it's on the menu." He led the way into the kitchen, more at ease surrounded by the simmering pots and the cutting board, stained green with herbs. The butter and chocolate. "Chardonnay?" He opened the fridge.

"Yes, please. It smells amazing in here." Wandering over to the stove, she peeked at the sauce, breathing in the scents. "How soon can we eat?"

Enjoying her enthusiasm, he said. "I need a few more minutes, but soon."

Cocoa roamed the room, sniffing at drawer handles, at the edge of the counters.

"Can I help with anything?" Charley asked.

"Next time I'll put you to work." He poured the wine into two long-stemmed glasses and handed her one. Raising his glass to hers, he said, "To dinner, and to your gallery opening."

"I'll drink to that." She clinked her glass to his.

"Are you excited?"

A smile broke across her face, bright and disarming. "Ask a silly question."

The lid on the pot clattered, the water reaching a rolling boil. He should put the pasta in. But it could wait, just one more minute. "So, you're in Oakcrest for the summer. Where's home?"

"Here." It came from the heart, no hesitation. "But my apartment is in Toronto."

Within driving distance, at least. "Which you'll be going back to, after the exhibit's over?" Casual curiosity? Probably better, if it was.

"I'm not sure yet."

Because he saw her gaze slide to the bowl of chopped bittersweet chocolate, he moved it further down the counter, out of reach. "Appetizer's on the table." Wafer thin olive crisps he'd made last night. "Hands off my chocolate."

Her laughter cruised along his skin. "How do you not eat half your profit?"

He looked at her seriously. "Self-control."

"Not my strong point. At least, not when it comes to chocolate," she confessed.

"In my books, that's a good thing."

"Says the owner of Chocoholic's." She took a seat at the table and chose a crisp from the bowl. Nibbling at it, she asked, "What are we having for dinner?"

"Linguini with prawns, cherry tomatoes and rocket. For dessert, individual chocolate cakes, warm from the oven." He turned back to the stove.

"Ask me again to marry you."

He shot a grin over his shoulder and shrugged. "You get turned down once."

She laughed. Then her eyes moved past him and widened. "Cocoa, no. Down!"

On a surge of panic, he spun to see Cocoa, paws on the counter, stretching toward the baguette he'd just sliced. He lunged for it, but the dog snatched the end piece off the wooden cutting board. And ate it. All four feet back on the floor, she sat on her rump and flashed him the doggy equivalent of a grin. There were breadcrumbs on her nose. Aghast, he stared at the dog. "Does she do that often?"

"I'd like to say no, but I'd be lying." Charley looked sheepish. "Sorry, I should have warned you. You might want to move the bread away from the edge of the counter."

Bread in safety, he turned to Cocoa. "In my kitchen, there are rules." She panted at him. "You want to stay" — he pointed a finger at her — "you've got to play by them." She licked his hand, and he sighed. "She keeps you on your toes, doesn't she?"

"She has a big personality." Charley clicked her pen and made a note.

His brows rose. "What did you just write?" He heard the tension in his own voice.

She glanced up at him. "It's not about you. It's a reminder for myself. I have a long To-Do list tomorrow. We can start the interview now, if you want."

"Yeah," he muttered as he moved to the stove. "That's all I want." He set a small pot on low heat.

"Hey." She aimed her pen at him. "No attitude. A deal's a deal."

"A man can sulk, if he wants to."

"I took the time to come up with some good questions. And I'm really busy right now, so that's saying something."

"All right." Resigned, he began heating the chocolate over the water bath. "Hit me with them."

"*Hamadryads*," she said and set his nerves on edge, "takes place in a post-apocalyptic world. What statement do you think your dad was making about the present-day society at the time?"

"Beats me." He stirred cocoa powder and brown sugar into the melted chocolate.

"Not the answer I was hoping for." She frowned at her notes. "What about the impact on the natural world? It's telling that the title refers to the Greek mythological beings that live in trees."

"Does it?" Working carefully, he mixed in the eggs, one at a time.

"Yes, they're bonded with the tree." Frustration filled her voice now. But that couldn't be helped. "Liselle is a strong female character," she said, "and the narrator of the story. Was she inspired by anyone your dad knew in real life?"

He opened the oven door, slid the ramekins on a rack, set the timer. "Haven't got a clue."

Charley put her pen down and crossed her arms. "You said you'd answer my questions."

"Sure," he replied easily. "But I can't answer those."

"Why not?"

"All of your questions are about the book." He gave the pasta sauce one last stir, tasted it. Fresh and fragrant, good punch of heat from the chili. Just a little lemon zest now to finish. He felt her looking at him.

"You've never read it."

"Don't like sci-fi," he replied. Transferring the pasta to a large serving bowl, he carried it to the table, Cocoa close on his heels. She danced around his feet, nose in the air, as he set the bowl down.

"But your dad wrote the book."

"Couldn't get into it." He hadn't even cracked the spine. "Pass me your plate?"

"But —" He could all but hear her grinding her teeth.

He served up the pasta. When he sat down, Cocoa rested her chin on his knee. He looked down at her. "Sorry, I don't have a plate for you."

As if she'd understood him, Cocoa heaved a sigh, turned twice, and curled up on the floor beside Charley's chair.

"You've read the book," he said, casually as he could, hating himself for asking. "Did you like it?"

"I loved it. It's passionate, brilliant and —" She searched for the right word. "— riveting."

"All that?" Matt picked up his fork. Relief, envy, and something else tore at him.

She twirled strands of linguini in a practiced move. "And more. You should read it."

Not in this lifetime.

But, before he could come up with a reply, she said, "This" — she gestured at the pasta with her fork — "is my new favourite meal."

He grinned. "If you want, I'll give you the recipe."

"Then I'd know all your secrets." She smiled at him over the rim of her glass and he wondered if that would be so bad.

"In that case, I'll have to keep some to myself. Otherwise, you might not come back."

"Speaking of recipes," she said, "when I visited Thomas the other day, I found one." Her eyes met his. "For nougat-filled Belgian chocolates."

That made sense. "Everyone in the class got a copy."

"But he kept his hidden in a sketchbook. And it was annotated."

The way she said it caught his attention. "You make it sound like the recipe was blood-stained."

"Maybe, in a way, it was." And, leaning forward, she explained her theory. About the padlocked shed, the sketches, and the house.

"You think Thomas killed Andrew?" He hadn't even considered the idea.

"It's a possibility."

They were valid points. But there might be a simpler explanation, too.

"You might be right," he said, knowing he was about to be the bearer of bad news. "But Thomas hoped the class would give him an activity to do with his granddaughter. After trying it himself, he decided the techniques would be too complicated for her. He asked me how he could simplify the recipe."

Looking disappointed, she leaned back in her chair. "That explains the annotations then."

"What about Kayla?" *Sometimes, I wish he was dead.* The cold fury in Kayla's eyes had been ruthless as the edge of a chef's knife.

"She didn't do it." No second's pause to debate or mull over the clues.

Still, he asked, "You're sure about that?"

"Completely. We were —" She paused, rephrased. "— we *are* kindred spirits."

The ties of friendship, strong and true? That single missed beat, the shift from past to present tense, told a different story. "Meaning?"

"From the first moment you meet a kindred spirit, you know that they understand everything about you, and you understand them. That they'll have your back no matter what, for as long as the sun and moon endure," she said it solemnly, as though reciting an oath of loyalty.

And maybe that's exactly what it was. "She's lucky to have you."

She grinned. "I know." Then she narrowed her eyes at him. "You briefly distracted me with the linguini and the questions, but I haven't forgotten about the interview."

"I had to try." He smiled, but his heart thudded.

"What was your dad like?"

Mouth suddenly dry, he reached for his wine. "Stubborn. Distant. Busy."

"So only good things," she said wryly. "You're not giving me much to work with here. If I return empty-handed, Meghan will come after you again."

"And that's a terrifying thought." It actually was. "I wanted to show you the first edition, but I can't find it right now." She was right. Best get it over with. Still, he hesitated. "When it came to writing," he said finally, "Nick Thorn was driven, prioritizing it over everything else. He escaped into it."

"And left you behind?"

Taken aback, he admitted, "It felt like it at the time." Unsettled, he forced himself to take another bite, to finish the plate of pasta. "He taught carpentry and renovation techniques at the college. Published a couple of articles on environmental factors. I can send you the links. You might be able to connect his theories to the book."

"That's a good idea. It's more of a review than a story, but I can sell it to Meghan. Did he write any other novels?"

"Nothing published. Whatever else he wrote, he kept to himself." Wasting all that time, with nothing to show for it in the end.

By now, the scent of chocolate had intensified, become richer. Matt started to relax. No need to look at the timer to know the cakes were done. "Ready to be impressed?"

"I'm prepared to be amazed."

No pressure.

He took the cakes out of the oven. Firm at the sides, and molten in the centre, exactly the way they should be.

He let them cool in the ramekins for a minute, then carefully unmolded each one onto a plate. Added a few fresh raspberries and a drizzle of crème anglaise as the finishing touches.

Charley tasted the cake and closed her eyes on a hum of bliss. "Amazed doesn't even come close. Also, I'm very, very happy."

Grinning, he picked up his own spoon. "Studies have shown that chocolate has a similar effect on the chemistry of the brain to what we experience when falling in love."

"I do" — she smiled impishly — "love chocolate."

On impulse, he reached across the table, tangled his fingers with hers. He ran his thumb over her knuckles, lingering over the faint smudge of teal paint. "I'm glad you came for dinner."

WHEN THEY'D WASHED THE DISHES and Matt ran out of reasons to convince her to stay longer, he walked her to the entrance. Holding the door open, rain still heavy on the air, he handed her the Tupperware container. "Leftovers. For you," he added, with a wry glance at Cocoa.

"I like you more and more." Charley placed a hand on his shoulder and stretched up to kiss him on the cheek.

But he turned his head just in time, brushed his lips over hers. Felt her breath catch on his.

"Oops," he murmured. Not completely innocent.

But before he could step back, she caught him by the shirt. "Want to try that again?"

The question jolted his system, like a thousand volts of electricity. Then he backed her against the door.

Mouth moving over hers, the hunger within him edged toward greed. The kiss was like tasting chocolate for the first time. Intoxicating, bittersweet, and addictive.

TWENTY-SIX

BAREFOOT AND STEALTHY, SNEAKERS DANGLING from her finger-tips, Charley stepped around the creaky floorboard. But before she could stop her, Cocoa raced ahead, paws scrabbling over the living room floor. "Ssh," she hissed.

Then again, the cottage was quiet. Maybe she'd escape without —

She stopped short. Cocoa kept going, faster now.

A kitchen chair, positioned in the middle of the entrance, front and back legs rammed against both walls, blocked her way to the front door. Meghan sat there, sipping a Thermos of coffee. A second Thermos rested on the ground beside her. The tips of her red hair were still damp from the shower, at odds with the cool competence of her white shirt, and the navy blazer draped over the back of her chair.

Meghan lowered the newspaper and levelled her reporter's gaze at her. "You snuck in last night."

She walked right into that ambush. "I did not sneak."

Her look said she didn't buy that one bit. "I waited up for you. But you never came in."

So much for the skills of the well-trained journalist. "Yes, I did."

Meghan had her canvas flats on and a head start on the caffeine. Odds were slim to none she'd be able to get away unscathed, let alone dodge the questions. Best she could do was dance around them.

She watched Cocoa sidle over for an ear rub. Meghan patted her head, avoiding most of the sloppy canine kisses. "The car pulled up, a door slammed. Then you disappeared into thin air."

"You probably dozed off."

Meghan shot her a knowing glance. "Did the thistles get you?"

She'd stumbled right over them in the dark and the rain. Cocoa knew enough to go around, but Charley's ankles still itched from the prickles. "You need to weed your garden."

Meghan threw her head back and laughed. "I figured as much. How did you get into the house?"

"Magic." It helped she'd found the key that unlocked the French doors in her room. One of the benefits of cleaning. "I didn't want to wake you." Or get the third degree.

"Thoughtful." Meghan leaned back, like she had all the time in the world to chat. "How was your date?"

Her pulse gave a traitorous leap, she tried to ignore. "Aren't you late for work?" Meghan was a firm believer in the early bird catches the worm.

"Talk fast."

Cocoa left them to lap at her water bowl, tags jingling against metal.

"I have an angle for the article." A safer topic for conversation that just might be interesting enough to distract.

Meghan sat up straight. "Scandal?"

"Environmental."

"I'll take it." She sipped her coffee. "Did he kiss you?"

She'd only been awake half the night thinking about it. But Meghan didn't need to know that. She looked at her watch. "You're now fifteen minutes late."

Meghan smiled slowly. "Was it good? And did you stay for" — she dropped her voice to a throaty purr that hinted at sin — "dessert?"

"Sixteen minutes," she counted down.

One innocent kiss, that's all it had been.

Oh, who was she kidding? There was nothing innocent about it.

Meghan held up the second Thermos, sitting on the ground at her feet. "This coffee here? It has your name on it. And the last of our cream in it. So, unless you want to drink your coffee black, you'd better spill the beans."

"You're holding the coffee hostage?"

She wriggled her eyebrows, Thermos in her hand. "Did your toes curl?"

Since Meghan's coffee could be like gut rot, even laced with half-and-half, she admitted, "My knees went weak." Like Jell-O. Or melted chocolate.

"Mm, the best kind." Good on her word, Meghan handed over the Thermos. "What are you going to do now?"

She popped the lid, breathing in the full-bodied scent. Why did coffee always taste so much better here than it did in the city? "Go to the gallery."

No matter how amazing that kiss had been, she couldn't let it distract her.

Meghan rolled her eyes. "I meant, what are you going to do about Matt?"

"Right now, everything is about the gallery." This summer was about her art. She'd made that promise to herself, and she wasn't about to break it for some guy. No matter how cute or charming he might be. Even if the heat of the kiss still sizzled through her veins.

"All work and no play... But" — Meghan sighed — "I get it. I'm bringing the crackers and cheese and" — she glanced at her watch and jolted — "is that the time? Shit, I am late!"

"Yes, you are." She made a point of taking a long, slow sip of coffee as Meghan leaped into action.

"If you'd dished the details last night, this wouldn't have happened." She dragged the chair back into the kitchen.

Cocoa padded over, a quizzical tilt to her head.

"You're right. It's my fault." Amused, Charley watched Meghan grab her purse. Then held onto her Thermos as she hugged her, hard.

"Luck!" Meghan dashed out, slamming the screen door hard enough to bounce off the latch.

Charley exchanged a glance with Cocoa. "Not as bad of an interrogation as it could have been." And now she had coffee. Not that she needed any caffeine. Her system was already on overdrive.

She heard Meghan's tires spin on gravel, then rumble down the road at a pace that pushed the speed limit.

Soon as Charley stepped out the door, the humidity caught at her throat. Mosquitoes buzzed around her, out for blood. It would be another hot day. And hopefully lure the crowds onto the streets for the Food Truck Festival, and to the gallery.

She opened the back door of the Jeep on a creak of rusted hinges. Cocoa hopped onto the seat.

Did she have everything she needed? Outfit for the opening, check. Red lipstick, check. *Hamadryads*, in case she had time to kill. Only two chapters to go, and she might need the distraction.

Bottles of Merlot, sparkling water, and glasses were already at the gallery. Was she missing anything?

Nerves of steel.

Thanks to the mysterious postcard, it was a safe bet things wouldn't go as planned. She had to be alert and ready for anything. And hopefully, by six o'clock, she'd also be cool, calm, and collected. Because this was it. Finally.

She met Cocoa's eyes in the rear-view mirror. "Ready?"

Cocoa panted. Charley figured she'd take that as a yes.

She put the key in the ignition and turned it. *Click*. Her heart sank.

Not today. "Come on." She turned the key again. *Click*. Nothing. Not so much as a tired whirr.

The engine was dead.

Charley got out of the car. "As if there wasn't enough to deal with already." Hands on her hips, she gave the Jeep a hard stare.

Then, with a sigh, she went around to the trunk to get the sturdy wooden stick she used to prop the hood open. If only she didn't need it so often. But it was better than having the heavy aluminum come down on her head.

Jamming one end of the stick against the metal rim and the other under the angle of the hood, she looked at the engine. Crusty blue froth around the battery terminals — that couldn't be good.

A jumpstart might do the trick, and she had booster cables, but both Meghan and Alex had already left.

If that didn't work, she'd have to find a mechanic in Oakcrest. And sink more money into the Jeep. If only she could go one whole month without having to track down the nearest auto shop.

She slammed the hood down, made sure the latch locked. Not always a given.

They'd have to walk to the gallery. Unless — It was a long shot, but worth a try.

"Come on." Charley tracked the path around the side of the house on the heels of a memory of barefoot races and whoops of laughter.

Cocoa coursed over the grass, hunting the ground for buttercups and bees.

Here in the shadows, orange slices dangled from the branches, strung on kitchen twine. Charley touched a finger to one of the rinds, still fresh with citrus oil, and sent it spinning. Meghan's doing, no doubt, although the vibrant strip of orange ribbon tied to the oak's trunk was so frayed, it might have been one of Grandma Reilly's. She hoped it was.

Dwarfed by the trees, the plywood storage shed stood there still, looking smaller than she remembered and weather-beaten. Red paint flaked off doors that no longer lined up perfectly. The concrete stepping stones almost hidden by weeds and sunk in the dirt.

Brushing cobwebs from the rusted latch, she yanked the bolt back with a grating snap that startled an oriole from its orange slice feast. The bird's rich, whistling song echoed over her head as it flew away, over the water.

With some effort, the sagging door scraped open.

A stagnant gust of old plastic, mouse droppings, and dried leaves hit her. Grey, indistinct shapes crouched in the gloom.

Before Cocoa could nudge past her leg, Charley said, "Sit."

An exasperated canine gaze met hers.

"Stay."

Cocoa's body quivered with barely restrained enthusiasm, but she stayed where she was.

Charley stepped inside the shed. Her eyes adjusted to the light and those shapes took on form, so familiar she felt the past squeeze her heart. The blue metal tackle box, like a puzzle box full of fishing lures. The inner tube, still inflated but sunk on one side. A mildewed life jacket, child-sized, hanging from a low hook. Hers or Meghan's? A foam pool noodle, gnawed and cracked. Dust and dead flies on everything.

Cocoa sneezed and shook her head, so hard her ears flapped.

Charley found the bicycle, half-buried behind a stack of empty flowerpots. Vintage and — as she wheeled it out, the morning sun hit the frame — more rust than anything else. The brake levers stiff from disuse. The thought tugged at the centre of her chest.

But Grandma Reilly would beam with delight — and shed tears

of laughter — if she knew Charley was pedaling her bicycle to her first gallery opening.

The tires were a little flat, but not bad. The wicker basket just the right size for her tote bag. Cocoa would love the run.

And Charley was pretty sure her tetanus shot was up to date.

TWENTY-SEVEN

FOR SO LONG, ART HAD been a way to look, to see, and remember. A way to process her feelings and experiences in paint. But art was also a form of communication. Hopefully her paintings would whisper, compel, and seduce. Because — in exactly fifteen minutes — Charley would finally have an audience.

They would judge her art. But that was the point. To let the critics decide her fate.

People liked to say it didn't matter what others think. But, to be successful, to make a living, of course it did. It was everything.

Despite the fact that her soul hung on these walls, she had to keep her cool. No matter what happened.

Kayla's high heels clicked over hardwood floor as she paced from one end of the gallery to the other. On the wrought-iron table by the entrance, Thomas set up wine glasses around the cheese platter. Charley had filled the tray with cubes of cheddar, red seedless grapes, dried cherries, and concentric circles of crackers — Table Water, multigrain, and sea salt.

Outside the gallery window, a row of white awnings fluttered in the breeze, shielding tables from the hot sun. Traffic on Main Street had been blocked off hours ago. The festival was about to start, and people milled around, a restless excitement building as necks craned to catch a glimpse of the first food truck.

Charley snapped a photo of the table laden with cheese and gilded glass. Playing up the similarity to Clara Peeters' painted banquet pieces, she cropped the image down and used the last chance to tease the gallery opening on social media.

Thomas bent to take a bottle of sparkling water from the box on the floor and she noticed the sunburn on his neck.

"How's it going with the house?" she asked, because someone had to say something. They were all on edge, especially Kayla.

"We made progress." His skin flushed darker with anger. "Now it's stalled."

Maybe not the best topic for small talk. "What happened?"

"Another delay." Knuckles white, his fingers strangled the neck of the bottle. Like the grasping hands of the villains lurking just outside the frames of *Black Mask* magazine covers. "I've been told it won't be a problem for long." His smile stretched thin. "I'll believe it when I see it."

Glass struck metal and shattered. Kayla jerked, the blood draining from her face.

The base of the bottle had knocked over a wine glass, sent it smashing against metal, toppling the others nearby like dominoes.

"Damn it." The scowl drew Thomas's brows together.

Two other glasses lay on their sides, one still rocking gently, balanced on the edge. Shards glittered on the wrought-iron table, caught in the sunlight pouring through the window.

Déja vu had a shiver running down her spine. A tipped over wine glass, like the one on the postcard. Was it a coincidence? Or a reminder.

Thomas began gathering pieces of glass.

Cocoa moved forward and Charley, worried about cut paws, caught her by the collar. Kayla stood there, as though rooted to the spot. She pulled Cocoa toward her. "Here, hold onto her. Make sure she stays there and doesn't come any closer."

Kayla jumped, startled into action. "Sure." She stroked a hand over Cocoa's head. "No walking on glass."

Charley grabbed the small garbage bin from by the door and crossed to Thomas. "Broken glasses, toppled goblets," she said casually, her heart slamming against her ribs. "It's like a Dutch still life."

"And just as ominous." His voice was terse. And gave nothing away. Not so much as a flicker of guilt.

"Do we need to reference *memento mori*?" Reminders of death. Kayla's face was pinched and drawn. And who could blame her? Carefully applied concealer almost hid the shadows beneath her eyes, but she couldn't gloss over her emotions. Not entirely.

"A still life of disorder," Thomas said, "seems fitting."

"Then let's restore order." The wine glass in Charley's hand shot prisms of light across the floor.

The gallery door flew open and Meghan burst in, with Alex a step behind.

Kayla shot a wary glance his way, Cocoa's tail beating against the skirt of her white linen dress.

"Missing food trucks." Meghan's eyes gleamed with excitement. "Gourmet street food: too little, too late." It sounded like a headline.

Kayla frowned. "What? But this event has been advertised for weeks. It should be perfectly organized."

Charley carefully swept splinters of glass into her palm. "What's with the food trucks?" The glass glinted as it rained into the garbage bin, a shower of sparks.

"One driver phoned in with mechanical problems, two are stuck in traffic on the 401, and one is a no-show. And can't be reached."

Kayla looked thoughtful. "I might make some calls, see what I can find out." Her dress swished around her knees as she disappeared through the door and up the stairs.

"She took off fast," Alex said, following her retreat with an assessing gaze.

"Only half of the food trucks are here?" Charley's heart sank.

"To feed over a thousand people," Meghan said cheerfully.

She knew her sister only too well. Charley pointed a finger at her. "Save some column space for the gallery opening." People would get hungry, impatient, and frustrated, fast. "The line-ups will be huge."

A couple of kids raced past the window, a flash of turquoise and yellow and sun-streaked hair.

Thomas filled the gap in the display with a fresh wine glass that rang with a cold, clean chime as he set it down. "They always say to manage your expectations. The reality of the opening reception is that it normally doesn't go the way you imagined."

She flashed on a mental image of a crowd of tourists turning into an angry mob. She fought the urge to ball her fists at her sides. Instead of benefitting the gallery's opening, the festival could spell disaster. "So, we'll problem solve."

Alex sighed. "I was looking forward to the wood fired, thin-crust pizza with pulled pork."

"You'll live." Meghan grinned with relish. "Conflict, human interest. This festival has it all."

"Seems the festival is more newsworthy than the gallery," Thomas said dryly.

Meghan shook her head. "Oakcrest's first pop-up gallery is getting pride of place in the Arts and Community section. And nothing gets the blood pumping like writing two stories at once." Her eyes shone, wide and bright.

She asked, "How much caffeine have you had?"

"A lot," Alex said.

"Coffee equals words." In her reporter voice, Meghan announced, "Oakcrest's first pop-up gallery drew an artsy crowd of locals and tourists —"

"We hope," Thomas said.

"Who sipped wine, while discussing the nuanced collection — no, the dazzling display of art."

"Would you like to see it," she teased, "or just make it up?"

"I resent that," Meghan said. "I deal in facts, not fiction."

They needed to get people into the gallery. And keep them happy. "We've got cheese and crackers. Could you spread the word on the street? Let's lure them in with snacks."

Meghan glanced at the tray and nodded. "On it."

Thomas muttered, "Because it's the serious collectors who will need to be coaxed into the gallery."

The sarcasm had Charley's back going up. "Have you got a better idea?"

"Need any help?" Alex asked Meghan. "Otherwise, I'll stay here, have a look around."

And seize the opportunity to corner Kayla? His eyes were on the open door, the glimpse of the stairs.

Meghan shrugged. "I've got this. Spreading news is right up my alley." At the front door, she paused. "By the way, that bicycle outside looks just like Grandma's."

"That's because it is." She sighed. "The Jeep wouldn't start."

"Don't they say bad luck comes in threes? Maybe you've met your quota for the day."

"The Jeep, the missing food trucks," she tallied. "Broken wine glasses."

"Cocoa just ate some crackers," Alex said.

A pink tongue flashed as Cocoa licked her chops.

"Great."

"You'll be fine," Meghan told her. "I'm going to go drum up a crowd."

As she headed out the door, Alex caught Charley's arm. He murmured, "I checked the postcard."

"And?"

He shook his head. "No fingerprints."

Somehow, that didn't surprise her. Today, nothing was going smoothly.

AS THE GALLERY DOOR OPENED, Charley's pulse quickened. Maybe now — but no. A young couple entered.

She had to stop looking at the door every time it opened, otherwise she'd get a crick in her neck. It just proved again that the kiss was a mistake. She couldn't let it distract her.

Sipping at her wine, she walked slowly around the gallery, looking at the paintings for what felt like the first time. The presence of strangers breathed life into the exhibit. The art fresh and new and real. Footsteps and murmurs pulsed through the space, quick as the beat of her own heart, drumming against her ribs.

"Darling," a male voice drawled in her ear, "Where did you get that outfit?"

Turning, she met electric-blue eyes. Cerulean or azure might come close to matching that vibrance, with opaque white highlights. "This little boutique in town."

"The owner has good taste," Eric said. "You look like a 1940s siren, straight off a Hollywood set."

"And I have pockets." She slid her hands into them with a grin.

"Make sure Meghan immortalizes that ensemble in the paper. It's screaming for a photo op." He looked past her, and his brows rose. "Could this be the start of a happy ever after?" he murmured.

She followed his gaze to where David stood, talking to Kayla. His body leaned toward hers, their heads close together. Radiating a force field of attraction, like rare earth magnets drawn together.

"What did I tell you?" Eric said. "Sparks."

"Looks like it." And yet, Kayla hadn't mentioned him.

Eric heaved a sigh. "I'm going to browse the art. Well done." He strolled away.

She watched David and Kayla a second longer, worry nagging at her.

"*Bar Line Shift* caught my eye," a man said from behind the partition. "You can almost hear the music, feel that tension between the notes, the rhythm."

"Yes, but look at this one," a husky voice replied. Male or female, it was hard to tell. "I heard she murdered her husband and got away with it." Filled with delight, the tone was pitched low, but not low enough.

Outrage simmering, Charley rounded the corner. And almost walked into Sarah.

Only three other people milled nearby and any one of them could have made that careless comment. She bit back the accusation burning on the tip of her tongue and focused on Sarah.

But when she saw what the woman was looking at on the opposite wall, her palms went clammy.

One of her newest paintings, of the woman kayaking on the lake. Maybe she wasn't quite as prepared for judgement as she'd thought.

"*A Voyage of Discovery*," Sarah murmured the title. "One can almost believe the story is hidden behind those layers of paint."

Charley stood beside her. "I like to think it is."

"I'd like to read it." A wistful smile curved her lips.

Through careful shading, Charley had imitated the worn seams and tattered corners of a well-read paperback. She'd layered acrylic paint on hardboard, the texture thick and rich. The raw, saturated colours picking up on the heightened realism and sensuality of 1930s cover designs. Waves splashed at the orange hull of the kayak as the paddle sliced through water, the woman frozen mid-motion. Tentacles of seaweed and jagged rocks lurked beneath her reflection. The boat skimmed over the surface.

"The woman" — Sarah's gaze was fixed on the figure — "why did you paint her?"

The question caught her off guard. "Because —" There had been something about her, something that caught her interest. But what? "— when I looked at her, I saw tranquility and adventure." A wide-brimmed straw hat hid her face from view, sunlight slanting low and hot over the water. The fine-boned hands gripping the paddle revealed the woman's age, but also showed strength. "Courage. And joy."

"How disconcerting," Sarah said, "to be the subject of observation." Goosebumps prickled over her arms. "What do you mean?"

"That, dear, is my kayak. And" — she gestured — "my hat. To think I posed for a painting without even realizing it."

"That was you?" The painting took on a new light.

Sarah said, "It's turned out quite well, hasn't it? You have a keen eye." Her expression sobered. "But it's easy to become sidetracked. To lose your way. Don't waste that talent," she warned. Her tone carried the weight of experience. A burden, heavy enough to crush.

TWENTY-EIGHT

MATT HESITATED OUTSIDE THE GALLERY, holding a box of choco-lates in his hand. Even though the cardboard felt dry and rough against his palm, the past seemed to overlay the present.

The shadow of wings on the wooden deck, too much like blood.

The seagull glided on a current of air, a sweep of black-tipped grey feathers against the clouds, the white underbelly. That dark stain drifted over the ground as the gull wheeled and soared overhead.

On the street behind him, white awnings snapped. The seagull squawked and plunged, diving for a crust of bread by the gazebo.

Matt blinked, shook himself out of it.

This was a gallery, not a crime scene. And he'd better be ready to celebrate, because that's why he was here.

Holding onto that thought, Matt shoved through the gallery door into laughter and the hum of voices. The colours hit him first. Then he saw the careful planning that enticed people in.

Charley had transformed the place. And drawn a crowd to witness it.

Scanning the room, he spotted her, and his heart stuttered. She looked like she'd stepped straight off the set of a film noir. Swept back hair, hands on her hips. Red lipstick that had him thinking of the taste of her mouth. When she turned, caught his eye, the grin she aimed his way had his heart skipping a beat. And that worried him.

She cut through the crowd toward him.

"You look —" Before he could finish, she grabbed his hand and pulled him back outside. "What's going on?" Concern shot through him.

But as soon as the door closed behind them and she turned to face him, he saw the thrill in her eyes. "I sold a painting," she whispered.

He grinned. They stood on the deck, in a hubbub of conversation, upbeat pop music and the crackle of sweet and salty kettle corn. It was unlikely they'd be overheard, but he dropped his voice low, to match hers. "You what?"

"To Sarah Felles." She beamed at him. "I'm hoping she didn't buy it just because it's a painting of her. But, still, a sale's a sale."

"That's huge!" They stood close enough together for him to catch that same cassis scent on her skin. "Why are we whispering?"

"Because I'm trying to pretend I'm taking it super-cool." But the excitement in her voice was barely contained.

"You had me fooled. Guess I'll have to give these champagne chocolates to someone else." He scanned the people strolling past, pretending to search for a likely candidate.

"Champagne chocolate?" Her eyes lit up. No poker face there. At least, not when it came to chocolate.

"Caught your interest, did I?" He laughed.

"And how."

"I meant to be here when the gallery opened, but Chocoholic's is packed." It had been hard to escape even now.

Charley took the box he held out to her. "Thanks. Matt —" She bit her lip. "— about yesterday —" A scratch of claws on the door interrupted her.

"Patience isn't Cocoa's strong suit, is it?" He'd picked up on the hesitation in her voice, that second's pause. It might be a good thing she'd been cut off mid-sentence.

"Never has been." Charley reached for the doorhandle, then turned back, eyes shining, like she was offering up a secret. "Would you like a tour?"

"Actually" — he couldn't resist shooting a casual glance past her — "someone said there were crackers."

"Very funny." She swung the door open. The glass panels reflected sunlight and white clouds, thick as Chantilly cream. Not a bird in sight.

Soon as he stepped over the threshold, Cocoa sniffed his shoes, his hands. "I probably smell like chocolate."

"You do," Charley said, then looked like she wished she hadn't.

He flicked his eyes to hers, felt that snap of electricity between them again. She glanced away first. But judging from the flush in her cheeks, she'd felt it too.

Matt tucked his hands in his pockets and followed her into the room with a grin.

She led him away from the crowd, over to the wall on their left. Her gaze firmly on the painted faces. "When art gets put on display in a gallery, that's when a piece takes on a life of its own. Everyone who looks at it sees it differently."

"Perspective, you mean?" The give of the floorboards distracted him. That squeak of wood yielding beneath his weight. A noticeable slope angled down toward one corner of the room.

"Yes, but it's more than just point of view. The natural instinct to want to find the meaning behind the artwork, to raise questions and search for answers. Every painting is a combination of choices the artist made. About the subject, the style, the size, the colours. To really understand an artwork, you have to pull it apart and figure out how the pieces fit together to make a whole."

"Like solving a puzzle," he murmured. Or a mystery.

But he was here for the art. Just because he'd been googling floor joists for the past few days did not mean this was the time to investigate.

She nodded. "It's all about noticing the details."

Sure, he saw the talent in Thomas's work, recognized it in Kayla's, but Charley's caught and held his attention. In fact... "I like these details."

The painting was small. Smaller than all the others. A femme fatale lounged in a hammock in the shade of oak trees, as deadly as a poison vial. But the gun rested forgotten on her stomach as she ate chocolates straight from the box. A distant smile on her lips, she stared up at the sky, as though lost in a daydream. *Choosing the Sweet Life*. To his surprise, he wanted it.

Charley glanced at him. "Art is more than just personal preference. It all comes back to emotions." And wasn't that true. "To provoking a reaction."

She moved on to the next piece. A vast, starry sky. Darkness and bright bone. A ragged shirt, silvered with frost.

She said, "That's why we say art, paintings, crackle with energy, with anger."

"This one does." He didn't need to read the artist's name on the title card to know this was Kayla's work.

That wasn't — He leaned in for a closer look. The similarity was impossible to miss. And that expression of suffering Kayla had painted on Andrew's face? He couldn't help but enjoy it.

Charley moved to the next wall. "Thomas's paintings are full of geometric shapes." She gestured at the musician painted on canvas. "That triangle could be a flat, abstract shape. But we see the angle of an arm."

A trick? Or wishful thinking. "So, we see what we want to see."

She grinned at him. "What the artist wants us to see."

A clever illusion. Like evidence, planted to mislead.

Stopping in front of the next painting, he tried to focus on it, but his gaze slid down the wall. Near the baseboard, spiderweb cracks ran through the drywall. Probably caused by seasonal changes in temperature and humidity.

"Those circles, those squares," she said, "remind us of the human form, of instruments. Thomas knew that."

"And used it." *There was something wrong with the structural integrity of the building. Then she died.* The words echoed through his mind, nearly drowning out everything else. "So, when we look at a painting, we're trying to uncover the truth?"

"The artist's truth, anyway."

Over her shoulder, he noticed a middle-aged couple turn toward them. The woman approached Charley with a smile. "Are you the artist? Could we ask you a quick question?"

"Go ahead," Matt said. "I'll look around upstairs."

"You're sure?" she asked.

"I won't get lost."

But when Cocoa followed him up the stairs, he was happy for the company. Especially when the man passing him on his way down said over his shoulder, "I swear I heard footsteps."

The man behind him laughed. "Straight from the afterlife?"

This might be harder than he thought.

But the room he stepped into was filled with colour and light. The bay window framed a blue square of sky. Despite all his better instincts, he moved to look out of it.

The floor dropped away beneath his feet. The room spun. Fighting the dizzying onslaught, he forced himself to look down at the deck below, the tops of the white awnings. To fall that far — Cocoa nudged his hand, cold wet nose to his palm.

His feet were on the ground. And there was a solid pane of glass in front of him.

He turned his gaze on the frame. Tried not to glance at the sky and the ground below. He focused on the seam in the sash. The patch job looked uneven. At some point, the window had been replaced. A shift in the foundation had caused the window to crack. And now it was resettling.

There was a reason the building was up for a temporary lease, why it wasn't for sale. All the signs pointed to framing deterioration — no surprise there.

Whatever Andrew had done to pull the job through had been a fast fix. Not meant to withstand the test of time. Then again, not much did.

The foundation Charley had built her dreams on was rotting.

Matt checked his watch. He couldn't linger. He had to get back, give Mrs. Callahan a break. Get away from that window. And pay for his painting.

Downstairs, Charley's laughter rose above the murmur of conversation. Following the sound, he headed her way, but checked his pace when Kayla cut in front of him.

She got to her first, Alex one step behind. "This was a mistake," Kayla said, her voice shaky.

Charley turned and looked startled. Then concerned. "What do you mean?"

"I don't know what I was thinking." She shook her head, looking a second away from bolting. "I can't do this."

"Hold on —"

"I have to get some air." Kayla pushed by him on her way to the door.

"What's going on?" Matt asked.

"That's what I'd like to know." Charley turned to Alex. "You've been watching Kayla like a hawk all evening."

"Yeah. And what I saw was a guilty conscience." Alex's gaze burned after her, and Matt thought of the seagull's steep and sudden dive.

What had Charley said? It was all about perspective. At a glance, it was easy to mistake flying for falling. Hunter for hunted. It all depended on how you looked at it. The questions you asked.

And all the answers kept leading back to Andrew. To Clarkston Engineering.

"You're paranoid," Charley told Alex.

"Realistic." Alex jerked his thumb at him and Matt raised his brows. "Even the chocolatier thinks I'm right."

"Hey." He put his hands up. "I didn't say anything."

"You didn't have to," she said.

Hopefully she'd forgive him, when he told her she could tally a second sale to her score for the day.

TWENTY-NINE

IF A RECIPE HELD THE secret to flavour, a blueprint held the secrets of a building. That's what Matt was counting on.

His dad had donated a bunch of architectural renderings and maps to the library's local interest collection about a year ago. Odds were good the plans for the gallery had been in the stack. If Jeffrey was right, and his mom was murdered to cover up a fault in the structure, the answers just might be in the blueprints. But Matt had to get his hands on them to know more.

As the screen door of the library banged shut behind him, he inhaled the musty scent of paper, chalk dust, and coffee. A standing fan whirred, working hard to circulate the hot air. Formerly a one-room schoolhouse, a blackboard still ran the length of the back wall, now used as a calendar for community events. A pot-bellied wood stove took up space in the centre of the room. Mint-green shelves strained under the weight of books, regatta trophies, painted rocks, boardgames, and puzzles.

He approached the circulation desk, the floor beneath his shoes gritty with sand. The small beach, just up the lane from the library, was a favourite gathering spot for families renting cottages on the lake. It wasn't unusual to see kids in flip-flops and orange life jackets, towels slung over their shoulders, browsing the stacks, but today, his footsteps echoed through the empty building. The Food Truck Festival had lured the patrons away from the books.

"Matt." Deb looked up from her computer screen. "I haven't seen you in a while."

She wore a floral blouse but had coiled her grey hair into a sculptural twist that looked set hard as stone. Deborah Hamlin had sat behind that desk and run the library ever since he started coming here, like she held the keys to a kingdom.

"I actually came to look at —" His eyes fell on the book she'd pushed aside. *Hamadryads.* "— the town archives." Under the plastic dust jacket protector, the hardback reprint was the same reddish-brown pigment as an old photograph. The woman on the cover a second away from taking a swan dive to God knows what fate.

Deb followed his gaze. "It's catalogued, labeled, and ready to go. Got any more secrets you'd like to share with us?"

More than she knew. But he said, "It was Dad's secret, not mine."

"And threw us all for a loop." The swivel chair bobbed as she leaned back. She tapped her pencil idly against the surface of the desk. "It's late in the day to start hunting through the archives. We close in twenty minutes. On the dot."

"I just want to look at the oversized materials."

She set the pencil down. "You have no idea what you're getting yourself into, do you? Opening up the archives is like going down a rabbit hole. Nothing is ever quick. Come back early tomorrow morning."

Not a chance. It had to be now.

"If you bring me one of your mochaccinos," she offered, "I might even help you search."

And that was something he wanted to avoid. "Bribe a public servant? I'm shocked."

She chuckled. "Bribery normally works on a grander scale than chocolate."

"It all depends on the quality. And mine's the best." Matt amped up the charm. "But my schedule's full for the next few days. I'd rather check now, if that's all right with you."

"What are you looking for?"

The largemouth bass mounted on the wall caught his eye. With a twinge of guilt, he lied. "Lake charts."

The land surrounding Blue Heron Lake was typical of the Canadian Shield, with bare rock ridges and shallow till. Even with an average depth of sixteen meters, fishermen had to navigate low wet areas, deep holes, islands, and bays.

"Planning a fishing trip?" she asked.

"Thinking about it." Close enough to the truth to pass.

With a sigh, she rose to her feet. "Right now, the Dewey Decimal System ends with the books. You're heading into unmapped territory. You'll need my help, if you want to find those lake charts."

He had to deter that. "Have a little faith, Deb. You've been on your feet all day. I'll be fine. Finish what you're doing."

She drew herself up to her full five foot three inches in a move that was surprisingly intimidating. "Oakcrest's first pop-up gallery opened tonight and I intend to be there, at least for the last hour."

"The pop-up gallery? I was just there." He grinned. "And witnessed the first sale."

Joy transformed her features. "Charley sold a painting?"

"Two, actually."

"Oh, that's wonderful." Then her expression turned stern. "I'm locking this door at eight thirty, whether or not you're still here. If I'm late leaving, even by a minute, it'll be your head that rolls."

The woman had absorbed thousands of pages of murder and vengeance. It wasn't an idle threat. "Got it."

"Everything, and I mean everything, gets put back exactly where it belongs. I'm not cleaning up after you."

"It'll be like I was never here."

"Famous last words," Deb muttered and turned back to her computer.

On his way through the shelves, he skimmed the watermarked spines for Marco Pierre White's *White Heat* cookbook. It was still there.

The black and white photographs made the chef look like a rock star, the kitchen like a war zone of adrenaline, cigarettes, meat cleavers, and passion. Unflinching and honest about the price chefs paid in blood and sweat to be the best. His library number was stamped all over that card. Dark chocolate sauce stained the white border of the recipe for *assiette* of chocolate on page 114. He'd checked out that cookbook too many times to count, before eventually buying his own copy.

He moved on, further to the back. To the oversized materials in the flat storage file. High shelves shielded him from view.

Building plans, once submitted to the municipality, were public record. His mother's words came back to him. *Blueprints are the bible for a project. It shows what everyone has to do, so you can plan and schedule the contractors. You can see possible problems in a build before starting and prevent them.*

Matt yanked out the wide, shallow drawers, one after the other. Local maps, lake charts. He checked over his shoulder, then moved right past.

Engineering drawings. Getting closer now. His pulse kicked up a notch. Architectural drawings.

Bingo. He pulled the drawer out further, flipped through the sheets.

And felt his heart sink. Deb was right. There was no system. At least, not one he could spot at first glance.

He'd hoped the plans would be sorted by contractor, or at least by date. No such luck. He'd have to go through them all. And the clock was ticking. Soon Deb would come looking for him and kick him out.

He pulled out the sheets, skimming, checking the names of contractors, engineering companies. He flipped past architectural drawings, looking for the structural drawings that showed the load-carrying members. The steel beams, framing materials. And joists.

The next stack of sheets laid the drawer bare.

By now his hands were damp with sweat. Ink stained his fingertips as he riffled, searching. It had to be here.

An architectural drawing caught his eye. He pulled it out, held it up to the light.

The project itself was nothing out of the ordinary. A three-story office building.

It wasn't what he was looking for. Not even one of Jeffrey's projects. But it was interesting as all hell.

Engineers and architects have to stamp their names and signatures on drawings, to give their final approval. The stamps were a guarantee of professional standing but also helped shift the blame, when necessary. If a contractor followed the blueprints to a T, any errors in construction came back to the engineer and architect who put their stamps on those plans.

Matt skimmed the highlighted text beneath the title block. *From proposed five story build on Water Street to three story build on Water Street.* Cutting two floors from the design.

Looked like the build was scheduled to begin in October. A risky time to start construction, with months of severe winter weather around the corner. He knew that much. Sub-zero temperatures, deeply frozen ground, high winds, and up to forty inches of snowfall. Even with the right precautions, blizzards and snow drifts could stop work. The foundation would have to be completed as much as possible before frost conditions set in, and they'd have to hope everything went smoothly. If the concrete wasn't cured to withstand repeated cycles of freezing and thawing, frost heaving would damage the building.

But a last-minute revision had been made to the fill material around the foundation.

The stamps on the blueprint, the names of the engineer and architect who approved those revisions, had his fingers tensing on a corner of the sheet. Andrew Clarkston and Thomas Kelley.

They knew each other. Had worked together before Thomas retired.

"Blueprints? I thought you wanted to see the lake charts."

"Ah —" With a guilty start, he turned to face Deb, angling to block her line of sight. He'd forgotten how silently she moved between the shelves on those rubber-soled shoes. Nothing compared to the stealth of a librarian. "I got sidetracked. Mind if I use the copier?"

"You've got two minutes."

It would have to be enough.

When Matt left, photocopies still warm from the printer, the realization hit him. He'd never found the plans for the gallery. Though they should have been there.

THIRTY

AT FIRST, CHARLEY THOUGHT KAYLA wouldn't answer the door. Knowing her, she'd be stewing over regrets. This had been their dream for so long, and she'd left the gallery opening before it was over.

Charley had gotten a ride back from town with Meghan and Alex. After dropping off her things, she took Cocoa out for her last walk of the day. And kept right on walking, all the way to Kayla's door.

Though it seemed like she might be left standing on the front step.

Somewhere, a wind chime pealed like distant bells. The solar lights gleamed along the path, although it was still too bright to need the light to see. The setting sun streaked the sky with orange, turning the trees behind her to a tangle of dusky shapes and vertical lines. Mosquitoes whirred, tiny flitting shadows on the high brick wall, a brush of wings against her neck.

She tried again, one more time. "Kayla, it's me!"

The lock tumbled and the door swung open. Kayla's face was bare, her hair tied back in a loose ponytail. A smudge of old mascara shadowed her lower lashes. She had changed into black leggings and an oversized sweater. "Charley. I was about to go to bed." She bent to pat Cocoa, who wriggled with excitement.

In the crease of Kayla's thumb and on the tip of her index finger, a dark grey smudge stained the arches and whorls of her skin like ink.

"And that's why you have charcoal all over your fingers?" she asked.

Kayla straightened and hid her right hand behind her back. "Look, I'm really tired. Worn out, actually."

"Guess I'll just have to eat these chips on my own then." She held up the bag she'd brought with, just in case. She'd swiped it from Meghan's stash, and would have to pay the price later.

"Are those sea salt kettle chips?" Interest flickered.

She held back the grin, tugging at the corners of her lips. Gotcha. "If you don't want them, I'll just share with Meghan."

"Fine." Kayla opened the door wider. "Come on in."

She never could resist those chips.

Stepping inside, Charley unsnapped Cocoa's leash. Like last time, the house felt cool. In the background, voices murmured. The TV? "Is the kitchen through here?"

"Yes, but —"

Undeterred, Charley headed through the living room, behind Cocoa.

A large, spiral bound sketchpad lay open on the white sofa. Conté pencils and pieces of charcoal were scattered over the coffee table. Pastel had been ground in a smudge of vivid green on the cream-coloured carpet. The closed curtains blocked the view of the sliding doors.

In the kitchen, Charley put the bag of chips down on the granite countertop, beside the coffee maker. The machine had a grinder, a milk reservoir, and a steam wand. It probably brewed a barista-worthy cappuccino at the press of a button but would be a nightmare to clean.

The rest of the kitchen was just as stylish. A magnetic knife holder. The table in the corner a sleek and modern tulip design with a pedestal base, most likely meant to convey a sense of balance to the interior design, but it felt forced.

Cocoa's nails clicked over stone tiles as she sniffed the spotless floor for crumbs.

"Bowls?"

"In that cupboard." Kayla washed her hands at the sink, scrubbing at the charcoal streaks. When she sat at the table and tucked one leg beneath her, her hands were clean and dry. "Did you sell another painting?"

Was that envy in her voice? Fighting a surge of guilt, she admitted, "Matt bought one too, after you left." She poured the salted chips into a wooden bowl and set it on the table in front of Kayla.

Where would the alcohol be kept? Probably expensive bottles, put on display in a — yes, there it was. A glass-fronted cupboard, at eye level. She scanned the contents. Did a double take at the label on the gin. A few levels up from the brand she bought.

Vodka, triple sec. Hmm, that had potential.

Charley opened the fridge and the bittersweet stench of rotting fruit hit her. "When did you last go grocery shopping?" The shelves were bare.

"I can't remember. It's hard to keep track of details right now." A little colour had started to come back to Kayla's face. And she looked at the chips with interest.

Charley took out something from the crisper drawer that might have been an orange or a grapefruit at one point and threw it in the trash. Same with the long-overdue container of cream.

"The other day," she said casually, "you left the gallery before

I did. Did you notice anything odd, see anything unexpected on your way out?" Like a postcard, taped to the glass.

Kayla frowned. "No. Why?"

"No reason." It was worth a shot. A bottle of unopened cranberry juice in the fridge door caught her eye. She held it up. "Cosmos?"

"Trying to get me drunk, so I confess to murder?" Her tone was bitter, defensive.

"I didn't think I had to trick you into telling the truth."

The door of the wooden cabinet above the counter swung open on a gentle click of inset steel hinges, revealing shelves filled with crystal-cut glassware. Tall stemmed wine glasses, delicate champagne flutes. But, in the back, something sparkled.

"The truth?" Kayla gnawed on her thumbnail. An old habit, a sign of nerves, she hadn't managed to polish away with everything else. "You do think I'm hiding something."

"You are." She held up one of the martini glasses tucked in the back of the cupboard. Rhinestone-encrusted stem winked in the light. And was exactly something the girl she used to know would have bought. "A guilty secret?"

That got a smile from Kayla. "Andrew thought they were hideous."

So, she'd hidden them at the back of the cupboard. "I think we could use some glitz."

Just enough ice cubes left in the tray. Working on memory, she mixed the ingredients, measuring out equal parts vodka, cranberry juice and a shot of triple sec. When the stainless steel martini shaker felt like ice in her hands, she poured the pink cocktail into the glasses.

Kayla stood, leaned against the counter. Crossed her arms. "So, are you going to report whatever I say to Alex?"

A lie would only do more harm. "He has to collect the facts."

She laughed. "Yeah, so he can make an arrest."

It sounded like she expected the handcuffs to close around her wrists at any second. "If there's anything you haven't told us about Andrew or —"

"Gotta love the blind faith." Kayla poured vodka into the shot glass and tossed it back. She winced. "You're right. This was a good idea." Picking up one of the cocktails, she sipped it on her way through to the living room.

Charley followed on a sigh. This would be harder than she thought.

Cocoa curled up on the floor, keeping the bowl of chips in her line of sight.

Kayla turned off the TV, throwing the room into silence. "What are you going to do about your Jeep?"

Shifting the conversation away from the gallery and the subject of murder. "Try to jumpstart it tomorrow." Pink drink, white sofa. A dangerous combination. She stood on the rug and hesitated.

Kayla dropped the remote onto the coffee table. "Jeffrey tinkers with cars. You should ask him to look at it for you."

"Is there anything the man can't fix?"

"Not that I know of. I can call him for you." Without waiting for a reply, Kayla reached for the phone lying on the end table.

And ask for a favour? No way. "I'm sure he's got better things to do. If need be, I'll call a mechanic."

"He won't mind. He does these things all the time." Kayla pressed a button, put the phone to her ear. "Speed dial."

"Seriously." He'd feel compelled to say yes, no matter how busy he was, because Matt had introduced them. Charley put her hands on her hips. "I don't need —"

She held up a finger, cutting her off. "Jeffrey? Hi. It's Kayla." With a thumbs up aimed Charley's way, she took the phone to the kitchen.

Too late. Hopefully Jeffrey wouldn't mind.

Charley picked up the wire-bound sketchbook lying on the sofa. She meant to move it out of the way, to clear space to sit, but the illustrations caught her eye. Dark colours and sweeping strokes, barely contained by the limits of the page. Curious, she flipped to the next page. Repeating patterns, exercises in blending. A forest of trees simplified into hard-edged shapes. A female figure dissolving into that of a wolf.

Cocoa's tail thumped on the floor as Kayla came back into the room.

Charley put the sketchbook down. "That was quick."

"If you can get the Jeep to the workshop tomorrow morning around nine, he'll look at it for you. You'll have to get it towed there, but I figured you have insurance."

"I do, but the battery might only need a boost."

Kayla waved a hand. "Then you call him and cancel. No problem."

Everyone's first reaction was to phone Jeffrey for help. If she was lucky, she wouldn't have to bother him.

Kayla took a seat in the wooden rocking chair, by the window. Light, filtered through the lampshade, caught her cheek, smoothing her skin to marble, free of expression.

Charley glanced at the sketchbook. "Are you working on something new?"

"Practice makes perfect." There was a dry note of irony in her voice.

"Perfect is a hard goal to reach."

"So is resurrection." Kayla took a sip of her drink and leaned her head back. "The time when the magic words were made," she murmured, half to herself, her eyes sunken and weary. "Do you remember that story? A word spoken by chance suddenly becomes powerful. Repeat that word every day, and it's all you hear. Like filling an empty glass up" — she raised hers — "with doubt. Course, you don't know what that's like."

Did she really believe that? "Everyone doubts themselves."

"Please. You know exactly what you want. And you'd never let anyone stop you. Or hold you back. And now, when I can finally look for the right words, the better words, to fill the glass, I can't seem to find them."

This was her chance. "Kayla, what's going on between you and David?"

"Who?"

Had that been a second of hesitation? "David Nadeau. You were talking to him in the gallery." With an intimacy that was easy to see, even at a distance.

"And that means I'm, what, having an affair with him?" She frowned. "I spoke to a lot of people tonight."

"I just thought maybe —"

"Wishful thinking." Kayla leaned forward. "Did you ever notice in grandmother's stories, when a hunter finds a woman alone, he always takes her as his wife? Women will marry boulders and eagles and whales. No one is alone for long." The chair rocked as she settled back. "Now I know why. It's hard to survive on your own."

Hard but not impossible. "Give yourself some credit. You're stronger than you think."

"I was at one point." With a glitter of rhinestones, Kayla raised her glass. "But Andrew wasn't the first murder." Her words were starting to slur. "Oh no."

A chill spread through her. "What do you mean?"

"I let it happen. I should have done something, but I didn't, and he killed it."

Her thoughts skidded on a slick of vodka and triple sec. "Who?"

"The old me." Kayla's smile was sad, wistful. "Let's turn into thunder and lightning, so that people will never catch us."

She flashed on summer nights, when they searched for rocks, to send sparks into the darkness, like in the story. The siblings in the legend feared people would kill them, so they became thunder and lightning to escape their fate.

Charley leaned forward, flipped the sketchbook open again to the wolf, wild and fierce. The contours unbroken, the broad black lines explosive and full of force. "Let's turn into wolves and fight."

Kayla gave her a tired smile. "It doesn't work like that and we both know it."

"These are good." She looked at the charcoal sketch, at the raw emotion spilled on paper. "You just have to believe in yourself. If it's important to you, you have to keep going, no matter what." And she recognized the hypocrisy in that as soon as she said it.

"Easy for you to say." Grief and envy hollowed out her features. "You sold two paintings. I used to be confident. I used to know exactly where to place the pencil. Now, with every stroke, it feels like I'm bleeding onto the page."

Something that once brought joy had turned to pain. And they both knew who was to blame for that. But it wasn't too late. "Kayla, the dead don't bleed. And wounds only need time to heal."

THIRTY-ONE

OLD WOUNDS. THAT'S WHAT THIS was all about. And Matt was about to pour salt on them.

Blueprint tucked in his back pocket, he grinned, nice and easy, as the door opened.

It was after nine o'clock and flour coated Jeffrey's jeans and hands. The strain around the man's eyes took Matt aback. Looked like it had been days, maybe even weeks, since he had gotten a full night's sleep. Nevertheless, his smile flashed quick and true. "Another unannounced visit?" He swung the door open wider, and Matt caught a blast of the sweet scent of baker's yeast. "Maybe I should put you back to work. You seem to have enough free time on your hands."

"Says the man with flour on his."

"Better than sawdust."

"I'll say. Seems like my timing couldn't have been better." Kicking off his shoes by the door, Matt strolled through in his socks, following the scent of freshly baked bread into the steam-filled kitchen. Curiosity had him heading straight for the oven. Turning on the light, he glanced through the clouded glass.

On the middle rack sat a round loaf, four slits in crust that was already golden and hard. Not much longer and it would have to come out. The baking sheet in the bottom he knew would be filled with a cup of water, to get that perfect glossy finish.

Turning around, Matt took in the large mixing bowl on the counter, lined with a flour-dusted tea towel and more dough, ready to be shaped. His brows rose. "You just felt like spending the evening making sourdough bread?"

"Pot, kettle," Jeffrey said. "It's Friday night. What are you doing here?"

"Hey, I was at a gallery opening earlier." And then the library.

"I can guess why the sudden interest in art," Jeffrey said dryly.

He grinned at the dig. "I was supporting a local event, that's all."

Jeffrey turned the contents of the bowl out onto the work surface. With the heel of his hand, he knocked the air out of the dough. Kneading bread takes energy, power, but he was putting his full body weight behind it. Applying force, although it wouldn't take much to reactivate the yeast.

Matt leaned back against the counter, biding his time. "How's the new project coming?" Thomas's house. Which was also a nice lead-in as to why he'd come.

Jeffrey slammed his fist into the dough. "Fine."

"Sounds like it," he said mildly.

Jeffrey shot a frown his way. "Don't get smart with me."

Because he recognized real worry when he heard it, he changed his tone. "There always seems to be a snag at the start. What's the problem with this one?"

"The backhoe." The timer shrilled. Jeffrey jerked his head toward the oven. "See if that's done, would you?

"You have a backhoe?" Through a blast of heat and steam, he saw the loaf was nice and dark, almost burnt in places. The scent of the bread had his mouth watering.

"That's the snag."

He winced. Jeffrey would need a backhoe to dig trenches for

a holding tank, haul material on site and any other landscaping. "That's some snag all right." He moved the loaf to the wire rack. "They're not cheap."

"It's an investment." Jeffrey put the dough onto the hot baking sheet, slid it into the oven. Reset the timer. "So, are you going to ask me about that paper hanging out of your back pocket, or are you going to carry it around with you all night?"

Caught on a grin, he spread the blueprint on the countertop, setting flour drifting.

"Building plans?" Jeffrey pressed the curled edge down flat, read the name. "What the hell is this?"

"I was hoping you could tell me that." He watched his face, waiting for that flicker of realization.

"You raided the town archives." Jeffrey frowned. "Why?"

"To find out more about Clarkston Engineering." Hard to believe he even had to ask.

"Always been too damn curious," Jeffrey muttered. His gaze flicked to the date. "These are from a while ago."

"After you stopped working with Andrew."

He nodded.

"Guess who the architect was."

Jeffrey shot him a glance, half-frustrated, half-resigned. Planting his hands on the counter, he leaned over the print. Then his head snapped up. "You can't be serious."

And there it was. "Interesting, isn't it?"

"No."

Not the answer he'd been expecting. "What do you mean? This proves Thomas and Andrew knew each other."

"So what? Did they make a point to hide that fact?"

Might as well have. "They didn't go out of their way to mention it."

"Why should they?" Jeffrey straightened. "This was years ago. And it doesn't mean much."

The thrill that had buoyed him all the way here — that his luck might be turning, that he finally might figure things out — sank inside him. Nevertheless, he said, "They acted like they'd never met."

"You know what they say when you assume. You make an —"

"Ass of 'u' and 'me'. Yeah, I get it. But look at this." He couldn't let it go, not yet. He placed his finger on the revision list. On the approved fill material. "Why the change?"

Jeffrey jerked his shoulders. "There's a reason revision lists are used. There are always alterations before a project gets underway."

"To meet deadlines, keep the bid low." But this was different.

"Turn a five-story build into a three-story and you cut costs, get the job done faster. Nothing odd about that. Just means you can win more bids."

"But why switch to this fill material?"

"No idea." Jeffrey sounded irritated now.

Still, he pushed. It was hard to believe that a man who had spent most of his life working on these sorts of projects, assessing foundations, didn't know the material. "You don't recognize it?" The heat from the oven had a trickle of sweat sliding down his spine.

"Does it matter?"

Balking him every step of the way. "Yeah, I think it does."

Jeffrey snarled a sigh. "Stubborn, as always. The change wouldn't have been smart, but it makes sense. The original fill material was a good choice. But the substitute material would have been cheaper and easier to get a hold of."

"And winter was setting in." The faster the build, the better.

Jeffrey nodded. "But the substitute material doesn't drain as well. It can retain water, which —"

"Expands when it freezes."

Flash of approval that he'd made the connection. "And cause cracking in the foundation walls," Jeffrey said. "They'd need to do remedial work later on down the road. Someone thought they were being clever, but this would come back to bite them in the ass."

That was one way to look at it, if you gave them the benefit of the doubt. "What if they hoped no one would notice? Using cheaper materials to lower building costs, that's more than cutting a corner. That's fraud."

"And you'd better be damn cautious about tossing that word around," Jeffrey warned. "Fraud is a repeated, deliberate action. To me, this looks like a judgement error. A mistake that someone paid for. You don't hang a man for that."

But you sure could fit the noose. "Yeah? What about holding paramount the safety, health, and welfare of the public?"

Jeffrey's hand fisted, the floured knuckles calloused and hard. "Are you quoting the code of ethics at me?"

The sheer force of his anger had Matt falling back a step, holding up his hands in defense. "Just thinking out loud."

"Seems you've been doing a lot of thinking since that artist showed up."

Shock wiped his face blank. "What's that supposed to mean?"

"That girl's really turned your head, hasn't she?"

Anger pulsed through him. "This has nothing to do with Charley."

"She asks for an interview about your father, you jump. She needs help at the gallery, you come running. Next, she'll have you rolling over and playing dead." Jeffrey's lip curled on a sneer. "Good dog."

Outrage and fury surged through him, had his fist curling in response. But he fought to keep his temper in check. "You're crossing the line."

"Am I? You're talking about accusing a man of murder."

"And this might give him motive."

"'Might'? Matt, you don't sic the cops on a man without proof. And this —" He slapped his hand on the blueprint. "— this isn't it."

"Not to mention the fact that you'd like him to pay his bill." He wondered how the hell things had gotten so out of hand, and how he was going to fix it.

"Yeah, I do. It's also clear as day to anyone who has eyes that Kayla killed her husband."

"Some people would disagree with that."

Jeffrey's brows rose. "I can only guess who. And she's got you chasing your own tail."

"Watch it," he warned through gritted teeth. "It's Andrew Clarkston I'm after and you know exactly why. And I'm going to keep asking questions. Because if Andrew really killed my mother to cover up a 'mistake' and got away with it, chances are good he did it again."

Jeffrey rubbed a hand over the back of his neck, his eyes suddenly tired. "Put that thing away."

End of discussion. So much for asking him about the blueprint for the gallery.

Matt rolled up the paper, felt the grit of flour beneath his fingers. "Seems like we keep talking past each other these days." Something had changed, though what and when, he had no idea. Maybe if he did, he'd know how to put it right.

"I don't like it," Jeffrey said.

"Neither do I."

On a sigh, Jeffrey went to the fridge, took out butter, eggs, maple syrup. "Make yourself useful and cut some of that bread."

Matt watched him line up vanilla extract, cinnamon, and sugar. "French Toast?"

"You want to argue about that, too?"

The familiar tone eased the stone-heavy weight in his chest. "Nope."

"Good."

"But it's better with lemon zest," he added on a grin.

A second away from cracking the first egg, Jeffrey paused, shot him a look beneath his brows. "You want to make it?"

"Nah. It looks like you've got this."

"Then shut up." A smile flickered at his mouth. "Or I'll get out the duct tape."

"Fighting words, Jeffrey." And because there'd been a lot of those lately, he let it go. For now.

THIRTY-TWO

ROUGH BARK STUNG HER PALM as Charley caught her balance against a tree trunk. Cocoa danced around her feet. "Whoops." Uneven ground. One more step and she'd be out of the pool of light shining from Kayla's house. Into the inky dusk beyond.

No longer a sun-soaked Renoir, this was Emily Carr's *Wood Interior, Old Trees at Dusk.* Overlapping layers of grey-brown tree trunks crowded, towering. Looming. A space-consuming wall of chiseled shapes and heavy foliage. Swirling ropes of growth.

Crickets chirped. Somewhere, a branch snapped.

At least she had her flashlight. She reached into the bag slung over her shoulder, lighter now that she'd left the rest of the chips — the little that remained — at Kayla's. Her hand skimmed the pouch of dog treats. A fine-tip pen. She rummaged, then yanked the bag off her shoulder to get a better look inside.

The flashlight wasn't there.

Cocoa waited patiently, panting.

Did she leave the flashlight at Kayla's? She must have.

Charley looked back, and the ground took a dive. She blinked, her vision swimming.

Cosmos seemed like a good idea at the time. Now, not so much.

Whip-poor-will. At the sing-song whistle of the bird, Cocoa whipped around, ears twitching with the last rising accent.

The canopy of branches and leaves hid the stars from view. The trees were a leaning presence. There were only a few cottages between Kayla's and their own, not nearly enough to light the way. In the distance, an owl hooted.

Sweat slithered clammy down her back and Charley felt panic tickle at the back of her throat. Cocoa's eyes glittered up at her.

One step in front of the other, that was all. "Let's go. We'll be fine." If only she could convince herself as easily.

It was black as night. And she couldn't see.

The thin soles of her sneakers crunched over gravel. She felt each stone beneath her shoes. Summer-warmed scents rose around her. Crushed grass, the sweet and spiced honey tones of phlox. The rustle of wild lilies, just a blur in the gloom.

The lands could not be seen, the animals could not be seen. Kayla's grandmother's voice echoed through her mind. *Everything was in darkness.* In the story, the magic words were made on a night just like this, when there was no light on earth.

A person could become an animal. A wolf, a bear, a fox. And an animal could become a human being. She gripped Cocoa's leash tighter.

A lone, chattering howl filled the night. A coyote, though still far away, she hoped. But the answering group's yips had the hairs on her arms rising, had her picking up her pace, even though the road wasn't quite steady beneath her feet. Cocoa growled, low in her throat.

This was such a mistake. What was she thinking?

The story stayed with her, kept pace with them.

The fox loved the darkness because then he could steal from the humans. But the hare wanted the light so that he could find food.

Darkness, darkness, darkness, said the fox.

But the hare's words were more powerful. Charley murmured

262

them like a chant as she hurried down the road, "day, day, day."

Close now. Just a little further. The weight of the darkness pressed against her back, urging her to go faster.

Sparks flew in the shadows. Rising like ghosts from the past, striking flint rocks in the night. A glimmer at first, then more and more flickered through the wildflowers lining the roadside. Drifting through clusters of Queen Anne's lace, glowing between the tiny white flowers.

Fireflies.

Charley laughed in relief. Just fireflies. God, all those sleepless hours leading up to the opening must be catching up with her.

Then night turned into day.

Caught in the glare of headlights, her heart thudded.

MATT SLAMMED ON THE BRAKES. He'd just barely caught the gleam of eyes, dead ahead.

Who the hell decided to stroll down the middle of the road in the dark? He scowled at the silhouette caught in his headlights. Then he spotted the dog and a jolt of recognition hit.

He frowned. What was she doing, walking the road late at night?

Never mind the cars. There were coyotes, wolves. Animals that didn't shy away from picking a fight with a chocolate lab.

He pulled over to the side of the road. Gave the knob on the stereo a twist, taking the edge off the hard rock, and got out of the truck. "Are you trying to get yourself killed?"

"What?" Charley shielded her eyes against the light, her shadow stretched out long behind her.

"Taking Cocoa for a walk this late at night. It's not —" Smart, he almost said. But he caught himself in time, rephrased. "A good idea."

In the low brush in the ditch, something rustled.

"We're not 'going for a walk'. We're going home." She waved an arm toward the cottage up ahead.

At the careful enunciation, he narrowed his eyes, moved closer. "Home from where?"

"Kayla's. What is this, the incqui—incquisi—"

"Inquisition?" Amused now, he rocked back on his heels. Cocoa panted up at him.

"That's what I said."

"Uh huh." Since he didn't want to come back to a truck full of moths, Matt slammed the door. "I'll walk you to the cottage." Because it was the right thing to do. Not because he was chasing after her, tail wagging, damn it.

"Thanks. But we're almost there." She turned, stumbled on the pivot.

Catching a hand under her elbow to steady her, he asked, "So how much did you drink?"

She shot him a glance. "Not much."

Enough though. "Celebrating?"

"And investigating."

Another tricky word. "I thought you didn't think Kayla did it." He kept a hand on her arm as they walked, avoiding the ruts and tire tracks worn into the gravel as best he could in the dark.

"I don't. It's David I'm not so sure about. And Thomas. Thomas is —" She paused for a second, concentrating on her feet. "— very suspicious."

Yeah, he was. What would she say to the blueprints he'd found?

She jostled against him, and the warmth of her body against his had other thoughts going through his mind.

"Sorry," she said.

There were more loose pebbles up ahead and all those uneven fieldstones, too. "That's it." He reached for the leash, looped the leather twice around his wrist, and swept Charley off her feet. And ended up with an armful of outraged female.

"Put me down!"

Enjoying himself, he said, "When we get to the door."

With a bark, Cocoa pounced around them, playfully tugging at the leash.

"Don't you dare drop me." Charley squirmed.

"Then stop fidgeting." A frog leaped out of the grass near his feet.

When she linked her arms around his neck, his thoughts scattered. "You smell like maple syrup and powdered sugar," she told him. It sounded like an accusation.

"That's probably true." He made his way carefully over the fieldstone slabs, trying not to focus on her heart beating against his chest.

"And you have a nice face."

Was that a compliment or a complaint? "I like yours too."

"Good, strong lines. Interesting angles." Her fingers skimmed along his jaw, light as a feather, making his blood run faster. "Especially up close."

"Don't do that." He stopped short and shifted the weight of her in his arms. "Keep doing that, and I'm going to drop you. Or kiss you."

"No." She shook her head, and her breath brushed his throat. "I've decided I'm not going to kiss you again."

She sounded sure about that. He looked down at her. "And why's that?"

"Because distractions are not allowed." It would have been more convincing if she didn't have her arms wrapped around his neck.

"I'm distracting?" He heard the grin in his own voice.

"I should be drawing you. Not kissing you."

"I gotta admit, I prefer the second option." At the door, he set her on her feet. Cocoa leaped between them, wagging her tail at the new game.

"My tongue is numb."

He bit back a chuckle. "I'll bet it is." At least someone had left the porch light on for her. Moths batted around the bulb. "Keys?"

He figured she'd have to search for them, but she pulled them out of her pocket. "Got them."

Taking them from her, he unlocked the door. "I'll wait until you're inside."

She smiled. Hesitated and said, "Thanks."

"Anytime." Matt watched as she let herself into the cottage, staying until he heard the latch fasten.

Heading back to his truck, he caught himself whistling a cheerful tune beneath his breath.

THIRTY-THREE

CHARLEY GROANED, DISORIENTED. GLANCING AT the clock she winced. Five a.m.? Why was she awake? Her skull felt like it was about to split in two.

The mattress dipped as Cocoa jumped to the floor. Just a shadow in the dusky room, she stood alert, ears forward, body rigid. Listening.

Something tapped against glass. A tree branch blown by the wind?

No. If the wind had picked up, the curtains would billow. But there wasn't a wisp of a breeze flowing through the room.

Nose to the ground, Cocoa raced to the closed bedroom door. Her low growl, the bristling fur, had fear skidding down Charley's spine. Something wasn't right.

She tossed the covers aside and swung her feet to the floor. The movement jarred her aching head.

She scanned the room. On the top of the chest of drawers, metal glinted. Her ruling pen. The two flexible metal jaws tapered to a lethal point. "That'll work," she murmured. Picking it up on the way past, she moved to the door.

Cocoa pressed against the doorjamb with an anxious whine.

Turning the handle, Charley got a good grip on the pen. She

wrapped her fingers around it, angling the metal tip up like a blade, wrist locked nice and square. "Ready?"

Cocoa pawed at the door. Charley swung it open and she took off in a flash, coursing over the ground, like she was stalking prey.

Charley crept through the dark living room, following in Cocoa's path. It was probably just a raccoon or a stray cat. Still, her pulse raced.

Her toe hit something hard and a flash of pain made her eyes water. Biting back a curse, she rubbed her foot.

Table leg. *Ouch.*

If ever there was a time to channel Liselle in *Hamadryads*, it was now. Think stealth and courage. Whip-smart reactions.

Cocoa's growl turned menacing.

Rounding the corner to the entrance, Charley's heart leaped into her throat. She raised the pointed tip of the pen, keeping it up and away from her body, ready to slash or stab, if she had to.

Nose wrinkling, Cocoa snarled and bared her teeth. Hackles up, the dog crouched, facing the front door.

Outlined against the glass pane was the tall and broad-shouldered silhouette of a man.

Knuckles knocked on the glass again. "Are you going to leave me standing out here?"

At the sound of his voice, Cocoa relaxed, and her tail began to wag.

He'd better have a good explanation for showing up this early.

Charley flung the door open and shivered as a gust of cool air skated over her arms. "What are you doing here?"

Cocoa scrambled forward to greet Matt.

"Morning," he said cheerfully. He looked wide awake. "How's the head?" He held two Thermoses and a butter-streaked wax paper bag.

"Still attached."

His blue plaid flannel shirt, white T-shirt, and Levis made her all too aware of the fact that she was standing there in her pajamas.

"Well, that's something," he said. "Did I wake you?"

"No, I've been up for hours," she replied, deadpan.

Matt chuckled. "Good thing I waited an extra hour before coming over. Are you going to stab me with that?"

She still brandished the pen like a knife. "I thought about it." But she lowered the makeshift weapon. "That's what happens when you show up at someone's house in the dead of night."

"Actually, it's dawn. And we're going to watch the sunrise from the dock." He held out a Thermos to her.

"You're kidding, right?" But she took the Thermos, because it might be filled with caffeine and her head was throbbing. "The number one carpenter," she read the side of the mug. "'A shelf made man'?"

Matt held up his own. "'Measure twice, cut once'. I raided my dad's collection of travel mugs and found these at the back of the cupboard. Woodworking humour. So, are you coming?"

"I'm in my pajamas!"

"Yeah, I noticed." He flashed his crinkly-eyed grin. "I could just eat these chocolate croissants myself."

Chocolate croissants? "Give me a sec. I'll throw on a pair of jeans and a sweater."

"No time. The sky's already starting to turn pink. Here." He shrugged out of his shirt and settled it over her shoulders. The flannel felt warm against her skin. She breathed in the scent of chocolate and soap. "Now you're set. Just grab some shoes."

Maple syrup. The memory pierced the fog clouding her mind. Last night, had she told him he smelled like maple syrup? It couldn't get much more embarrassing than that.

"You're bossy. Did you know that?" But she set the Thermos

down and slid her arms through the sleeves of the shirt. If her brain were functioning, she'd be able to come up with a better reply.

"You look good in flannel," he said.

"Who knew all a girl needs to make an impression is flannel and pajamas?" She slipped into her flip-flops and closed the front door with a quiet click.

Cocoa roamed ahead of them to the water, paws swishing through dew-tipped grass.

Charley took a sip from the Thermos as she walked, then winced at the bitter taste. "Matt, what is this?"

"English Breakfast tea."

"Why —" It hit her. The Coffee Nook. She told him she preferred tea. Damn. And he'd remembered. She'd have to drink it. "Mmm, so good." Karma.

He threw her a glance. "Too strong?"

She took another sip, swallowed hard. "It's great."

Matt shook his head. "Did no one ever tell you you shouldn't lie?" He held out his own drink. "Here, swap."

Caught out, she grinned. "Lesson learned." She took a sip of sweet, creamy coffee and wrapped her hands around the mug. "But you make really good coffee."

Matt lifted his Thermos with a wink. "Luckily, I make a mean cup of tea, too."

The old wooden dock, streaked green with moss and faded as driftwood, swayed as she sat beside him.

With a splash, Cocoa leaped into the water. Wading through the shallows, her tail wagged furiously.

Sunbeams hit the mist. Not just warm streaks of morning light but sun-shot gold, straight to the vanishing point. The surface of the lake shone, smooth as glass. The peace and solitude broken only by the ink-dark shadows screening the far shoreline.

"It's like there's no one else in the world," she murmured.

Somewhere a loon called to its mate.

Matt shrugged, but the lazy movement seemed tense. "That's because they're all still sleeping."

She nudged his shoulder with hers. "Ha. Funny." The coffee was starting to hit her system. The croissant flaked apart in her fingers and tasted of toasted caramel and bittersweet chocolate. "This is nice."

"Can't beat a sunrise at the lake."

Colours bloomed like paint on damp paper. Crimson, Burnt Sienna. Indigo, Yellow Ochre. Insects hummed, the drowsy sounds of a hot summer day. Ripples spread toward them from where Cocoa splashed through the water, brown fur already wet and gleaming.

"I didn't drag you out of bed just for the company." Matt reached into his pocket, pulled out a folded square of paper and passed it to her. "Take a look at this, tell me what you think."

Glancing away from the horizon, she took the paper from him, smoothed it out on the dock. The edge fluttered in the breeze and she pinned one corner down with her Thermos. "A blueprint?" A legal-sized photocopy, faint in parts.

When he leaned over to tap the sheet, his arm grazed hers, sending a current of electricity tingling over her skin. "Check out the names."

"Andrew Clarkston." The second name had her heart rate kicking up a notch. "Thomas Kelley," she murmured. She checked the date on the stamp. "This was drafted ten years ago. They worked together, knew each other." That put things in a whole new perspective.

"Not only that," he said. "Take a look at the changes. This was originally proposed as a five-story build but it was scaled down to three."

"Why?" Fewer materials?

"It would be a faster build, meaning they'd be able to start other projects sooner. The workforce would be smaller and, because of that, the company would be able to have multiple projects on the go and a lower labour base rate. And, see here?" Matt shifted, pointed at one of the revisions. "Someone made a last-minute change to the fill material around the foundation. The new material was a hell of a lot cheaper and more readily available than the original one. But not the same quality. It was known to retain water, which would expand when frozen and cause cracks in the foundation walls. The project was scheduled to start in late fall."

So, Clarkston Engineering had cut corners and Thomas was a part of it. The realization prickled at the back of her neck. "Engineering fraud?"

"Or lousy research." His eyes had gone hard as flint, his jaw tense. "But I'd assume so, yeah. It would be easy to apply pressure with the cold weather setting in. To put a rush on the project, and get the material approved. Up the profit margin."

The edge to his voice had her asking, "How did you find out about this?"

"I was searching for something else, stumbled across this instead."

Something else. It was vague enough to jar. "You were looking at blueprints?"

"It's not important." He brushed the question aside. Fast.

"Did no one ever tell you you shouldn't lie?" She quoted his own words back at him.

A smile flickered at the corners of his mouth. "Okay." He shifted so that he faced her, and their knees bumped. Sunlight played over his face, glinting golden at his jawline. "But it's about your gallery."

Her heart thudded. "You went looking for the gallery's blueprints? Why?"

He looked at her, his expression impatient. "I could tell you if you'd stop interrupting me with questions."

"A side effect of spending too much time with Meghan. Sorry." She waved a hand. "Keep going."

"Clarkston Engineering built it. Jeffrey was Andrew's general contractor, and my mom worked for him as a framing carpenter."

Lizzie. Her ghost in the Mews. "So, all three were involved in the job."

He took a breath. "I found some photos she took on the site, late in the day. Of the joists."

"But why would she —"

Matt shot her an exasperated frown. "You said you'd let me finish."

"Right." She slid her hands under her legs and fought the urge to rock impatiently. "Go ahead."

"She spotted an error and documented it. Then she died." His voice was flat, his expression calm, except for his eyes. In them she saw the pain, the anger. Carefully tamped down and ready to explode. "An accident on site."

Dread settled in the pit of her stomach. "Are you saying what I think you're saying?"

"Andrew killed her."

Oh my God. She sucked in a breath. "Are you sure?"

"I'd ask him, but he's dead." A muscle leapt in his jaw. "Yeah, I'm sure. She discovered an error in the structural integrity of the building. She wouldn't have backed down until it was fixed. But, before she could make it public, she fell to her death from the second-floor window. Only thing is, she was careful. Followed all the safety regulations. I don't think she fell. I think she was pushed."

"You're saying Andrew committed murder to cover up a mistake." The man Kayla had married.

"That's my guess. And it's got me wondering if his death has something to do with the past."

Fraud and murder. She looked at the blueprint. "In other words, Thomas might have a motive that's more than just anger over the delays on his house."

"You found the recipe, so I thought I'd get your opinion on this."

Thomas had easy access to the gallery and knew enough about art history to turn a *vanitas* painting into a threatening message. "Alex needs to see this."

"Not yet." He folded the blueprint again, sharpening the crease with one swift slide of his fingers.

"But this is the clue we've been looking for."

"It also gives me one hell of a motive."

That gave her pause. He had a point. Alex might decide the evidence proved his theory of revenge.

Matt said, "You know he's going to ask the same questions you did. I need better answers. Otherwise, this won't play out well. I want all the cards in my hand before I take this to the police."

He'd have a hard time tracking down answers from a holding cell. "We need to figure out what happened between Thomas and Andrew in the past. And fast." She thought of the postcard on the gallery's door.

"We?" He skimmed his thumb over her cheekbone, just a brush of contact. A shiver ran through her at the gentle touch.

Someone cleared their throat nearby, loudly.

"Nice timing," Matt muttered.

Alex walked over the grass to them. Cocoa gave a happy woof and shook her head, ears flapping. Drops of moisture spattered over them.

"Charley." Alex's face was grim. "Someone tripped the alarm at the gallery."

The statement, the meaning behind it, seared through her. "What?" She jumped to her feet, pulse scrambling.

He jiggled his car keys in his hand. "An officer's already on the scene. I'm on my way now."

God, she couldn't think straight. And Cocoa was soaked. "I need to get Cocoa inside first. Throw some different clothes on." Take an aspirin.

"Make it fast. Meg's coming too."

"So am I." Matt raised his brows at the look they both shot him. "I'll follow you there."

Adrenaline coursed through her veins. "Was anything taken?"

Alex's expression was stony. And all cop. "We'll find out when we get there."

THIRTY-FOUR

"VANDALISM," CHARLEY HEARD THE POLICE constable say to Alex. The young woman reported the fact in a clipped, dispassionate tone. The cold hard truth, simple as that. "But, now that you're here," she said, "we'll have to do a thorough search to rule out theft, too." Document the evidence, the crime scene. Her gallery.

The partition wall blocked Charley's view of the rest of the room. Her glance met painted eyes. Veronica Lake hair, red lips. An intense stare of almost scientific interest. She had painted the woman so that she seemed to be leaning out of the canvas, to look at reality. Larger than life itself, she appeared to be a second away from reaching a hand out, into the gallery.

The title of the piece took on a whole new meaning now. *The Witness.*

What had she seen? A trick of the light changed the woman's expression, her eyes widening, as she moved past her, deeper into the gallery.

Anger churned inside Charley. Her steps echoed as she scanned, looking for marks, for damage. And braced herself for empty spaces.

A canvas lay face-down on the ground. One of hers? Dry-mouthed, she forced herself to move toward it, to her section of the exhibit.

The painting on the wall. The torn canvas gaped like an open wound.

Grief slammed its fist into her, hard and fast.

Because her vision swam, she bit the inside of her lip, tasted blood. And stepped closer.

Not torn. Cut. Something sharp had sliced through the canvas, lacerating the careful brushstrokes. The diagonal incision ran from corner to corner. Just like the visual effect she'd created on the gallery's poster, revealing the exhibition title. A deliberate reference?

Only this time, words had been scrawled on top — thick and red and gleaming — over the paint she'd built up, layer by layer.

BITCH

The letters glistened, with the plastic sheen of a lacquer. The permanence of varnish.

She struggled for calm. Tried to see past the hurt, take stock of the situation. And realized what she'd missed as she entered.

Only hers.

The thought ran through her like a knife.

Not Kayla's. Not Thomas's. Their work was intact, untouched. This wasn't theft, and it wasn't just vandalism. It was another message. Another threat.

Charley heard the sharp hiss of an indrawn breath as Matt came up behind her. "Jesus."

Heart aching, she swallowed hard. "Yeah."

Alex rounded the corner, and his step faltered. "Hell, Charley." He'd gone pale, and she could guess why.

Close on his heels, Meghan asked, "What happened?" And gasped when she saw it. "What kind of a scumbag does this?" She looked at the painting, at the reporter working moonlit hours to beat her deadline, and crossed her arms. "Did you tick them off or did I?"

The reporter in the painting was Meghan. The cut slashed across her face. The red letters trailing like blood on her cheek.

"That's a lot of anger there," Matt said.

"Or envy," Alex remarked.

Someone who wanted what she had. Enough to destroy it? Someone filled with doubt. Grieving for a life they should have had.

He killed the old me.

No. She shook the thought off. Kayla would never butcher a work of art.

Meghan scowled. "Whoever did this deserves to be throttled."

Charley's hands balled into fists at her sides. "Worse." Torn limb from limb.

Alex sighed. "I'm going to pretend I didn't hear that."

"What's the title of the piece?" Matt moved closer, read the print on the label. "*The News —*"

"*Never Sleeps,*" she finished.

Meghan stared at the slashed canvas. "I liked that one."

"Me too," Alex said flatly. No surprise there.

Meghan glanced at her. "Are you okay?"

"I'm not going to cry, if that's what you're asking." But damn it if her voice didn't wobble, just a little.

Flanked on either side, they stood in a row and took in the destruction. The ragged canvas curled back to expose the drywall beneath, scarred too, nicked by the blade.

Meghan draped an arm over her shoulder. Meant to comfort but Charley felt the anger vibrating through her. "You can paint another one."

Alex studied the scrawled letters, the large print, taking up as much space as possible. "You sold a painting, but Kayla didn't. Her life is in turmoil. Do you recognize the handwriting, Charley?"

Of course he'd leap to that conclusion. But Kayla's writing was small and neat, her dots always placed directly above the stem of the 'i'. Not an off-centre afterthought like this one. "We spent the better part of last night drinking Cosmos. I doubt she woke up this morning with revenge on her mind."

"There's only one target — your art. This attack was planned, purposeful."

And vicious. But the motive wasn't jealousy. "She wouldn't have tripped the alarm system getting in."

"Neither would Thomas," Matt murmured at her side. For once, his mouth was unsmiling, his brows furrowed.

Alex snorted. "Only a complete idiot would use their key to enter the gallery. Might as well hold up a sign, saying 'I did it.'"

She had a hard time imagining smashing the glass pane was the more subtle route, even if it was just a single panel. "What about the alarm system? How could they do all this before the police showed up?"

Alex grimaced. "It's not a perfect system. Our target response time is ten minutes. In an ideal world. Realistically, it's impossible. Response time is a combination of two factors: the allowed time to enter a code before the alarm goes off, which varies between companies, and the time it takes for the security provider to be notified that the alarm has been triggered. Then they call us. All in all, it takes about eight minutes before we even get the call. Then we have to get here."

"So, the alarm is useless," she said flatly.

He shook his head. "Only if the perp has balls of steel. It takes confidence to carry out a burglary — or destroy a painting — while an alarm is going off over your head. In most cases, it's enough to stop the crime and send them running."

Twenty minutes, fifteen even, would be more than enough time for someone who knew the building. Who had helped design the layout of the exhibit.

Meghan asked, "Did anyone hear the alarm go off? If so, maybe they saw something."

Outside the window, the wooden deck, the courtyard was deserted.

Alex said, "On a residential street, that might be the case, but on Main Street at 6 a.m. on a Saturday? We'll look into it, but I doubt it." He slid his hands into his pockets. "I told you to take the postcard seriously." His voice was calm, matter-of-fact. "I told you to leave it alone."

Charley opened her mouth to reply, but Matt was quicker. He asked, "What postcard?"

Meghan crossed her arms. "That's what I'd like to know."

No way to deflect attention now.

Alex's smile was grim. "Care to answer that one, Charley?"

Put on the spot, she had to tell them. "This isn't the first —" Threat? "— message, I've gotten."

Matt and Meghan rounded on her, both talking at once.

"What's that supposed to mean?" Matt asked. The tone accusing, and no wonder. He'd confided in her and she'd kept this from him.

"I want details," Meghan said. "Right now."

Or else. Alex met Charley's eyes and raised his brows.

Fine. "Someone left a postcard of a *vanitas* still life inside the gallery door the other day." Was it possible to feel both numb and furious at the same time?

"Inside the door," Matt repeated, his brows drawing together.

Alex said, "The painting was full of *memento mori*. Reminders of death. Go on. Tell them about the note on the back."

"I was getting to it." Charley shot him a look that she hoped would shrivel his toes. She would have told them eventually, but not here and not like this. "There were only four letters, cut from newspaper and pasted on, like a clichéd ransom note. M-Y-O-B."

Meghan frowned. "Poison. A postcard in the gallery window. Wrecking the painting. There hasn't been any real violence."

"No violence?" Alex waved his arm at the painting. "Megs, whoever did this slashed a knife through your face."

"A *painting* of my face," Meghan said.

"Who's to say it'll stop there?"

"This is simply murder of a different kind." At the new voice, Charley turned around. Sarah stood beside the face-down canvas on the whitewashed floor, surveying the damage done in her building with a fierce glint in her eye. "To destroy art" — she stepped forward — "is unforgivable." She pursed her lips. "Has anything been stolen?"

"I'll have to check," Charley said, "but so far, it doesn't look like it."

Matt said, "Seems odd someone would go to the effort of breaking into an art gallery without stealing anything."

"Senseless," Sarah agreed. With slow steps, she walked the length of the wall. Her lips moved silently, as though tallying a score to be reckoned.

Charley hoped she wouldn't blame her for this. "I must have hit on something," she murmured to Matt. "But what?"

"A clue," Alex said, fast and off the cuff.

Meghan nodded. "Have you noticed the way Matt and Charley keep looking at each other?"

Matt tensed beside her. She had to force herself not to glance his way.

"Hard to miss it," Alex said.

"It almost makes you think they're hiding something."

"I'm with you on that one." Alex prowled around them. "Maybe they heard something, saw something —"

Like two lions stalking their prey, Meghan circled counter-clockwise. "Or pieced something together."

Sarah stood at a distance, head tilted. The scavenger on the sidelines, waiting for scraps of knowledge.

Matt rubbed a hand over the back of his neck. "There's —"

Charley cut him off. "Why not pastel?"

Matt was right, they couldn't tell Alex about the past just yet. They didn't have enough facts. But they would soon.

Alex paused. "What?"

"The writing." She gestured at the word scrawled over her paint-ing of Meghan. "It looks like some kind of varnish. And a quick-drying one at that. Why not oil pastel or oil paint squeezed straight from the tube?" She had both in her kit. It would only take a second to grab a tube of scarlet oil colour, shove it in a pocket.

"Why not a permanent marker?" Matt asked.

"The ink would smear. You'd need to use an oil-based paint marker." An artist would know that.

Meghan studied the letters. "Varnish, like nail polish?"

There were no brush marks. "The lines are too precise for that, and thicker."

"Car lacquer?" Matt suggested.

Touch-up paint. Similar to nail polish, but more potent. Laced with chemicals. "Maybe."

"Another mystery." Sarah's voice echoed through the gallery.

Alex snapped a photo of the painting on his phone. "This whole thing reeks of desperation." His grin was sharp and feral. "And that's a good thing."

"How do you figure that?" Matt asked.

But Charley knew what he meant. "Because that's a sign the murderer has stopped thinking straight."

"And that's when mistakes happen. Which is when I" — Alex emphasized the word — "catch them."

Sarah met her glance, a sudden flick, and away. Had that been dread, fast as a shadow and gone just as quick?

Or just another trick of the light, changing an expression.

THIRTY-FIVE

WAIT FOR ALEX TO CHECK Thomas's alibi? No way. Not when she could do it herself, and faster.

Charley shot a glance over her shoulder, back at the cottage. She sat cross-legged on the sun-warmed dock, Cocoa beside her. A hot, mineral smell rose off the lake. Silvery fish rippled in the water. Between the gaps in the warped boards, something darker scuttled. A dock spider, stalking the minnows.

Thomas had motive, means, and opportunity. The recipe and the blueprint were evidence. He had access to the gallery. He could have taped the postcard to the door, could have slashed her painting. It was time to strike. For Kayla and for herself.

It was him. All she had to do was get him to confess.

She'd rather catch him off guard, confront him in person, but that wasn't an option. If she drove the Jeep somewhere, she'd be stuck. The engine died as soon as it was turned off. Without being able to jumpstart it, she'd be stranded.

But she could phone Thomas, and there was safety in distance. Anger had her fingers trembling as she dialed the number.

Thomas couldn't paint the way he did without having a conscience. And, hopefully, it would haunt him.

Her fist clenched as she listened to the dial tone. He would lie, but even a lie could be used against him.

The phone kept ringing.

Answer already. She laid a hand on Cocoa's soft fur, felt the steady beat of her heart. And willed him to pick up.

The call went to voice mail.

"Okay, think."

Cocoa glanced up at her, cocked her head.

"Maybe," Charley said, "he ignored my call. But why?" He'd assume she was calling to tell him about the break-in at the gallery. Wouldn't he seize the opportunity to witness the effect of his actions, to gloat?

The distant grind of a boat's trolling motor startled the fish, sent them scattering.

The postcard and the slashed painting were meant to scare her. And Thomas would be confident that she had no idea who was behind them.

Which meant she still had time.

Cocoa rested her chin on Charley's knee and gave her a pointed stare.

"You can't come with me."

The dog's eyes narrowed.

"Sorry." Oh, she'd be punished for that one later.

She'd get the Jeep to Jeffrey's workshop, as planned. Maybe he would be able to work his magic. Then she'd drive to Thomas's house.

And get the facts they needed to seal his fate, once and for all.

THIRTY-SIX

EVERY MOVE MATT MADE SEEMED to dredge up more secrets that muddied what should have been clear as the lake on a summer day. But sometimes, when the silt settled, you found gold. And he was prepared to sift through the murk to find it.

Cellphone clamped between ear and shoulder, he opened the door to the basement. "I'm going to be late." Again.

"Do what you have to do." Mrs. Callahan's sigh was loaded with disappointment that did nothing to ease his guilt. "I'll hold down the fort here."

"I appreciate it. I'll be at Chocoholic's, soon as I can." He hung up the call, flicked on the lights. The bright wattage of new bulbs flooded the stairs, filling the rec room below with a welcoming glow.

He'd come down here often enough when Dad was sick, to sit and think. To get the chance to breathe, in at least one room in the house.

The bar in the corner gleamed. He'd wiped it clean, gotten rid of the cobwebs. Added a six-pack of Canada Dry to the shelf that had only ever held pop. That one act felt like a ritual. A home-coming, more so than when he'd filled the cupboard in the room upstairs with his clothes.

Cold seeped up from the concrete floor. No matter the season, they used to double-layer boot socks when they came down here, to keep their feet warm.

Most of the space in the room was taken up by the ping pong table, scavenged from a garage sale. No net. Mom hadn't even considered buying the paddles, too. Not for a second.

She bought that table for the sheer scale of it. Because it was cheap and because it was big.

When the surface wasn't spread with blueprints, they'd built civilizations on that green terrain, one Lego block at a time. The farthest corners of the table the only limit. The edge of the world.

He ran a hand over the scuff marks. The faded rings of condensation from glasses of ginger ale she'd garnished with maraschino cherries and plastic swizzle sticks.

Together, they'd built skyscrapers, castles, and spaceships. Entire cities, on a miniature scale. Telling stories of good versus evil. Sieges and intergalactic battles ended only by selfless acts of bravery. Heroic deeds that restored peace and order.

Listening to her, you'd have thought she was the storyteller in the family. Maybe if she'd had the patience to write them down, but for her, it was all in the spinning of the tale. Right up to the moment justice reigned. Then they'd architect the universe all over again.

He headed to the cardboard boxes, pushed against the wall. The corners damp with mold, stacked on planks, and raised off the ground. He'd spent hours down here in the past few months but hadn't had the energy to sort through more memories. It was harder here, to make the call of what to keep and what to discard. One day he'd have to, depending on what he did with the house, but not yet.

Now, he figured it was a stroke of luck that he hadn't had the heart to throw anything away. Because here might be the gold he was looking for.

He should have thought of it sooner.

All they needed was one damning piece of evidence. A project Thomas was involved in. Another document hinting at fraud, or the gallery blueprints.

Matt hefted one box after another onto the ping pong table, keeping an eye on his watch. An hour, that's all he had. Then he'd have to leave for Chocoholic's, continue this later.

He only had to glance inside the boxes that rattled with plastic bricks before setting them aside. The heavier ones, filled with old papers, were the ones he wanted.

He spread each page out, scanning. Searching for the gold in the silt.

Tax returns. Manuals for appliances no longer in the house. Receipts.

Nothing jumped out at him. Not a single link to Clarkston Engineering. No facts to trap Thomas. To restore justice. Not even the flicker of a memory that could take him down a different route.

He'd been so sure, if there was anything to be found, the answer would be here.

Not just dust and Lego pieces, more like rubble after a demolition than building blocks.

The hour was up, and he'd only made it through a few boxes. He had to get to Chocoholic's, let Mrs. Callahan off the hook. Then tackle the rest, if he could, after work.

A stack of yellowed pages slid off the edge of the table, spilling onto his shoes and onto the floor.

Matt bent to scoop up the scattered papers. Piled them in a heap on the table. He'd figure out what to do with them later.

His fingers brushed over glossy cardstock. The back of a photograph?

He tugged it loose and felt the grin catch him off guard.

Colour-faded by time, but recognizable, was Jeffrey. Younger. The picture probably older even than the negatives he'd found in Dad's office. The lines just starting to fan out around Jeffrey's eyes. He sat at the helm of a motorboat, arm slung over the wooden steering wheel. White T-shirt. Dark hair cut in a style that would have been classed as cool a few decades ago. Full-blown laugh crinkling suntanned cheeks. Closer to carefree than he'd ever seen him.

Matt slid the photo in his back pocket. Jeffrey would get a kick out of seeing it.

He wondered who took the shot. Whoever was behind the camera sure knew how to make him laugh.

THIRTY-SEVEN

THIS TIME, THERE WAS NO music. Just the dull thud of hammer striking wood. Inside Jeffrey's workshop, light prismed through the stained glass window and onto the concrete floor. Charley walked over the shimmering pattern of green and gold and red, following the sound, past steel-tipped power tools and heavy wooden planks. The sawdust layer was thicker here, scuffed by the snaking imprint of extension cords and footprints.

She found Jeffrey leaning over the workbench, assembling a wooden table, a rich reddish-brown hue. Three legs were finished. The joints fit together like puzzle pieces.

Rubber mallet in his hand, he turned to face her. The flicker of annoyance was quickly hidden by a grin that fanned laugh lines around his eyes. Judging from the gleam of sweat at his brow, he'd been hard at work for a while. And she was interrupting him.

As though reading her thoughts, he said, "I'm playing catch-up with this project." A coarse grain swirled through the wood, interspersed with darker marks. Sun caught on the razor-edged teeth of the table saw. He rested the rubber head of the hammer on the scarred work surface. "I hear you've got car trouble."

"Again."

"Happen often?"

Only all the time. "Let's just say it's surprising when everything's running smoothly."

"Then let's take a look at the patient." Solid *thump* of the hammer as he set it down. "See what we can do." He led the way back out through a maze of planks, unfinished cabinets, and stools. "Shame about the gallery."

She should have expected it. News of a break-in, at a building on Main Street, would spread through Oakcrest fast, but it caught her off guard anyway. "I'm with you on that one."

He glanced back at her over his shoulder. "Did someone use the opening to scout out the wares?"

She shook her head. "Nothing was stolen. But they damaged —" She hesitated. "— some of the art." Took a knife to it.

"Vandalism?" He sounded surprised. "That must have been one hell of a shock."

She stepped outside after him. "That's an understatement."

Their steps crunched over gravel as they walked to the Jeep.

"Start the car," he said, "and we'll have a listen."

Sure, easy as that.

She slid behind the wheel and turned the key, expecting that same empty *click* as before. But after a few seconds, the engine cranked. A slow start, but it turned over. Wasn't that just typical?

She was about to warn him about the hood when he popped it open, leaned his weight against the rod, and locked it in place. The hood stayed open.

Leaning over the engine, he said, "Alex must have an idea who did it."

Oh, he had an idea all right. "Yeah, he does." She watched Jeffrey examine the parts with the confidence of someone who knew his way around the inner workings of a car.

"Local kids?" he asked. "Or cottagers?"

A stranger, that was always the easiest solution. But both guesses were off the mark. "Kids didn't do this."

"You think?" The rumble of the engine muffled his voice.

"This was different, targeted." Purposeful.

"Is that Alex's opinion?" He flicked a glance at her, his brown eyes thoughtful.

"His. And mine."

"You've been in Oakcrest how long?" Casual, his focus on the battery terminal. "And you managed to piss someone off already?"

Something felt off. An uneasy feeling tingled at the back of her neck. "Seems like it."

"What are you going to do now?"

"Put together the clues and hunt them down."

Jeffrey straightened and pulled a threadbare cotton rag from his back pocket. He wiped his hands. "Things go wrong often enough, maybe it's not meant to be."

Speechless, it took her a second to recoup. Her spine stiffened. "Is that what you told Matt when he wanted to open Chocoholic's?"

He gave her an assessing gaze. "Sometimes obstacles are signs."

And she'd been too dead set on fulfilling her dream to see them? "When the going gets tough, the tough get going."

"I always wondered if the message there is to rise to the occasion. Or leave."

That was blunt. "And that's what you think I should do? Leave?"

Clouds scrolled through the blue sky. A chorus of birdsong spilled from the trees shading the edges of the driveway from the brunt of the sun.

He considered her. "What's the point in dealing with all these challenges when you're just here for the summer anyway?"

So that was it. Charley put her hands on the frame of the Jeep, felt the heat of the metal burn her palms. "You don't like me much, do you?"

"Matt seems to."

Seems to. "But?"

"Oakcrest is a stepping stone for you."

And how could she argue that?

Before she could reply, Jeffrey said, "The alternator cables don't look cracked or frayed. You've got some corrosion around the battery terminal though. How old is it?" His shift in tone, lighter again, seemed like an offer. An olive branch she was happy to accept.

"Three years, probably."

"Then that's your problem. Friend of mine owns a wrecking yard. He tends to have spare parts, sells them on the cheap. I bought a decent battery from him last year. He might have one lying around. Then it's just a matter of installing it. I'll clean the tray and the cables for you so we can get a better look at this thing." He flashed his devil-may-care grin at her. "Too bad we can't simply pop a Tylenol in the gas tank."

Surprised into a laugh, she said, "I wish."

"I'll just grab a socket wrench from the shop."

"I can get it." He was helping her out with the Jeep. The least she could do was the footwork.

"Do you know what it looks like?"

She shot him a glance. "Please."

He chuckled. "Fair enough. But it'll be faster if I look myself."

"Try me."

The frown was quick, then gone. He shrugged. "There's a rack of storage boxes by the workbench. They look like drawers, clear tops. They're all labelled."

"Then it shouldn't be too difficult. I'll be right back." She left him standing by the Jeep, balling the rag between his hands.

Despite the clutter, the workshop was well-organized. She saw that now. Tools were laid out neatly on the workbench, within easy reach. Like a chef's *mise en place*, everything in its place and all the set-up done beforehand. No wonder Matt felt at home here.

There, that must be the rack Jeffrey meant. It was filled with storage drawers. Although neatly labelled, some stickers had worn off, leaving behind darker sections in the sun-faded plastic. Bearings. Nuts and bolts. Screws. Lots of different screws. But no sized sockets.

She hesitated for a second, then opened the drawer. Inside were sharpened bits of steel and brass that had her thinking of androids and spaceships. She grinned at that. The next drawer was filled with more screws, all sectioned off in inset compartments.

Further down, almost at the bottom of the rack now, she pulled out another drawer. And froze.

Through the clear plastic lid, she saw the rectangular shape of a book.

That was odd. Why would a book be kept here?

Condensation fogged the inside of the lid, drops of moisture beading at the edges.

Leave it alone.

She checked over her shoulder. She shouldn't — but one quick glance couldn't hurt.

She pulled the drawer out, set it on the stool. With a snap, she opened the lid. And felt her breath catch.

She'd looked that book up online just days ago.

The black and white photograph on the cover showed a sky-scraper shrouded in mist. The image delicate as a charcoal drawing, moody and atmospheric. She ran her fingertips over the leaf-shaped cut-outs in the dust jacket that gave way to the bright green board beneath. Felt that change in texture from glossy paper to rough binding.

The cover was visual and tactile, and more expensive to produce, which was why a different design had been used for the reprint.

She held a first edition of *Hamadryads* in her hands. In pristine condition. The edges still crisp as they'd been on the day of publication. But they wouldn't be for long, if the book stayed in that plastic container in the workshop.

She flipped to the copyright page. Checked the date, the name of the cover artist. A memory she couldn't catch hold of teased at the back of her mind. There was something familiar about the way the photograph was composed. Soft-focus and almost painterly. That silver typography, too.

Why was the book — this rare first edition — here, in the workshop? Tucked in a drawer. It should be stored on a bookshelf, not in what was essentially a plastic box in an environment full of sawdust.

Socket wrench forgotten, she strode outside, book in hand. Jeffrey glanced up, eyes narrowing against the sun.

She said, "I found this with the tools."

Jeffrey had his hand on the hood, knuckles white. Hot light glared off the metal. "A book won't help us much here."

"I've never seen a copy in person before." Still good as new, for now. "The workshop might not be the best place to keep it."

"Last time I checked, it was my business where I kept my things." His face had gone carefully blank.

"Moisture and heat can lead to foxing or warp the paper."

"I'll keep that in mind. It's chaos in there, as I'm sure you noticed." He held his hand out for the book and she stepped back on instinct. A flash of something in his eyes set off warning bells in her head.

It was organized chaos. Lots of labels. Everything in its place. Except that book. "This edition is rare. How did you manage to track one down?"

"Luck," he said with a simmer of anger that surprised her.

"I'll say." A once-in-a-lifetime strike. "This copy of *Hamadryads* is hard to find. And valuable."

"Only if someone's willing to pay the price." An undertone of bitterness there that had her wondering.

"How much did you pay for it?" She watched him, caught the twist of pain before he hid it.

"More than you'll ever know."

And to think, in a span of a week, she might have seen that rare cover twice. "Matt had a copy of the first edition, but —"

"Life's full of coincidences. Hand it over." His voice was low, threatening.

She took another step back, more than an arms-length away — farther now from the Jeep, too — and held the book tighter.

Then something changed. The tension seemed to drain from him, leaving him older, less substantial. "That book's been nothing but trouble." He looked her in the eye. "I was going to return it."

To who? The guilt on his face could only be for one reason. Her heart thudded. To Matt. This was his copy. "You took it from him."

He shook his head. "I borrowed it."

Without telling him. "Why?"

"To get a second chance," he said simply. "I needed the cash to get the equipment, to get a fresh start."

"You planned to sell it." Highest bidder wins all.

The silver lettering glinted beneath the title. The original by-line. *Sam West*. Nick Thorn's pen name.

"I was going to buy the book back, when I could." He dragged a hand through his hair, with the rough, restless movement of a caged animal. "Matt was giving the damn thing away. Didn't have a clue what he had. Thanks to your comment the other day, I did. So, I took the opportunity. Better me than someone else, I figured." A smile hitched his mouth. "Only reason he noticed it was gone was because he wanted to use it to impress you." She'd heard him use that same tone before, to tease Matt.

"But you couldn't find a buyer."

"Couldn't keep it in the house either. I had a hell of a time sleeping while it was in the other room."

"The telltale heart beneath the floorboards," she murmured.

He blinked. "What's that?"

"Nothing. So, you brought it to the workshop." And got in deeper.

Jeffrey looked at the big green building behind them. "Not my wisest move, I'll admit," he said, with a self-deprecating honesty that was unguarding. "I was trying to figure out how to give it back to Matt without him realizing what I'd done." For one second, she saw past the quick grin to the regret beneath.

"I could help you with that." She spoke without thinking.

"Are you trying to tell me you can turn back time?"

She smiled. "No, but I might be able to return the book for you."

Wary still, he asked, "Without him knowing?"

She could try. "It's worth a shot."

Hope, and something else she couldn't read, flickered in his eyes. "Fixing my mistakes for me?"

She thought of the gentle brush of Matt's thumb over her cheekbone. "If I can."

A cellphone rang. Jeffrey pulled it out of his back pocket, checked the screen and his brows rose. "Sorry, I need to take this." He turned away, listening.

His shoulders tensed. "But I just saw him the other day. Right." Careful edge to his voice. "Yeah, been burning himself out."

Another pause. "Keep me posted." He hung up the call, his face pale.

"Something wrong?" she asked.

"I'll say." He looked at the phone in his hand. "That was Jennifer, Thomas's daughter. He" — Jeffrey shook his head in disbelief — "he's in the hospital. Chest pains had him calling an ambulance last night."

"Last night?" Two words and her theory flew apart in pieces.

THIRTY-EIGHT

THOMAS WAS INNOCENT. AND THAT left her with nothing.

Worse. It left her with a pissed-off killer and no idea who it might be.

Instead of walking back to the cottage along the road, Charley cut through the ATV trail that sliced a narrow path through the oak trees bordering Jeffrey's property.

Sunshine flickered through the branches above, but she saw only the ragged edges of slashed canvas. Glistening red letters. Proof she'd come close to the truth. And missed it by that much. Or hadn't even recognized it.

Maybe she really had been playing detective. And now she was losing the game.

Humidity pressed in on her, sticky and cloying. Instead of providing relief, the heat seemed trapped between the trees, thicker here. Mosquitoes swarmed around her. A line of sweat trickled down her spine.

What was the last clue they'd found? The blueprint. But someone had already slashed a knife through her painting when Matt told her about it. The timing didn't match up.

Last night, she'd asked Kayla to tell her the truth.

Trying to get me drunk, so I confess to murder? Charley's stomach twisted at the memory of her defensive tone. The anger in it.

If Thomas didn't murder Andrew, that only left one person. One suspect with the most motive. Maybe Alex was right all along.

But no matter how the facts added up, she couldn't believe Kayla did it.

A staccato hammering broke the silence, followed by a shrill, raucous cackle that slammed her heart into her throat. The sound echoed through the trees. She glanced at the shadows crowding around her, then up.

A red-headed woodpecker drummed against the tree.

High above her head, worn and weathered boards crossed the sky. A deer stand. Built by hunters to give them a better vantage point. She noticed now the sections of ladder, still bolted to the trunk and slowly rotting. A remnant from when this was just forest, without cottages or roads.

Even these familiar trees held secrets that whispered of violence. Of bloodshed.

She skirted around a patch of low growth with clusters of three leaves on each plant. Poison ivy. Green as the binding of the book, weighing down her bag.

What had Alex said? *You have to find out how a person lived to find out how they died.*

The blueprint Matt found hinted at engineering fraud that spanned years. And started with a death Andrew had a hand in. Another murder, but one Alex knew nothing about.

The leaf-shaped shadows moving over the ground reminded her of the cut-out leaves on *Hamadryads'* dustjacket. Nick Thorn's wood nymphs had spread their roots beyond the page.

Maybe it was as simple as tracing those roots back to the source of inspiration. To Lizzie. And Clarkston Engineering.

In the distance, kids shrieked and splashed. The joyful sound carried across the water.

Who would know more about the past? Someone who watched people, all the time.

Sarah had been surprised — no, horrified by the destruction in the gallery. Still, Charley had seen that flicker of dread cross her face when Alex said he'd catch the murderer. The woman was hiding something. Maybe the clue they needed.

Stepping from the trees onto gravel, her heart lifted at the sight of the cottage's earth-toned siding and red shutters.

Hadn't Sarah said it was up to the observer to uncover the secrets?

She had to take a bike ride into town.

THE BELL CHIMED AS CHARLEY pushed through the door of the B&B into the scent of bacon and freshly brewed coffee. She'd left Cocoa tied up outside, so this would have to be quick.

Mirrors — wooden and rustic, gilt and ornate — hung on the walls, reflecting glimpses of the lounge and the few guests who lingered over brunch. And sunlight. Even on a wet and gloomy day, there would be light here, glimmering in those frames. A horseshoe shaped bar took up the back corner of the room. Narrow floor-to-ceiling shelves, filled with tattered paperbacks, tempted guests to borrow a book, to get lost in a story.

The Blue Heron B&B, inside and out, was all charm and tongue-in-cheek whimsy, from the terracotta archer kneeling in the garden to the vintage hostess stand in the lounge. The stand held a stack of menus and a glass jar filled with assorted silver-wrapped chocolates she recognized from Chocoholic's.

A middle-aged woman carrying a tray, loaded down with a teapot and bone china cups, paused on her way passed. "Here for a late breakfast, hon?"

"Actually, I'm looking for Sarah Felles." She'd expected to find her in the centre of activity, talking to the guests. People watching.

"I'll let her know. On second thought —" She hesitated, seemed to toy with an idea, then said, "Why don't you go on up? She's in the Royal Colonnade."

"The what?"

Porcelain clinked as she shifted the weight of the tray on her arm. "All the rooms at the B&B are named after Regency circulating libraries. Hookham's, Meyler's, and Donaldson's. The Royal Colonnade has a fireplace and a view of the lake, fit for the Duke and Duchess of Cambridge. At least, it was. Right now, it's in shambles."

Shock jolted through her. More vandalism? First the gallery, now the B&B.

Sarah owned both. Had she been the target? The attack to the gallery not a threat to her after all, but to Sarah?

She must know something.

"Well." The smile dimpled the woman's cheek. "You'll see for yourself. Maybe she'll let you help." Help with what? "God knows, we've all tried and been shot down for the effort." She nodded at the cased opening on the other side of the room. Curved letters in eggshell blue paint spelled out *Hotel*. "Head on through there, up the stairs. Second door on your right. You can't miss it."

"Thanks." Charley took a chocolate from the jar, the foil crinkling between her fingers. Maple melted on her tongue as she crossed the room, but even the sweetness couldn't mask the bitter taste of adrenaline.

Steep, narrow stairs creaked beneath her feet. Pausing on the landing, she looked down a hallway of shelves. Inset bookshelves lined the walls, filled with paperbacks, row upon tightly packed row. A Persian rug protected the hardwood floor. She followed the faded centre line worn into the elaborate pattern. Running her fingers along the creased spines, she skimmed the titles.

All romances. Why was she not surprised?

From the second room she heard an electric whine. Catching a break in the noise, Charley knocked on the door. It swung open, onto the yellow glow of artificial light.

Mid-morning on a cloud-free summer day.

The room would have been brighter if the queen-sized mattress hadn't been leaning against the wall, covering half of the window. Sarah stood in the heart of the timber bed frame. Slats lay on the ground at her feet. A floral silk scarf tied her grey curls back from her face. And she held a cordless drill in her hand, finger on the trigger.

"Don't even think about it," Sarah said, without looking up. "I'm more than capable of — Charley." She lowered the drill, sounding surprised. "I thought you'd be in the gallery, putting things to rights."

"It can wait."

A wingback armchair faced the fireplace. A stack of crisp sheets and pillowcases lay folded on the dresser. The cozy room smelled of furniture polish and fresh flowers. But the heavy mattress pinned the cotton curtains against the window frame and the bed was far from usable. The room was in shambles, but this wasn't an act of vandalism.

"What happened?" she asked.

"A broken bedrail." Sarah's eyes twinkled. "I doubt it was a pillow-fight, but one never knows."

She kept underestimating the woman. Of course, she'd never be content to run the B&B from a distance. "You're fixing the bed." Had she moved the mattress herself, too? She must have had help with that, at least.

"You'd be surprised at how many slats, rails, and tenon and

mortise joints I've repaired in my time. I've had years of experience" — she met her eye briefly — "in putting things right."

Charley thought of the waitress's comment. "Would you like some help?"

"No, thank you." She picked up the glue, spread a thin layer over the strip of wood. "Novices make clumsy mistakes. And tend to make matters worse."

If you want the job done right, do it yourself? "How else will anyone learn?"

Sarah bent to fit the reinforced rail against the frame, pressed it in place. "By watching from a safe distance." She adjusted the position of the wood and nodded, satisfied. "Pass me those clamps."

She figured the *please* was implied and handed them to her.

Sarah secured the clamps to the wood, one on either end. She tightened both, distributing the pressure evenly. Concentrated on the task at hand and obviously busy.

But Charley didn't have the patience or the time to wait for a better moment. "I came to ask you about Lizzie."

Humour lit her face. "I don't think she damaged your paintings." Then she looked at her more closely and her smile slipped. "Why?" Not surprised. Resigned.

"I know Lizzie worked for Andrew." She had some facts, but not all, and they needed the rest. "I know she died on site, while the gallery was being built."

Sarah bent to gather the drill bits into the palm of her hand. "A tragedy that occurred long before I bought the building." She straightened. "I said it once and I'll say it again, it's best not to stir up old hurt."

"Someone already has."

"The murderer, you mean?" Irritation crossed her face. "You're throwing caution to the wind. Taking a risk."

Charley blinked. "Excuse me?"

"You're ignoring the warning. Asking more questions."

If she didn't, who would? "You said it yourself. Destroying art is just another form of murder. And I won't let them get away with it."

"Justice takes many forms and perhaps it's already been served."

On that shimmering hot summer day, in that comfortable room, a chill crept over her. "That's it? That's all you have to say to that?"

"Vandalism was a threat. To you and to Meghan. The message left for you in the gallery was clear. Unmistakable." Sarah's fingers tightened on the handful of steel. Metal ground against metal. "Nevertheless, you're choosing to ignore it."

She looked at the old bed frame, the brackets strengthening loosened joints, the reinforced rail. "Wouldn't you do the same? Repair what's broken?"

Shoulders tense, the woman's posture radiated indignation. "There's a difference between fixing a bed and solving a murder. You came here looking for answers, but I'll share some words of wisdom, instead. Let it go."

"Don't tell me you didn't try to find out everything there was to know about the ghost haunting your building."

"*My* building, dear. And all I discovered is that she's missed by many."

"Some more than others." She thought of Matt.

Startled, Sarah pinned her with a calculating stare. "So, you noticed it. I wondered if you would."

Noticed what? She searched her memory, but she had no idea what Sarah meant. It could be anything.

Fake it. She had to play along, act like she knew. Don't blink. Don't react. Her pulse sped up. "It's obvious, isn't it?"

"Only to those perceptive enough to see it." Sarah shrugged. "He hides it well. Until he talks about her and then the look in his eye says it all." She paused, left a beat to be filled.

Charley let it slip by, waited for her to speak.

Sarah said on a sigh, "That's the look of a man who knows he had the most incredible thing in his life and nothing else will ever come close to it."

Nick Thorn? But he'd passed away weeks before Charley arrived in Oakcrest. No, Sarah was talking about someone she had met. Someone who loved Lizzie. But who? She felt like she was stumbling her way through the dark. Carefully, she asked, "How do you get over a loss like that?"

"By spending time with her son."

An icy wave of realization washed over her. "You're talking about Jeffrey." The name seemed to reverberate, hum in the air. "He was in love with Lizzie?"

Sarah's eyebrows arched in stunned disbelief. "You didn't know."

Knees weak, Charley sank into the chair. Her thoughts felt as muddy as the water she soaked her paintbrushes in. "She had an affair with him?"

Sarah shrugged. "They worked together for years. It's not a stretch of the imagination to think that there might have been more than friendship between them."

She'd spoken to Jeffrey twice. They'd never talked about Lizzie. "Are you sure that wasn't all it was? Friendship?"

"You mean, could I be romanticizing the past?" She seemed amused by that. "It's possible."

But unlikely. She didn't have to be good at reading people to pick up on the subtext. "Lizzie never left Nick."

"You've read *Hamadryads*. You know as well as I do why."

Sarah stood in the dismantled frame, drill bits scattered at her feet. A corner of her mouth curled up, just a fraction. "That book is a love letter to his wife. Published after her death, he brought her back to life on the page."

As a tough and determined heroine, bent on saving the day, no matter what. And she'd taken on Clarkston Engineering by herself. "Rumour has it, there might be more to Lizzie's death than meets the eye."

"And you, of all people, understand just how easy it is to trick the eye. The only thing connecting Andrew's murder and her accident is grief. Keep up the chase and, sooner or later, you'll find yourself face to face with a killer." Sarah met her gaze. "In a situation you can't control."

Fear skated down her arms. "Not if I lay the groundwork carefully. And trap them first."

"Trust me, you'll regret being the driving force behind the investigation."

Anger stirred within her. "Is that a threat?"

"Advice, and I hope you'll take it. You're better off putting your energy into fulfilling your dreams. A once-in-a-lifetime opportunity doesn't come around twice. Why risk it?" Sarah's lips pressed into a thin line. "Now, I need to get back to work, and I'm sure you do, too."

Charley came here hoping to get information about the past. And she had. But what she found out wouldn't help solve Andrew's murder. It would only cause pain. Shatter trust.

It was just a guess, she reminded herself as she left the B&B. A romantic story pieced together from fragments of the truth. But it didn't feel like fiction.

Warmth and pride filled Jeffrey's voice when he talked about

Matt. They moved in step through the workshop, without needing to say a word. Had that same crooked lift to the right side of their mouths when they grinned. That same hip-shot stance.

Like father and son.

She had to get the book back to Matt.

THIRTY-NINE

"IT WASN'T THOMAS," CHARLEY SAID when Matt opened the door. The first edition of *Hamadryads* weighed down her purse, heavier than it should have been.

"Run that by me again?" He leaned against the doorjamb. Chocoholic's had closed for the day about an hour ago. He looked as tired as she felt.

At her feet, Cocoa's tongue hung out as she panted, eyes bright after running alongside the bike.

Charley dragged a hand through her hair, fingers snagging in windblown tangles. "Thomas had a minor heart attack. He's being kept for observation. Meaning, he was in the hospital this morning and couldn't have been at the gallery."

Matt looked stunned. "He has an alibi?"

"It's watertight."

"That changes things." A frown knit his brows. "Come in. I just put a pot of coffee on."

The book felt like a ticking time bomb in her bag as she stepped past him, into the house. Instead of setting her purse down on the wooden bench, she kept it with her. If the right moment came up, she'd have to seize it.

She couldn't stop thinking about the shame, the regret in Jeffrey's eyes. The fact that Matt's grin mirrored his.

In the kitchen, a cookbook lay open on the counter, notes in thick black marker scrawled around the recipe. Cardboard boxes covered the Formica table, some stained with water marks.

"You're busy," she said. "Sorry, I should have called first."

"I was going through some old files I found in the basement. Thought I might find some more evidence tying Thomas to Clarkston Engineering. I didn't get far." He lifted one of the boxes and put it on the floor, clearing space. "Grab a seat."

She took the closest chair.

A photograph lay on the table. A four-inch print with the orange cast of degradation, corners curled from damp. The hazy grain pattern and low-contrast background was about thirty years shy of high-resolution. Despite the oxidation, the dust marks, she recognized Jeffrey's face before Matt palmed the print. The shock of dark hair. The grin, so wide and bright you could hear that laugh echoing across time.

How could she have missed the similarities before? The bone structure, the mannerisms so alike, now that she knew.

Restless tension coursed through her. "I was sure he did it." She drummed her fingers on the table. The book more on her mind than murder, right now. But she'd have to be patient. Wait for the right opportunity. "He could have hired someone to break into the gallery for him." The thought had hit her at the gallery that afternoon. "But why risk getting someone else involved?"

Matt grabbed the cereal bowl drying in the dish rack. He filled it with water and set it on the floor for Cocoa. "It wouldn't be smart. And yet, he seemed like the kind of guy who prided himself on being two moves ahead of everyone else."

"Except with his house."

Matt took two mugs down from the cupboard. Steam rose as he poured the coffee. "That was out of his control, depended on someone else. If he could have done it on his own, I'm sure he would have."

"And that's probably what put him in the hospital. He's been working too hard. The stress was wearing on him. You could see it." Carving lines into his face. "Put that much pressure on yourself, you're going to crack at some point."

Could she leave the book here, in the kitchen? Tuck it into one of the boxes sitting on the floor? Only if Matt left the room. But if he'd already gone through that box, set the contents aside to recycle, the book could end up in a landfill by accident. If that happened, she'd never forgive herself.

"And you're putting pressure on yourself right now." Matt brought the mugs to the table, then took the other chair. "Feet."

"What?" She blinked.

"Do you ever do anything without asking a million questions first? Put your feet up." He swung them onto his lap, and his fingers zoned in on the pressure points beneath her arch. His thumbs worked over the muscles and she felt the tension melt away under the warmth of his hands. "So, Thomas didn't break into the gallery," he said. "But he could still be the murderer."

"How? The two events are connected." They had to be. Matt peeled off her sock, and his hands touched bare skin. "It's cause and effect." She lost her focus as his thumb stroked down her toe. "Why else would someone leave a threatening message in the —" Her brain stuttered as his fingers pressed on her instep. "— the gallery?"

"But what if it wasn't a threat?" he asked. "What if it really was just jealousy? You sold a painting."

"Two, actually."

Matt grinned. "Right." He sobered. "But others didn't. Kayla could have damaged the painting out of spite."

"Alex took Kayla in for questioning today," she told him.

"What did she say?" His fingers rubbed the length of her arch, from heel to toes.

"I don't know. I haven't been back to the cottage yet." From the B&B, she'd gone to the gallery, then straight to Matt's, soon as she knew he'd be home.

"You came here first?" His whole attention aimed on her. His fingers traced slow, distracting circles over her ankle, under the hem of her jeans.

"I thought it would help if we" — okay, that felt really nice — "talked it through."

Matt slid forward on the chair, so her legs were on either side of him, his hands resting just above her knees. "Did it help?"

"It did when I could think straight." The weight of his hands on her legs, the heat of his touch, didn't help. Her insides felt like a pot on a slow simmer.

"Maybe not thinking is a good thing," he said in a low voice.

He was close enough for her to see the flecks of gold in his eyes. "Not when it comes to solving a mystery."

"We might have to postpone that for a bit," he murmured. Then his mouth closed over hers.

This was a bad idea. She just couldn't remember why.

SO MUCH FOR SELF-CONTROL. MATT'S breathing was deep and even and warm against her neck, his arm heavy over her waist. Every part of her was hyper-aware of him. And of the fact that she'd happily stay there forever. A dangerous thought.

Her heart already skipped a beat when she saw him. Now they had entered the mind-blowing physical relationship phase. Distracting was an understatement.

Biting her lip, Charley eased out from under his arm, and waited. His face was half buried in the pillow. He was sound asleep.

She was tempted to stay there, but she'd never get a better chance. She could put the book in a spot where he'd find it later and be back before he even realized she was gone.

He had the quilt draped over him, but the cotton sheet was half on the floor. Snagging the edge, she gave it a tug, then wrapped it around herself. It would have to do.

She tiptoed toward the door. *Creak.* She winced and froze. Floorboard. Nothing was ever silent in an old house.

Matt shifted, stretched out an arm.

Holding her breath, she opened the door and slipped out into the hall. Closed it carefully behind her. Now she just had to figure out where to leave the book.

Nowhere obvious, otherwise he'd wonder why he hadn't seen it earlier.

The office off the kitchen. His dad's office. Matt wouldn't question it if he found it there. He was fast asleep. She'd have time to look for the right place.

She tiptoed down the stairs, quickly, quietly. Heart pounding in her ears, jackhammer loud.

On the carpet below, Cocoa leaped to her feet, and turned in three excited circles. "Shh." Charley bent to pat her head, soothing her.

She picked up her purse, slid the book out. The glossy cover felt cool in her hand.

At the office door, she hesitated with a twinge of guilt before pushing it open. It felt like aiding and abetting. But she was righting a wrong. The book belonged here.

Had Nick Thorn written *Hamadryads* at that desk? The hairs on her arms rose at the thought. Most of the bookshelves were empty, but a few titles remained. If she could just leave it in a desk drawer —

"What are you doing?"

With a sharp gasp, she whirled around.

MATT WATCHED FROM THE DOORWAY as Charley hid something behind her back. With her other hand, she clutched the white sheet to her chest. The green stem of the dandelion tattoo on her wrist marked a watercolour line along her pulse.

He hadn't expected to find her here, of all places. And not with that look of guilt on her face.

He stepped into the office, and asked again, "What are you doing?"

He'd thrown on a pair of jeans before going to look for her. The carpet felt rough beneath his bare feet. The old oak tree outside the window shook on a breeze, sending shadows skittering from the corners of the room and up the walls to the ceiling.

"I was going to reheat the coffee," she said.

Maybe that was true, but — "Kitchen's the other way." Standing beside his dad's leather armchair, he crossed his arms. "Looking for more info for Meghan?" Disappointment did a quick pitch and roll in his stomach.

She went completely still. "That's your first thought? That I was spying?"

He moved forward, two more steps. Just an arm's span away from her now. Charley tensed but didn't back away. "I know one thing for sure. You're hiding something. What is it?"

She held her ground. "Nothing." And looked him right in the eye when she said it. But the lie had a flush spreading over her collar-bone, up her neck.

"Okay." He leaned a shoulder against the bookshelf, prepared to stay there until he got an explanation. It struck him that they'd stood like this before, in The Coffee Nook. "I'll wait."

"It's not important."

"Show me, then." This was the second time she'd kept something from him. The postcard, now this.

A breath lifted her shoulders. Leaving a second's gap of silence big enough for panic to creep into. He debated dropping the whole thing, when she said, "It's just a book."

He flicked a glance at the shelf behind her. "Which one?"

Charley bit her lip and hesitated. Then drew her arm out from behind her. "*Hamadryads*."

The sight of the black and white cover, those green leaves, knocked the wind out of him. "Yeah, I recognize the book." The iron-grey title glinted like fool's gold. She held the book out to him. He didn't touch it. "What I'd like to know," he said, "is why you have it. And what you're doing in here."

"I found it."

That, at least, had the ring of truth to it. "Where?"

She shook her head. "I can't tell you that."

More secrets. "Why?"

"Because I promised."

"Promised who?"

Eyes sparking with frustration, she took a breath and spoke in a calm tone that annoyed the hell out of him. "You just have to trust me."

It was never a good sign when someone said that. He tried to think past the anger, the doubt. "That's a little hard to do right now."

"Fine." Not so cool now. The edge to her voice had Cocoa trotting into the room.

The dog cocked her head at them.

"Here, take it." Charley shoved the book at him. "I'm sorry I tried to help."

The corner of the spine dug into his palm. "It would help if you told me what's going on."

Cocoa sat at her feet. A united front.

Charley said, "Sometimes, it's better not to know."

Seemed like everyone was singing the same tune these days.

"I disagree."

Light broke through the branches outside the window, throwing shadows over her face. "Normally I would too but, this time, you really don't need to know."

Oh, was that so? "I don't like it when people make decisions for me. Is this why you came here today?" Because that was what was getting to him, he bit off the words. Hurt flickered in her eyes, but all he could think about right now was his own needs.

"Believe whatever you want." She stepped around him. "I should go."

Right. Because that was easier. "I was going to make dinner for us, but yeah, that's probably best."

He stayed where he was as he listened to her footsteps, the scamper of Cocoa's paws over the floor, fade into the distance. For the first time, he flipped the book — that damn book — open.

No dedication. That figured. Rather than use the space to honour someone else or single anyone out, he'd left the page blank. No generic niceties for Nick Thorn. No *in memory of.*

What the hell was it about *Hamadryads*?

FORTY

TO SAY THAT HADN'T GONE well was an understatement.

Charley steered the bicycle around potholes as she pedaled down Fire Route 22. Cocoa, let off the leash for the last stretch, prowled through the dense growth of wild lilies along the roadside.

Up ahead, two young girls with lake-tangled hair tore around the side of the rental cottage. The one in the lead shouted, "You'll never catch me." Her taunt rose through the trees like a battle cry.

The breeze tugged at Charley's T-shirt, with the snap of a storm to it.

The wide garage door of Jeffrey's workshop was closed. No truck parked out front. Not a sound from inside.

So much for good deeds. She'd only made things worse. A few hours ago, Matt didn't even know *Hamadryads* was missing.

She'd lied to him. Her stomach clenched. And she hadn't even come up with a convincing excuse. The only thing she'd done was give him an incentive to investigate.

He wouldn't let this go.

At their cottage, she wheeled the bicycle over the fieldstone slabs and leaned the metal frame against the weathered siding.

"Argh!" Alex's cry of horror carried clearly through the open window.

Cocoa barked, an urgent, nervy tone.

What now? Blood running cold, Charley slammed through the screen door, Cocoa right behind her.

Down the hall, the string of curses became louder.

On images of blood and open wounds, Charley burst into the master bedroom. The sky-blue dresser, beat-up at the corners now, stood against the wall. The wide windows, the water beyond the same as ever. Honeysuckle and vanilla caught at her throat. Grandma Reilly's perfume, gone again on the next breath, leaving only the scent of fresh air and clean sheets behind.

Alex stood in the middle of the room, holding something clenched in his fist. He looked livid. Balled up socks trailed from the open cupboard door, over the rug. It looked like a whirlwind had torn through the room.

"What's going on?" she asked.

"Your dog." His voice shook with frustration and disbelief.

Beside her, Cocoa sat on her rump and cocked her head.

"Is that a baseball?" Charley had a sinking feeling that the whirlwind might have had four legs.

"Catch," he snarled and tossed it to her.

The ball landed with a *thwack* in her palm. She felt the pock-marks in the leather before she saw them. The telltale teeth marks. "Oh no."

"I'll say."

A gouge ran through the smudged and faded scrawl. "It was signed."

"Damn right, it was signed." Alex raked a hand through his hair. "Of course, it was signed."

"This isn't so bad." Meghan stood in the doorway. In one hand, she clutched a tea towel. In the other, a wet plate that dripped onto the floor. Equal parts relief, amusement and horror filled her voice. "I almost broke the plate when I heard you."

"Not that bad?" His arm swept over the mess. "Look what the dog did to my socks." Wadded up and hardened with drool. "To my shoe." He picked up the running shoe by the heel. The high-end sneaker with cushioned soles now looked more like a favourite chew toy. "She put a hole in my concert T-shirt."

Meghan flicked a glance at the balled-up heap of fabric in the corner. "The one you left lying on the floor all week?"

"I didn't expect the dog to go on a rampage."

"Hey, Cocoa was with me," Charley defended her.

"Yeah, where were you?" Meghan dried the plate with the towel and set it on the dresser. "You missed dinner."

"It's a long story."

Alex glared at Cocoa. "I doubt you've got an alibi for the whole day."

She didn't. Not for this morning. "I left her here, when I took the Jeep to Jeffrey's." She looked down at Cocoa. "Did you do this?"

Cocoa pinned her ears back.

Alex snorted. "The evidence is adding up and it all points to you, my canine friend. I only wanted to take a shower, for Christ's sake. Not clean up after the dog." Charley didn't like the emphasis he put on the last word. "Conveniently enough, she didn't touch any of your things, Megs."

"That's because she loves me." Meghan rubbed Cocoa's ears.

Charley grinned. "And she doesn't have a death wish. I'm really sorry, Alex. I've been busy with the gallery, and she hasn't been getting enough attention."

"Fact of the matter is, a guy can't win in this house. Not any-more. I've had it." He paced the hardwood floor, shoe gripped in his hand. He shot a glance at Meghan. "I barely move in when your sister comes to stay. Not for a day. Not for a weekend, or even a long weekend. But for the summer. The whole summer. I know,

I know." He held up a hand. "Don't say it. Let me." He pitched his voice higher, "The house is half hers."

Meghan straightened. Her eyes narrowed dangerously. "Is that supposed to be me?"

Charley told Cocoa, "You're in big trouble."

"Never mind," Alex said, "that it's my toothbrush on the side of the sink, and my TV in the living room. I'm the guest here. That much is obvious. And I'm tired of having it thrown in my face. I'm going out."

"Where?" Meghan crossed her arms.

"Just out." He dropped the shoe on the floor. "Sometimes a man's gotta have some space." He slammed the door with enough force to rattle the picture frames on the wall.

Charley squatted down on eye level with Cocoa. "It would help if you showed some regret." The dog licked her nose. "Oh, you're good. At least try to look guilty when he gets back."

Meghan picked up the concert T-shirt. She poked her finger through the hole in the fabric. "Really guilty." The mauled cotton looked soft and vintage.

She sighed. "We'll work on it." They'd made Alex feel like the third wheel.

Meghan folded the T-shirt. "He's either going to the shooting range or the Three-Corner Pub. He cracked."

"Like an egg."

"Porcelain, baby. The case is getting to him."

"Funny," she said. "I thought it might be us."

"You think we're breaking him?" Meghan's brows lifted in surprise.

"Could be. We're a lot to handle."

A smile crossed her face. "Especially Cocoa."

"That's true." She nodded. "It's probably more her than us."

"That's what I'm thinking." Meghan dragged the wicker laundry basket into the centre of the room. "Alex took Kayla in for questioning today."

"How'd that go?" she asked casually. Although a seed of doubt had taken root. Maybe Kayla wasn't as innocent as she'd thought.

"Did you notice the mood he's in?" Meghan rolled her eyes. "If he'd solved the case, he'd be flying high and this wouldn't phase him."

"So, not well." Charley tossed the gummed-on socks into the basket.

"I think he's starting to face the fact that he's hit a dead end." Hands on her hips, Meghan cast another glance around the room. "Good enough, for now. Did your mystery errand involve food?"

"No." It might have, if things hadn't gone so wrong.

"Hmm." Meghan studied her face thoughtfully. "There are leftovers in the kitchen, if you want them."

"Actually, I'm not hungry." She couldn't even think about food right now.

Meghan blinked in disbelief. "Who are you?"

"I'll have something later." When the guilt wasn't churning inside her.

"Suit yourself. But I'm going to get out the vanilla ice cream and chocolate sauce," Meghan said. "I'm going to put out two spoons. You can have some or not. It's your choice. And if you want to tell me about whatever's bugging you — and where you went or who you saw or what you did when you saw them — I'd be okay with that, too."

"Subtle."

"Always." Meghan grinned.

Maybe comfort food wasn't such a bad idea. "Well, I can top your ice cream and offer chocolate." Forget the sauce. This was a day for a bar of chocolate, straight up.

Meghan cast a glance at her. "A secret stash?"

"One I'm willing to share."

"YOU SNUCK INTO HIS DAD'S office to return a missing book?" The citronella candle in the centre of the wrought iron table cast flickering shadows over Meghan's face. Lemongrass-scented smoke rose into the air. "Sure," she said, "your intentions were good but, you have to admit, from Matt's point of view, that had to look bad. And then you didn't tell him why?"

How many times had she sat out here with Meghan in the past, after cannonballing off the dock? In the distance, white-capped waves crashed toward shore. On the tree by the shed, the ends of the orange ribbon fluttered and snapped. So far, the rain had held off.

Charley broke off another piece of caramel chocolate. The grocery store bar didn't taste as good as it once had. "What was I supposed to do, tell him Jeffrey had it?" Not after the blood ties Sarah had hinted at.

"You're in a pickle."

"Thanks, Meg." And that was just the half of it. She'd censored the description of her visit with Matt, leaving out a few minor details. There were some things her sister didn't need to know.

Cocoa dropped the soggy tennis ball at her feet and wagged her tail in anticipation. Charley picked it up and whipped it into the trees again.

Meghan watched Cocoa chase down the toy. "Jeffrey really thought he could buy the book back, and Matt would never know?"

"He was sorting through his dad's office, giving all those books away. You can see why Jeffrey thought it wouldn't matter. That it might even go unnoticed." Cocoa returned the wet and muddy ball to her, like a prized possession. She pranced and bounced until she threw it again.

"Only, things didn't work out the way he hoped, and he was stuck with the book," Meghan said. "Until you showed up."

From the lane came the slow grind of tires over dirt and gravel. Game forgotten, Cocoa raced along the length of the picket fence to the front of the house, barking wildly.

Instead of driving past, the car stopped. Cocoa's bark turned fierce at the slam of the door, the approaching footsteps.

Charley raised her eyebrows at Meghan. "You should go see who it is."

She shook her head. "Can't. Cocoa wouldn't listen to me."

"Oh, really?" That was doubtful.

"She'll eat them alive." Meghan broke off another square of chocolate. "You'd better go."

"Call off the guard dog? Sure." With a sigh, mostly for effect, she walked around the cottage. If someone came all the way down their lane, they normally had a good reason.

But she wasn't expecting to see David standing on the other side of the picket fence.

"Hey. Is Alex around?" He kept a wary eye on Cocoa. She lay on her haunches, straight as an arrow trained on him.

"Not at the moment." Charley rested her elbows on the fence. Since when did he swing by to hang out with Alex?

"Do you know when he'll be back?"

"It's hard to say." Judging from his reaction before, Alex would need a couple hours to cool off.

"Seems like I'm always missing him these days." That focus

she'd noticed in him before was charged now with nervous energy.
"I should have phoned first, instead of just dropping by." David
paused. "Only I was hoping to do this in person."

"Do what?"

He looked tense, the lines around his eyes strained. What was
this about? A tip? A confession? People didn't stop by to visit a cop
at home without a reason. Maybe he came to debate the results
of the latest Blue Jays scores, but there was bound to be more to
it than that. And she'd love to know what.

Where was David this morning, during the break-in at the
gallery?

He asked, "Think there's a chance he'll be home soon?"

"Sure." It couldn't hurt, to let him think a cop might show up
at any moment. "You can wait with us. Meghan and I are sitting
out back." She unlatched the gate. There were two of them, after all,
and a dog.

Cocoa launched herself forward. He froze as she sniffed the
hem of his jeans. Then, as though he'd passed some test, she backed
off, let him enter.

Meghan came up behind them. "David." She sounded surprised.
"What are you doing here?"

"Looking for Alex, actually."

Charley cut in. "I suggested he sit with us until Alex shows up."

Meghan frowned. "All right, but —"

Charley grabbed her arm and squeezed hard. "Can we get you
something to drink, David?"

Meghan hissed through her teeth, "Ouch."

"Water would be great, thanks," he said.

"Just follow Cocoa, she knows the way." Charley lingered a step
behind and murmured to Meghan, "I want to know where he was
this morning. And why he wants to talk to Alex."

Her eyes narrowed, glinted. "Fishing for intel? I love it."

"But no going rogue, got it?"

"Fine, fine," she muttered grudgingly.

Charley gave her a nudge toward the house. "Don't forget the water. And throw some ice cubes in." Moving fast, so she was a step ahead of Meghan, she dropped into the chair across from David. Then gave Meg a subtle tip of the head toward the cottage.

She rolled her eyes. "I'll be right back."

The candle guttered, the wax a melted pool near the wick. A wasp buzzed around the chocolate wrapper.

She'd start with small talk. Then work the conversation around to murder. "Thanks for coming to the opening last night."

Cocoa dropped the tennis ball at David's feet. He leaned forward to rub her ears and picked up the slobbery toy, without hesitating. "I had to see the place. You've done a great job with it." He lobbed the ball into the grass and Cocoa took off after it. He shot a glance at Charley. "I heard about what happened this morning."

What happened. That was nice and vague. But he'd broached the topic for her. "Yeah? What did you hear?"

"Someone broke into the gallery." His eyes tightened at the corners. "Damaged the art." He lounged in the dainty iron chair but his fingers resting on the tabletop curled, flexing and releasing. The tendons in his forearm rigid.

"You're well informed." Too well? The ribbons on the tree crackled on another gust of wind that blew the scent of orange rinds her way.

"The rumours are getting out of hand," he said, "but there's a kernel of truth in every version. And those details always stay the same."

"Except that it wasn't all of the art. Just mine."

David nodded like he'd known that too, and something inside her snapped to alert.

Cocoa returned the toy, then backed up and did a playful lunge. He threw the ball again, harder this time. A breeze rustled through the branches above them.

"They destroyed something that's important to you." For a second, he sounded thoughtful. "Happens all the time in the primary cloakrooms. You expect that from third graders. Not adults."

"I guess some people never grow up."

"Actions have consequences." It sounded like he was trying to convince himself.

She leaned forward.

But that tension, that almost-had-it moment, shattered as Meghan came back outside. One more minute and she would have discovered what David was hiding.

Meghan placed the glass down in front of him and sat in the other chair.

"Thanks." He took a sip of water.

She raised her brows at Charley, and said casually, "So, actions have consequences?"

Thank God, she'd always had ears like a bat. And this time, her keen sense of hearing came in useful. Tension settled over the table again.

Might as well turn the screws. "When someone does something wrong," Charley said, "they have to deal with the repercussions. Right, David?"

"That's how it normally works," he agreed cautiously.

She said, "Funny how people forget that."

Meghan picked up on her thought. "And do stupid things."

"Like murder."

"Thinking they can get away with it." Meghan smiled, a dangerous, feline curve to her lips.

Charley watched him closely. "Even though —"

"They always get caught in the end," Meghan finished.

Smoke rose in tendrils from the smoldering wick, along with the burning reek of melted wax.

David held up his hands in defeat, palms out. "All true."

"Why are you here?" Charley asked.

He looked from one to the other. Cocoa stood at his knees, eyes glinting in the growing dusk. Her ball lay in the grass. "To tell Alex something."

"Tell us," she said. It wasn't a request.

He shook his head. "You won't want to hear it."

Meghan leaned forward, propped her elbows on the table. "Try us."

"Or maybe you will." He looked thoughtful. "Either way, you won't like it."

Meghan heaved a long-suffering sigh. "Spill the beans, teach."

"All right. But you won't talk me out of going to Alex with this."

Talk him out of telling Alex? Why? She exchanged a puzzled glance with Meghan. "Agreed."

"I found —" He broke off on a frustrated breath. Then muttered to himself, "Fast, like ripping off a Band-Aid." He paused, then said, "I found a container of nougat paste in Kayla's kitchen. After Andrew died."

The silence that fell was heavy with shock.

"Where was it?" Charley asked, trying to process the news.

"That top cupboard, beside the fridge. The one where she keeps extra pots, the larger ones. The container was small, almost out of sight."

"But you spotted it." How convenient. "What were you doing in her kitchen?"

"Looking for mugs. I made coffee for us." Sweet and handsome and innocent as can be.

"Cozy," Meghan said.

He shot her an angry glance. "She needed a friend."

Friends. Sure. Charley asked, "What did you do with the nougat?"

"I threw it away."

She stared at him. "You what?"

Meghan shook her head. "You destroyed evidence."

"Look," David said, "I don't want to condone what she did, but I understand why she did it. She needed a way out."

An alkaline taste hit the back of her mouth. She remembered the little girl at the cottage, laughing as she ran. *You'll never catch me.* "And now?"

"The gallery changes things."

"So, you came to rat her out?" The toe of a shoe connected with her shin. She glared at Meghan, who mouthed back, *cool it.*

"I know you're on Kayla's side," he said, "and so am I, but she's gone too far. And you of all people should want to see justice done."

Oh, she wanted to see justice done, all right. But before they told Alex anything, she needed to hear Kayla's side of the story. Because there had to be more to it than that.

David downed the rest of his water, then looked at them. "Alex isn't showing up anytime soon, is he?"

"No," Meghan said, "he isn't."

He stood. "Making excuses for the people you care about, that's easy." A punch of morality to his voice that would have suited a classroom setting. "It's a lot harder to admit you can't save them from themselves. And you can only turn a blind eye for so long. At some point, you have to face the facts."

FORTY-ONE

WHERE HAD CHARLEY FOUND THE book? And why had she lied about it when he caught her returning it?

Words on paper, that's all that book was. But, as it turned out, those words were valuable, with the right cover. Matt had looked it up, and still couldn't believe a book could be worth so much.

The Three-Corner Pub was already busy, filled with cottagers looking to spend a Saturday night away from the lake. Kill an hour here, and maybe he'd get Charley off his mind. In any case, it beat staring at those boxes of files again.

He leaned over the bar and caught Jules's attention. "I'll have a Guinness." He pitched his voice over the acoustic guitar riff her husband was playing on the small stage at the back of the room.

"You got it." She began building the pint from the tap.

Jules and Ben O'Keefe had been the proud owners of The Three-Corner Pub for the past three years. Jules had kind eyes, a nest of fine-spun blond hair, and a no-nonsense attitude that could clear the pub at last call, quelling the complaints of even the most stubborn stragglers.

Matt leaned his elbow on the bar, taking in the sights and sounds of the crowded pub. All the gimmicks that appealed to cottagers, but with enough authenticity mixed in to ensure the locals felt just as comfortable here. Honeyed oak tables, fireplace, canoe paddles hanging on burgundy walls. Tiny black loons stamped on three corners of the white paper napkins. The scent of grilled burgers and caramelized onions filling the air.

He probably should have come here sooner. It helped to get out of the house, escape all the memories and the questions.

Jules set the glass down in front of him, froth licking down the sides and onto the napkin. For a second, she watched her husband on the stage with a grin, then said, "So, where've you been hiding?"

"In a chocolate shop." He took the closest wooden stool, propped his heel on the rung, and settled in.

Wiping her hands on the cloth hooked into the pocket of her jeans, she chuckled, like he knew she would. "And we appreciate it. Especially Cody. I was hoping when he hit his teens he'd grow out of that sweet tooth. Then you showed up, opened shop, and that was that."

"Hey, your kid's got a good palate. Knows what he likes." And appreciated the unusual flavors too. Even his turmeric and cinnamon bar.

"And here I thought he was just a picky eater. I have no idea where he gets his taste buds from."

"I do." It was no secret that the pub's varied menu was her doing. Raising his glass, he was about to take a drink when Alex stormed up beside him.

"Bourbon, whatever you've got," Alex ordered.

On his own on a Saturday night? And itching for trouble if his expression was anything to go by. Though he didn't think a cop would need to go hunting for more on his downtime. "How's it going?"

"It's not."

Ticked off or brooding from the sounds of it. Riled up, in any case. "You'd better state your preference or you're going to rack up a hell of a bar tab."

Alex scowled. "You're right. The cheaper, the better. Doesn't matter what it tastes like, so long as it gets the job done. Don't worry, I'll order enough."

Despite the appraising look she gave him, she poured a glass, on the rocks. Alex probably would have preferred it neat. "No offence, but you both" — she included him in the comment — "look like hell."

Alex claimed the barstool beside him and shot him a curious glance. "She's got a point."

"She only said it after she saw your face," he replied easily.

Alex took a healthy swig from his glass. "Well, I'm here to get drunk, not to chat."

Jules leaned her weight against the bar. "I hate to deter a paying customer but drowning your sorrows won't work. Sometimes, it does more good to talk."

"I could talk about it until I'm blue in the face," Alex said, "but it won't change a thing. And if I'm going to be sleeping in my car tonight, I'd rather be drunk when I do it."

"Have it your way. Just don't forget to tip your friendly bartender before you're two sheets to the wind." She sidled away, to take the next order.

He watched Alex knock back more bourbon. "What's wrong with your house?"

"It's overrun by women."

"Ah."

"And it's not my house. I just happen to live there."

"You and Meghan have a fight?" It seemed like Alex's luck ran pretty solid there.

"It's more of a personal space thing. The dog was the last straw."

"Cocoa?" He hadn't expected that.

Annoyance drew Alex's brows together. "The hound mauled my signed baseball."

She had good taste, then. "Player?"

"The whole team. Blue Jays, 1993 World Series. Collectible."

He winced in sympathy. "Ouch."

"Yup. I thought moving in with Megs would help lay the groundwork, let her get used to living together. Before I popped the question." Alex sighed, brooding into the liquor. "I bought a ring."

"No way! Congrats, man." Though he looked less than happy about it.

"Yeah, except now that her sister's here, that has to wait. And the ring has been burning a hole in my pocket for weeks." He picked up his drink, narrowed his eyes at it. "My stomach lining too."

Matt turned a chuckle into a cough. "Nerves?"

"I love Megs. I like living with her. It's a house full of women I can't handle. Too many x-chromosomes, and everyone else is always right." He suddenly sat up straight. "I'm getting one of Jules' club sandwiches. With all the fixings, hold nothing."

The skyscraper sandwich was normally stacked high with roasted chicken, strips of bacon, tomato, and lettuce between thin slices of toasted bread. "Can't beat the food here." Maybe he'd get one too. He never did eat dinner.

Alex leaned forward to catch Jules's attention. "Hell, I'm going to get a side of bacon, too."

Probably a better plan than spending the night drinking cheap liquor.

On the stage, Ben's fingers flew over the guitar strings, sliding into a whirlwind Celtic reel without pausing or missing a beat.

Matt took a thoughtful sip of his beer. Alex was sharing a

house with Charley. Was in on any intel Meghan had on her sister. Chances were good he'd know why Charley had the book, maybe even why she'd lied. Alex had all the info he needed. And he was in the mood to vent. It couldn't be more perfect. "Grab a booth?" he suggested.

"Yeah." He nodded. "Why not?"

They'd need a table quiet enough for a decent conversation, but loud enough so that they wouldn't be overheard. Farther from the stage, but not in the back corner. The free booth by the window would work. Matt led the way.

When they'd taken their seats, Alex leaned back. He said in a low, musing voice, "The real kicker, the real" — his mouth twisted — "blow to the ego is that I'm starting to think Charley was right."

Ready to lend an ear, he asked, "About what?"

"The case. That Kayla didn't kill her husband. And that" — he tipped his glass at Matt — "is hard to admit."

Hit a wall while making chocolate and you burned the cacao, maybe ruined a saucepan. Hit a wall in a murder investigation and you let a killer walk free.

He looked at Alex. "If Kayla didn't do it, who did?"

"That's the big question, isn't it?"

FORTY-TWO

"I'M COMING WITH YOU," MEGHAN said.

Heart beating a shallow rhythm, Charley clipped the leash to Cocoa's collar. "Kayla won't talk if you're there and you know it."

"That's true. Damn." She paced the narrow entranceway. A sharp wind gusted through the screen door, catching at the sleeves of the jackets hanging from the cast iron hooks.

"Give me an hour before you tell Alex about this —" Meghan's guilty expression had her pausing. "You already did, didn't you?" There went her advantage.

"He didn't answer the phone."

Relief washed over her. "Good. I want to hear Kayla's side of things before we go around telling people David's version."

"He had me convinced," Meghan muttered. She caught Charley's eye and sighed. "What if she did kill Andrew? I don't think you should go over there on your own."

Kindred spirits, through thick and thin. *I need someone on my side.*

Charley said, "I have Cocoa with me." Warm brown eyes blinked up at her. "Besides, it's not like Kayla's going to poison me. Look, if she did kill Andrew — and I'm not saying she did — it means she felt like she was backed into a corner with no other way out." Like the girl in the drawing, standing in an Arctic tundra, watching her hands turn to stone. She pushed the thought aside. "But this time, she's got people who can help her figure out what to do next. I want her to know that."

"I have a bad feeling about this." Worry was raw on her face. "She's either going to confess to murder or keep lying."

"Or prove her innocence." Annoyance simmered inside her.

"Always the optimist."

"She'd do the same for me." She pushed past Meghan, stepped outside. The setting sun blazed over the road, sparking off gravel.

"Are you sure about that?"

The question caught her mid-step, stopped her short on the fieldstone walkway.

"What happens if she does confess?" Meghan asked. "Do you really think she's just going to come to the police station with you?"

Charley turned back to face her, a chill sliding down her spine, despite the heat, the humidity. "If it turns out she did it, I'll convince her to talk to Alex."

"Who will arrest her."

The wind buffeted the trees, fierce now. And dangerous.

"Worst case scenario." On impulse, she hugged Meghan, squeezed tight. "Stop worrying so much. It's Kayla." She started down the path. "I'll be back soon." With a battle plan.

This time, she'd convince Kayla to fight. And make her believe they could win.

MUSIC, THE SWEEPING TONES OF an aria, spilled through the open windows. Charley rang the doorbell again.

Still no answer.

It was instinct more than anything that had her reaching for the handle. The door swung open. The soaring voice of a weeping soprano poured out. She shot an uneasy glance at Cocoa.

An unlocked door. Not unusual in cottage country, but a house like this tempted fate.

She hesitated on the threshold. Cocoa strained forward and she kept a firm hold on the leash. The note rose an octave higher, trembled there, on the brink.

"Kayla?" The hairs on the back of her neck prickled. She stepped into the dark entrance. A breeze wafted over her arms from deeper within the house, raising goosebumps.

Where was she?

In the living room, one of the lamps by the sofa cast a yellow glow. The sliding doors were wide open, the curtains billowing, like they had on the night Andrew was murdered. The dying sun stained the sky and water red.

The conflict between soprano and baritone rose to a crescendo.

Charley stepped out onto the patio and caught movement out of the corner of her eye. Cocoa turned, tail wagging with a full body quiver.

Kayla sat with her back to the wall, a large sketchbook propped on her raised knees. Cocoa scrambled forward to greet her. "Hi." She scratched behind the dog's ears, then glanced up at Charley. "I'm surprised to see you. You must be exhausted after dealing with the incident at the gallery. I know I am."

Had that really only happened this morning? "Actually, I'm still wound up."

Sharpened coloured pencils rested on a Blue Willow porcelain plate, to stop them from disappearing into the cracks in the stones. A second sketchpad lay open beside her, covered with a few fleeting penciled impressions. Practice, although they used to call that second sheet of paper the sabotage page.

"This is the first time I've been back out here since —" Kayla inhaled, long and slow. "This is as far as I got," she admitted.

Charley sat beside her. The patio paver had stored up the afternoon heat and felt sun-warmed beneath her jeans. Cocoa settled down nearby. "David came to visit us tonight."

A dark bank of clouds rolled in over the lake. In the distance, a white sail flashed. The boat speeding toward shore in a race against the storm.

"What did he want?" An undertone sharpened the casual question. Kayla's pencil scratched over the thick paper. Above their heads, the wind chimes crashed.

Had it always been this hard to get her to open up?

Charley glanced at the drawing. Still a bare-bones sketch, the shading a mixture of parallel straight lines and contours. Colour-blocked shapes, in the shades of the setting sun, made up the background. A woman with long, black hair stretched her arms to the sky. She had the wings of a raven and they were spread in flight. Her feet lifted off the ground. In profile, her upturned face was one expressive line. In the distance, still just a vague outline, lay the prone form of a body — a man. The tip of Kayla's pencil worked over the figure, adding details, dimension. Life.

No, not life. Realism. In all its painstaking precision.

"Actually," Charley said, "he wanted to talk to Alex."

"That's odd."

She searched her face but saw only curiosity. "He said he came to visit you, at the house, after Andrew died."

Kayla's pencil pierced the paper, leaving a small round hole in the man's chest. Like a gunshot wound. "People seem to think that dropping by will somehow help the grieving widow. It doesn't."

"But you weren't having an affair with him." Half-statement, half-question, to take the edge off her words.

"Marriage is a promise and I kept it." Kayla's voice was flat. Her face cold and hard and luminous as a statue. "Nothing happened between us before Andrew died."

Before Andrew died. "David said he found something. In your kitchen."

She put the sketchpad down with barely restrained force. "He found something here? And he told you about it?" Betrayal flashed in her eyes.

"It was nougat paste."

She laughed, a quick, startled sound. "You're kidding. Why would I —" The laughter faded, falling away, as Charley kept her gaze steady. "He made that up."

Maybe. Hopefully. "Why would he do that?"

"I have no idea. But he's lying." Fear stripped away some of that perfection. Made her look younger, more like she had before. "Did he show it to you?"

"Apparently, he threw it out. To protect you."

"And they say chivalry is dead." Sarcasm there, chisel sharp.

"David was quick to cover for you."

"Until today," Kayla said, her composure chipping. "When he changed his mind. But why?" The clang of wind chimes filled the silence. "The gallery." She stood. "He thinks I did that? That's bullshit."

Charley felt the force of her fury finally let loose. And about time. She rose, too, planted her feet, and faced it. "There's only so much I can do. The evidence keeps adding up and all I've got to go on is trust." And she was running low on that.

"I went over all this with Alex already," Kayla said. "I was here, at home. I wish I could prove it, but it's the truth."

"The only alternative is that David lied." But why? Her thoughts raced. "If he murdered Andrew, he'd want the attention on someone else." Maybe he thought he had a chance with Kayla, if Andrew was out of the picture. But that theory had one flaw. "If he got rid of Andrew to be with you, why would he now blame you?" It didn't make any sense.

"I don't know. I still can't believe he didn't just ask me about this." Kayla's expression turned bitter. "David has strong opinions about what's right and wrong. This isn't just about the vandalism. He thinks I killed my husband. That's it." Her voice was flat and hard. "That's exactly what he thinks. And so do you."

Guilt caught between her ribs, stabbed through her like pencil through paper. Leaving a small hole behind. "If that's what happened, I'll help you." A beat went by. "Kayla, it's the lies that make it hard to trust you. And I know you've been lying about something."

She pressed her lips together.

Charley took a breath. "The night Andrew died, you told me you killed him."

Kayla looked at the drawing lying on the ground. The paper fluttered as another gust of wind tore at them. "I did. But not in the way you think."

This was it. Dread seeped through her from the heart out. But she said, "Tell me."

"When I found him —" Kayla stopped, started again. "Andrew always had an EpiPen on him. He knew a reaction could be fast and deadly." She twisted her fingers together, looked out toward the lake — no, to where they found Andrew. The red chair striking as a grave marker against the water.

"But he didn't have it on him," Charley said. "You can't blame yourself for that."

Kayla turned, met her eyes. "You don't get it. If I'd gotten there earlier, looked for him sooner, called for help in time, he'd still be alive. When it counted, I did nothing. And, when I found him, I was glad. That he'd suffered."

Taking pleasure in his pain. She had changed. But she wasn't a murderer. "Whoever made those chocolates killed him. If David really found nougat paste in the house, then the killer planted the evidence." Meaning, they'd had access to the house. A thought hit her. "The door was unlocked when I got here. Is it normally like that?"

"When I'm at home. Though Andrew always hated it when I left the door unlocked. Said it wasn't safe." Kayla smiled a little. "I guess he was right about that."

"Maybe." Someone could have walked right in. "If you'd been distracted, while painting, you'd never know anyone was there. Although that would take guts." The break-in at the gallery had, too.

Kayla shivered and wrapped her arms around herself as though to ward off a chill. "Someone was in the house, prowling around, while I was here?"

Charley glanced back, at all those windows. A view of the lake for the price of a sheet of glass, separating inside and out. "Did you notice any signs of forced entry? Scratches around the lock?"

"No, nothing like that. And we have an alarm system. It would have gone off if someone tried to break in."

Even in those old stories, doorways couldn't be walled up. Men brought monsters to life and brought them into their homes.

Anyone on their suspect list would have been welcomed into her house without a question.

"Maybe you invited them in." All it would take was a moment alone in the kitchen to leave a container of nougat paste in a cupboard.

Kayla laughed, a brittle, broken sound. "And you're still trying to tell me this isn't my fault?"

"Yes. And together, we can catch the killer." They'd always been more powerful together. There was strength in numbers. "Did you have any visitors, just before Andrew died?"

The chocolates they found had been fresh, just a few days old, at most.

Kayla stood on the patio, but she was no longer statue-still. The wind tore at her hair. The black strands flying around her head like scattered feathers. "Once chocolate was in the house, it never lasted long. Andrew always had to have his within easy reach while he worked, in the bottom drawer of his desk."

She'd read enough crime novels to know that habits and routines made for easy targets. "If there were more chocolates in the drawer than before, would he assume you put them there?"

"Sure." She shrugged. "If he was distracted, focused on work, he might not have even noticed the difference."

Something scurried through the bushes. The air was denser now, thickened by the scents of earth and ozone and the brewing storm.

Adrenaline coursed through Charley. "So, the killer could have put the chocolates in the desk in his office, then left the nougat paste in the kitchen cupboard."

"It would be hard for a visitor to do that though, without getting caught."

"Let's see." They could put the theory to the test by going through the motions themselves.

Walking into the house, electric with the discovery, Charley headed straight for the kitchen. Cocoa followed, an anxious dance to her step as she fed off their nervous energy.

The top cupboard by the fridge, David had said. High up.

Charley stretched, reaching. But the handle was an inch too far above her head, out of her grasp. But that told them something, too. "Whoever did it would have to be tall enough to reach."

Kayla nodded. "I need a stepladder to take a pot down."

"What about Andrew's office?" Might as well try the whole route. "It's down the hall."

As Kayla led the way, Charley timed the distance, counting the seconds. How long would someone need? How well would they need to know the house?

In the office, Kayla switched on the light with a pull of the metal chain on the standing lamp. An energy-saving bulb spread a muted glow through the room. A glow that seemed weak and pale in comparison to the darkness gathering outside the window. Pressing closer.

The wood-paneled walls and built-in cupboards would have suited a cabin on a luxury cruise liner. Imposing wood and leather, meant to intimidate whoever entered through that door.

Shoes sinking into the plush carpet, Charley walked to the desk, pulled out the bottom drawer. She checked her watch. "Barely a minute, all in all."

Inside the drawer, there was a stapler, three ballpoint pen refills, a handful of paper clips. And more than enough space for a box — or a bag — of chocolates.

"Someone tall," Kayla said slowly. She twisted the lamp's pull chain, winding it around her fingers. "Who came to the house. Two days before Andrew died." She frowned. "But I really don't think —"

"Who was it?" The drawer slid in the tracks, latched with a nearly inaudible *click*. She straightened.

Kayla let the chain go. Metal rattled against the lamp. "A lightbulb had burned out."

Her chest tightened on a hard squeeze that snatched her breath. It couldn't be. But suddenly, everything made sense.

And she wished with all her heart that it didn't.

Cocoa turned to the door, fur bristling, ears on alert. The last note died in the soprano's throat and the CD ended on a beat of silence.

Inside the house, a floorboard creaked.

FORTY-THREE

"I GOT AN INTERESTING LEAD on the case today. One that had me rethinking things." Alex paused as his phone vibrated on the table. He put down his sandwich and checked the screen with the speed and resigned expression of the off-duty cop. Then relaxed. "Megs." He pushed the phone aside, let it ring unanswered. "I'll call her back later."

Matt cast a thoughtful glance at Alex. His copy of *Hamadryads* could have ended up in the box on the curb outside Chocoholic's. And Meghan took some of them home. "Meghan picked up some books from Chocoholic's the other day." Though why Charley would feel the need to cover up for her, he had no idea.

"You're dealing in fiction now?" Alex asked.

The pace of the pub around them worked up to a faster pitch, quickened by loud voices, the clink of cutlery, and the breakneck speed of the fingerpicked guitar notes.

"A short-lived side hustle, without pay," he said. "I gave them away. Did you get a look at them?" The question sounded odd, even to him.

"The books?" Alex lifted a shoulder. "Haven't had much time to read lately, believe it or not."

"Right." Dead end again. "Only, Charley returned ... one of the

344

books. Turns out, it was pretty valuable. But she wouldn't tell me where she found it." Or who had it.

"Did she say why not?"

Trust a mystery to pique his interest. "Just that she made a promise. Seems to me she's protecting someone."

"From the wrath of the chocolatier?" Alex grinned. "I can tell you this much, no matter who she made that promise to, you won't get her to break it." He crunched a strip of bacon.

"Word of honour?"

"That and an iron will."

Which only meant he'd have to find out another way. "Any updates on the break-in at the gallery?"

A hard-to-read expression crossed his face. "One painting is taking on a whole new light."

"The one of Meghan?"

Alex shook his head. "The woman kayaking."

Matt thought back, to his walk through the gallery. "The one Sarah bought?"

"Yeah. She phoned me this afternoon. Apparently, she saw something while kayaking one morning. Before Andrew's death."

The tone, too casual, caught his attention. Alex was working his way up to something. "Yeah?"

"It's amazing how much voices can carry when you're on the water. People don't realize how easy it is to get a good view of the shore, the properties, from a boat. Even the houses."

But Andrew's house was set a ways back from the shore. "You're saying she saw something?" The charged atmosphere of the pub seemed to push in on their booth.

Alex raised his glass. Condensation left a bullseye ring on his paper napkin, dead centre between the three black loons. "She overheard parts of a conversation — well, argument, taking place on the dock. According to her, it was heated."

"Who was he arguing with?" Wouldn't surprise him if it was Thomas. But they'd already ruled him out.

Alex took a long swallow of his bourbon before setting the glass back down with careful precision. He leaned forward. "He was arguing with Jeffrey. You know anything about that?"

He laughed. This was Alex's hot new lead? "Those two were at each other all the time."

"Petty disputes the whole town was well aware of. Only Sarah said this was worse. Jeffrey sounded furious."

Seemed like her favourite pastime was spying on people. "Why didn't she report it earlier?"

Alex shrugged. "Happens all the time. People stew over a clue, don't want to bother the police with false accusations. She said she didn't think it was important until today."

His gut twisted. He pushed his plate aside. "Yeah, well, it's not."

Alex leaned back, eyes gone hard and sharp. "It's interesting though. He'd know how to make the chocolate, wouldn't he?"

"Are you listening to yourself?" But fear caught hold of him, had his stomach jumping in his throat. "That's bullshit and you know it."

Alex's phone rang again.

CHARLEY NOTICED THE GUN FIRST. The shotgun pointed at the floor, hanging loosely at Jeffrey's side.

He followed her gaze. "For safety. My own. And I'll only use it if I have to." He stood in the doorway to the office, shoulders filling the width of the frame.

A low, constant growl emanated from Cocoa's throat, her hackles raised. His glance shifted to the dog.

Fear shot down Charley's spine. She grabbed Cocoa's collar. "Sit," she told her. She couldn't risk him using the gun on her.

Jeffrey's eyes were no longer kind, no longer calm. But they weren't filled with anger either. Instead, she saw resignation in them. He looked like a man who had walked out onto a ledge and could no longer turn back to save himself.

"But why?" Kayla's voice was raw. "I don't understand." She shook her head, eyes gone blank with panic and shock.

But Charley understood, now. "You killed Andrew." She kept her voice calm, level. No sudden movements. Nothing to make him feel threatened. So long as Cocoa didn't lunge.

"Pointless to try and deny it now, isn't it?" A crooked tilt to his smile, so like Matt's. "But I was counting on Kayla being alone. You weren't supposed to be here."

So, he could tie up a loose end? Her pulse scrambled. "Sorry to ruin your plans."

"You've been making a habit of it." The accusation strained against the tight control in his voice.

Her heart thudded against her ribs. "Not intentionally."

"Oh, I'm well aware of that." Jeffrey made a dismissive gesture and Kayla drew in a sharp breath at the movement. "Doesn't change the facts though. Things would have turned out fine, if it hadn't been for you."

"You mean, you would have gotten away with murder."

Thunder rolled in the distance, booming across the water.

"Thanks to you, the cause of death was questioned," he said it simply. "When you opened that gallery, Matt started digging into the past."

Where the pain festered. "You broke into the gallery."

"To give you a warning. And yet, here we are."

A necessary evil? Maybe, to him, it had been.

He said, "I knew you wouldn't leave well enough alone."

"The message" — those red letters — "what did you use to write it?"

"Car varnish. One of those pens from a repair kit, in Poppy Red." A little bit of that familiar humour slipped through. "The same colour as your Jeep, in fact."

Scrawled over her painting, like gore in a slasher film. "The postcard wasn't enough?"

Jeffrey frowned. "What postcard?"

Kayla steadied herself with a hand on the desk. "You used to be friends with Andrew."

"A lifetime ago." He suddenly looked haggard. "Literally. Don't tell me there weren't days you wished him dead." Her face went a shade paler. "Hit the truth, didn't I? Which is why, when they find you, no one will question whether or not you did it."

Kayla pressed the back of her hand to her mouth.

Find you. Charley fought a clammy wave of terror.

Cocoa snarled and jerked forward, jolting her arm.

He angled his body toward the dog. Feet planted, he trained the shotgun on Cocoa. Finger on the trigger. Canine teeth flashed in the light as Cocoa bared them.

"No." Charley struggled to keep the fear out of her voice. She had to get him away from her. "Let's take this into the other room. I'll close her in the office. She won't hurt anyone." And maybe they could talk him down.

"Fine." He lowered the gun. Stepping aside, he swept his arm toward the door. "You first, Kayla."

With jerky movements, she crossed the carpet.

"Sit." Charley told Cocoa. It took a second before she listened. Then she looked up at her with trusting eyes, and her heart broke. She ran a hand over the dog's head, felt the warmth of fur beneath her palm. "Stay here. Be a good girl." She'd figure out what to do. But they had to buy time, and Cocoa had to stay safe.

They'd overpower Jeffrey somehow, get the gun away from him.

She kept her eye on Cocoa as she moved to the door, making sure she didn't budge.

She had to walk past him to leave the room. And, for a second, she debated. It was possible. He was taller, heavier, but she had the element of surprise on her side.

He was so close, she felt the heat radiating off him. She just needed an opportunity to wrest the gun from his hand. But Cocoa would come to her defense. And there was no guarantee she'd get the gun in time. She couldn't risk it.

She watched him pull the door closed on Cocoa's keening whine.

"If only you'd left well enough alone." There was no heat to the words. Instead, they were filled with regret. He'd do what he had to do. "We're going to stop by the kitchen first."

Charley felt the presence of the gun at her back. Heard Kayla's breath turn quick and ragged as they walked down the hall.

The magnetic knife holder over the kitchen counter. If she could just get her hand on one of those knives, maybe they'd have a chance. Some leverage, at least.

He pointed at the floor by the kitchen table. Well away from everything else. "Sit there. On the floor. And don't even think about moving."

They knelt. What else could they do? Beneath her knees, the tiles were hard and cold.

He opened the glass-fronted cupboard, surveyed the bottles of alcohol. Gun pointed their way, but his attention on the labels.

Eyes off them for now.

Her muscles tensed, ready to spring. She kept her gaze on the handles of the knives.

But the second wasn't long enough.

"Andrew always said nothing took care of his back pain like Oxycodone," Jeffrey said conversationally. "Swore by it. Did you know that an overdose can be fatal? Especially when taken with alcohol. I've heard it's just like falling asleep. Ah." He took a bottle off the shelf. "Eighteen-year-old Scotch whiskey. Aged in bourbon casks. We'll take this with us. All right." He closed the glass door. "Just one more thing." He squatted to rummage in the cupboard under the sink. "Ha! Thought so. Trust Andrew to keep some in the kitchen." A roll of duct tape. "Charley, if you'll stand."

He gestured with the gun. "I can't leave marks on Kayla's wrists, but I'm more concerned about you playing the hero anyway. After all, your paintings are all about heroics, aren't they?"

And courage. She got to her feet, slowly. "You don't have to do this."

"Believe me, I wish that were true. Turn around." He tossed the tape to Kayla. "I'll have to ask you to do this. Tight as you can, please."

With a wrenching tear, the tape peeled off the roll.

"There's always a choice," Charley tried again.

"Not this time." Certain, as though he'd gone over every option in his mind, and this was the only way out. "I'm sorry, but I can't let you go. You're a problem I have to decide how to solve. Some minor adjustments to the Jeep and a long drive might do the trick. We'll deal with that later."

The tape bit into her skin as Kayla wound it around her wrists, twice. Not too tight, but tight enough. It held fast.

"Why did you do it?" Kayla asked, her voice shaky.

Jeffrey took the tape from her, put it back where he'd found it. "Well, that's something to discuss over the Scotch, isn't it?" He tucked the bottle under his arm. "Let's head outside. It'll be better if they find you where he died."

Charley had to buy them time. "This isn't the solution. It'll only make things worse. Alex will figure out what you did." They walked ahead of Jeffrey into the living room.

"I don't think he will," he said. "Not after Kayla slashed your painting at the gallery."

At the sliding door, Kayla stopped short. "I had nothing to do with that."

"But that's not what he'll think." He gestured for her to move forward. "You're the obvious suspect. Emotionally unstable. Wracked with guilt."

Charley said evenly, "You're not thinking straight." Alex was wrong. Reckless behavior didn't make the murderer easier to catch. It only made him more dangerous.

"Oh, but trust me, I am." The muzzle of the gun pointed down, but his fingers trembled against the stock. "Someone has to take the blame. And it won't be me."

That desperation, his fear, had panic clawing at her own throat. She wouldn't — couldn't give in to it.

Outside, darkness had fallen, black as night. Thick rain clouds hid the stars from view. The air was moist, cloying with humidity. Electric. Shadows loomed everywhere.

She blinked, willing her eyes to adjust. *She couldn't see.* The old terror caught at her, had her breath rasping. A trickle of sweat slid down her back. But she wouldn't let it consume her. Not now.

In the distance, Cocoa began to bark, a frantic sound.

Jeffrey walked behind them, urging them forward, toward the solitary chair, down by the water. Alcohol sloshed in the bottle, like waves against the shore. "You've always been quick to ask for help, Kayla. But slow to return it. Unless it brought you something. Same as Andrew."

The whites of Kayla's eyes flashed as they widened in fear. Thunder cracked overhead.

"It took me a while to notice," he said, "how selfish you are. I'm sure you have though, Charley. After all, she used you to investigate her husband's death. Did she thank you?"

Not once. But did that make her selfish or just distracted?

"I didn't think so." Certainty warmed his tone. "Your friend does things to serve herself. No more, no less. It's why she married Andrew. For security and a life of leisure. Everything money can buy. Only that backfired, didn't it? Because Andrew was selfish too. Ego-driven. Nothing but the best for him and to hell with anyone who stood in his way." Betrayal, fed for years, had grown, become all-consuming.

Maybe that resentment could help her get through to him. "Andrew made a lot of enemies."

"Pissed people off all the time. He had a talent for it. If he saw an opportunity to stab someone in the back, he'd do it, then walk right over their cold, dead body."

Like Lizzie. Could she use that somehow? But push too hard and she might tip him over the edge.

There were no boats on the water now. No sound of an approaching motor. Nothing but the shaking branches, the crash of waves breaking against the dock. Across the lake, lightning sliced through the dark sky, silver as an old scar.

Jeffrey stopped at the red Adirondack chair, where Andrew sat as he ate the chocolates that killed him. "Take a seat, Kayla. We'll stand."

Charley stayed where she was. With a slight shift of her foot, she moved back, closer to the rocks leading to the shoreline.

He swung the gun toward her, sending a skitter of fear down her spine, but she held her ground. "Stay right there."

"Do you mind if I sit?" Tremble in her voice, just a little. Let him think she was weak. "I can't — I feel faint."

He weighed it. Dismissed it. "Fine."

She lowered herself to the ground until she sat cross-legged. Her hands touched the sharp edges of the rock behind her. She held still and waited.

"Go ahead." He set the whiskey on the armrest beside Kayla. "Have a drink." From his back pocket, he took out a bottle of pills. The contents rattled as he set it down beside the alcohol.

Kayla angled her chin up. "And what if I don't?"

"There's a flaw in your plan," Charley said. The jagged rock scratched her wrist, wearing at the tape. "You can't make her take those pills."

"True. But I can give her a choice. The pills or a slug." He stood on the grass, the lake at his back. The wind tore at his hair. It would only take one move for him to shoulder the gun.

"If you shoot either of us, you'll be left with another body to get rid of. One that can't be passed off as an accident."

Shadows scraped his face, hiding his expression. "Did you know that Andrew used to hunt? Years and years ago now. Open season and he'd be out with the rest of them. Deer mostly. Wolves and coyotes too. Only a semi-automatic rifle is a lot better for that than a shotgun. So, he gave me his. It's still registered under his name." And he had yet to aim it at one of them. Though it would be foolish to think he wouldn't. "It's barely half an hour past sunset. It's not hunting season yet, but people won't question a single shot. It'll take a while before anyone comes to investigate. If they even hear it over the thunder. And when they do, it'll look like suicide."

Kayla made a strangled sound in her throat.

"A shotgun," he said, "isn't a pleasant way to go. I'd take the pills. But, in the end, it's your choice."

Slowly, Kayla reached for the bottle of Scotch, unscrewed the cap. And stared at him with hatred in her eyes.

She had to stall him. The casual tone had Charley thinking of the first day she met him, in the workshop. "Sometimes," she said, "kindness is a weakness."

He smiled, and there was nothing kind about it. "Wiser words were never spoken."

"LIKE HELL," MATT SAID TO Alex. "You're way off the mark."

The cellphone vibrated on the table, ignored. "Maybe. Once I've checked the facts, we'll know for sure."

"Do it now," he suggested. "We'll go talk to him together." And stop this before it went any further.

Alex looked at him. "Are you serious?"

"He'll either be at the workshop or at home." He dropped some bills on the table, enough to cover both their orders. "Let's go." He wouldn't take no for an answer.

"Investigate a case on my time off?" Alex raised a brow. "What else is new? Okay." He looked down at the half-eaten sandwich in front of him. "But I'm finishing my food first."

"I'll wait." *As long as it takes.* And he'd ignore the panic, the doubt, rising inside him.

FORTY-FOUR

A WARM TRICKLE OF BLOOD ran over Charley's fingers as the rock, knife-edge sharp, cut into her skin. She had to keep Jeffrey talking. "This will destroy Matt."

That threw him, she could see, almost had him. But he shook his head. "He'd understand. But he won't have to. Because he'll never know."

In her mind's eye, she saw the rough sketch. The shotgun in the hands of a desperate character. The raging wind and white-capped waves. The villain with an all-too-familiar face.

Her shoulders ached as she strained to work the tape against the rock, while staying as still as possible. "Why did you replicate his recipe to commit murder?"

Jeffrey tensed. "I didn't mean to kill Andrew. I had no idea he'd already used his EpiPens."

"You put the chocolates in his desk," she said, "when you came to change the lightbulb. Planted the nougat paste in the kitchen."

"A fail-safe. It all should have gone off without a hitch." He looked at Kayla, sitting in the chair. "You were used to leaving me alone in your house. Going off to paint while I worked to fix whatever Andrew was too busy to get to."

Kayla took a swig of the Scotch, grimaced at the burn of alcohol. Pills still untouched. "I trusted you."

"We all put our faith in the wrong people." His tone was careful and controlled. "Do you know how your husband made his money? By cutting corners and cutting losses."

Kayla's face stood out, pale against the red chair behind her. "You worked with him."

Wind surged off the lake, spraying mist. It seemed to blow straight through Charley.

Jeffrey dragged his arm over his cheek, wiping away the dampness. "Andrew needed a partner, someone to help him beat out the competition. He was young, had charisma, could bait clients like no one else. Reeling them in though, that was another matter. The lowest bid wins the contract, but he couldn't offer it, not every time." He spoke to Kayla, his attention on her. "He lured clients by pointing out risks, then promising security, solutions. A fast fix."

The bottle knocked against the armrest, glass against wood. Not quite steady, Kayla said, "He'd offer the moon and convince you he could build it."

"But to do it at cost" — flash of that wry one-sided grin that spread lines around his eyes — "he needed help from a contractor. I agreed to give him a discount, on the condition that I would be the general contractor on all of his projects. So, we came up with ways to make his bid lower, then lower again. But he wasn't content, wanted to find ways to make a profit on that, too."

The blueprint Matt found. The change to the material turned a profit but came at a risk. "You helped him," she said.

"The structures we built were always safe — safe enough to meet standards."

"Until Lizzie died on site." The rock missed the tape, nicked her wrist again. Her skin stung.

But Jeffrey was the one who flinched as though cut. "I wasn't comfortable with that one, even before she —" He broke off.

Started again, "The joists were too small for the weight load. Andrew knew it would affect the structural integrity of the building, and lead to repairs later on. But, by the time anyone noticed, it would be out of our hands."

If Matt could see Jeffrey now, would he even recognize him? It was hard to believe the same blood might run in their veins.

Cautious, aware of the shotgun in his hand, she said, "Lizzie noticed."

"And it got her killed." The wind shredded his words, scattering them over the water. "Construction continued. The weakened joists were hidden behind the drywall. Then, after all that, he forgot our agreement and dropped me." Hatred, old and hidden and buried, reared its head. And snarled. "I couldn't get the same kind of business on my own. I'm a builder, not a slick-talking salesman. I went from commercial jobs to residential, fix-it jobs. Honest, yes, but downgraded to the local fucking handyman. That everyone used, but no one wanted to pay." Fury twisted his features.

Kayla sucked in a breath as Jeffrey stepped closer. Charley froze, held still, heart hammering.

He carried the weapon as casually as any other tool. "I took out a mortgage on the house to pay the bills. Alone and heading toward ruin, I had to watch Andrew hit the fast track to success. From right next door, because I couldn't afford to move away. When Matt found those photographs, I thought it was finally my turn to make him pay."

Anger, betrayal had led from one bad decision to another, until it was too late. "Blackmail." Charley felt the tape fray, just threads left. Almost there.

"Andrew laughed in my face. Said he'd accuse me of fraud. He threatened to produce new drawings in hindsight and fake the specifications, to lay the blame on me." His voice rose, rough now and bitter. "He'd gotten away with worse before, he said, so why not this time? So damned sure he was invincible." Thunder rumbled, louder than before. "I just wanted to give him a taste of fear."

The temptation too much to resist. "But the chocolate killed him." The rock cut through the last of the tape.

"A mistake," he said, "and one I'll have to live with."

"What about us?" She gave it one last try. Maybe she'd get through to him. "There's a difference between manslaughter and murder."

A blue fork of lightning split the sky. In the blaze, his eyes glittered. Before she could search his face, darkness closed in. More impenetrable than before.

"The storm's about to break." He stretched his back, looking up at the dense clouds. "It's time. What's it going to be, Kayla?"

Gathering her energy, Charley took a breath and exchanged a glance with her.

Let's turn to thunder and lightning, so people will never catch us. Sparks flew through the sky as another bolt streaked toward the lake.

Kayla levelled her gaze at him. "I won't die."

"I'm afraid that's not an option." He was no longer acting on reason. He was far beyond that.

Charley stiffened, ready to leap. Hoping the element of surprise would be enough.

Up at the house, something dark exploded out of the doors and onto the deck. With a flash of white teeth and a ferocious snarl, the shadow shot toward them.

With a vicious oath, Jeffrey pivoted toward the dog.

STOMACH CHURNING, MATT STEPPED OUT of the car as Alex slammed the driver's side door. The workshop was deserted. They were trying Jeffrey's house next. But something inside told him to run the hell the other way. And that voice was getting louder by the second.

Something wasn't right. Only one window glowed on the main floor.

Kayla's house, on the other hand, was bright with lights.

In the distance, lightning forked toward the water. Soon the storm would break. But, instead of thunder, a loud crack split the silence.

A gunshot.

The lake bounced the sound, so it echoed. From the shore? No, from the direction of Kayla's house.

He hit the ground running. With a muffled curse, Alex followed, slowing only to yank out his phone and dial.

"Shot fired," Alex said, his voice curt, efficient.

Over the sound of his own breath, the beat of his footsteps, Matt heard him report the location, request backup.

Shadows shifted. Lightning flared again and he blinked away spots. A booming roll of thunder shook the ground. He ducked beneath branches, felt the sting as a twig lashed his cheek. A raindrop splashed on his arm. With a crash of leaves, Alex came up behind him, keeping pace, fighting for the lead.

The next flash of lightning lit the world like an x-ray and what he saw had his heart stopping.

Three people and a dog, down by the water. One standing, one sitting. One aiming a shotgun.

Matt forced himself to go forward. After all, he'd gone looking for the truth. And now he'd found it.

He always knew Jeffrey had the answers. Dread closed a fist around his heart, squeezing tighter with every step.

Charley held the shotgun. It took him a split-second to realize that the low, threatening growl came from Cocoa's throat. Kayla pushed herself out of the chair but kept a hand on the back of it, for support. She looked unsteady on her feet.

Alex scanned them. "Everyone okay?"

"We're fine," Charley said, though Matt figured they were anything but fine. "The gun went off in the struggle."

Cocoa snarled and Jeffrey fell back a step. "That dog was supposed to be locked up."

"She can open doors. And, this time, I'm glad she did." She kept her gaze on Jeffrey. "Matt —" Sorrow, sympathy filled her voice. Or was it pity?

He met Jeffrey's eyes. The man who had taught him to cook, who he'd looked to for guidance, support. Had looked up to. The faith he'd had in him, unshakable in its strength, began to crumble.

Jeffrey spoke first. "Someone had to do something, and I did."

The truth, raw and blood-red. And easy to recognize, in the end. "This is your idea of justice?" With a sweep of his arm, Matt took in all that had happened there.

"As close to it as it'll ever get." He spoke to him like the others didn't exist. Like it was just the two of them.

"You killed Andrew and used my recipe to do it." It took time to make chocolate. To temper it, pour it into molds. To cool and set, and still he'd gone through with it.

"He wasn't supposed to die," Jeffrey said. "I just wanted to scare him."

Bring him back from the brink of death, a changed man? "Tell me one thing. Did he kill my mother?" The words scraped his throat raw. "Or did you?"

Jeffrey's head snapped back, like he'd been punched. "You have to ask? Of course it was Andrew. When I showed him the photographs you found of those joists, he confessed. Said Lizzie confronted him, accused him. They argued. You know what he was like. He'd crowd in, get right in your face. Force you to back away."

Matt noticed Charley stiffen with a sharp intake of breath.

Jeffrey said, "Lizzie stepped back, and fell. He called it, 'an unfortunate accident.'"

Sick at heart, Matt said, "An accident." Not murder. "That sounds familiar." Full circle. One death led to another.

"You should have heard him. Confident, smug, and untouchable. He was always good at covering his tracks."

"So are you, it seems."

A shadow of the old grin crooked his mouth. "Could have been better." The ironic tone, the same one he'd heard so many times before, caught at Matt.

Anger flared, white-hot. Almost seared away the pain. "What the hell were you thinking?"

"He killed Lizzie," Jeffrey said. "I saw your face when I told you what Andrew did. You would have strangled him with your bare hands. The only reason you didn't is because I got there ahead of you."

And hadn't he thought the same thing? "I would never have done this." There was water on his face. Rain, he realized. Steady drops now, that brought out the smell of the earth.

"Andrew planned to blame his actions on me," he argued. "He was going to accuse me of fraud. And take away any last chance I still had."

Matt laughed. The sound scraped in his throat like sandpaper. "Fraud is an intentional deception. What do you call this?"

"Self-defense."

He figured he should feel something. But everything inside him had been singed away. "That day I left you in Dad's office. You took the book." The pieces fell into place. Charley had made a promise and lied to protect someone. Turned out, it was Jeffrey.

"I needed the money."

It was that simple. And he wished again for the power to change the past. "You could have asked. I would have given you everything I had." And prevented this.

"And risk my pride?" Twist of that familiar grin for a second, before it slipped. Normally tall and straight-backed, Jeffrey's shoulders seemed hunched beneath the weight of an invisible burden. "I was going to buy the book back, return it to you, soon as I could."

"A man of honour." Sarcasm left a sour taste in his mouth.

"Don't give me that." Jeffrey took a step forward. Cocoa's growled dropped a register lower and Charley raised the shotgun, stopping him in his tracks. He held up his hands.

"I don't care if it was unintentional or not. You committed murder." Matt made no attempt to soften the words. "And it looks like you were prepared to do it again tonight."

"In my position, you'd have done the same thing, picked the same method. Because we're alike." There was a raw desperation in his voice. A plea for understanding Matt couldn't give.

"For the first time ever, I hope that isn't true."

"You see right and wrong the way I do. I did what I felt was right." It sounded like he was trying to convince himself. "What I had to do."

"I doubt that." Jeffrey had made good on his promise and sliced through the Gordian knot of loose ends. Solved the cypher. And driven the dagger straight into Matt's heart. "If you're looking for redemption, you won't get it from me."

Alex stepped forward. "Jeffrey Haste, you're under arrest for the murder of Andrew Clarkston."

Chocolate. It all came back to that.

Sirens sounded in the distance, coming closer.

"Guess it's time to pay my debts, after all," Jeffrey said.

Everything came at a cost.

"For what it's worth Matt," he said, his voice gruff, "I'm sorry. You're a better man than I am."

"And I'm sorry to say, that's true."

The rain came pouring down as he turned his back on Jeffrey.

"I HOPE YOU REALIZE" — MEGHAN paced the living room floor — "you are never leaving me behind again. Next time you decide to confront a murderer, you can bet your ass, I'm going to be there, too."

"Noted." It was late — or was it early? The shallow cut on Charley's wrist throbbed under the bandage, along with the dull ache in her heart.

The storm had blown over, leaving the cottage windows beaded with rain. The darkness trapped on the other side of the glass. The lake obscured.

She dropped onto the sofa. Cocoa hopped up beside her, ears pinned back at Meghan's tone. One paw knocked the paperback lying on the sofa cushion to the floor, pages riffling as it fell.

Charley picked up the book — *The Demise of Lady Red* — and set it on the coffee table. The femme fatale on the cover smirked, although the title didn't bode well for her. Her silvery nails matched the lettering.

A memory teased at the back of Charley's mind, just out of reach.

Alex took the armchair and stretched his arms over his head, easing stiff muscles. "How about next time, you both leave the detective work to me?"

She caught Meghan's eye and knew they were both thinking the same thing. *Yeah, right.*

Meghan sighed. "Do you think Jeffrey was really going to kill Kayla?"

"I don't know." The comforting weight of Cocoa's chin settled on her knee. "In every scenario, he left the end result up to fate. If Kayla had used the EpiPen, Andrew would have survived. To murder her, Jeffrey needed her to take the pills. Tampering with the Jeep to get rid of me would have depended on chance, too. Any number of factors could have prevented death."

"That doesn't absolve him," Alex said.

Meghan wrapped her arms around herself. "I still can't believe he killed Andrew."

He nodded. "It just goes to show how easy it is for reason to be overpowered by hatred."

"And envy." Charley thought back to what Jeffrey told them. "Until it corroded everything else. And broke the bond he shared with Matt." The biggest sacrifice of all.

"There's no way Matt will stay in Oakcrest now," Meghan murmured. "Not after this."

She was right. Why would he? Her chest tightened. "Jeffrey thought he was taking justice into his own hands. Fighting for a second chance. But all he ended up doing was betraying Matt."

"And how."

All it took was one batch of chocolate.

Slouched in the chair, Alex drummed his fingers on the arm-rest. "What's still bothering me is, if he didn't leave the postcard in the gallery, who did?"

By the window, Meghan paused. "Seems someone else wanted Charley to mind her own business."

But she and Meg had never been good at that. "Turns out, Oak-crest is full of secrets."

Alex aimed a frown her way. "And too many people afraid of discovery."

Secrets. Afraid of discovery. That sense of déja vu nagging at her. The connection she'd missed.

Charley leaned around Cocoa and grabbed the paperback from the coffee table. The one Meghan had been reading. That cover. All those similarities. How had she not noticed it earlier?

"What is it?" Meghan asked.

"Just a hunch."

"Another one?" Alex groaned. "I give up. You're both hopeless."

Hopeful, actually. Fingers tingling, she flipped to the copy-right page. Could it be? The writing style of *Hamadryads* seemed so familiar, like she'd read the author's work before. Maybe she had.

She ran her gaze down the page, to the cover artist's name. Her breath caught.

Same designer. Different publisher. Only a year or two later. Different author. But the name could be a pseudonym.

The acknowledgements might tell her more. Or the dedication, if there was one. Please let it not just be blank space. Not again.

She turned the page, blood roaring in her ears.

For Matthew and Elizabeth, with love. Always.

FORTY-FIVE

DRIVING DOWN MAIN STREET, CHARLEY followed the pull of her heart as it led her deeper into town. She'd taken the Jeep to a local mechanic that afternoon and gotten the battery swapped out. Then she stopped by the library. It took some searching before she found what she was looking for. But she had.

Her pulse kicked up a notch as she turned onto Union Street.

There it was. Chocoholic's. Only, today, the store was dark inside. The CLOSED sign hung in the window, but, knowing Matt, he'd be here.

She parked the car, took a breath. If she had told him that Jeffrey took *Hamadryads*, that he planned to sell it because he was strapped for cash, would things have ended differently?

But she knew one thing without a doubt. She couldn't tell Matt about Jeffrey's affair with Lizzie. Not after last night. Sarah was right. It was best not to stir up old hurt.

Then again, she might be about to do exactly that.

A cloth bag rested on the passenger seat beside her. Charley drummed her fingers on the hot steering wheel.

Just go for it. There had to be some good in all of this.

She got out of the car and stepped into the blaze of afternoon sunshine. Moisture steamed off the pavement, still dark with rain. She slung the bag over her shoulder and the contents banged against her hip.

She peered around the sign. At the back of the store, a rectangle of sunlight glowed from a doorway. Matt's workroom?

She knocked, knuckles against glass. Nothing. Nervous energy coursed through her. She paced the sidewalk.

Digging her cellphone out of her bag, she typed a text. Hopefully Matt had his phone turned on.

— *I'm outside Chocoholic's. Can we talk?* —

She waited. Finally, there was movement inside.

Matt unlocked the door but kept his hand on the frame. "We're closed." Stubble shadowed his jaw and his eyes looked tired.

"I know. Can I come in?"

"I'm not —" He broke off, rubbed a hand over the back of his neck. "I'm not very good company right now."

Pushing her away. She tried not to let it hurt. "Just for a minute."

He hesitated. "Yeah, okay." Matt stepped aside, to let her through. "Where's Cocoa?"

"With Meghan." The scent of dark chocolate, chili, and black cherries hung in the air, faint as a memory. The shop quiet and empty, without the murmur of voices, the laughter and crinkle of plastic wrappers. "How are you doing?"

"Been better." A twist of humour caught at the corners of his mouth and fell short of his eyes. "Are you sorry you asked?" He threw the bolt, locking the door again.

As though the sign wasn't enough to deter customers.

"Actually, that's why I came. Could we sit?" She thought of the barstools at the counter.

"Better not."

Her heart squeezed. Of course. Sitting would take more time.

She was already nodding when he added, "Not here, anyway. If someone sees me through the window, they'll never leave. Come on, we'll be safe in the back."

This was it. Maybe she should have thought this through more. Planned out what she would say and how.

Two steps behind Matt, she pushed through the plastic curtain strips hanging over the door. And walked into a rich, heady aroma of cocoa and vanilla. Fresh as though scraped from the pod. The air almost cold here, after the heat outside.

She stopped short and dragged in a breath. "Wow."

The shiny appliances, all that chrome, might have seemed sterile anywhere else, but the red floor tiles added warmth. Stacks of chocolate molds filled the metal shelves. A marble cutting board rested on the work surface. The counters, the sink, were spotless.

He hadn't been working. Not this morning, anyway.

"Impressed?" The touch of humour in his voice had her smiling. That sounded more like him.

"Maybe." She set the bag on the floor and couldn't resist running her fingers over the scarred surface of the wooden table.

"I got that table secondhand," he said. "It's a little beat up, but serves the purpose."

"I like it."

One stool butted up against the table where a mug of coffee rested, almost empty now. Two more stools were pushed against the wall. The refrigerator gleamed, throwing back reflections.

The photographs on the wall caught her eye, drew her closer.

Matt shifted his feet. "Those are just some old pictures." Was that a hint of panic in his voice? "Ancient history. You should see the tempering machine. Or the guitar cutter, for slicing ganache."

Both were on the other side of the room. If she didn't know any better, she might think he was trying to distract her.

The cobblestones in the first photograph had an unmistakable old-world charm. "Was this one taken in Paris?" Matt — younger there — sat at a round café table. He was laughing, the tone easy, comfortable. Legs kicked out on the *terrasse*.

In the next picture, he stood in an industrial kitchen, flour smeared and sporting a cocky grin.

Moving quickly, Matt slipped one of the frames off the wall and tucked it behind his back.

Smooth. Subtle. "Is it that embarrassing?" she asked.

"What?" He widened his eyes innocently.

"The picture you're hiding." She made a grab for it.

Matt dodged, lifting the frame up high. But not high enough.

The glimpse of bare skin had her biting back a grin. "Are you only wearing an apron in that picture?"

"No." It sounded like he'd deny it to the day he died.

She shouldn't laugh. A giggle rose inside her, threatening to spill over. "Are you standing outside?"

His lips curved in a sheepish smile. "Some of the guys in the pastry class thought it would be funny —" He paused, his ears flushing pink. "— to steal my clothes and only leave me with an apron." He returned the frame to the wall. "It's a complicated story involving a lot of French wine, and probably isn't something I should tell you."

"Nice friends." She grinned. Looking at the photographs, she tapped the one that was unframed and pinned to the wall. "How old were you there?"

"Seven." Matt's smile died and his tone turned sober.

"That's some cake." Joy radiated from the image. A party. Balloons, cake, and a whole lot of love. "Is that your mom?"

"Yeah." He looked at the picture. It was hard to read his expression.

So, she finally got to meet Lizzie. "She had a wonderful smile. But there aren't any pictures of —" *Your dad.* The words caught in her throat. "— Nick."

He laughed. "With good reason."

It was now or never. She turned to him. "You should sit."

Matt blinked, startled. "Why?"

"Do you ever do anything without asking a million questions first?"

That got a flicker of a smile. "Fine." Watching her, he grabbed the stool, chair legs scuffing over the tiles.

Charley picked up the bag she brought with her. One by one, she laid the contents on the table, facing him.

He stared at them blankly. "Library books?"

A fizz of excitement built inside her. "Thrillers. In the hardboiled tradition."

MATT SCRAPED A HAND OVER his jaw. Charley was beaming at him and he had no idea why. "What's this got to do with —"

"Ever heard of Philip North?"

"Should I have?" The tattered paperbacks laid out on the table looked like they'd been around the block. A remnant of the '90s. "I feel like I'm failing a test here." She was waiting for a reaction, like the books should mean something to him. But he didn't have a clue.

"There were seven books in the series, starting with *The Demise of Lady Red.*"

A sultry knockout with platinum hair, soulful eyes, and a hard smile. The image grey as the smoke from a charcoal barbeque.

Charley tapped the cover. "The paperback originals were printed by a small publisher, holding onto the pulp tradition. Print 'em cheap but go all out on the covers. Each design has that black panel of space, silver lettering, and monochromatic photography. The images are soft-focus and moody. Similar to the work of Edward Steichen, they're almost Pictorialist —"

"Charley." He appreciated her enthusiasm, but his head was pounding. "Believe it or not, I didn't get much sleep last night. You're going to have to spell it out for me, because I have no idea what you're talking about."

He reached for the cup at his elbow. The ceramic was cold. The coffee, too. Cream floated on the surface. He debated drinking it anyway, then set the cup back down, pushed it further away.

More slowly, Charley said, "Pictorialists took the medium of photography and reinvented it as an art form, prioritizing beauty, tonality, and composition, trying to elevate it to the same level as painting." She sighed at his expression. "Oh, never mind. The important thing is that the cover artist also designed the first edition of *Hamadryads*."

That comment hit like a jolt of caffeine. He picked one of the books up, turned it over in his hands. But he still didn't get why this was so important. "So, the guy worked for a few publishing houses. Look, if this is the big reveal —"

"Philip North is a pseudonym."

He put the book down, his mouth dry. "Go on."

"North is an anagram for Thorn. Nick Thorn." A bright lift to her voice. Blue eyes practically shooting sparks. "He wrote *Hamadryads* under the pen name Sam West. Notice a theme?"

Cardinal directions. "So, my dad did publish more books." The closed door, that muffled strike of keys, late into the night. Maybe there'd been a reason for it. A deadline. Not just an excuse to escape, to avoid him.

She flipped one of the books over and read the praise quote.

"'The unselfconscious eloquence of the prose is a nod to Raymond Chandler. A writer with vision —'"

"'A visionary,'" he murmured. The critics seemed to agree about that. They'd said the same thing about *Hamadryads*.

"'And a sentimental wised-up hero.'" She drew a breath. "It's obvious Chandler influenced your dad's writing."

"How do you figure that?"

She put her finger on the byline. "Philip."

He couldn't stop the grin. "You mean Marlowe?"

"It's a guess, but it would be a nice touch, if Chandler's protagonist inspired his pen name. Most importantly." She leaned forward, the smile lighting her face. "Philip North dedicated each and every one of these books to his son and wife."

"What?" Matt froze. "Say that again."

"Every one of these books is dedicated to you and your mom."

"Let me see that." He took the paperback from her, flipped through the pages. "Here it is."

For Matthew and Elizabeth, with love. Always.

He swallowed hard and reached for the next book.

For Matt and Lizzie. You give my life meaning.

His dad's secrets, finally exposed. And they were anything but dark. "How did you find this?" His voice rasped in his throat.

She shrugged. "Someone donated the series to the library the summer I worked there, and the covers caught my eye. I read all of these. They're perfect cottage page-turners. When I saw the first edition of *Hamadryads*, the cover artist seemed familiar. Then that pen name had me wondering. It was just a guess. But, when I saw the dedication in *The Demise of Lady Red*, I knew. I looked the author up, to see what else he'd written. These books showed up in the search results. Luckily, the library hardly ever weeds their collection, so the books were still there."

"You make a pretty good detective."

"All I did was see past the cover."

"You saw through Jeffrey." If he'd looked closer, maybe he would have too.

She hesitated a beat, then closed her hand over his. "I'm sorry about —"

"Me too."

She leaned forward and pressed her lips lightly to his. It wasn't enough. He caught hold of her, drew her in. Deepened the kiss. But the spark of happiness it kindled inside him caught him off guard.

He eased back. "I have to decide what to do next." He had a hell of a lot to deal with right now. It would be unfair to drag her down with him.

Her expression sobered. "So do I." She glanced at the clock on the wall. "I should go. I still want to visit Thomas."

"I hear he's on the mend."

"He is. I'll leave the books with you." She bit her lip. "Call me, if you need me." Humour lit her eyes as she quoted his words back at him.

"I do need you." But, because it was too soon to tell her exactly how much, he added, "To help me with something."

"Sure, what?"

"A social media post." He glanced at the books fanned out on the table. "Speaking of photography."

"Tomorrow?"

Warmth, slow and steady, spread in his chest. "I'll be here."

FORTY-SIX

HAPPY BIRTHDAY TO ME. CHARLEY walked Cocoa to the gallery door for the last time. She didn't feel like celebrating.

How had the summer disappeared so quickly? Soon the lazy buzzing drone of cicadas would give way to the wild honk of geese flying overhead. Red treetops ablaze in heavy autumn light. Mist settling on looking-glass clear water, on bright splashes of wet leaves, like splotches of paint. And she wouldn't see it. Back to rush-hour subways, crowded streets, and grey pavement, she'd have to imagine it and hold onto that.

The magical turning point had come, and she didn't feel older or wiser.

She was an artist. This summer had proved it. She could create paintings other people wanted to own. It was a heady realization. Powerful. But to make the dream a permanent reality, she had to figure out how to finance it. Because selling a few paintings had barely covered her share of the lease.

Nothing had changed. The summer was coming to an end, and she'd have to leave Oakcrest. It would be hard. Harder still, to say goodbye to Matt.

Don't think about that. Not yet.

She'd get through the day and, when the time came, she'd move on. There was no other choice.

She fit the key in the lock. And froze.

The door was unlocked. But she'd double, triple-checked it last night. A habit she'd picked up since the break-in.

But, instead of snarling, Cocoa wagged her tail and pressed her nose to the doorjamb.

Braced for anything, Charley gathered her courage and flung the door open. Cocoa bounced ahead, dragging the leash out of her hand.

"Surprise!" A chorus of voices shouted.

Heart thundering, she entered the gallery. Instead of the faint fresh paint smell of canvas, chocolate filled the air, warm and fragrant, with an undertone of butter and sugar.

The room was full. Matt stood there, grinning at her. Alex and Meghan, too, with that glow she got when she was flying high on a secret kept too long. Eric, all in black, and Kayla. Sarah and Deborah. Even Thomas, looking thinner but rested. Posed like a tableau in a painting, they stood together, gathered in one spot.

Meghan broke away and slung an arm over her shoulder. "You're looking a little pale, sis."

She dug an elbow in Meghan's ribs. "My heart stopped, that's all." And was just now starting back up again.

"This was Matt's idea, so you can blame him for that."

"Blame?" He leaned down and brushed a kiss over Charley's lips. "I'm taking credit. I figured it's time to focus on the good."

And bury the hurt? Only two weeks had gone by since Jeffrey's arrest. The grief was still there, still fresh. You could see that just by looking at Matt. Pretending everything was fine might seem like the easiest solution, but it was like applying paint to unprimed wood. Eventually, the underlying surface would show through the cracks.

Alex said, tongue-in-cheek, "Shame you have to resort to scare tactics, Matt, to get a woman's heart to skip a beat."

He shrugged. "You're just jealous, because Meg's going to expect you to do the same for her one day."

A grin spread across Meghan's face. "He's right. He's set the bar pretty high."

Charley shook her head, her pulse starting to settle back into a normal rhythm. "For a second, I thought I was about to find another *vanitas* still life."

"There would be no point," Sarah said. Backlit by the sun streaming through the windows, her face was in shadow. "It didn't work the first time."

That proprietary tone, the trace of annoyance. It sank in. "You put the postcard there?"

Sarah drew herself up taller. "I was under the false impression that Kayla had removed her husband from her life. And was the better for it. Your sleuthing, Charley, would have altered her story-line for the worse."

Arching an eyebrow, Kayla asked, "So you decided to use a painting to save me from a life in prison?"

Sarah glanced at the wall of framed illustrations on their left. "I thought it appropriate, all things considered."

No one would have questioned Sarah. She owned the building. And yet… "You told me it was up to the observer to make sense of it all."

"Oh, my dear." Sarah shook her head, smiling as though the very idea amused her. "I wasn't talking about you. I was talking about myself. Editing is an art in which the best work goes undetected."

And it almost had.

Alex grimaced. "I should have figured that one out."

Sarah dismissed the comment with a flick of her hand. "You had a homicide to investigate. Hopefully the first and last the Oakcrest police department will be called upon to solve."

Deborah pivoted away from the painting she'd been studying. "As a reader, I appreciate the work you do, Sarah, but I'm not sure you can apply the same methods to real life as you would to fiction."

"And that," Sarah replied, "is the narrow-minded comment of a bookworm who can't visualize the creative process."

Deborah took one step forward. "I beg your pardon?"

"Let's leave death at the door," Eric drawled. "And cut the cake already."

Cake? If that's what smelled so amazing then, God, yes.

Thomas rubbed his hands together. "Now that's a good idea. Thanks to this damn diet they put me on, I can't remember the last time I had cake. But you can't live like a saint every day. And one piece won't clog the arteries."

Charley glanced at Matt. "Chocolate?"

He held her gaze a second longer. "What else?"

"The cake is a work of art," Meghan said. She never could resist a good pun. "Fudgy and decadent." Catching hold of Charley's arm, she tugged her over to the wrought iron table, where they'd set up the snacks on opening night.

So that's why they'd all been standing there like that. To block her view of the glass plate. The cake rose from it in a light and airy cloud of whisked egg whites and bittersweet chocolate.

Matt came to stand beside her. "A chocolate soufflé cake, served with vanilla-scented whipped cream and" — he gestured at the cooler on the floor — "a scoop of espresso ice cream." Picking up the small glass dish filled with bone-shaped cookies, he added, "The milk bones are for Cocoa." The dog looked up, gaze fixed on Matt and the treats he held. "Filet mignon flavoured."

"Because you promised her steak." So much for not being charmed. And, as for Cocoa, she'd been a lost cause from day one.

"When did you find the time to do all of this?"

"I baked early this morning," he said. "And when I say early, I mean really early."

Alex grumbled, "Now you're just milking it."

"And it took some work to get all of you here." Matt clapped a solid hand on his back, hard enough for Alex to grunt and take a step forward.

Beside the cake rested a bag from the Blast From The Past Boutique, a few small packages done up in birthday paper, and a box, wrapped in newspaper. The front page of an old issue of the *Oakcrest Courier*. "Nice gift-wrap, Meg."

"You're just going to tear it anyway," she said. "And you should. Right now."

"Bossy much?" Charley picked up the box. "It's heavy." Really heavy. "What is it?"

Meghan rolled her eyes. "You don't need to make three guesses. This isn't a game of Clue. Just open it, already."

She tore through newspaper to the cardboard beneath and lifted the lid on the box. From a bed of scrunched tissue paper, she freed the cool weight of cast iron. "A doorstop?" It had a curved tail. She laughed. "In the shape of a squirrel."

"A souvenir from Oakcrest," Meghan said with an impish expression.

"And it's red." Don't cry.

"For luck."

Oh God. Tears pricked her eyes.

Sarah stepped forward. "Which you won't need. I've been mulling over what to do with this building now that the pop-up gallery is ending."

With my building. But she no longer had any right to be

possessive. This place, when the walls were stripped of the paintings, wouldn't be the same. "What did you decide?"

"That a gallery, featuring the work of local artists, is an asset to Oakcrest."

Afraid to even breathe, she asked, "A permanent gallery?" Here.

"This building deserves a happy ever after. You promoted the gallery well. Drew visitors," Sarah said, all business now. "And it's obvious you have a keen artistic vision. I would like you to run it. You don't need to answer right —"

"Yes." Curate a gallery? As if she even had to think about it. "Yes, yes, yes."

Meghan grinned and tucked her hands in her pockets. "Told you she'd do it."

Kayla said, "And Oakcrest will be a destination village, soon." She spread her arms, reminding Charley of the woman in her sketch, who spread raven wings and took flight. "You're looking at the newly appointed Community Events Coordinator. There won't be any missing food trucks at the next festival, I'll make sure of that."

"You're going to be perfect for the job." Maybe Kayla had found the magic words after all, her antidote to doubt.

Thomas poured sparkling water into a glass. "About time things shaped up around here."

Nearby, Matt murmured to Alex, "What about you?"

"I can wait," he answered cryptically. "A little longer."

What was that about?

Sarah said briskly, "We're in agreement then. Renovations will need to be done. But, this time, they'll be done right."

Matt's hand closed over Charley's. He gave her fingers a squeeze. "I can help with that."

She glanced up at him, a flicker of hope catching in her chest. "You're staying?"

"Looks like we both are," he said. "Besides, what would Oakcrest do without a chocolate shop?"

Thomas eyed the cake. "It wouldn't be the same, if you ask me."

A smile curved Sarah's lips. "A wise person pursues her passion."

Eric rocked back on his heels, blue eyes twinkling. "Passion is an honourable pursuit. And I've always found the end justifies the means."

"I think she meant other passions," Thomas said dryly.

"Did I? Perhaps." Sarah swept her gaze around the gallery. "Life calls for many sacrifices, but a dream should not be one of them."

To think, she'd almost given up on hers.

Instead of an end, this was a beginning. What would happen next? Charley couldn't wait to find out.

Matt lit the candle on the cake. He turned to her with one of those crinkly-eyed knee-jerking grins only certain men can muster. And said, "Make a wish."

She already had.

ACKNOWLEDGEMENTS

Thank you to the team at Cormorant Books, and especially Marc Côté, for making this real. I have to also thank illustrator Nick Craine for creating a cover that promises an escape to cottage country.

Ellie Alexander, Ginger Bolton, Vicki Delany, and Daryl Wood Gerber generously took the time to read my manuscript and provide blurbs. Crime writers may spend their days plotting murder and mayhem, but they truly are the kindest people.

A series of serendipitous events led me to Sleuth of Baker Street Mystery Bookstore and a lasting friendship with Marian Misters, who played the role of literary matchmaker for *Cover Art*.

Thank you to my mom, for loving art and hanging a print of Renoir's *Dance at Moulin de la Galette* in my room, before I was even old enough to appreciate it.

And, last but not least, thank you to my family, for the best cottage memories.

We acknowledge the sacred land on which Cormorant Books operates. It has been a site of human activity for 15,000 years. This land is the territory of the Huron-Wendat and Petun First Nations, the Seneca, and most recently, the Mississaugas of the Credit River. The territory was the subject of the Dish With One Spoon Wampum Belt Covenant, an agreement between the Iroquois Confederacy and Confederacy of the Anishinaabe and allied nations to peaceably share and steward the resources around the Great Lakes. Today, the meeting place of Toronto is still home to many Indigenous people from across Turtle Island. We are grateful to have the opportunity to work in the community, on this territory.

We are also mindful of broken covenants and the need to strive to make right with all our relations.